Praise for Brad Watson's *The Heaven of Mercury*

FINALIST FOR THE NATIONAL BOOK AWARD

"Extraordinary. . . . Mixes whimsy and hard truth in a way that's heartbreaking. . . . Pungently erotic, and as affectionate as it is acidic . . . a perfect modern southern gothic."
—Mark Rozzo, *Los Angeles Times Book Review*

"An intensity reminiscent of Faulkner, a bleak humor that recalls Flannery O'Connor, a whimsy inspired by Eudora Welty and a spontaneity suggesting prime Barry Hannah. . . . Reading *The Heaven of Mercury* certainly restores one's faith in Southern literature's ability to startle and surprise . . . the risks pay off with insightful observations, dynamic relationships and scenes that crackle with tension and possibility." —*Memphis Commercial Appeal*

"[A] lushly written novel of Deep Southern dream and landscape." —Richard Eder, *New York Times*

"A vivid mythology of a small Southern town that moves to a strange, electrifying beat. Think of it as an Irish blues . . . as something that goes beyond the literal—and way beyond the pale of most contemporary Southern fiction." —*Atlanta Journal-Constitution*

"Sort of a calm wail. Each page a deep pleasure. A book at life's pace yet somehow without any of its tedium. Only the Irish geniuses wrote like this."
—Barry Hannah, author of *Airships, Ray,* and *Yonder Stands Your Orphan*

"*The Heaven of Mercury* possesses as sharp an ear for Southern speech, both black and white, as any novel published in the last 30 years. . . . A superb novel, graced with lush and exciting prose in the Southern high rhetorical tradition."

— *Raleigh News and Observer*

"A rich history of Southern literature just became richer with Watson's first novel. . . . Moving and mystical. Watson . . . moves deftly between now and then, and occasionally between now and the hereafter, to map new literary territory." —*Orlando Sentinel*

"Death, sex, supernatural spells, and bad marriages are among the essential elements for a Southern Gothic novel. But like the masterpieces penned by the writers who developed this celebrated literary tradition, Brad Watson's first novel, *The Heaven of Mercury*, feels anything but formulaic. . . . Watson's simple, compelling prose . . . resonates with emotion."

— Liza Weisstuch, *Boston Globe*

"As mythic and miraculous as Faulkner and Marquez. Amazingly original, and a sublime delight for the lucky readers who get their hands on it. A novel so fine you don't want it to ever end."

— Larry Brown, author of *Father and Son* and *Fay*

"Thrillingly ambitious. . . . Watson does not merely invoke Faulkner and García Márquez, but seems at times to speak straight through them." — *Book*

"*The Heaven of Mercury* reads like the love between its two principal characters. The story is ethereal yet comforting, intangible but somehow permanent. It has the necessary components of love, anguish and magic, and it incorporates the dramatic and the unreal. Watson imbues his work with an elegance that sets it apart from the rest." —*Boston Herald*

"Watson has written a novel at once intimate and epic, magical and real—a dazzling Southern gothic in which love and hate claim equal hold on the human heart. . . . Slipping easily between heaven and earth, between fanciful dreams and waking nightmares, Watson has given us a bravura performance. *The Heaven of Mercury* is an astonishing novel, one that burns with passion, color, and breathtaking prose—one that cements Brad Watson's place among our great American writers of fiction." —*Jackson Advocate*

"The Southern novel, with its ear for the music of words and its delight in off-kilter characters, returns with gale force in the pages of this sparkling debut. . . . Watson tracks decades in the small town of Mercury, Miss. (based upon his hometown of Meridian), spinning indelible tales and characters with magic, poetry, empathy and sour mash." —John Marshall, *Seattle Post-Intelligencer*

"The best thing to come out of the South since *A Confederacy of Dunces*. I haven't seen or heard such an eloquent flow of just-right words since Odysseus was caught lying to Athena." —Gregory Rabassa, professor at Queens College, City University of New York, and translator of Gabriel García Márquez's *One Hundred Years of Solitude* and other novels

"A fast-paced, myth-echoing, tragic-comic commentary on our modern lives." —*Bookpage*

"A strangely beautiful book that resonates with echoes of William Faulkner and Flannery O'Connor, with mythic touches of

Gabriel García Márquez thrown in here and there. . . . Watson's writing is lush, earthy, drenched in atmospheric detail. . . . A strange novel, this one—strange and uncommonly fine."

— *Charlotte Observer*

"Seamless . . . superb. . . . Southern storytelling is alive and well in Watson's capable hands." — *Kirkus Reviews*, starred review

"Finely wrought. . . . Ruefully romantic." — *Booklist*

"*The Heaven of Mercury* is a tragicomic story of missed opportunities and unjust necessities that wittily explores the souls of its highly colorful cast of characters. It is suffused with an almost savage lyricism that illumines every accurate detail and nuance of place and speech. The light this novel casts is so brilliant it makes even its own shadows luminous. Brad Watson has struck a fresh and thrilling note."

— Fred Chappell, author of *Look Back All the Green Valley*

"Gimcrack storytelling . . . grounded by generous humanity." — *Entertainment Weekly*

"Watson's keen eye for the human condition alone makes *The Heaven of Mercury* a worthwhile read, and you may find yourself accruing a particular type of knowledge that not even Faulkner could impart." — *Literal Latte*

"What a delectable treat this novel is, on every level. Large-spirited, raucous, darkly comic and comedically dark, and above all, just plain fun, this fable will stay with me the way personal experience stays with me—a wondrous elaboration on the theme of love." — Richard Bausch, author of *Someone to Watch over Me*

"Lovely, poignant, funny first novel, a book filled with fascinating, unpredictable, original characters. . . . Watson has a Faulkneresque understanding of human nature in the employ of an earthy, lively prose style that limns his characters with nuanced sympathy and wit. . . . *The Heaven of Mercury* finally is about love and loss, grief and remembrance, rage and caring. In other words, about the business of living, a subject on which Watson is well worth hearing." —*The State* (Columbia, S.C.)

"How thoroughly Brad Watson understands that emotions have no expiry date and how elegantly he writes about them. Vividly peopled, full of surprises, *The Heaven of Mercury* is a deeply satisfying novel."

—Margot Livesey, author of *Eva Moves the Furniture*

"[A]n unforgettable story. . . . The accidents, the disappointments, the corrections, and the secrets each life contains are woven into a deeply sympathetic portrait of small town life at its worst and best." —*Nashville Advocate*

ALSO BY BRAD WATSON

Last Days of the Dog-Men

THE

HEAVEN OF

MERCURY

a novel

BRAD WATSON

 W. W. Norton & Company · New York · London

For Mimi, Sissy, Velma, and WEW,

bless their sweet, conflicted hearts.

Copyright © 2002 by Brad Watson

Printed in the United States of America
First published as a Norton paperback 2003

For information about permission to reproduce selections from this book, write to Permissions, W. W. Norton & Company, Inc., 500 Fifth Avenue, New York, NY 10110

Composition by Amanda Morrison
Manufacturing by Quebecor World, Fairfield
Book design by JAM Design
Production manager: Andrew Marasia

Library of Congress Cataloging-in-Publication Data

Watson, Brad.
The heaven of Mercury / by Brad Watson.
p. cm.
ISBN 0-393-04757-1
1. City and town life—Fiction. 2. Mississippi—Fiction. I. Title.

PS3573.A8475 H43 2002   2002023103
ISBN 0-393-32465-6 pbk.

W. W. Norton & Company, Inc., 500 Fifth Avenue, New York, N.Y. 10110
www.wwnorton.com

W. W. Norton & Company Ltd., Castle House, 75/76 Wells Street, London W1T 3QT

1 2 3 4 5 6 7 8 9 0

Acknowledgments

I'D LIKE TO thank the following people and institutions: the Seaside Institute, for a month at Seaside, Florida, where I began this book and had a wonderful time; the American Academy of Arts and Letters; the Great Lakes Colleges Association; the Department of English and American Literature and Language at Harvard University; the Department of English at the University of Alabama; Jack Shank, for his three-volume history of Meridian, Mississippi, which was valuable for facts and information; the staff at the Foley Public Library, for help finding documents about early Baldwin County history; my students, for reminding me of what's important. For reading manuscripts and offering wise advice and encouragement, my enduring gratitude to Helen Vendler, Julie Anne McNary, Kim O'Neil, Karl Iagnemma, Sam Shaw, and Nell Hanley; thanks to David Gessner for urging me to get on with it. Other friends who lent support and encouragement are too numerous to name here, but I am grateful for their many kindnesses. I once again thank the members of my families— Collins, Watson, and Nordberg—for their patience, love, and support, especially Jeanine for infinite patience in addition to the rest. Thanks to Peter Steinberg, of JCA Literary Agency, for sound advice and advocacy. Finally, I'd like to thank Stefanie Diaz, Bill Rusin, Carolyn Sawyer, Ashley Barnes, and everyone else at W. W. Norton & Company; most especially I'd like to thank my editor, Alane Salierno Mason, *sine qua non*.

Although the town of Mercury, Mississippi, in this book bears some resemblance to my hometown, Meridian, I have taken many liberties with regard to historical, geographical, demographic, and other facts. Meridian, Mississippi, is farther from the Gulf coast, is more populous, prosperous, and demographically diverse than the town represented here as Mercury. In a few cases I have used the names of real places as they stand or stood in Meridian, or referred to real historical incidents, but their use here is not meant to represent the facts about them any more or less realistically than they might be represented in an actual dream.

Contents

II.

III.

1

Finus ex Machina

FIVE HUNDRED FEET above the highest building in downtown Mercury, thrust up amidst the light and swirling, lifting fog, the tower beacon for WCUV-AM glowed on and off with the regularity of a low pulse. Its red bulb illuminated a sphere of fog, so that it looked as if some throbbing, miasmic planet were drifting in the nebulous field of another, yet unformed. But then the huge red sun rose behind it all, the fog dissipated in wisps and curls, and you could see the skeletal structure of the tower, its base attached to the tip of the Dreyfus Building, at fifteen stories the closest thing to a skyscraper Mercury had. From a great distance it appeared to stand like a lone building left after a cyclone, though actually surrounded by all the low and empty-eyed smaller buildings in this slowly dying downtown, where few even of the remaining residents shopped or strolled, a town of twenty thousand that had been twenty thousand now for almost the entire century, a static death in a growing region, all migratory growth flowing around it. The aging downtown buildings, homes, railyards and junkyards, fairgrounds, car lots, truck stops, drab shopping centers, and small factories of Mercury were strewn east and west from this locus along a narrow valley one hundred miles inland from the Gulf coast, as if hurled there by the tornado that actually had destroyed the old section of downtown by the railroad tracks in 1906.

That being the blow that both stalled the city's momentum as a growing rail and trade center and drove nearly all its black population out of what had been a discrete and sprawling neighborhood around the tracks and (destitute) to a wooded area around a long and broad wooded ravine north of town owned by the scion of a decrepit and brambly once-plantation there, a man who claimed that since the Case family had brought all the black people to Mercury in 1837, a Case should take care of them now when they had nowhere to go. He allowed them to squat in his woods, gave them rough materials with which to build little shacks, gave them food in the beginning, and there protected they huddled and intermarried and developed a reputation among Mercury whites as being insular, strange, and half-wild creatures of the wood, domesticated only to the point of performing household chores. Just in the previous thirty years or so, the last Case descendants either long dead or moved on to another kind of life, they had begun to trickle out to homes in old neighborhoods around the ravine and quietly slip their best (as wood creatures slip into our midst unbeknownst) into the local public schools and state universities and beyond, to live as real human beings in the real world. Mercury was still a curiously segrated town in that way. At this point, only its odd enervation knew no ethnic or social constraints.

The valley was a river basin once thicketed with tall pines and broadleaf and run by bear, panther, deer, raccoon, bobcat, coyote, and flown by all manner of bird. In downtown anyway, only the birds remained, with the occasional disoriented, desperate coyote or coon. The deer ran the woods around. The bear were gone north, the panther south and west, the bobcat to near extinction. When one spied a bobcat in the woods, the bobcat seemed as surprised, even alarmed by his own presence as the one who spied it. Again it was as if the 1906 storm, marking the new century's change, had tossed all the old far around and left it ravaged for the new. But the birds returned, unfazed, to flick and flit through the streets and around the old blank-eyed windows of downtown, to crisscross the air above the dwindling number of humans who toddled along its sidewalks, who stood dazed in its dusty windows, not long for this world, who seemed but images left behind, photocopied in little pockets of palpable humidity. The birds lived on with a sublime unawareness of oblivion or genetic continuity, an ever-present life form that would never go away as long as the earth remained the blue-and-green planet we all know. The old saying went the cockroaches would outlive everything, but Finus Bates, for one, knew the birds would feed on cockroaches easily, happily, forever.

Inside the tiny studio on the Dreyfus Building's fifteenth floor, Finus's burled and veiny, spotted hand flipped a switch and sent a signal up the tower and into the air. He left his finger on the switch for a long, symbolic moment. He was the medium between electric power and radio wave. He would give the senseless impulse speech, and speech which was the words of not just Finus but the whole community, which was for some in effect the whole world. He felt as if he tapped the strength of life itself, with which he could infuse his listeners as a tonic against the possibility of not rising to meet the day.

He had the ironic, wizened face of a vaudevillian straight man, which he actually had been a few times in his late teens. When traveling vaudeville acts would stop in Mercury on the circuit, they sometimes wrote him in as a kind of punching bag for their roundhouse jokes because his somber dignified expression, onstage, was funny. He'd even gotten to know George Burns, in those days before George had made it. Old George would sometimes call on the phone during Finus's radio show and they'd talk for a while, about vaudeville and Gracie and George's memories of visiting Mercury, and about George's revivified fame as Hollywood's favorite geezer. Finus's audience in Mercury, mostly old white folks, had gotten so used to hearing George Burns call him up every month or so that in unguarded moments they almost thought of George Burns as a fellow resident, someone with whom they shared a collective knowledge of their histories, their individual lives. After all, Finus would talk to George about them, George knew many of their names. These people wouldn't have been surprised to see George tottering along Mercury's cracked and cantilevered sidewalks looking for someplace to get a good martini. Some of the old men caught themselves at times pretty sure they had actually met George, stopped to shoot the breeze with him outside Ivyloy's barbershop, watched him screw one of those plastic tips onto the crown of his cheap cigar.

After vaudeville, Finus stayed off the stage until radio offered another, of a sort, in his old age. WCUV's owner asked him to just come in for a few hours each morning, talk to folks, play some music. Over the years his sense of his audience had become more and more personalized, as he developed a sense that the only ones willing to listen to him these days were the people he actually knew, who were many, and so he spoke to them directly, saying, -Alberta McGauley, this little number's for you in memory of the time you rode that hot air balloon all the way across the county and into Alabama, supposing just to land at the local fairgrounds, or, -All right, Ed Kruxmier, it's bean time so we're going to string together a few little numbers in honor of all you truck farmers already out there weeding your beans. Hear me, Ed? Got your Walkman on? Just wave if you read me, Ed. Just tap on the headset. I must be talking to myself, today.

He was a literate man and his favorite poet was Wordsworth. He'd read "Intimations of Immortality" and had a sense of how as he'd grown up from a child he'd moved further and further away from his spiritual self, his spiritual origins, and he sensed that most people experienced the same thing, a slow uncoupling, like someone stepping out of the rocket for a nice space walk, secure in knowing the life cord kept them connected, however tenuously, to the ship. And then one day they realized that the floating cord was only that, attached to nothing but their own ass, and that they were at best more like a moon held detached but distantly in tow to its planet. A body of pale memories of when they were part of the world.

Because he was a newspaper man by trade, a morning radio announcer by choice and local popularity, he kept up with the news. In addition to local items, the *Mercury Comet* printed any bit of interesting science news Finus got through press releases from the government and private labs. His latest fascination was the scientists' recent belief that there were other planets in other solar systems capable of supporting earthly life. There was water and oxygen. There were clouds and sunsets, seasons, the cycles of storms. Gave new meaning to the phrase "another world." Now they were trying to explore Mars, to see if there'd once been some form of life there, preserved cryogenically beneath frozen oceans in evidence of God knows what. One of the scientists said, Take a good look at Mars, it's what the earth will look like one day. It had all made Finus reflective. He'd been on the air now with his morning show for twenty-five years. Was it not possible that some of his earlier shows had made their way to antennae on other worlds, through far-flung space travelers just passing through, or via some slip between or among dimensions that diminished time and space? If anything, radio waves would be the medium to slip through. Whether the antennae be metallic rods for electronic receivers or some delicate, antlike, cephalic appendage among a people for whom radio waves were the primary means of communication, he wished he'd come across as a little more intelligent. But at least if they heard his show they'd have to recognize that he was representative of a friendly race, kind and considerate of one another, willing to spend time in resisting the isolation of the human soul.

He felt the power move through him as he put on the first record, listened to its familiar bars, cleared his throat, and spoke into the microphone as if into the ear of an old friend nearly deaf —close, and loud enough to be heard, but not too loud, in his deep rich baritone twang, -Good morning Mercury and surrounding environs, thinking, Who knows how broad an environ may be? For if radio waves were not a manifestation of a Creator's presence in the universe he didn't know what was, and if there be a God well then his environ is Everything is it not? He felt the frequency run in his veins from the tips of his toes and fingers to the top of his head, vibrating the horny cartilage in his throat, -Good morning in the a.m. to y'all, each and ever one of you, and it's a beautiful morning, and he played his old 45 of "The Star Spangled Banner" and looked at the notes he'd scribbled on his pad: those who were born, those who had died, those who were winning at bridge these days, and those who had traveled and come home. There was a cancer-screening vehicle coming through for the outlying rural areas. He'd note that the garden club would be planting a tree downtown and that the Mercury Heritage Library had gotten in a large shipment of new books thanks to a grant from the Selena Grimes Foundation. He'd talk a little about what the almanac said as compared to the way things turned out to be, and chat with himself about the possibility of global warming, about the national debate over Social Security and medical care, and offer some words of wisdom for the millions of baby boomers already showing signs of being perplexed with a generation of youth who were making the impetuous sixties seem quaint and tame. Finus would put the world into perspective. There wasn't anything better for that than good conversation. It was how everything that happened in the world got filtered down into ponderable reality, considered and thereby experienced by all. It was important to understand you were a part of the world, and of everything that happened in it. After the president had addressed the State of the Union and gone on to bed and dreamed about being a naked child standing onstage having forgotten the words to "The Midnight Ride of Paul Revere," after an astronaut had walked in space and come back and touched down and gone home and made love to his wife in passionate exhilaration and mortal fear, after a serial killer had murdered some innocent stranger and slipped back into rational life and gotten his hair cut and had a meal with his friends and maybe even gone to church on Sunday, was the experience soon any more his or hers than it was everyone's who'd heard about it, imagined it, envisioned it, and mulled it over in his or her mind? It didn't necessarily seem so to Finus, for whom all experience now seemed to have been filtered through his own blood and bones. He'd lived through eighty-nine revolutions around the sun. Long enough for the residual energy of millions of years to have mingled with and charged his own as if his body was a rechargeable cell.

But it would all become particulate, and slough away as dust adrift on the earth. The world would spin on, and toss and mix such dust as had been him and Albert Schweitzer and George Washington and Thomas Jefferson and the poor souls of the Dust Bowl depression and the dead frozen Russians in Siberia, and poor Midfield who'd died the day before. And Birdie Urquhart, too, with whom he would visit nearly every day, sometimes for an early coffee before his show, when she would part the little curtains at the kitchen table, *It's candlelight, soon be time for Finus Bates to go in to work.* Even Birdie would be more a part of him than ever before, now that she was gone. Everyone would be filtered through the eyes, skin, and lungs of the living, into the very fiber and sap of the trees, mingling and mixing and some finally slipping back out into what was not emptiness after all, but was the vast, articulate space between beautiful worlds.

Cephalantus Accidentalis

Late morning, second day of a July Methodist youth retreat to a wide and lazy stretch of the Chunky River, 1917, young Finus Bates felt the effects of a little shine he and the other boys had sneaked off to consume the evening before. He rushed from the campsite down a trail and slipped inside the thick-leaved cover of a buttonbush beside a tiny clearing. Hadn't been there long, voided but still too shaky to leave, when he heard voices come along the path, and through the slivers of space between the whorled, elliptical buttonbush leaves he saw two girls, Avis Crossweatherly and Birdie Wells.

Finus went absolutely still. Birdie was soaking wet because (he would find out later) she'd slipped on the bank and fallen into the river fully clothed. Avis looked up into the air, then all around. Finus squatted under the dense, low cover of the shrub, pants around his ankles, ass cooling in a low breeze. Avis straightened and said, -My Lord, what is that smell?

-Something died, Birdie said.

Finus quietly began to scoop sandy soil and dead leaves between his legs over his sick scat.

But just after she'd made her comment, Birdie had peeled off the last of her wet undergarments and stood naked and pearly white in the light-threaded shade from the taller trees and this is what Finus looked up again to see. She had that shape and look all around of the actresses and models of the day, just fleshy enough to make a man think of reproduction. And that which had seemed merely ordinary inside her clothing now took on a baroque sensuality Finus could not have imagined in the abstract, much less in the reality of chattery Birdie Wells. Ample in the hip yet augmented in protruding carnality of bone, pelvic jut like a smooth white plow, a sweet little benaveled pooch, and shoulder blades beautifully awkward as the small futile wings of a hatchling. He gazed through the leaf lattice at the immaculate cradled shading of her visible ribs, smooth and defined of faint bone shadow, and the delicate scoop from which her long slim neck rose into an oval face made beautiful in this light and unself-conscious nakedness. A plum-shaped mouth, her sad and impish pale blue eyes. Not the face of a girl given to governing herself without considerable chaperonage and whackity discipline across the open palms—at least that was the way Finus imagined it.

Her dark brown hair curled about her ears in a bob, fleeting red hues in the slim rays of sun that slipped in and fell upon it. Compared to Avis Crossweatherly's hard angularity, Birdie seemed like a regressive dream. Finus felt himself go curved and firm as a summer squash. He watched, his heart heavy with the grief of longing, as Avis approached Birdie with a white bath towel. But something struck Birdie at that moment. She turned away from Avis and did a naked cartwheel, her legs and low, scanty pubis flicking through the dappled light, the motion quick and graceful as a child's, the child she still was in ways he would never see again, and she landed upright with a look of surprise and conquest on her face, little breasts aquiver. They were hardly more pronounced than little halves of peaches, he'd never seen a delicate color brown like the brown aureole around her nipples.

Upon landing she gave a little yelp of surprise, and then laughed out loud, spreading her arms for imaginary applause. Birdie's face seemed so free of all self-consciousness and open, in a way he'd never seen before, to all the possibilities of her beauty. And never before that moment had he really understood beauty, or been able to look beneath or beyond the masks women wore over their beauty like veils—not just makeup, but the masks of conventional behavior and attitude, of modesty, of keen privacy, and of coy lust. He never really considered Birdie to be "beautiful" in the conventional sense, but he'd felt some kind of discreet and inarticulate longing for her, which he'd vaguely imagined had something to do with their kindred spirits. And then Avis stepped up to Birdie with the towel and began to buff her down, vigorous rubbing with the towel all over her shoulders, her back, and then gently under her breasts and between her legs. They were giggling. Some sound almost escaped him, some sort of muffled carp, and he closed his eyes then and thought he'd actually made no sound but maybe he had, since before he could detect her approach the leaves of his hideaway rustled and he opened his eyes to see a pair of hands parting the branches.

It was Avis. Her long, kangaroo face peered at him with no more emotion in her eyes than the animal she was often compared to. For a long moment, they stared at one another. My God! All the requisite proprieties between him and this girl vanished in that instant, as if a mischievous god had tossed some sort of magical clarifying dust in their eyes. Finus's horrified humiliation was brief, for the look of cool, detached appraisal in Avis's eyes—the gaze of an animal one realizes has no interest after all in eating one at that moment—both calmed and created a sort of detachment in him. He thought, Maybe she'll stop paying so much attention to me now, stop embarrassing me with her flirtation when everyone knows I'm not interested in her. But she stared at him so long, her look penetrated him so precisely, that he understood this wouldn't happen. She knew exactly what he had seen, as if through his own eyes. *Her* eyes, at that moment, were on his waggling member, which in spite of discovery still asserted itself. Avis Crossweatherly's eyes went back to Finus's own, and he sensed that she knew exactly what had happened inside him, beyond pure sexual infatuation, that he'd been imprinted with something beyond a simple, lustful fantasy. Years later, he would understand that she knew he'd been struck with an image of the ideal form as surely as if Birdie Wells had been a bathing goddess there in the wood, and she—plain Avis Crossweatherly—the goddess's attendant maid.

-What is it, Avis? Birdie had called out then.

-Nothing, Avis said, and the leaves closed up again as she turned back to the glade. -Something dead, like you thought.

He would remember all this keenly years later, when he learned how Avis subtly worked on Birdie to accept the insistent but unwanted courting of Earl Urquhart, how Avis spoke so glowingly of Earl to Birdie's parents, how Avis even hinted to Birdie that if Earl were to shift his affections to her, she would feel like the luckiest girl alive. But by then he figured it didn't matter. He came to believe, in the late evening of his life, that it was all finally unavoidable. As fates will be.

Self·Reliance

He'd confronted Birdie in a manner of speaking, about her imminent marriage, at the Potato Ball, spring of 1918. It was held at the old country club, now defunct and returned to pastures but for the lodge-style clubhouse. Men were a little scarce, most boys off to war. The stars and moon were out, the skylights open beneath the eaves of the hall, and the soft light spilled in upon them. They'd turned down the gas lamps. Finus had cut in on Earl, who let him so he could go smoke with some boys out back nipping raisin jack.

-You're speaking to me again now? Birdie said, teasing him.

He said nothing, gave a grim smile. They danced, and Finus said, -So you are going to marry Earl for certain. And she said, looking at him with that gap-toothed lighthearted frankness she had, -Well I reckon—it's all set. I wish they could do it all without me, though.

Finus said, -Are you sure you don't just want to run off with me?

She stood still and stared at him, astonished. It wasn't all astonishment, though. He thought he could see in her eyes that she might really consider doing such a thing if he was serious. He'd caught hold, for the moment, of some loose line in her that would attach itself to stray wildness. And then, he couldn't explain this at all, something in him had panicked at the whole idea, of how much his life would change if he did that. Some current of reticence went down through his hands and into her bare shoulders. And Birdie sensed it, he could tell in an instant that she did, and before he could quell it as the momentary rationality of a sensible man that would always, of course, buck away from the acquiescence of love, it was over, she was knocking him on the arm and turning away.

-Here's your sweetheart, she said, and Finus saw Avis Crossweatherly headed his way across the floor, her eyes pinning him to the spot. She came up and stood before him in a pale blue skirt and navy cashmere sweater.

-Dance with a girl? she said.

He smiled weakly, and took her hand.

~

A MONTH LATER, the night before Earl was set to marry Birdie, Finus got drunk at a card game in Earl's honor at Marie Suskin's whorehouse on 9th Street. The drunker he got, the less he felt like honoring Earl, so when he got Earl down a hundred dollars at stud he demanded that Earl go double or nothing and put up his fiancée as collateral. Earl, who never drank but had a temper, didn't really like to gamble, knew Finus had long been sweet on Birdie, accepted and lost—three kings to Finus's full house. Earl threw his cards down and they fought. Finus was bigger, knocked Earl down with a roundhouse and went outside, climbed into his old Model T. He meant to go out to Earl's house, where Birdie was staying with her mother until the wedding there the next day. He would get her out onto the porch, and tell her that he loved her and there wasn't anything he could do about it, and ask her to marry him, instead. They could move to some other town, if she wished, even to the Gulf coast, live in his father's beach house, he'd work out of Mobile. He would tell her he was serious even though he was drunk. He would tell her he'd call on her later in the week, and then he would leave.

He carried a pearl-handled .32 revolver in his pocket, his father's pistol, with which he meant to shoot Earl's father, old Junius Urquhart, if he stood in the way. The Urquharts lived out past southside, beyond the highway, out the Junction Road. Finus roared across the highway hardly checking for traffic, fishtailed in the gravel on the other side, and then while trying to light a cigarette on down the road he slipped a wheel into the ditch, ramped into a thicket of sapling pines, and flew from the car through the old fabric roof like a circus performer on a vault. His head banged hard on the ground and he lay insensible for a while with a broad knot swelling up through the gash in his forehead.

A couple of his friends had followed him some five minutes behind. When they saw the lights of Finus's car in the stand of pine saplings they went in and found Finus lying a few feet away on the ground, bleeding from the ear and the bump on his head, a burning cigarette stuck to his bottom lip, and so they at first thought him conscious, smoking beside his crashed car, which would have been just like Finus. They sat down in a ragged circle around him for a minute before they realized he was out, and about that time Finus opened his eyes anyway and asked where they all were.

-In a little set of pines just off the ditch, Curly Ammons said.

Finus noted the cigarette still in his mouth, spat it and asked for another. He lit up, pushed himself off the ground, touched the bloody knot on his head, and walked over to look at the car.

-I don't imagine it'll start again, not now, he said.

-Not likely, Bill said. -We can tow it in. I got a piece of cable.

-All right, Finus said. -Take it to Papa's house. And he started walking.

-Better not go on out there, now, Curly called. -Old man Urquhart is waiting on you. One of Earl's buddies called him on the telephone at Marie's.

Finus gave a wave and kept on. Shoot him and his goddamn telephone too, he said to himself, righteous in the drunken certainty that Earl and Birdie's was a marriage illegitimate in the highest moral sense. Contrary to natural law. There was a moon and he could follow the road easy. He smoked the rest of the fresh cigarette, and when he'd finished it he picked up his pace. He kept to one of the well-packed ruts. In the bright moonlight he could see the Urquhart house where it sat low in a grove of old oaks that seemed to guard the sprawling house like hulking gnomes. He walked into their shadows as the dogs started up. Old Junius's rabbit dogs, beagles. They shot out toward Finus as if unleashed.

Junius stepped onto the porch, a stout man with an egg-shaped head gleaming in the porch light, toting a shotgun at the ready. When he saw Finus approaching at the edge of the grove by the highway, he hollered at the dogs to stop, raised the gun to a level above Finus's head, and fired. He was a tough old man but he did not shoot to kill, he'd long ago had enough of killing. The gun was shooting dove load. One pellet dipped away from the rest like a dove itself and flew into Finus's right eye. It felt like a grain of sand flung in a gale.

After Finus stopped screaming and the dogs had been put up, Junius helped him into the house and laid him on the sofa in the parlor.

Junius said, -Son, you're lucky about that eye. He leaned forward to peer at it, then straightened up. -It don't look so bad. I could've killed you if I'd wanted to. No riffraff is going to presume to win my son's fiancée in a goddamn poker game.

Finus, though in pain, managed to get out, -Well, sir, what about the fool who would put her up in the kitty?

-Earl loses his temper, don't think straight, Junius said. He sat in a chair next to the sofa, a stout man with a little tuft of graying hair on the top of his bald head, looking at Finus with small, glassy eyes.

-It's a bad marriage, Finus said. -She doesn't know what she's doing. He knows every one of those whores by name.

-Hear tell it wasn't just him by himself out there at Marie Suskin's, speak of your attitudes toward females, Junius said. -My own opinion is every good woman could use a weekend in a whorehouse. And what was he to get if he won?

-Just to keep her. I had him down.

-Boy's no gambler, Junius said.

Junius left the room and came back in a minute with a cold wet rag for Finus's eye. He sat down, produced a worn deck of playing cards, and began to shuffle them on the coffee table between them. Finus held the cold rag to his eye, which was throbbing now and still hurt like hell. There was a sound been digging at him, tic tic tic, and when Old Junius pulled his pocket watch from the fob pocket in his vest it got much louder, TIC TIC TIC TIC, and when he put it up it was back to tic tic tic. Finus stared at where the chain disappeared into the folded generosity of the vest around old Junius's girth.

-What kind of cards was y'all playing? Junius said.

-Stud, Finus said. -I was winning.

-Let's see how you do with one eye then. He dealt onto the coffee table. -You win, I tell Earl a deal's a deal and maybe he ought to think about calling it off, marry a woman better suited to him. I win, you buy me a drink next time we meet up in town and forget this foolishness.

The vast absurdity of the whole situation just then swooped down on Finus, and he was aware of the old man patronizing him. He sighed, said, -You want to go that route, I've already won her.

Junius ignored him, a placid look on his hamlike face. He dealt each of them two down and one up. Finus showed a two, Junius a queen.

Finus looked at him. Junius was without expression. He dealt two more each, up. Finus had his two and an eight and a jack. Junius had his queen plus an ace and a seven. They checked their cards. Finus squinted his good eye, saw a queen and a three. A pain shot through to the back of his head and something throbbed on the top of it. He tapped the table. Heard a tic tic tic tic. Junius dealt them each two more facedown. Finus checked his last cards. A queen and a two. Pairs of queens and twos, then.

-Just this hand? he said.

Junius nodded.

-Nothing to do but show them, then. Hearing in the silence that tic tic tic. He showed his two pair.

Junius turned over his cards. Full house, three aces and a pair of queens.

-All them queens, sitting pretty high in the deck.

-Make it bourbon, old Junius said. He stood up to leave the room. -I'm hungry now.

A car roared up into the yard outside and in a second Earl banged in the door, stood there lean and wild-haired, and pointed at Finus.

-You son of a bitch, I'm going to kill you.

-Let it go, now, son, Junius said. -Man knows he's beaten.

Earl looked at his father, then at Finus.

-What happened to his eye?

-I winged him, Junius said. -Now go outside and cool off. I'm handling this.

Earl stood there staring at him, then at Finus, for a minute. Then turned around and went back outside.

-Where is Birdie? Finus said to Junius then.

-With her family, by the grace of God I suppose, Junius said. -Her mother took her back home this morning, didn't want to spend her last night away from them. They'll bring her over for the wedding tomorrow at noon. He took a half-smoked dead cigar from his jacket's handkerchief pocket and lit it with a kitchen match. -With family is where she belongs, you ask me. Earl'll never be happy with that girl.

-Why don't you just tell him that? Finus said.

Junius puffed the cigar and waved the match out, tossed it into the fireplace.

-Nobody could ever tell Earl anything, he said.

In a little while Finus's father came out in his car and took him to the hospital. He would keep the eye, they said, but it would be slightly defective, a spot or a blurry patch in its vision.

-I won't ever see properly again, Finus said.

-You'll see well enough, old Dr. Heath said. -You're lucky. Man chases a woman into the path of a shotgun and comes out alive has got something to ponder. You ponder it, son.

The afternoon after the incident, he awakened in the hospital to see his father standing at the foot of his bed, wearing his business suit with the watch chain hanging from the vest pocket, which caused him to sense a peculiar gloom. His father's hair was slicked down as if he'd just arrived at the office and Finus could smell the hair oil. With his long bony nose he looked like an oiled blackbird. He pulled the chain and extracted his gold watch, looked at it. He put the watch back into his vest pocket, straightened the vest. Finus cocked his head to listen, but this watch was silent to his gauze-covered ears. In addition to the patch over his eye, the entire top of his head was wrapped in a bandage—he'd suffered a concussion when he was pitched from the car.

-I'm going in to work, his father said. -You rest around the house, if you like, after you leave here. But don't speak to me again until you can resolve not to act a damn fool in public. I'll not tolerate that kind of behavior in my family.

Finus started to protest, then just said, -Yessir.

His father squeezed the bridge of his nose between finger and thumb for a moment, then released it. He looked out the hospital window, and seemed to Finus to have a sadness pass over his features. Outside the window it was a Saturday, and a few motor cars and some supply wagons in from the country passed by on the street, the shod hooves of the dray horses and mules clopping in the still, heated air. It was hay-cutting time, and where they had come from, where his father had grown up, tractors droned and mower blades clicked in the air domed high, blue-hazed, and empty.

-Do you really love that girl? his father said.

Just the question itself caused a wave of heat to rise from Finus's spine into his aching head. He was haunted by the night at the Potato Ball, when he actually had her for a moment in thrall to the idea that he loved her, and that she should throw off Earl, and how he'd backed down. Jesus Christ! What had that been? What had caused him to hitch his emotions and blow his chance at happiness?

-Yes, he said to his father, I think. He felt overwhelmed. -I don't know what I think anymore.

His father looked at him a long moment, made a face and looked away out the window.

-I tell you, son, he said. -It doesn't pay to bank too much on the rightness of one woman or another. It's all a difficulty, in the long run. He looked at Finus, picked up his hat.

-It's not for me to tell you not to follow your heart, but I can point out this girl is simply not available to you. And you are still just a boy, whether you like the idea or not. I want you to go off to the university, make something of yourself.

Finus said nothing for a minute. Then said,

-You know I'd rather just stay here and help you run the paper.

-There'll be plenty of time for that, you still want to after college.

His father shook his head.

-What about that girl you been seeing, now? What are you doing with that poor girl, if you're so in love with this Birdie Wells?

Finus frowned and looked away.

-Well, what? his father said. -You think you can just jack people around like that, play with them like that?

-I'm not doing that. We just run around together some, that's all, he mumbled. The last thing he wanted to think about right then was Avis Crossweatherly, with her determined if low-key tendency to attach herself to his arm somehow whenever they all went out in a group, and often when he was planning to head somewhere alone.

-Mind that's all it is, then, his father said. -These things have a way of getting serious on a man before he's aware of it. Especially if his head is lodged far up into his ass.

He picked up his hat from the chair and walked out.

Later that afternoon Avis Crossweatherly came into his room and stood at the foot of his bed. Though she was a tall girl with a narrow and somewhat flat face, hence the kangaroo jokes people made behind her back, she had a noble nose, which helped somewhat in close quarters to give her an odd kind of beauty. Though later Finus would think she'd never resembled her hard old father as much as she did in that moment. The old man was a self-made hardscrabble cattle trader whose only words to Finus when they would go out to his farm to ask his permission to marry (a moot point, her being a month or so along, pure ceremony) would be: -Have you any money in the bank, then? And when Finus said,

-Yes, sir, a little, and business is pretty good, the old man nodded, said, -All right, then, and the two of them sat there on the porch for another ten minutes with the old man rolling cigarettes and smoking them and saying not another word until Finus got up, joined Avis, who'd been standing in the front yard holding her purse and pair of white cotton gloves in her hands, and left.

At the hospital, Avis was wearing a green dress, a green hat, and her white gloved hands held the handle of her white leather purse before her. Finus, surprised to see her there, didn't know what to say.

-How are you feeling? she finally said.

-Well enough. They say I'll keep the eye.

She stood there saying nothing, until Finus filled the silence and answered her unstated question with a lie about a bachelor party that got out of hand. Her face was like a nickel Indian's set in stone.

-Where was the party?

-Out at Urquhart's, he said. -We were shooting tin cans, drunk.

She stared at him a minute.

-Was Birdie there?

He shook his head. -Home, getting ready for the wedding.

In a moment, she nodded. Then she looked to see if the hospital-room door was closed, and walked over to his bedside.

-I know how you feel about Birdie, she said.

He didn't reply, but looked away with his uninjured eye. He heard her sigh, and then in his good eye's peripheral vision he saw her white-gloved hand reach over the hospital sheets, and to his astonishment he saw and felt it press gently against his groin, find his prick, and give it a gentle but firm squeeze. And what he couldn't believe, in the context of the moment, was that under her strong fingers' gentle pressure he responded like a bull at stud. He looked first at the hand, at the bulge of sheet beneath it that was himself, and then at her face, which wore an enigmatic expression of mischief and tenderness, something he'd never seen in Avis's features before.

-You'll get over her, she said then. She brought her gloved hand back to its demure position on the handbag. -I'll help you, if you like.

It was a spell, in spite of his somewhat passive resistance, that would last through a strung-out period of dating some seven years in length, and through a long and unhappy marriage, and more than thirty years would pass before he would truly escape it. It was a moment that precipitated what he came to see as a long journey through a tangled wood, all as if in a semiconscious dream, a pretension of life. He would walk through it like a ghost, present but unaffecting of others, there but stirring no other's blood aside from in memory, a softening shape about to molt and pass into what passed for the spirit, a free traveling current or pulse in the passage of time.

Giddyup

THE DAY BIRDIE WELLS gave in to Earl Urquhart, she and her friends had picnicked at the river in Finus Bates's father's old 90-T Overland. The car got stuck in a mud hole and trying to push them out Finus was covered head to toe, Pud up there trying to drive and slinging the mud all over him. Finus came around and hugged Birdie, shouted, -I love you, Birdie! and everybody laughed because she had mud on her clothes exactly in the shape of Finus Bates, according to Pud, and they all made him go back and jump in the river before they'd let him back in his own car to drive them home.

Earl's car sat parked on the lawn in front of the gallery at her house. Pud and Lucy jumped out and ran into the house, but Finus grabbed her arm and said, -Birdie don't go in there. Let's ride around a little longer.

-Well I got to go in, she said, we were supposed to be home an hour ago. She turned to look at Finus sitting there behind the giant wheel of the Overland, looking like a pouting little boy. -Well maybe you do love me, she teased. -Are you jealous?

-I am, Avis said, her arms crossed. Then she tried to smile. -I'm jealous you got a man like Earl Urquhart in there just waiting to see you.

-Ooo, now, the others said, listen at Avis! Finus turned and gave Avis a curious look.

Birdie jumped out, and they all waved and hollered to her as Finus drove them away, scowling, looking back at Birdie as she went up the porch steps.

In the parlor Earl was dressed for Sunday, hair oiled and parted down the middle. He held a bunch of wildflowers she recognized from the patch they'd just driven by coming from the river. She'd even pointed them out and said Look how pretty, though it was just false dandelions. From the center of the yellow blossoms rose a stem of purple phlox he'd apparently found somewhere, and he didn't seem to notice its sap leaking onto his fine suit pants. When he stood up to greet her she said, -Did you have an accident? He looked, flushed, and saw it was the flowers then and laughed. She liked him in that moment, shouldn't have let on, for then he wouldn't leave that day until she agreed to marry him, no matter how many times she said she didn't want to, he was just crazy, followed her around the house, onto the porch, out back to the pasture where they kept the horse, would even have followed her down the woods path if she'd taken the chance and gone there. He was like a pesky fly or gnat in the shape of a man, swat and miss and he's right back again. So finally it was almost like she promised to spend the rest of her life with him just to get rid of him for the time being.

It was later that night when she was in bed and Mama came to stand in the door, looking at her in that way, that she realized what she'd done.

Not long after that her grandfather, ancient one-armed white-bearded sweet Pappy, took her out into his garden, where he liked to walk with her and tell her stories. Everyone said the war had made him a little crazy, though she didn't think so. There they were in the pale gloaming, supper done. He took hold of her arm and looked at her in that way that used to scare her, like he wasn't looking at her but at something in his mind. -When I was a scout in the war, he said, one evening like this I came upon a Yankee soldier alone in the woods and laying on the ground.

-What was he doing? she said.

-Something un-Christian, Pappy said. He looked at her oddly. -I can't tell you.

-Was he hurting somebody, or something?

-No, he was alone. He was committing a sin, is all I'll say. But I could not blame him, it was war, though I thought it strange.

Her scalp and the back of her neck prickled, though she dared not pursue it but vaguely. Suspected she shouldn't. She could hardly believe Pappy was even telling this story.

-Well what did you do?

-I laid my musket down and knelt there to say a prayer for him. He was God's child, though a Yank. Well when he was done sinning he looked up and seen me and jumped, but I had his musket laid next to mine. I said, Don't be afraid, I won't shoot you. I took him back to camp and they shipped him to a prison in Georgia after asking him some questions.

-What kind of questions?

-Oh, about his company, what he was up to.

-Did you tell about what he was doing?

-No, it was a private thing, I respected that. I said he'd been asleep.

She could picture this Yankee soldier lying down on the forest floor and doing something to himself, something almost but not quite unimaginable. Her Pappy standing by, not her Pappy yet, a young man.

-Well it's a strange story, Pappy. I don't understand it much.

He looked away. Later she reckoned he was trying in his strange way to tell her something about men's desires, how strong they could be, how they could be twisted into something awful, but in her family they simply didn't have the words, trusted to God you might say for all that.

She wouldn't have known a thing about sex if it hadn't been for Pud, four years younger than her but would try anything. Put herself to sleep every night giddyupping, she called it. Would put both hands down there and rub herself, and say, It feels so good!, not a care in the world what anyone would think. Pud, *stop* that! she would say, and Lucy would bury her face in the pillow, screaming in a funny way. But then Birdie caught not only Pud but Lucy herself doing it one night. Lucy! Of all girls. As soon as Birdie walked into the room and saw them, each in her own little bed, Lucy screamed and ran out of the house and into the yard, they had to go fetch her from the crook of a mimosa tree, sitting up there like a little skinny monkey, making mournful monkey sounds. They talked her down.

-It's just something feels good, Pud said as they tramped across the dewy grass back to the house in their nightgowns. -There ain't a thing wrong with it, I don't care what anybody says.

Birdie hadn't been any good at it, herself. But then one evening at one of their family gatherings around the fireplace, she was closest to the fire where their old dog Bertram lay sleeping. She sat astride him, for she'd always ridden him like a horse when she was small, before they even moved from the coast, before the hurricane. Now she was too big to do that, and he was old. So she kept her weight off him, most of it, with her legs. But his old backbone was touching her. And when he sighed it moved against her and gave her an odd feeling, a little shock. The talk around her faded to something like murmured talk in another room, or memory of people talking in a dream where she couldn't see herself the dreamer, didn't even know if she was there. She moved herself against Bertram again and the old dog groaned a little in his sleep. And again. And when it happened, it so took her that she cried out, not in pleasure exactly but more a mortal fear of what was she knew a forbidden and shameful pleasure, fear of it happening there in front of everybody in the room, who'd come slamming back into her awareness. She shrieked, as if the dog had bitten her, and fell into confusion and convulsive tears. And that's what she told the others when they rushed to her, as the poor old dog scrambled away, his claws scrabbling on the worn wooden floor. -He bit me! Bertram bit me! -Where? her mother said. She wouldn't answer. Pud stood up then, pointed at Birdie and shouted Giddyup! and ran out of the room screaming with laughter. -Pud, hush! their mother said. -Somebody go chase down Pud. -He bit me! Birdie kept insisting until they finally calmed her and put her to bed.

-Bertram wouldn't bite you, darling, I can't find a mark anywhere, her mother said.

-I know, Birdie said softly.

-Well what happened, then, her mother whispered.

-Nothing, Birdie said. -I think I fell asleep sitting there. I must have had a bad dream.

Her mother kissed her and went out, closing the door. And later, when she was half asleep and heard somewhere distant in her mind the opening and closing of the bedroom door again, and a shuffling of little bare feet on the floor, she heard Pud's voice whisper hot in her ear, *Giddyup*, and the two of them giggling as they ran back to their beds.

-Shut up, you hear me, she whispered loud back. -You just shut up, the both of you.

~

ONLY A FEW years after that, just married, she and Earl drove to Pensacola for their honeymoon. He was yippy the whole drive down, along those dusty country roads, and she could tell it was nervousness, and come to find out nervousness made his feet sweat, first time she had realized that, bad timing. He was undressing in the room, taking off his shoes, she in bed in her nightgown with the covers pulled up to her chin and trembling herself, but it struck her and before she thought she said, -What's that smell, is that your feet? And he flushed red and went into the bathroom, she heard the tub water running, splashing around, he comes out in a minute with his trousers rolled up, his white bony feet on the hardwood floor. They were in the San Carlos Hotel.

-My feet sweat me sometimes, he said.

-Well, she said. -That's all right. You're human.

He finished undressing, she looked away, then peeked.

-My lands!

-What?

-Oh! She pulled the covers up over her eyes.

-That's what it's supposed to do, he said.

-Well I don't want to *look* at it, she said. -Turn off the light. He did and got under the covers on his side, then sidled up and started kissing on her, rubbing himself hard against her.

-It feels like a *bone* or something, she said. Terrified he would stab her with it.

But he didn't say anything else, passion just came over him, she guessed. She was too frightened to feel passion herself.

-Stop! she said. -Wait. I'm not ready.

-You have to be ready, he said, it's our wedding night. Like he was all out of breath, and hoarse, and his breath stinking of cigarettes.

-Did you brush your teeth? Your breath smells so of those old cigarettes.

And something else, just the hint.

-Is that your feet, still?

-Well *hell*, he said, I *washed* them.

-Well maybe it's just in my nose. Don't cuss.

But then he was pushing on in her and she kind of screamed before she could stop herself. She'd found out later, much as she and her friends would talk about that sort of thing, much as old Dr. Wilson would tell her about it, that you could be *ready* for such as that, but she had little idea at the time, and the same went with Earl, the way he acted. And the pain. She tried to push him off her but he was too strong. Maybe some girls had muscles, girls like Avis, but she was spoiled. And she hadn't ever liked a man enough to make her feel that way, to get *ready*, she just hadn't. Spoiled that way, too, she guessed. But he kept on, didn't take long but seemed like forever, like when the doctor went to work on you but even worse, the old snorting devil having his way, just a nightmare. And later that night, too, and the next morning. She could hardly stand up, much less walk. Didn't want to leave the room, anyway, ashamed. After that just the thought of it scared her so, she wouldn't let him touch her for a long while.

That's what passes for sex, they can have it, she said to herself. She'd thought it would be tender, like a kiss, but down there, a gentle touching or pressing, a joining. Her childhood had just vanished. Of course Ruthie came along not too long after that, she was a mother at the age of seventeen. Sometimes she'd wake in the middle of the night, Earl sleeping beside her, Ruthie in the basinette at the foot of the bed, and she'd want to cry a little bit. Though she'd go into another room and do it. No sense in letting him see how unhappy she was. There was nothing to do about it but try to be happy, or satisfied anyway with her lot. She'd allow herself to grieve for the things that she missed in her life, as long as she was the only one who knew.

Aunt Vish

SNOW FELL SPARSELY on the frozen dirt road from Mercury out to the country, where they were going, dusting in the wind across the pastures. Creasie was cold inside the quilts Aunt Vish had given her. She was then just turning twelve years old, in two days. Aunt Vish had given her the women's secret that week, about the miseries, having babies. They were headed out to a house where Aunt Vish was going to midwife for a woman she knew.

Aunt Vish didn't like cold or snow. She had wrapped herself in two or three old gray horse blankets, hard to tell how many, and wore a pair of clean, frayed cotton gloves so her hands wouldn't freeze holding the reins. Every now and then she picked up an old riding crop, set in a knothole on the seat beside her, and flicked it against the rolling haunch of the big work horse that pulled their buckboard wagon along the road.

It was the first time Creasie'd seen snow. It didn't come here often, Aunt Vish said, sometimes not for twenty years, not enough to stick, anyway. There was a hush over the land. Every ragged isolated call of a crow, every faintly piercing hawk whistle, stood alone in the mind for that moment, the only sound in a silent world. The little road was clean and white, their buckboard wheels first to mark the snowy ruts. Creasie's nose was cold, but she kept the blanket parted to see the stark pastures, so pretty, the bare and veiny lone pecans and oaks, the long narrow pines.

Aunt Vish flicked the crop and nodded her head. Creasie looked up to see the little shack in the snow-dusted yard, beneath the splayed heavy bare limbs of a single oak. A cold black washpot sat on black dead coals below the leaning porch. A curl of gray wispy smoke rose from the narrow brick chimney. Three small black faces peered out from plain colorless curtains. Going to be cold in there, too, Creasie thought.

But inside, just one big room with a fireplace full of seething coals, the air was overly warm and smelled strong and ripe, like a squirrel just after Aunt Vish skinned it fresh in her little kitchen, and bad, too, like poop. An iron kettle hung low over the fireplace coals, something inside it steaming.

A dozen or more pairs of black eyes looked at her from faces nearly hidden in the gloomy light. Children from big to small, standing against the walls and squatting on the floor, all of them looking at Aunt Vish and then at her, at Vish, at her. She stuck to her spot where she'd stepped just inside the door.

Aunt Vish shed her coat and went straight for the steaming pot to ladle some of what was in it to a basin. She took a bar of soap from the hearth, dropped it in the basin, then went over to the big bed where the woman lay under a pile of quilts and blankets. A bright round copper face shiny with sweat, its brow furrowed, peered from where it was sunk in a dirty-looking pillow.

A big man she hadn't seen got up from a little wooden chair in the corner by the door and went outside. Creasie went to the window and looked out. The man walked past their buckboard and horse and walked straight into the woods across the road and didn't come out. She saw, didn't notice when he'd got up, that he wore no shirt, the gray-black skin looking frozen on his back. A lit-tle wisp of steam seemed to rise from his short, crumply hair. A gray tufty cat, trotting like a dog, followed the man across the road and into the woods. The cat had come from under the house. Creasie slipped back out the door and went to the edge of the porch, leaned over, and peered under it. The eyes and impassive faces of a small colony of cats and dogs peered back from curled, puffy forms laid about on the packed earth.

She heard the woman inside screaming. Just one loud scream and then nothing. The wind blew in gusts and whipped the light snow into little snow devils across the bare yard. She straightened up and looked at the horse. He shifted his haunches in the old cracked harness. Long dreamy puffs of warm air frosted from his nostrils. She wished she could fit there, in that warm air from his horse nostrils. A cold blast of wind came round the house and hit him broadside, whipped his mane and tail. The horse shifted footing and his hooves squeaked in the shallow fallen layer of snow. Aunt Vish's old leather crop rested in its knothole beside the seat, and the stringy tips of its braided horsehair flickers rested on the horse's chestnut flank. They were made from the horse's own tail. His name was Dan. A long, slow fart flabbered from the proud black lips of Dan's hole, and the smoke from it too trailed off in the air.

Her feet and hands were stiff with cold. Be like this when I'm old like Aunt Vish, all the time, she thought. She didn't want to go back inside. She listened. Still no sounds in there. She got too curious, went back in. Maybe the woman had died. She wanted to see her, see if her eyes stayed open. Aunt Vish said some peo-ple closed their eyes when they died, some didn't. Depends on what they seeing when they die, Aunt Vish said. They like what they see, they close they eyes. Don't like it, can't stand to look off.

All the eyes and faces of the children were in their same places and Aunt Vish was again washing her hands in the basin. Her sack was tied and set beside the door where Creasie stood. And next to it was a little bundle, like a loaf of baker's bread wrapped over and over in a stained and yellowing sheet. The woman lay in the bed with a rag on her forehead. Her eyes were open. She was looking at Creasie. Then the woman blinked. Creasie almost jumped back into the door she'd closed behind her.

Aunt Vish dried her hands on her skirts and went over, checked the woman's forehead, said something to her and patted her cheek. Then came over to Creasie.

-You take my sack, she said to Creasie.

-Yes'm.

Creasie picked up the lumpy sack full of Aunt Vish's tools. They clattered and clanked and clinked.

-Careful, child! They's glass in there.

-Yes'm.

Aunt Vish picked up the bundle wrapped in the dirty sheet, held it cradled in one arm, and opened the door. Creasie heard a quiet voice behind them, -Thank you, Miss Vish.

At the buckboard Aunt Vish lay the bundle on the seat between them, picked up the reins and the crop, flicked the crop against Dan's butt and said, -Hup. Dan pulled them away.

They followed their own ruts back toward town. Crows winged over moving faster than their wings, seemed like. A wind behind them. Their black heads looking this way and that. Creasie looked at the bundle, the edges of its sheets touching her quilts.

-Is that the baby?

Aunt Vish said nothing, then glanced at her, looked ahead.

-Mmm hmm.

-Is it dead?

-It's dead.

-Aunt Vish. How come the woman to thank you if her baby died.

Aunt Vish looked down her nose at her for a minute.

-I saved *her* life, she said. -That's something. If I could have killed that husband, now, I'd done some real good. Should have called me early on.

Creasie looked at Dan's behind, the tail lifted off it again. Here it comes, she thought. But nothing happened. Dan's tail dropped back down.

-Why you want to kill that man? she said to Aunt Vish.

-I don't. I expect *she* might.

In a minute, looking at the bundle.

-Can I look at the baby, Aunt Vish?

-No.

They rode on.

-Is its eyes closed or open?

-Who? What you talking about, child?

-The baby.

Aunt Vish gave her a fierce look that said hush up or else. She hushed.

-How come it died? she said real quietly after a time.

Aunt Vish didn't answer. They rode on. They made the turn toward the north part of Mercury, climbing the hill.

-How come we taking the baby with us?

-Hush up all your questions! Aunt Vish said. She nicked the crop tails against Dan's flank.

They rocked behind the clopping horse back to town, past the old Case mansion and the trail to the ravine, Creasie looking but holding back her question. Down winding Poplar Avenue, into town. Vish stopped in front of Dr. Heath's house. She reached around behind her for a little paper sack.

-Take these in to Dr. Heath.

Creasie jumped down and bounded up the steps, knocked on the door. Dr. Heath came in his robe, his hair up funny on his head.

-Hello there, Creasie, he said, looking down his nose.

She held the sack out to him. He took it, looked up, and nodded to Vish, who nodded back.

-Bye, Creasie said, and ran back to the wagon.

They clopped on into downtown. White people stopping on the sidewalk to look at them, to laugh at their rig, at Aunt Vish sitting proudly there with the reins in her hand. Past the fire station, where the firemen came out to call out to her, Hey old Aunt Vish! Vish didn't acknowledge. She pulled up before the white funeral home. Aunt Vish handed Creasie the reins, stepped down, reached back and picked up the dead baby in the bundle.

-You wait here with the wagon.

She went inside. Creasie waited. Old Dan shifted, clopped a hoof on the slushy pavement. Creasie burrowed down into her quilt. After a few minutes Aunt Vish came back out, climbed back onto the wagon seat and took up the reins.

-Hup.

Creasie ventured, -He going to bury the little baby, Aunt Vish? A colored baby?

Vish said nothing for a moment.

-Something like that, she said.

They made their way back north of town to the ravine, Dan clopping carefully down the narrow trail. She wanted to ask why the white home would take in a colored child. She unhitched Dan and led him to the little shed Aunt Vish kept for him beside the creek. When she came back up Aunt Vish reached into the pocket of her dress, fiddled there a second, peering in, and came out with a paper dollar, handed it to her. It was more than Aunt Vish had ever given her at one time.

-I give you that. You going to have to go to work soon, though. Getting old enough.

She nodded.

-Thank you.

Thinking of what she might buy.

-You going out in the world, such as it is, Aunt Vish said.

Vish was looking at her.

-Don't you ever let no man mistreat you, now. Long as I'm around, no man ever going to mistreat you. You just come to me.

-Yes'm.

Aunt Vish smiled her black-toothed smile at her. Creasie looked up at the awful teeth in wonder.

-Why your teeth so black, Aunt Vish? she had once said to her.

Aunt Vish had cocked her head at her like a sleepy-eyed owl.

-Cause my heart's clean and white, Aunt Vish said. -Count your blessings it ain't the other way around.

Birdicus Urquhartimus

SIN WAS EVERYWHERE and serious for Mrs. Urquhart. She was a scrawny and sallow woman, set upon by demanding spirits, a tight brown bun in her hair like an onion God drew forth from her mind, a punishment and reminder of evil's beautiful, layered symmetry. Her heart though good was a shriveled potato, with sweet green shoots of kindness growing from it, a heart gone to seed.

-As long as Earl has to work that job in New York, she told Birdie, you're welcome here, and I'll love you like my own. But you have to pull your weight.

That meant most of the cooking and cleaning, as Mrs. U was always off to some camp meeting or another, rolling in the dirt and speaking in tongues, for all Birdie knew. Something far from the Methodist mumbling she grew up with, anyway, or even Pappy's odd way of seeing the world.

The Urquharts had moved into town, to a two-story Victorian near the hospital, so that Earl's younger sister and brother could go to the town schools. Earl had insisted Birdie stay with them while he had to work in New York with his new job. He didn't say it, but Birdie figured he worried she'd get too fond of her own family again, if she stayed with them, and would leave him.

She could stand on the porch balcony in the evenings and watch cars and wagons go down the hill to the center of town, see the smoky outline of the buildings there, and the sun's glow sink and fade behind the bluff to the southwest, inflaming the distant sandy ridge full of beeches, white and blackjack oak, mockernut hickory, hemlock, and pine. She tried to get a few minutes to herself every day, before suppertime in the winter, and after supper in the summer, after Earl's family had settled into the living room to listen to the radio and talk. She didn't separate herself rudely but when she could get a moment alone she did.

When she could get away to town with Ruthie in a stroller, she pushed her down the hill to the drugstore or maybe to see a picture show at the Strand, stop in at Loeb's department store to look at clothes. Sometimes when Earl'd had a good month she bought a little outfit for Ruthie or herself, but not too often, as Mrs. Urquhart would frown on her vanity, say she ought to be sewing her own. Merry tagged along some days, usually when they were going to see a show, and when Birdie would stop afterwards to look at a dress Merry would make a face, standing there with a hip stuck out, not unlike a pretty version of her mother's bitter Holiness wrath.

-You just don't have the figure for that dress anymore, Birdie, she'd say. -It'd look a lot better on me.

She was just fifteen, just two years younger than Birdie, but already a tart. She almost had no choice about being bad, it seemed to Birdie, with her mother so obsessed with sin and wickedness.

Mrs. Urquhart was Holiness. Anything worldly was a sin, especially anything to do with the flesh. She was obsessed with the idea of a whore. The way Merry would stare at women in bright clothes and makeup, sauntering along the sidewalk below the porch, Birdie knew that's what fired her imagination. She, Birdie, had never even heard that word until she married Earl. But after they moved in with the Urquharts she heard it all the time, came to know it was about to twist from Mrs. Urquhart's mouth just from her expression, came to know just what a whore looked like, by Mrs. Urquhart's lights.

So little Ruthie grew up hearing the word and of course delighted in it. One day long after Earl had moved them out, she and Ruthie went over to visit, and Mrs. Urquhart's neighbor Mrs. Estes came up to see them. Mrs. Estes was a good woman, but she had a male friend who would visit her, and word was she'd once been pregnant out of wedlock, lost the child—a punishment, to Mrs. Urquhart's mind. -She ain't our kind, she'd say when Birdie protested Mrs. Estes was good. But she came up that day wearing rouge and eyeliner and lipstick and a bright dress imprinted with all kinds of fruit like bananas, peaches, and clusters of grapes, going downtown. Little Ruthie jumped up and blurted, -Oh, Mrs. Estes, you look so pretty, you look just like a whore! Tickled Mrs. Estes but Birdie like to died.

Earl's little brother Levi was puny with a big round head and hound-dog eyes, dark circles underneath them, laying about the house and complaining of polio. Polio! *Lazy-o* is what you got, she'd say. I'll tell Mama you whipped me, he'd say. He'd go to the toilet and cry, constipated, she'd have to go in, sit with him and then clean him up—he was far too old for that – and help him back to his bed. She'd see him smiling out the corner of her eye, and dump him there so he could wail she was mistreating him. Made him drink prune juice for the constipation and he threw it all up in the middle of the hallway out of pure spite.

Mr. Urquhart, old Junius, wasn't home much, out wandering the town and county all day, selling insurance or pretending to. Everybody said he was such a whoremonger, he'd pull a woman in off the street. He came in evenings smelling of whiskey and cigars, sat down to supper and ate it without saying a word, just looking at everybody in turn with those pale gleaming squinty eyes, wicked eyes she came to believe, always some kind of mischief going on, laughing to himself every now and then. Just his sitting there had

Mrs. Urquhart interrupting every meal two or three times to say an extra grace over it, his wickedness was such a presence, it seemed. Kind of comical, really, when it wasn't scary, when he was in a good mood and seemed almost kindly. But one evening after supper, when everyone else was out on the porch resting and Birdie was alone in the kitchen with the dishes, he came in there. She heard something then felt him come up behind her, put his hands on her shoulders and give them a squeeze. And kept them there a good minute, her scrubbing away harder than ever.

Finally she said, -What are you doing, Papa, for he made her call him Papa (as if he could hold a candle to her sweet, gentle Papa) like his real children did.

-You got a fine shape, he said, I'd say my boy's a lucky man, to have a good-looking young gal like you.

-Well, she said, shifting her shoulders trying to suggest he let her go. She could smell and even feel his whiskey and cigar breath on her neck he was so close.

-Let go, now, I'm trying to do these dishes.

He held on, but after a minute gave a little har har under his breath and let her go, not before patting her behind on his way out.

Merry said to her one day, -You don't like my papa, do you?

-What makes you say a thing like that? She was sitting by herself in the swing on the porch and Merry had come out, the little harlot in the making with her sleepy eyes.

-I can tell by the way you act around him. And he likes you, she added.

-Merry, you say the awfulest things. I ought to wash your mouth out with soap.

-I'd like to see you try.

-Well I could. Or get your mama to do it.

-I wish I had a cigarette, Merry said.

Birdie got up and went inside, left her out on the porch. Ruthie was asleep in their room. She picked up the moldy old book she'd found on the shelf in the foyer downstairs, *Extraordinary Popular Delusions*, and opened it to her mark in the chapter called "The Slow Poisoners," all about how way back in England and Italy and whatnot people had discovered how to kill a body slowly with different poisons. They'd started to use it on their enemies, until it became so common in Italy for a while the story said a woman wouldn't think any more of doing it to a lover or husband than someone would to file a lawsuit today. It was interesting to her because Pappy had grown hemlock in his garden and told her about how people used to use it for poison in this wickedness or that, he'd been fascinated with it.

In the book she found, it was mostly women who did it. One old woman in Italy was like the queen of the poisoners, saw it as helping out poor women who had no other recourse. It was horrible, but funny too, and she had fantasized about doing something like that to old Junius, and watching him get more and more poorly until his skin boiled over and his eyes popped out. She laughed out loud, almost woke up Ruthie sleeping beside her on the bed. But the longer she was forced to stay there alone, Earl on the road, the more miserable she was, and scared of Junius, too. She wanted to tell on him, but if she did Earl would kill him. Mrs. Urquhart wouldn't be able to believe him capable of such a thing, anyway, in spite of his reputation and her tending to see evil and wickedness all around her. Birdie knew that for Mrs. Urquhart, evil was everywhere but remote, surrounding her and hers like a siege held off only by the force of her constant prayers, muttered under her breath every second of the day she wasn't gabbing aloud about one thing or another. It would be Birdie who seemed evil to her, coming out with such a wild story. She decided she had to get out of there before things got worse.

When Earl came home the next weekend she didn't give him an explanation or a choice. Just said, -Either you move us out of here of I'm going home to my family. So they moved to a little apartment on Southside on a day when the dogwoods were ending their bloom, and their white withering petals were strewn across the yards surrounding downtown. A flock of cedar waxwings like a rustling visible yellow-brown gust of a breeze rushed over their heads and into a chinaberry tree beside the Urquharts' porch, then out the other side red-flecked before the last one entered, a breeze delayed or caught in the branches and swirling on its way. And they were gone, she and Earl and Ruthie, from that house. She kept the bad blood to herself, though Earl knew something vaguely of it, and they didn't speak of it for some time.

After that it was easier, when he was away, because she'd fetch Pud and Lucy and bring them to town to stay with her, and run them back and forth to school in Earl's car, and would bring Mama in sometimes, too. And Sundays they'd go out there and make a big Sunday dinner so Mama and Papa could see little Ruthie and she, Birdie, could walk with Pappy in the garden and hear his wonderful awful stories.

Earl would be gone for months at a time. It was like she wasn't married, or maybe a widow already, such long nights ticking by in the lamplight, Ruthie sleeping, Pud and Lucy gone home. Here she was married, and pretty much alone. When he came back, she did her best to make it seem a good home, and to show him she appreciated him, though it seemed he had a hard time readjusting to being there, himself. She had the idea he was more comfortable with himself out on the road or working alone in the city.

Finally, though, Earl got the chance to open his own store in Mercury, and he bought them a little house just outside of town on the old Macon highway. It stood right across the road from where he'd build the big house with the deep front property during the war. One night in early June, the end of a hot day, they'd taken cool baths and lay in the bed with an oscillating fan blowing back and forth over them, and didn't talk for a while, just lay there. There was a big honeysuckle bush between their house and the one next door, and the sweet smell of it drifted in the window, and for the first time ever she let Earl know, instead of him letting her know, that she wanted him. He turned on his side in the faint light and soon she could see his handsome eyes just looking at her. His coming home for good, and making them a real home, had tendered her toward him. They'd grown ever more remote during his years on the road. She touched him. Something about the way it happened—he was so gentle, and took his time, and maybe for the first time it felt as natural as could be, their being together like that. She forgot the night outside, Ruthie snoring childlike in her room, and the scent of the honeysuckles became something else not-honeysuckle, just became something all through the moment, and she cried out softly. It made Earl cry after, just silent tears she could see in that faint light, a glistening. -I love you, Birdie, with all my heart, he said, and wept, and she held him in her arms until they both fell asleep.

She'd thought he'd been so happy and relieved that it made him cry. But later she'd think it must've been guilt and shame. That he must've gotten started with other women when he was on the road, and had a whole history of passion that'd had nothing to do with her. That, in this way, he had already left her far behind.

She blamed herself, as much as him. He'd never had any real love around his house, no tenderness, not like her when she was growing up. One day not long after that evening, she went into town, caught a ride with Hazel Broughton in her new little coupe, and went into the store and all the girls looked up like she was a robber come in with a gun. She said, -Where's Earl? No one said anything. -He's up checking stock, one of them—a girl named Arlenie—finally said, and fairly rushed up the stairs. In a few minutes here comes Earl down, and when she kissed him she smelled a kind of perfume on him, a scent she'd smelled in the store before. She said nothing, just looked at him, and he looked away, said, -Well it's real busy today, I'd better get to it, I need to work on some orders, and went into the office and left her standing there, all the girls avoiding her eyes.

-Where's Cinda? Birdie said then, of the girl she knew he'd hired not a month before.

Another long silence. Then Arlenie, again, mustering a smile, says, -Oh, she took a late lunch, I think.

And Birdie didn't say a word after that, just left and walked in a kind of blindness all the way to the library and stood there in front of the main doors until someone spoke to her. It was Finus Bates, standing there smiling a kind of fond, ironic smile at her, his expression changing when he saw the way she looked at him.

-Birdie, he said, reaching out to touch her shoulder, leaning toward her just a bit. -Are you all right?

She felt a little chill go through her, and stepped back. She was carrying Edsel, almost two months along. She hadn't quite found the right time, just yet, to tell Earl.

She nodded at Finus, standing there perplexed, and started back toward Woolworth's.

-Birdie? she heard Finus call out after her.

She was supposed to meet Hazel there for coffee. And then Hazel would drive her back out to the house, so she could start cooking, and have a decent meal ready before Earl came home at seven, regular as clockwork, for supper.

-Birdie? she heard Finus call after her again. -Is something wrong?

She lifted her hand, without looking back, in a feeble gesture could have stood for any number of things, I'm fine, No time, Got to run now, bye.

The Dead Girl

ARNELL GRIMES, SON of Mercury's most prominent local funeral director, possessed a general grief for such as those unclaimed and unmoored in the world. By the time he was fourteen he'd developed a working fascination with his father's profession, and had begun to sneak down into the preparation room to see the corpses who would be embalmed and presented the next day. And on some few occasions during that time, and always when the people had been mauled in accidents or contorted in some terrible death, he'd gone down in the wee hours to find them simply gone, disappeared, and had fled back to his room terrified that these walking dead would grasp him at every corner. The next day, their funerals would go on as planned, closed-casket. He'd been too terrified to say anything or ask, except once, and then never again. He'd pushed it deeply into a place where he would not have to think about them all the time. He was able to do that. Until the time he thought himself to blame.

The summer he was sixteen years old, he had been awake in his room one night and listening out the window to the occasional automobile rumbling past on the street. He'd seen the oscillating red of the silent ambulance light before he'd heard the car's engine, and knew then he'd heard the telephone ringing earlier, as he'd thought, though it had awakened him from a deep sleep and he hadn't been sure just then that it hadn't been a dream. But he heard it now pull up out back, the whining sound of its transmission as it backed up to the preparation room doors, heard the two doors of the ambulance open and shut, heard the longer creaking of the heavy rear door, and then the rolling of a cart being removed and the voices of his father greeting the men quietly, and the men greeting him in return. And then the closing of the doors, and the ambulance driving off, with no red light now flicking, and then quiet. He rose and slipped into his clothes and shoes and crept down the stairs, in case his mother hadn't awakened.

This was in the year before the strange and mysterious illness of first his father, who died a horrible suffocating death about which no one had an explanation, followed just a week later by his mother. He'd been horrified by the strange noises they made in the room outside of which he crouched fearfully, old Dr. Heath going in and out, weary, and washing his hands, it seemed the old man washed his hands so furiously in the pail in the hallway outside the room. And the doctor would not let him assist with their preparation, not that he'd wanted to but he'd thought it proper, almost an obligation. Dr. Heath laid a hand on his shoulder and said, -Son, it may be catching. And when first his father, and then his mother, lay in their caskets and he stood over them one after the other in the parlor, as he had over so many they'd prepared themselves, he felt a separation of himself from something he couldn't pin down, death reversed upon itself, become something less clinical and more strange, as if all the making way they'd done for other people to that point had been slowly absorbed by them until it became them, too. And so he felt it then, himself, that he'd already gathered some of his own dying, and it would be a lifelong process of accumulation.

There was no explanation of what had happened for some two years until Dr. Heath saw the article that led him to suspect the psittacosis, and then investigated to find out that the gypsy woman his father had embalmed just before he got sick had been a breeder of imported parrots. And had died in much the same way. And when word leaked out, a veritable posse of men from town, friends of his father's, went out to the camp with torches and drove the gypsies away on foot, warning gunshots popping the air, burned the gypsies' wagons, tents, and all their belongings in a conflagration of hatred, grief, and fear. Parnell had seen it from some distance away, having run to follow the men at a safe distance. What he remembered was the terrible sounds of the birds in their cages, trapped there and burning, their shrieking like women and babies, which settled into an awful silence replaced by the quiet crackling of the burning wagons—and the stench, faint but coming to him in little waves, of burning flesh and feathers. He could not stand a bird in a cage to this day.

But on the night he'd awakened to hear the ambulance bring its cargo he'd crept downstairs and quietly opened the door to the preparation room to see something that made him catch his breath. The figure on the table was a girl near his age that he knew from school. He'd never spoken to her as she was a year older and a quiet girl, though he'd admired her. Her face seemed a sleeping face, not one with the contortions of pain or even the blankness of death, but with her mouth parted and her chin lifted just so, she seemed to be in an expectant sleep, as if she might wake any moment from the dream she kept alive by somnambulent will. His father turned and saw him, and pulled the sheet back over her face.

-I know her, Parnell said.

-You go on back to bed. You can't help with this one.

-What happened to her?

Her father looked down at the form beneath the sheet.

-Nothing, he said. -This one's a mystery. Her parents are beyond grief. She went to sleep and never woke up.

-How long has she been asleep?

-She's dead, son.

-I mean, how long was she asleep.

-A week or more, his father said. Then after a moment he said, -She's too close to your own age, Parnell. I don't want you helping me with the young ones. There's time later in your life for that sad business.

-Yes, sir. There won't be an autopsy, then?

-The parents said they can't abide the idea. There's no evidence of foul play.

-Will you do the embalming tonight then?

-No, his father said after a moment. -I've had my toddy tonight. I think I'd better wait till morning.

-Yes, sir.

-You go on back to bed. Here, I'll wash my hands and come up, too.

So he waited while his father washed in the sink, though Parnell's eyes never left the vague figure of the girl under the sheet. He looked at the shape of her feet beneath it and could tell she wore no shoes. He imagined she was in the nightgown she'd put on the night she lay down to sleep from which she would never awaken.

-Father, he said. -Was she even sick?

-Ran a little fever, is all, nothing much. His father turned, drying his hands and looked at the girl. -I cannot imagine anything more awful. I hate to know it can happen. But I knew it before. I'll try to forget again, if I can. Though you should, more than me. He smiled at Parnell. -It's you with your child-rearing days ahead of you.

Not something Parnell could imagine, though. He walked with his father back up the stairs to the parlor level, then up the curved staircase in the foyer to their living quarters, and his father kissed him on the forehead before leaving him in his room and going back to bed with Parnell's mother. Parnell undressed, took off even his underwear and socks, and got into his bed. Some minutes later he heard his father's steady sonorous breathing, and some minutes after that, stepping into his slippers and pulling on his cotton bathrobe, he stole back down the two sets of stairs and into the preparation room. He felt his way in the dark around the wall to the sink, switched on the little lamp there above it, and turned around.

She was like a ghost there under the sheet. He could imagine, felt almost he had been there with her when she had drawn her last breath. The sweet expiration. This loss to him, to Parnell, of that which had never been his nor could be in life, and now here alone with him in death, she was. His heart ached with it.

He drew the sheet away from her face, his hands trembling, and the shock of her features, more alone with him than he'd ever imagined a girl could be, moved through him like a mild electric current.

He hadn't noticed her much, but a few times, passing her in the hallway at school he had observed her shyness, how she walked with her chin tucked down in her neck, her dark brown eyes glancing up to make sure she didn't run into anyone or get run over in the between-class rush, hardly daring to make eye contact with anyone. Glance up with a smile that seemed almost apologetic, then look down again and make her tentative way along. She was beautiful, he could see now, but no one would have noticed this, she'd been so demure and invisible. Now so visible it seemed a crime that she had never been admired by anyone but her parents, or maybe some boy just as shy as she was, someone who'd never have had the nerve to talk to her or ask her to a game, or ask her to dance at one of the dances they sometimes held at evening in the gymnasium.

Someone like Parnell. She was a little dark, and her dark eyebrows were narrow but thick and defined, with a little arch like a V pointing upward in the middle of each one. And her eyes, closed, were wide-set. But it was her mouth that transfixed Parnell. It was broad and full, her lips a little dry and cracked, and now parted in death he could only imagine how expressive it must have been when she was at home, with family, and uninhibited by her shyness, how much joy she must have given to her mother and father, how much they must have hoped for her.

It was the hint of exotic in her features that began to sink into him now. What exotic locale they suggested he could not imagine, but someplace different. It was not the look of a gypsy. Until the woman with parrot fever, which ended it all, his father had often embalmed and buried gypsies; he had a friendship with the old gypsy queen's son. He'd buried the queen, in that grand ceremony they'd conducted down 8th Street to the old cemetery west of town, Rose Hill. But she was not a gypsy. Her name, now he remembered, was Littleton, that was fitting. Constance Littleton, they called her Connie. Little Connie Littleton, here alone with Parnell. He leaned down and kissed her lips. Dry as desiccated clay. No give there. No, there was the faintest. She was not entirely cold. Still fresh in death, still sweet in passing. Still between the living and the dead, her spirit not entirely removed. He gently pulled the sheet down across her body, and off her small toes.

She was all small. And if she'd worn her nightgown in death his father had removed it, to prepare for embalming. She barely had feminine breasts. Her arms and legs were thin, her wrists no bigger round than stalks of sugarcane. Her shins and ankles almost bird-narrow, ending in the slim flat feet. Her waist was like a boy's, not narrow and flaring into her hips. Her hands were turned up, as if she were consciously laid out in sacrifice, merely drugged by the high priests who'd laid her there.

He imagined that if he had known her, they would have walked to a little clearing in the woods. She would be silent, as always, and hardly able to look at him in her shyness. And in his own, little else to say. They would have sat together in slanting afternoon sunlight and let the quiet sounds of the woods gather around them for their company. He took the robe off and stood there a long moment with his eyes closed.

-I love you, he said to her. -You have to know that.

He began to cry a little, his eyes welled up. He had loved her and he hadn't even known it. He began to be flooded by memories of her. He'd seen her eating by herself or with a couple of almost equally silent girlfriends in the school cafeteria. He'd seen her sitting on a bench beside the stadium reading a book and eating an apple one day. She wore a sweater and a tartan skirt and penny loafers. He imagined her helping him remove them, one by one, the light sweater, the skirt and shoes and socks off her feet, her underwear and a little brasiere there more for modesty than support.

The table hardly creaked when he climbed atop it and lay in the narrow space beside her. -I do love you, he whispered. He had hardly to push apart her thin legs, she was in the attitude to receive him already. At her neck, and behind her ears, in her hair, the musty sweet-and-sour smell of a week's neglect in her bed. He could hardly hear the sounds he made for the louder sound of the blood rushing behind his eyes.

As he laid his weight upon her, her lips parted and an almost imperceptible exhalation escaped them, the odor of something strange and familiar too, an animal's breath, and rotten flowers, the scum of an iron-rich creek near the swamps, the odor of richly decaying life, life in death, the dying always overtaking the living so the richness of the roots of life must push up unevolved from the earth and into an almost instant decomposition. She was thick and solid in her tissue, hard in parts of protruding bone like stones beneath a mat of firm moss, and cool but dry. Inside her was thick and cool and close but not entirely unyielding, his hard prick like a rigid fetus inside a cold womb. He moved himself deeper, slowly, with a wild restraint born of his barely contained respect and love for her, which fought within each second in his mind with a violent lust. He gripped the delicate knobs of her shoulders, which fit snugly into the palms of his own small, childlike hands. His mouth was at her ear, and into it he whispered desperate declarations of his passion, her beauty, oh how she was giving more of herself to him each moment. Some heated current ran its hot millipede fingers up his spine, shocked through his brain and out his scalp, his follicles pure heat valves, his jaw thrown open as if to eject his own heart, some shout must have rolled out of his diaphram though he could no more distinguish sound from some other force than if it had occurred in a world yet to know any living, breathing thing, his drool on her neck making a wet spot he could see, when he could see again, spreading beside her lank dark hair on the table beneath them.

He closed his eyes and lay there, his breath returning slowly to normal, his heart returning to a dreaded calm, when he heard the little noise that made him open his eyes again. It was a sound like the first little cheep you hear sometimes outside your window at dawn when a bird wakes up in its nest. And when he looked he saw first her mouth move, the lips press together, and then her narrow brow furrow over her thick dark eyebrows. His own breath caught in him like he'd been delivered a blow just as she caught her own, and her eyes opened like those of a child who's been sleeping long and hard and he was up and off her still thumping gently with the last of what he'd done, and standing there watching her.

She lay there blinking for a long moment, then sat up.

-Mama?

Her voice small and crusty, weak. A thick gray cloud in her eyes, clearing.

-Where am I?

Parnell had retreated further away from her into a darker corner. Now she was blinking her eyes and looking at him.

-Where am I?

He couldn't move. She stared at him a moment, then felt on her right shoulder where Parnell had drooled, looked at the faint glint of moisture on her hand. She looked down and tentatively touched her lower abdomen, her tummy, felt herself, made a quiet hnngh sound, an almost delicate expression of puzzlement. She saw the sheet still bunched at her feet and reached down to get it. She pulled it up over her waist, and then held it while she got down from the embalming table. Her bare toes flexing as they touched the cold concrete floor. She fixed the sheet around her shoulders like some kind of biblical robe and found the door with her eyes and started for it slowly, like a sleepwalker. She had forgotten him. She was not fully awake. He did not know what. He did not know what this was. Her hand found the doorknob and she opened the door and then stood there a minute in the doorway, looking out, looking up the stairs. And then she started up the stairs, going slowly, a little shaky, her hand on the railing. At the top of the stairs she opened the door to the main floor and stepped through.

Parnell snatched up his robe and put it on and followed her quietly in his slippers. When he got to the top of the steps she was almost to the front door at the end of the entrance hallway. She pulled on the door a second, and Parnell almost cried out, thinking she would not be able to open it and his parents would wake at her rattling the knob. Then he heard the lock tumbler click and the door creaked open, not too loudly, and she walked out into the streetlamp light on the front porch. He hurried forward to catch the door before it shut to and just did catch it and opened it to look out. The girl was out to the sidewalk now, still looking about her as if in a dream.

He was paralyzed with terror, but what could he do? In the mist of the bare light before dawn she was a diminishing figure wrapped in a white sheet, her dark hair and bare white feet exposed, a slip of leg when she took her steps, wavering, like a child drunk or a poor corpse wandering toward its gloom as a ghost, until she disappeared in the faint light, a wisp becoming one with the misty fog, and he closed the door quietly, leaned against it trying to catch his breath, and then stole up the stairs and crawled back into his bed and lay there for what seemed hours until he heard his parents stirring.

He lay there curled in his bed unable to move, his mind a wild jumble of fear and horror. What had he done? What would become of him now? He was more alive and awake and full of terror and wonder than he had ever felt in his life, and waited for the news to spread to the proper authorities who would come to arrest him, and thought about what he would say.

It could have been a few minutes later, it could have been an hour, he couldn't tell, when he heard the telephone ring. And in a minute he heard the door to his parents' room open, and his father rushing down the stairs. And then his mother calling down to his father, and he heard her go by his room and down the stairs. And he waited longer, lying under the sheets and awaiting whatever would happen. He heard their car start and leave. Then nothing. And he stayed there until some long time later, it seemed, his mother opened the door to his room and stuck her head in, a queer look on her face.

-Parnell, hon, come on down to breakfast.

-What is it, Mama? I heard Papa leave.

She stood there a second, looking at him.

-That Littleton girl, she finally said, and looked then as if her senses came back. -She just up and walked out of here sometime last night!

-The dead girl, Mama?

-Well, his mother said slowly then, I suppose that's what she was. But now she's alive and down at the hospital.

-She's at the hospital? He lay there breathing hard and looking at his mother, but she seemed distracted. -How can that be? he said barely above a whisper.

-How can anything be, darling? she said. -My good Lord, to think we came close to burying that child, and her alive the whole time.

Parnell could hardly find the words, but finally he said, -How did she come to wake up like that?

His mother looked at him oddly then, and his heart seized up for what seemed the hundredth time that day.

-I don't know, she said slowly. -I guess she'd just slept long enough.

When his father came home and went downstairs, Parnell waited until he was alone and went down there and went quietly into the preparation room, where his father sat on a stool looking over some papers beneath the small lamp he had set up there.

-Papa? he almost whispered.

His father looked around at him over his glasses, then turned back to his work.

-Your mama tell you what happened?

-Yes, sir.

-Very strange business.

-Papa, he said after a minute. -Is that what happened to those other people?

His father turned slowly to look at him, removed his glasses.

-What other people, Parnell?

-The ones that would be gone.

His father said nothing, just stared at him. Then he saw him glance at the dark corner over the by the sinks and he saw old black Clint, his helper, standing there staring at him also, and a chill ran through him.

-The ones, I would come down and they would be gone?

His father continued to stare at him. Then he spoke slowly.

-It's been a hard night for all of us, Parnell. I don't know what you're talking about. You need some sleep, son.

-I'm sorry, Parnell said. -I wasn't spying on them.

-You should never come down here alone, Parnell, his father said. -Not yet. There are things you don't understand. He paused. -Will I have to put a lock on the door?

-No, sir.

-Go on to bed, son, he said then.

His father watched him as he turned and walked out of the room and closed the door behind him and stood there a moment, and heard murmuring conversation between his father and old Clint but couldn't make out what they were saying. He went upstairs to his room and lay there all day with no coherent thought in his head until sometime in late afternoon he dozed off, and would not come down to eat supper. His mother brought him a sandwich up to his bed and sat on his bedside smoothing back his hair as he ate it, and whispering, -Poor boy, sometimes I wish we weren't in this business, it's no place for a little boy to grow up.

-Yes, ma'am, he said, and forced some bites of the sandwich down, though his mind still raced wildly, and for the next several days, when he feigned sick to stay out of school, terrified to go there lest the other children see in his face what he'd done. Until finally he was forced to go back, and he crept the halls more fear-fully than ever, more invisibly than ever, and spoke to no one, and became again simply the strange Parnell all the children had always known, who kept to himself and would be a mortician when he was older, and was therefore an oddity to be abided with some amusement and unarticulated dread. And after some time, late in the year, the dead girl returned to school, as well.

He would see her in the hallways, after that, but like Parnell she was more the way she had been than ever before. She clutched her books to her thin chest, she kept her eyes down at her feet, and moved quickly from class to class. But Parnell, when he saw her now, saw more than he could bear. Her life, her living, the vital self she carried through the drab hallways, seemed a continuous miracle and the source of a deepening shame, even as the horror at what he had done became for him in his private and unchallenged thoughts something commonplace. Replaced, as it was, by simple shame, a secret and unmentionable embarrassment. In what little niche of her memory was she aware of what had happened? In what dream that visited her in the hours she could not recall, long before she would awake, this miracle of awakening every day? What part of Parnell existed in there, to be known by no one but Parnell and a part of Constance Littleton that might never resurface, and if it did could not be believed? Some students, some of the boys, called her the Dead Girl and would laugh. Other students said she had no memory of anything from when she went to sleep until she woke up in the hospital. Wandered from the funeral home like some risen mummy and went straight to the hospital. It was like an angel had guided her there, some of the pious girls said. But if it was an angel, Parnell said to himself, it was a fallen one, awakened now to see the darkness of the world all around him.

Finus Connubialis

SEVEN YEARS FINUS and Avis Crossweatherly spent in a desultory dance with one another, a rutting seven years in which they scratched whenever possible at an itch neither seemed able to truly satisfy for the other, yet they tried. In the seventh year Avis conceived and they married quickly in a ceremony at his parents' beach house on the Alabama coast. They bought a small home in north Mercury and set about what would later seem to Finus the time-honored practice of slow connubial dissolution.

At a barbeque Earl Urquhart put on for several couples at his lake house one year, Finus and Avis lounged about on the patio of the little concrete block cabin sipping beer while the children ran in and out of the water, romping on the bank until they got hot again and then running back and jumping in. Only Finus and Avis's little boy, Eric, did not join them. They'd forgotten his swimsuit, and he stood on the lawn looking awkward in the sailor boy outfit Avis had purchased for him the day before at Marx Rothenberg and which she'd forbade him to get dirty or wet. Finus watched as Eric stood in the sun there—a seven-year-old boy slightly pigeon-toed in his meekness, little hands by his sides, his pale straight hair almost glowing in the sunlight, looking more like a fragile gathering of light in the shape of a child than a real, a corporeal, child—as the other children shrieked and flopped onto the grass beside him and ran crying chasing one another back to the water, where they splashed around and screamed in delight. Every now and then Finus would see him glance back at the adults up on the patio in the shade of the loblolly pines.

In that moment Finus felt all his own failings as a father well up inside him and he lost his appetite for even the cold can of Falstaff in his hand, which he'd so relished just a couple of seconds before. He judged that his paternal failings emerged from his seemingly terminal distraction, his tendency to daydream his way through the days and to resent insistent intrusions along those wayward paths. He was moody, melancholy, and took a kind of joy in solitude, a well of this inside him that must be filled at regular intervals. And if it was not, if the demands upon his attention caused this well not to fill each day or week or month or season, he felt edgy and irritable—and, ironically though with perfect logic, somewhat empty inside.

He stole occasional looks at Birdie, who seemed entirely self-possessed and content sitting in her green metal patio chair and sipping a glass of lemonade, bouncing one leg over the other and talking to Cicero Sparrow's wife, Cornelia, who took slugs of her third or fourth Falstaff and wore a ridiculously wide-brimmed straw hat and sunglasses, to hide the wreckage of her alcoholic, insomniac eyes. Avis stood beside Earl, wearing her cream-colored summer dress and her new canvas summer shoes from Earl's store, her short light brown hair swept back behind her ears, her so-often-suspicious or angry green eyes alight with good humor and eager attention. She was still a handsome woman. Finus had at some point in their past let himself let go, stopped comparing her to Birdie in appearance and attitude, and resolved to love Avis for who and what she was, to open his heart to her own clenched one, to open his longing to her long and harder-edged beauty, for he knew it was something to appreciate. Avis tossed her head back at some joke Earl had made, her slightly hoarse voice rising in high laughter, and when she glanced over at Finus he gave her a little smile, and she gave him a big broad one back in just the moment before her eyes registered all their troubles again swiftly like some hole in the sky sucking day into dusk, their dimmed and diminishing happiness, what little there was. She turned back to Earl somewhat sobered.

Though Earl already had turned away and gone down to the lake bank to check on something in the johnboat he used to fish for bass and crappie in the lake. Avis stood there all alone for the moment, no doubt feeling slighted, feeling cheated by Finus for distracting her from one of the few openly pleasurable moments she'd had in some time. She came over and stood next to where he sat on the little parapet wall around the patio. And was about to say something to him when she looked over his head at the children and saw Eric out in the water up to his knees, his sailor-suit shorts rolled up high to keep them from getting wet.

Finus turned as Eric looked up toward the sound of his name, his mother's voice. He looked shocked, as if he hadn't expected to get caught. Then he called out in his own defense, -I took off my shoes and socks!

Avis set her can of beer down on the wall, stepped over it, and strode down the bank toward him even as Eric, a mild child's panic causing him to hold the rolled ends of his shorts between his thumbs and forefingers almost as if they were a skirt, started pulling his feet out of the muck and high-stepping toward the bank himself.

-Avis, Finus said, hoping to check her.

But to his horror she met the boy as he came out of the water and had him by the ear pulling him up the bank, everyone on the

patio now stopped to watch them. Finus saw her let go of his ear
and get down in his face. He saw Eric bunch up his face in a
frown and say something and stomp his foot, big mistake. He saw
Avis's hand draw back and slap him across his cheek, and then
Eric opened his mouth wide and closed his eyes tight and let out
a heartbreaking wail, and that's when Finus went over the parapet
himself, grabbed up Eric in his arms, muttered a furious *Let's go*
to Avis's astonished face, and headed for their old Ford, whether
she would follow or not. She barely had time to get into the car,
mute and furious herself, almost didn't get in at all when he hissed
at her torso through the open passenger side window where Eric
sat sniffling, *You ride in the back.* He popped the clutch and tore
out of the gate and down the dirt road back to the highway. On
the way home no one said anything until Eric, still sniffling,
asked, as children will do when they know the advantage is in
their court, -Could we stop at Brookshire's and get some ice
cream? Finus almost laughed, and said finally, -Later on this afternoon, I'll take you. And he could feel the waves of intensified outrage from Avis in the backseat that he would take one step further
to ostracize her in this situation.

Later, after he had taken Eric to get ice cream and had sat with
him in the parking lot eating it, tall fountain glasses of ice cream
and nuts and chocolate sauce and pineapple pieces and a cherry
on top of whipped cream—Cupid's Delights, the shop called
them—and after he and Eric had driven out to the airport and
watched an old biplane come in to land over the roof of the car,
its wings wobbling slowly to stay on the center-line track of the
runway, and they'd gone home with dusk approaching, Avis had
come up as he sat reading the paper and drinking a bourbon and
water in the den and stood there.

-I know I was wrong to do that, she said.

He looked up at her over the paper without replying.

-But you have no right to shame me for it, she said. -You know I love him as much as you do.

-Then why don't you show it? he'd said.

She stood there a moment, her eyes moving back and forth between his own. Then she said,

-You have the gall to say that to me, when you hardly give him the time of day unless it suits your own fancy. When you stay at that newspaper office fiddling around until he's almost ready for bed each night or already in the bed, and come in and tell him a story or just kiss him good night, then go to get yourself a drink and sit in this chair and ignore me. Meanwhile I get him ready for school in the morning, after you've gone early to have your coffee and breakfast with other men at Schoenhof's and had yourself a shave at Ivyloy's barbershop, and I take him to school and kiss him if he will let me and let him off, then go to school myself and teach a bunch of snotty brats all day, wishing a tenth of them were as sweet-natured and intelligent as my own child, and then I get out and go to pick him up again and take him home and fix him a snack, and let him go out to play, or I even play with him myself, help him put together his model airplanes, even throw him the baseball sometimes and chase his balls and comfort him when he frets he's not as good as the other boys his age, and then I make his supper and make him do his homework and make his bath and make him say his prayers and put him to bed, and then sometime along in there you come home and fix yourself a drink and make some half-empty gesture toward being the most important man in his life and make no gesture at all toward pretending that you could ever want to be that in mine, and then sometime along around ten or eleven o'clock you go to your own room and go to bed. Sometimes you come in to tell me good night and sometimes you don't. We are neither of us very important to you and yet you sit there like some righteous fool and lecture me on how I ought to show more affection to my son.

He'd had no reply to all that, for right then it sounded like the truth.

-I don't know why you stay with me unless it's for Eric's sake, she said. -But I swear it doesn't seem to me that you even care enough about him to stay for that reason anymore.

He grew hot over that and said through his teeth, surprising himself at the surge of emotion that nearly brought quick tears to his eyes,

-Who are you to say I don't love my own child?

-Well if you do, she said, you might do a little more to show it.

~

ALSO AT THE barbeque had been Earl's sister, Merry, now married to the hapless R. W. Leaf, who sold insurance with old Junius Urquhart. She'd sat apart from everyone in a reclining lawn chair, surveying the scene from behind a pair of sunglasses, her long dark hair curled and brushed back, her lips a bright red, fingernails and toenails to match. She sipped what looked like a glass of bourbon on ice. Whenever Finus's glance happened to fall on her, she caught it like a fish he'd cast a line to and sent back along that line the tactile reverberations of a slow, salacious smile. He absorbed it into his own tight grin and cranked his gaze away from her legs, crooked and slightly askew up on the footrest of the chair.

Two days later, while Finus's father was out for lunch, Merry strolled past the plate-glass window of the *Comet*, paused to look, then came in the door, little bell tinkling behind her like a fairy sprite announcing her entrance.

-Hello, Finus.

-Merry.

-I'd like to place a classified ad in your newspaper, if the rate is right.

She smiled, then unclasped her purse and pulled out a little notepad and tore off the top sheet, folded it, and handed it to him.

He took it, looked at her standing there with an expression he could not quite read, then unfolded the paper and read: Meet me at 4:00, back lot of Magnolia Cemetery, in the oak grove.

What he would say to Avis in his mind when she had demanded, once—just once she had allowed him to see how this had hurt her, and he couldn't remember too many times she'd shown her vulnerable side—demanded to know why he had done it, was: Because Merry was beautiful. Not pure, by any means, but she had a flowing, let-down, buxom, long-legged beauty that just made a man want to get down in a glade with her and rut. Let loose the wildness. Her hair was dark and long and full of wavy curls, and one of her dark brown eyes was cast just a tad inward. She kept her mouth parted in the company of men, just barely, as a silent and private signal to desire her. And always the not-quite-subtle eye contact, always looking at you at just the moment, and for the moment, that you happened to look up at her, as if she had been thinking privately how much she would like to give herself to you, and was now caught at it and secretly glad.

They met in the far back and then-unoccupied lots of the new Magnolia Cemetery north of town. There was a sharp downslope and little more than a packed dirt path leading to the woodsy brush around the creek, and still plenty of trees between there and the fresh graves up on the hill, and one could just see the steep Victorian gables of the new widows and orphans' home above the tops of a thick and leafy oak tree if one looked up over Merry Urquhart's bare and sculpted delicate shoulders as she rode him, eyes closed and head hung forward in pleasurable concentration on the ride.

It was true what they said about her breath, it was awful, but Finus had determined early on a way around that, and had taken to bringing along a half-pint of bonded bourbon and made it a ritual that they take a few swigs apiece upon first meeting, so the halitosis was somewhat alleviated, for long enough anyway. When she got to breathing hard it sometimes seeped its way through again but by then he didn't care so much anymore and when they were finished and lying there first thing he would do was bring the bottle up again for a ritualistic toast to what they'd just done. Merry liked a drink enough that she never suspected the reason. And it made Finus a little more daring in his attitude, anyway, and assuaged the guilt for long enough to get home, clean up, and ease into the forgetting of what he'd done, on into the evening.

Maybe the more interesting question was why had Merry chosen to have a thing with him? Usually, Birdie would later say, it was just with men who'd come fresh to town, didn't know a thing about her, and whom she wanted to buy insurance from her husband, R.W. That way when she was bored with them, which would take about two or three weeks, maybe a month, she'd have gotten something material out of it and R.W. in his ignorance would be pleased at how she'd sweet-talked a man into buying insurance from him. Oh he knew she was a flirt, he'd say, but couldn't conceive as how his darling would go all the way. She kept up a charade with him her whole married life. And just what kind of a person can do that, day and night?

It was because of Birdie, he knew that. They were always jealous of Birdie because they were all in love with Earl, his whole family, in love with him and in hate with him at the same time. He was the oldest sibling, and the smartest, and the handsomest, and had the most drive. And he made the most money and had thereby control, in an implicit way, over them all. Even the old man, old Junius, was worshipful in a way and bowed to Earl's power.

And so seducing a man like Finus, whose attraction to Birdie was similar to Earl's, was next best thing to seducing her brother himself. At least Finus figured it that way. Once he and Merry

took a ride out the Macon highway, nipping from a pint of bourbon, and he'd made a joke about her reputation, and added, -Ah,
you'd fuck your brother if you thought you could get away with it.
They were in Finus's Ford, but Merry was driving. She gave him
a look. He noticed they were gathering speed. Ripped through
Lauderdale at about ninety. Somewhere on the other side, she
threw the wheel so hard to the left that he'd been thrown against
the door, a miracle it didn't open and tumble him out. A miracle
the car didn't capsize and roll, killing them both, before she could
get it out of fishtail and slow to seventy, and neither of them said
another word about it. They rode back to Mercury in the oppres-
sive dark coming on, silent, radio off, looking ahead at the road
and placid, as if content enough in knowing the corrupt complic-
ity of their union, and did their duty in the cemetery after hours,
evening insects cheeping and chirring around them as the hot
engine of the Ford ticked toward cool, and she shouted like she
never had before and held him pinned beneath her strong hands
on his shoulders, fucking him with a vengeance for having had
the audacity to speak the truth about her enterprising nature. And
when she'd finished, and before he had, she'd pulled up off him
with a merciless lack of care, a heartless sound like a foot being
pulled up out of muck, and stepped out into the deep green of the
darkening graveyard and stood naked among what would be the
plots of the dead come forty years hence, her bare long slim feet
splayed in the gathering dew on the grass, her shape hippy and
beautiful, the long dark hair a thick gout against her pale back,
hands resting on those hips as she looked up at a canted half-
moon, and waited while he shamelessly finished himself into his
own palm, watching her, until the passion of the moment was a
mockery of itself, and a chill set in, and that was the last he'd
heard from Merry till she waltzed uninvited and late into a tea
Avis had thrown, and let Avis know simply by her familiar ges-

tures, by picking up the last half of a cookie Finus had left on his plate and eating it, looking frankly at him, what all had occurred. His whole head had been clanging with alarm from the moment she stepped through the door. And Avis had finally and just as frankly walked up to Merry and said, -I'll thank you to take your whore self out of my house and never come back. Merry had smiled as if Avis had falsely praised her hair or her dress, dusted the cookie crumbs in a delicate way off her fingertips, retrieved her purse from where she'd set it, conveniently, on the floor beside her chair, and walked out, head held up in victory and hips rhythmically inventing the balance she needed to stride elegantly out the door in her high-heeled shoes, given her no doubt by her brother Earl and definitely superior to any other woman's shoes in the room. And Finus had never wanted her more than in that moment, when he knew she would never even look at him with the slightest hint of familiarity again in his life.

~

AVIS OPENLY HATED him after that. He offered to divorce her, but she refused. So he moved out under cover of an unofficial separation and moved into the empty apartment over the *Comet* office downtown.

Mercury downtown was pretty lonesome at night, but pleasantly so. Few cars, so that when they passed on the street below their tires made an airy sound that he found comforting. The stoplights clocked through their preset changes, he could hear the clunking switchboxes as if over water, so clearly, and their red, yellow, and green glows were cast upon the asphalt in air heavy with the dissolving heat of the day like silent, benign messages of no import. And sometimes he would walk to the window and look out on them and if cars were stopped at them, at the courthouse intersection, he could see the people inside them, shapes variegated in black and white, sashed by the streetlights, and he saw arms crooked at windows, legs propped up on dash-boards, bare feet sticking out sometimes, and heads turning to say something to one another and thrown about sometimes in animated talk or laughter. And it didn't make him feel lone-some, it made him feel good about things, comforted by the presence of these people passing. He was surprised at how few of them he recognized. Very few. It was a larger town than he'd always thought, with more people in it and passing through it. Sometimes looking down on them he was amazed at the simple awareness that here were people with lives as complicated and multifaceted and connected by a web of acquaintances, friend-ships, and kin as his own, mostly with no connection to Finus at all. He felt silly at his age coming to this awareness so cleanly, so late. The world felt vast right within his hometown in a way it hadn't really, before.

He did miss terribly seeing Eric every evening, tucking him in. He had a Frigidaire in the kitchen and sometimes its hum-ming was the only other presence in the rooms. He sometimes had women to come over and he sneaked them in like crimi-nals. Or like *he* was, receiving them. He guessed he technically was. When the telephone rang at night it was as loud as a fire alarm. Mostly his life at home was filled with silence. His rela-tionship with Avis during this time was chilly but civil. He would call before going to pick Eric up, and he called to talk to him during the week, most nights. He didn't always call, though, because sometimes the whole situation depressed him so he couldn't bring himself to break that particular silence and pick up the phone.

Weekends, and the occasional weeknight when there was some-thing the boy wanted to do with Finus instead of Avis, he had Eric with him in the place. And Eric loved coming to see him there, though he couldn't understand why Finus wouldn't move back home. Finus bought a radio, a nice wooden Motorola, and together they listened to local and national variety shows and the news broadcasts in the early evenings. They took walks in the quiet downtown and would stop in at the drugstore fountain for a Coke or ice cream. They took long drives in the country on the weekend days, just driving for long periods without talking much.

One late spring after school was out Finus took Eric on a boys' vacation down to his family's old beach shack out on the Fort Morgan peninsula. They threw their suitcases and floats for lolling in the Gulf swells into the 1931 Model B Ford four-cylinder car he'd bought new just a few years before, and rolled through Mercury just after dawn, climbed the high bluff road, and Eric turned in his seat to see the sunlight slanting in on downtown. He sat back down, and in a minute he looked over at Finus and said over the sound of the wind through the windows, -Only boys are allowed on this trip, Pop. Finus grinned and said, -That's right, buddy. No girls allowed.

It was early June and so by ten o'clock the breeze coming into the car was hot and Eric's cheeks flushed red as he laid his head down on the seat beside Finus and napped, his child's lips parted, and Finus glanced down in wonder at how beautiful his little boy was, with his light blond hair and long golden eyelashes, his thin and delicate, perfect skin, faintly freckled across his small nose. He could hardly stand the idea that he had failed to make a good home for him.

Just before noon they stopped in Citronelle for lunch at a little roadside diner, and he and Eric pepped up with a Coke on ice and a hamburger apiece. They put the sweaty-cold Coke bottles on the table beside the glasses of ice, short little glasses with a roll in the glass near the rim, and Eric regarded it before he picked his up in one of his little hands and drank. Finus marveled at the boy's fingers, so narrow and delicate at the ends, soft child's fingers. There were moments such as this when he knew that he'd never love a soul like he loved this boy. Those moments when he could escape himself enough to know. All his life (he considered in such moments) he had imprisoned himself within himself, hardly aware of the world outside the small sphere of his terrible self-absorption. He did not consider himself to be a selfish man, a man incapable of caring for others, a man sleepwalking through his emotional life. But he was most often limited by an inability to see the world except through the dingy filters of self-conscious need. It was the most niggardly existence he could imagine, and he was filled with self-loathing and a desire to be some other way. To not be who he was. Which was akin (he thought at his most ironic) to some pathetic embodiment of the Old Testament Father: strong, selfish, jealous, vengeful, proud.

~

WHEN THEY'D EATEN he stopped for fuel at a station down the street, and they headed on.

Below Mobile the going was slower but the route prettier, through long flat fields of wheat, beans, and corn, till they crossed the canal. He took it slow down the old winding, wavy-surfaced, sand-shifting military road out the peninsula. By the time Finus stopped to let some air out of the tires for the sandy path from the road to the beach house, it was late afternoon, just in time for a late cooling-off swim in the Gulf.

He flung open the front and back doors and all the windows to let the Gulf breeze run through the screens. They stripped down and got into their trunks and went down the old splintery steps and Finus raced him to the water, let him win, and when Eric pulled up waist-deep Finus took him up and went out farther until the swells reached his chest, and he held Eric out and let him flail his arms at the waves. It was a calm day and there were hardly any breakers at all except right at the shore's edge.

-Don't let a jellyfish get me! Eric shouted.

-I won't.

-Do you see a jellyfish?

-No, no jellyfish today. I see a shark there.

-Pop!

-Just kidding.

When they'd swum awhile they went back to the cabin and Finus got the ice chest from the back of the car and hauled it up the steps into the cabin and put on a pot of water and boiled the shrimp with some small new potatoes he'd picked up in Foley. When the shrimp had boiled he drained them and peeled them and set them out on plates with a sauce he'd made from ketchup, a little horseradish, lemon juice, and Worcestershire sauce, and he drank a cold beer with it, and they ate bread with the shrimp and potatoes, and he took his empty can and filled it mostly with cold jug water from the chest and poured a sip of beer in there from his own can and gave the water-beer to Eric. They sat out on the deck watching the sun go down in the water, two fellows having a good old time, and Finus wished every moment in their lives together could be like this.

~

BUT OH HELL the short of it was that in 1943 Eric was drafted into the army and shipped out to a training base in North Carolina. Finus and Avis both felt a little numbed by his absence, his infrequent letters, the sense that not only the reason for their (barely) surviving marriage but also the last medium for their animosity had disappeared. When they received word that Eric had died in a training accident at his base, never even sailed to France—or in the strange aftermath of it all—Finus felt almost as if their child had never existed, as if Eric's whole life had been some kind of shared dream.

After the funeral, with military honors, Finus and Avis sat in her living room, he in the chair where he used to sit to have his bourbon and water at the end of a day. Avis was looking at him not with hatred or even plain anger, but with something more weary and resigned.

-I needed you, she finally said. -I did need you. I don't know what it is in a man who seems to lose his feeling for someone, that's if you ever really had it, as soon as that person really gives in and lets herself feel something for him. That's what I think happened. She stared at him, waiting for a response. -What do you think? she said.

He tried to think, to respond to that, but it seemed his thoughts were just gears slipping, refusing to engage. His distraction was intimate and remote at once. He couldn't really say what he felt.

-I think it's more complicated than that, he finally said.

-I feel sorry for you, Avis said. -I used to think it was just that you fell in love with Birdie when we were only children, teenagers, and you never got over it. But now I don't think it was just that. I think something in you makes it impossible for you to really love another person. God knows it's a hard thing for someone like me to do, too, I know I'm far from perfect. But I think you're worse, I'm sorry to say.

-Well maybe you had a little something to do with that, he said.

Avis said, very deliberately, -Go to hell.

He asked, this time, for a divorce, and again she refused. Something in her couldn't give him that. He closed up the apartment above the *Comet* and moved to Tuscaloosa, Alabama, across the state line, took a job on the city desk. He drove from Tuscaloosa to Mercury to visit his parents once a month or so, but otherwise never went home. Attended his mother's funeral in '52. When his father died of a heart attack two years later, he quit the *News*, packed up, and went home to take up where his father had left off, with the *Comet*. Moved back into the apartment above it, nothing changed but the dust and two or three new creaks in the floors.

He wasn't sure when he'd started thinking about Birdie again. He'd not exactly put her out of mind, especially since her friend Alberta McGauley wrote their community's column for Finus's paper, and was always including Birdie in her gossipy ramble. But he had spent some two or three years thinking of her only peripherally, as some vague recurring figure spinning past, as past, on fortune's ever-spinning wheel. One early February, as if he'd poked a stick in the spokes of that wheel and stopped it, he ran into her on the sidewalk outside Schoenhof's, chatted her up for half an hour in the windy chill before he let her go to walk the two blocks to Earl's store, where she was headed. She was aging well. They both were. Her hair still long, and braided, pulled up onto her neck. A wool coat buttoned up, calf leather gloves. The wide gap in her smile. Pale blue eyes easy and unguarded, unaware, it would seem, of the slow accretion of rekindled interest in Finus. She gave him a peck on the cheek. He watched her cross the street, turn the corner, disappear, the small round spot in the hollow of his cold cheek tingling as if infused with warm, charged particles fine as powdered steel.

Negro Electric

WHEN EARL BUILT the new house across the road he let stand an old cabin out back, hired a maid for Birdie, and let the maid live out there during the week so she could stay later and help with supper, and be there earlier to help with breakfast, too. Said he could afford it now and wanted life to be easy for her, Birdie. Well just guilt, that. The maid, a girl named Creasie, got on her nerves, shuffling around the house in her bare feet like an old woman though she was only twelve years old. Because of his interest in herbs, Birdie's Pappy knew the old medicine woman who lived down in the ravine at the north end of Mercury, and knew she had raised this girl and wanted to put her to work. So Earl had gone and picked her up. But from the beginning Birdie had doubts about her fitness.

In those days around Mercury, when you wanted one of them you just drove your car to the front edge of the old ravine, up where it was still woodsy and there was a little dirt turnaround in the lot next to the old Case mansion, and honked your horn. Directly one of them would poke his head out of the trail leading down in there, a boy or a young man usually, and you'd say, I need somebody to dig me a ditch, or whatever, and the boy or young man would say, How big? Oh not big just about ten foot long, yea deep, and the head would go away and in about fifteen minutes or half an hour up out of there would climb one, two, three of them, male or female depending on the job (you could ask for a washwoman or even a midwife in a pinch). But unless there was a specific job to do you rarely saw them outside the ravine. They did their trading in town on Saturday afternoons. This girl Creasie was some kind of perfect example of a ravine nigra, seemed not only to be in her own strange little world but hardly communicated outside of it, either, just a lazy Ye'm, or No'm, or a noncommittal Mmm-hmm, or just a vague and inscrutable heh heh heh. Never really making eye contact. Kind of insolent, but nothing you could really nail down. Everybody said the ravine nigras were half wild animal, anyway, and half something else like wood spirit.

They hadn't been in the new house a year before the day Junius brought the dummy home from the trip to Little Rock, had sat him up in the backseat of his car for the drive like he was a real nigra and so everybody that saw him driving back into town thought he'd brought a strange nigra home with him. He let everybody think he'd brought home a real nigra man from Little Rock, Arkansas, and put him into a shed behind their house, Earl and Birdie's house, and kept him there like a prisoner. One of his practical jokes. Mercury was small enough even then so that everybody knew what everybody else was up to, and people would say Well he was not just a strange nigra he was a strange-*looking* nigra. Mr. Urquhart would drive through downtown at a good clip so they couldn't get a hard look at him, just see this black head poking up in the backseat with seemed like a funny expression, but who would ever think it was a wooden man, a dummy? If white people couldn't tell strange black people apart then how were they to distinguish between the wooden and the flesh? Being driven around town like with a chauffeur, which even she thought it was odd the way black people got driven around by white people, the reason being there was no sitting on the same seat together no matter what, but wasn't it funny. People knew this nigra was not from the shanties down in the ravine unless they'd been hiding him down there for some reason, and so for a brief period people were speculating that Creasie's people had been hoarding this strange nigra down in the ravine, maybe because he was dangerous, maybe because he was crazy, or both.

But all of it died down when Junius got tired of the game and took the nigra out of hiding and showed him around before bringing him back over to their house, sat him up in one of her cane-bottom chairs out on the back sunporch, till he could figure out what to do with him. Mrs. Urquhart wouldn't let it in her house. Birdie had to walk past this grinning abomination whenever she was coming from the back of the house, and got to where she couldn't stand it and started going through the living room instead. When Junius got tired of her pestering him about it, he finally just took Earl aside one day and said Earl could just keep the nigra. Birdie said, -Well what in the world are you going to do with such a thing?

Earl said, -I don't know, maybe some kind of advertising.

-But you sell women's shoes. How is a colored dummy going to help you sell women's shoes?

-I said I don't know, Earl said. -Maybe stand him up in the display window, waving people on inside.

-Waving?

-He's an electric nigra, Birdie.

-A what?

-He's supposed to operate an electric saw, kind that you pull the saw blade across the board. So his arm moves like that.

-Like how?

He showed her.

-That doesn't look like waving to me.

He just looked at her.

-It almost looks nasty to me, without the saw or whatever's supposed to be in his hand.

Earl looked at her and didn't say anything, she thought he might blow up, then he walked off. And not two days later put the electric nigra back out in the shed and there he stayed.

Creasie was spooked by it, she could tell. If she was heading to the back of the house via the sunporch she'd pull up shy of the French doors from the dining room and veer off into the living room instead, take the long way around. Birdie'd thought she'd be glad too when Earl put it up, but when she said something Creasie mumbled, -No'm, Mr. Junius likes to take us out to the shed and talk to it.

-Say what, now? You and who?

-Me and the children.

Meaning her grandchildren, Ruthie's two and Edsel's little boy, Robert.

-What do you mean, talk to it?

-Yes'm. He talk to that dummy like it's real, then make like it talking back.

She told Earl about it and he said, -So what? He's just playing a game with the children.

-Well don't you think it's strange to keep a wooden dummy locked up in a shed behind the house and to take little children back there and pretend it's real and can talk to them? And then to leave and lock it up in there again, them all the time thinking he's got a nigra man locked up in a shed behind the house, sitting up on a shelf like some boogie man?

Earl just laughed to himself. -You tell him to quit it, if you want to. I don't see anything wrong with it.

She tried to let it go. Then Earl brings home the new vacuum cleaner that day, odd contraption like some kind of metal basketball on wheels with a hose and wire coming out of it, and Creasie doesn't like it, of course, says, -Ye'm I'd just rather sweep, me, but Birdie says -Now they say these things will clean the rugs so you don't have to haul them out and beat them every week, so I want you to try it. And they plug it in and Birdie pushes it around to show her how, and pretty soon Creasie, who's standing there with this scowl on her face, big pout, takes the handle from her like to snatch it away and starts pushing it around. Then just to get her back, won't stop vacuuming. Every day before Birdie's even finished her coffee good, Creasie in there firing that loud, whining thing up, giving her a headache, till she hears a pop and a little scream and runs into the living room to see the wall smoking and the vacuum hose flung aside and Creasie laid out on the rug with her eyes wide open and quivering like a freezing person, can't breathe.

Birdie jumped on her and started pushing her chest, be dog if she was going to put her mouth on a nigra to revive her. But she came to, blinked and smacked her lips a while, sat up. Birdie helped her to stand up, and got her a cup of coffee. And about halfway through the cup of coffee Creasie started cutting her evil looks. -Well I didn't make it shock you, Birdie said, and Creasie stalked off back to the cabin and wouldn't come back to work for two days. She told Earl, called him where he was in St. Louis on a buying trip, -I'm putting that thing out in the garage and when you get back you just don't even stop, take it straight to the junk pile if it's going to shock the nigra maid and make her even stranger than she already is.

-You can take that durned old nigra dummy too, while you're at it, she says.

Which she repeated when he got home.

-It's not out there anymore, he says, starting to eat his dinner and not looking up. -Papa took it and sold it to somebody.

-Well thank goodness for that.

-Thank goodness my foot, it wasn't his to sell.

-I'm glad to be rid of it.

-That's not the point. Point is he gave it to me, then turns around and sells it. He takes another bite of chicken and mashed potatoes. -I'm going to get it back. He won't tell me where it is, said the man was just passing through. I'll find out.

-You do no such thing. Why in the world would you bother to do that? I hate it! Why can't you just let it go, if you know I hate it around here.

-It's the principle of the thing, he says. -That son of a bitch never gave me anything when I was growing up, and now after all these years miracle of miracles he's given me an electric wooden nigger and I don't give a good goddamn if it's a worthless piece of junk or not, he gave it to me and I'll be goddamned if he's going to just reach into my shed and take it back and sell it, because it's mine.

-Well now you got a real nigra man living here, so you ought to be satisfied, she said.

The real nigra was that Frank, who'd just appeared the week before — a black ragged ghost, there in the yard raking leaves in the scant dark gray light of a late afternoon. -You there, she shouted out to him, what do you want? -Yes'm, he said, I's just raking the leaves, something like that. She told him to talk to Earl, they couldn't hire another nigra around the place. But Earl says, -Well I'm sure as hell not going to rake the leaves, and it's hard enough to get someone over here to do that. Besides, he's staying with Creasie out there, looks like, maybe she can use the company, better to help keep her around.

She'd have liked to be done with the both of them, with the lot of them, there were plenty of white people, even old people, could be got to do that work. She didn't like them skulking around. If she hadn't gotten to where she liked for Creasie to fetch her sassafras for tea from old Vish—it was good for her stomach trouble and other ailments, too—she might have just let her go, but then too firing one of them could be harder than hiring, so she didn't.

Earl got to where he'd take Frank off fishing with him, down to the coast, where she knew he was seeing the woman he'd hired at the store that year and sent off to manage the new store in Tallahassee, so Frank knew that about him, about her, which was humiliating. She knew Earl was seeing her down there, but said nothing, it was out of her sight. But it made her feel all the more lost in her life, what she had become, and she would find herself sometimes on weekends when he was down there thinking she had slipped into another life where he wasn't even alive anymore, had disappeared almost as if he'd been gone for a long time, and she wandered the grounds around the house picking leaves from the trees and bushes and memorizing their vein patterns, their shapes, and digging earthworms from the black earth at the base of the magnolia tree out by the road to take fishing by herself out at the lake. At the lake sometimes she would stay into the dark, and lie on the cot in the living room of the cabin smelling the rank smell of the bedding bream and would want to touch herself but when she did felt nothing, no desire, as if she were physically numbed as well, just made her think of her sisters and being girls together and she'd feel sad, and she would get up and drive in the darkness down the dirt road back to the highway.

She wanted to escape it all, go back to the past. To be a girl again. When she turned into the long winding driveway to the house and saw the bleak light spilling weakly from the curtains in the kitchen and den where Creasie sat there like a black shadow in the dim electric lamp's penumbra with little Ruthie's children in irregular orbits around her, she felt she was a stranger reentering a world she would have to remember all over again when she stepped in the door, by sight and touch and by things the others said that might bring her back to who she supposedly was, like someone lost her memory and struggling always against her own will to know something of this place, these people, these lives.

Discussion with the Dummy

CREASIE HAD HATED the dummy from the start. Mr. Junius would round up all the little grandchildren, Ruthie's two and Edsel's Robert, bring them out there and walk them out to the shed to see the dummy. Come on, let's go see Oscar! he'd say. Come on, Creasie, you come along. And out they'd troop back to the shed, Miss Birdie fussing at him from the kitchen door the whole way, she didn't like that dummy. Mr. Junius would rattle his keys and open an old hasp lock on the shed door, call out, Look alive, now, Oscar! Company coming! and he'd cre-e-e-eak open the big wide door that was nothing but another sheet of roofing tin on a frame made into a shed door. Blade of light would slice slowly into the shed's darkness. And up on the highest shelf, feet dangling, eyes looking off to his left like a happy blind man, sat Oscar. He wore a dingy white shirt with no collar, shabby work britches with faded red suspenders, white socks, and a pair of knobby-toed work shoes that came over his ankles, if indeed he had ankles, she couldn't say.

All of them looked up at Oscar in dread and a kind of wonder, though hers of a slightly different kind than theirs, wondering just what it was made this white man want to keep a colored dummy locked up in a black-dark shed like that, up on a shelf. Something about it very odd.

-Well hello there Oscar how you doin' today! Mr. Urquhart's most jolly voice would boom in the tiny stuffiness of the shed.

And there in a second would come Oscar's voice, strange and muffled as if strained through cheesecloth: -Oh I's fine Mr. Junius, how you?

-Well we doin' all right here Oscar what you been up to?

-Oh nothin' much Mr. Junie I guess I been busy with this'n'that, here'n'there.

-Well I just thought I'd bring the chulluns out to say hello to you, Oscar, it's Sunday.

-Well they looking mighty fine Mr. Junie, mighty fine!

-Y'all say hello to Oscar now.

Hello hello hey they peeped, barely audible.

-Y'all want to touch old Oscar? You want to feel of his leg?

Silent, little heads barely waggling no, big eyes stuck on the dummy, hands clutching one another's hands, and little Robert holding tight to Creasie's.

-Well I reckon we better get on back to the house Oscar, is there anything I can get you, anything you need?

-No sah Mr. Junie I don't need a thing!

-All right now.

And gently he would shoo them out and cre-e-e-eak the door would gently shut and rattle the lock back onto the hasp and she, Creasie, would be staring at the door and directly one of the children would always ask, GranPapa, don't he mind being shut up in that shed all the time?

-Oh, no, Mr. Urquhart would say, old Oscar is a happy nigger. And she thinking how horrible it would be to be locked up in the dark like that all the time, dummy or no, it gave her nightmares, she'd be locked in there with him and he'd turn his old head at her and his awful red lips and white teeth would make her cry out in her sleep. He was going to bite her head off.

And then he'd taken her out there one Sunday afternoon Miss Birdie and Mr. Earl and the children gone into town, and she was going to head down to the ravine and see her mama but then he come driving up in his old automobile without honking the horn, had been to town but come back, said he'd thought she might be wanting a ride in. She said, -Thank you, sir, I'll get my things from the cabin, and he followed her halfway there, stopping at the shed. She comes back and the shed door's open, he's in there, calls out, -Hey, Creasie, come here and help me with something. And when she steps in there he closes the door, nothing but dark and a cleaver blade of light through the black, across the dummy, and old Mr. Urquhart begins to run his hands all over that dummy, showing her this and that, though you could hardly see in there, just that blade of light from the door ajar. Then saying, -See this here plug in his heel here, this here's an electric nigra, and then saying, -Why look here, I do believe this's a horny old nigger here, too, my my I believe just the sight of you has put a spark in him, got him all worked up! -No, sir, she said, I don't think he all worked up. -Oh, I believe he is, Mr. Urquhart said, and then he'd started doing something else—to her. He pushed her up against the wall and began to run his hands over her, and grabbing her, she was too frightened to breathe. When he pushed her down onto the floor of the shed she shouted and struggled, but he held her down and yanked at her clothing, and then he was lying heavy on her and pushing himself into her, the pain first sharp and hard down there and then cutting into her brain behind her eyes, and all the time looking up at that wide-eyed dummy up on the shelf, his amazed eyes wide open and dull in the blade of light from the door, and after what seemed a long time, a loud

roaring in her head receded slowly into a distant noise and she
heard a sound, a tic tic tic, and she could see a little gold chain
disappearing into the little pocket in his vest which had ridden up
on him and was close to her eye, a tic tic tic of the hidden watch
in there, though this moment seemed outside of time, so that
when he was at some point up and off of her and she was lying on
the floor of the shed, she couldn't have said how long she'd been
lying there just staring at the dummy, not in her right mind. She
said,

-You didn't see nothing.

Dummy didn't even blink.

-Son of a goddamn bitch! she heard old Mr. Urquhart say outside the shed door, his pocket change and belt buckle tinkling.
And then in a softer voice, -Little nigger bitch, just talking to himself. -Bled on me like a stuck pig.

-I been stuck, she would say to herself later, when the capacity
for reason had slipped back into her like waking up from a dream,
but you the pig.

She heard him jingle off with his coins and keys. Heard the car
start up. Heard him call out in a minute, -Come on, now, I'll take
you to town! Heard nothing but the car motor for a while. Heard
the car door shut and heard him drive away. The dummy sat there.

She said, her voice strange to her own ears, -Why don't they
plug you into the electric? I know what you'd do. Go kill them all.
Cut they throat.

She lay there a long time no longer in pain, as if drugged or
drunk, and then pain came back dull at first and then sharp and
an ache all over. She gathered herself best she could and hobbled
back to the little cabin and washed up, changed clothes, and put
a bunch of rags in down there, found a powder and took it and lay
down awhile, and since it was too late by then to go to the ravine
she figured she'd better go on back over to the house and fix sup-

per, since Miss Birdie and Mr. Earl and the children would be back soon. And that day, wasn't too cold for a day in December, but nearly dark at five o'clock, she finally gets back to the house, walking slow, hurting, a wad of rags stuffed into her drawers, and Miss Birdie is in there rushing about with supper.

-Creasie! she says. -Where have you been? Hurry up and help me here with supper before Mr. Earl throws a fit. And so she pitched in, feeling like the whole world was dark dark outside the kitchen in which they labored, feeling like she might faint anytime, and when she heard a car crunch up in the drive and heard old Mr. Junius hail from the driveway she slipped out the kitchen door and ran back to her cabin and wouldn't come out at all that evening though Miss Birdie called her from over there, called out two or three times, but she lay in the dark that was the whole world outside that little bit of light in the kitchen across the yard that even itself was fading now into nothing.

A Tree Spirit

AUNT VISH KNEW the herbs, and when Creasie missed her period she went to the ravine to see her. Vish gave her a smelly green potion in a little wooden cup, told her to drink it and wait twenty-four hours there in her little cabin next door, where Creasie's parents had lived when she was born, before her mother died and her father left her with Vish and went away. The next morning, Creasie left whatever there was in her of Junius Urquhart in a hole she dug in the loamy ground next to the creek at the bottom of the ravine. She never let herself get lured back to the shed again, never saw that dummy again but in her nightmares. Staring at her like he did the whole time it was happening. She tried to blank it out of her mind.

But she had nightmares all that year, after. She was still having them the night Frank came in through the window, silent as a ghost.

She was sleeping in her nightgown on top of the sheets, hot, having the dream, and woke herself trying to cry out. It took her a second to know where she was. She cleared her throat and had reached down to pull the covers up over herself when she saw him sitting there in the chair across from the foot of the bed in the wooden chair, black but for the faintly gleaming whites of his eyes, and screamed. He was up and onto her in half a second and had his hand over her mouth, whispering -Shut up now, I ain't going to hurt you, I ain't going to do nothing to you, hush up.

It was dark, he was flesh and blood, holding a big hard hand over her mouth. He was flesh and blood but for a second all she could think was the dummy. He took the hand away when her breathing slowed enough so he must have trusted her not to scream and they lay there like that, his breath on her hot and sour, smelled like liquor and a fresh-cut pine tree. He held her shoulder bones with big knotty hands and looked away as if listening for something, then his big eyes turned her way and he looked at her.

-What you want? she whispered, hardly able to gather the breath for speech.

-I just want to know the man own this big house need a nigger to work for him around here.

-Get off me.

-Just tell me.

-Get off me, I'll tell you.

He rolled off her slowly and stood at the edge of the bed, looking ready to spring on her again if she started shouting. She couldn't speak, thought to run. He made like to come at her again and she said, -He might need somebody to rake leaves and cut the grass. He hires it out whenever he thinks of it but Miss Birdie's always on him to get it done, he don't think of it himself.

He stood there a second, then nodded.

-I'll speak to him in the morning then, he said. -You mind if I stay here tonight? I can sleep on the floor.

She didn't say anything, but was thinking if he didn't do what she thought he was going to do before, then she guessed he wasn't going to do it later, either, and how could she keep him out anyway if he wanted in, and let him out couldn't go for help as he'd be out there waiting on her, her heart like a bird fluttering the mites out of its feathers and wouldn't stop. Then calmed again. Something about him, turning away toward the window, like she wasn't even there. She changed, wasn't afraid. Something about his face in the pale light from the window, like he was a man too far away in his mind to be a danger. She said, -I'll make you a pallet with a quilt I got in the chiffarobe.

So she did, and gave him one of her pillows, and lay there wide awake and listening to him breathe and then snore, and at some point fell asleep in spite of herself. When she woke the next morning he was gone and the quilt folded with the pillow resting on top of it on the floor. She washed in the basin and got dressed and went over to the house and was cooking bread and Miss Birdie comes in the kitchen, says, -Creasie, Junius come by sometime, I don't know when, and took that dummy off, and I know you're as glad as I am about it, that old thing was evil. She looked at Creasie. -Is your lip busted? What happened to you?

She tasted the dried blood for the first time, ran her tongue over it. Stopped and had turned to Miss Birdie.

-What'd he do with him? she said.

-What?

-What did Mr. Junius do with the dummy?

-I hope you're not sneaking out and going honky-tonking on me. Now don't look at me like that.

-No'm. I just bit it, accidentally.

-You start acting like trash, now, I just can't keep you on.

Miss Birdie looked just like a doll in a store when her eyes got big like that, little doll mouth. She thought maybe she would have laughed at her but she was fixed on what she'd said, about the dummy.

-Yes'm. What did Mr. Junius do with the dummy?

-Sold him or give him away, one, some man took him away. I don't know where and I don't care! Listen, she said, and gave her a five-dollar bill, if you go home to the ravine get me some more sassafras for my tea. I'm about out.

-Yes'm.

That evening lying there with the window open again, she had closed it but the room was just too hot, and a warm damp breeze blowing in from the black evening. And sometime late when she's drifting off, in he comes, a quick shadow upping one bare foot onto the sill, and crosses the room without so much as a word and goes to where she'd left the quilt and pillow and makes up his pallet again and lies down, soon enough she could hear his gentle rasping, no more than a child's snore coming from such a big man. Come dawn she crept in and looked him over good. He was sleeping with his mouth wide open and the morning light glinted off a gold tooth partway back in his mouth. Who puts a gold tooth way back in his mouth where can't nobody see it? She stared till his eyes came open and he looked at her and closed his mouth and swallowed. -I'm Frank, he'd said in a hoarse dry voice. She said, -I'm Creasie. -I know, he said. Then she said, laughing kind of to herself, -I got a crazy notion about you.

Looking at her he says in this husky quiet voice like he wasn't so used to saying much, -What?

She just shook her head.

-I thought you done gone.

He didn't move, eyes droopy with sleep, and in a minute said in that same voice, -Where to?

-I don't know. Nowhere. Just a foolish notion I come by.

-Ain't nobody run me off. Not yet anyway. I'm on see if Mr. Urquhart won't give me some work.

She looked back toward her little kitchen for moment, nothing but a corner where the cold iron stove sat like a big iron toad frog staring at her, wanting to croak.

-You can use the door next time you come in, unless you just like coming in people houses through the window.

She looked back but he was gone, out the door this time, his bare feet making no more sound than a breeze tippling through last fall's leaves dry on the ground.

Which he would show up raking later that afternoon.

She watched him out the Urquhart's kitchen window and whenever he would glance up she would turn quickly away, her face burning. She went out back to rinse some old rags in a washtub. She heard Miss Birdie holler at him from where she was in the kitchen, You there, what are you doing? And he says, Yes ma'am I'm raking the yard. Creasie was listening without looking up from the washtub. Miss Birdie says, Well I see you are raking, who are you? Name Frank, ma'am. Well you talk to my husband about getting paid, I don't have any money for you. Yes, ma'am, he said, I will. And he did. Mr. Earl, home that afternoon, just looked at him for a long time, his short moustache twitching every now and then and his eyes kind of squinted, then he lights a cigarette and gives one to Frank, goes away. Next day, same thing, Frank weeding the beds, Mr. Earl coming home and standing there looking at him, gives him a cigarette, goes on in the house. Finally he comes out a little later and says to him, -You staying with Creasie now on my property?

-Yes, sir, Frank says.

-No sir! Creasie hollers from the breezeway between the kitchen and garage. -He ain't staying with me. I'm not like that!

-Well, he says, ignoring her and just looking at him a while longer, I don't care where you stay, but if you're going to hang around here you might as well do some work I need done, and jangles his keys and change just like his old papa. And so Frank was on the payroll, such as it was, a dollar a week and sharing the leftovers with Creasie, who always had too much anyway and ended up throwing it out. It was enough for the time being. You couldn't expect a whole lot more. It was just work and what little bit of pleasure you could find at the end of a day. If Creasie was working late with cooking for the next day, pies or baking a ham, Frank might come over to the Urquhart house and knock on the kitchen door and ask if there was anything he could do, or come fall and winter make sure the fire in the sunporch fireplace was going good, getting the coals so hot he could roll a big round log in there and it'd burn all night, Mr. Earl asleep in a chair across from it after his evening coffee. Then he'd lurk like a ghost in Creasie's pantry till she was done and walk her back to the cabin.

Even as lonely as she was, it took her a while to find pleasure with a stranger. He was fairly tall, and with a head like a brick, hair kind of squared off on top, and a sleepy, wise look on his face. Not kind eyes but not hard, either, just eyes that would look at her without saying anything, and then turn to the peas and the greens, the pot roast or pork chops, the cold cornbread she brought back from the house. The Urquharts ate well, and so did they on seconds.

-If we they dogs, Frank said one evening, dogs eat well.

-Well Mr. Earl or Miss Birdie neither one much like dogs. Mr. Earl had him a hunting dog but he give it away to somebody. Miss Birdie hates dogs for they smell.

-Reckon that's why they like the niggers around, he said.

She came to like him. A long and knobby man, knees and elbows as dry as dust and gray as ash, voice like the sleeping grumble of some panther beast.

-Only part of you still wood, she said to him that evening, giving him a squeeze.

He didn't know what she was talking about and just mumbled, -What you talking about wood, and not much else as he wasn't a talker.

She said, -Wooden man can't make no babies.

He looked at her like he might say something sharp then, so she shut up.

Miss Birdie says the next day, -I don't want you living in sin back there. If that man's going to stay with you, you ought to get married. It ain't right.

-Ye'm, we married, she said.

-I mean in a church, Miss Birdie said. And later she heard her saying to Mr. Earl, -Well where'd he come from?

He says, -I don't know.

-He might be a thief.

-I think he's just one of them turpentine niggers, come up from Florida to work the trees.

Mmm hmmm, Creasie thought, back in the kitchen scrubbing the stove. A tree spirit, come out of the tree when somebody carves themself a wooden dummy, been cooped up in a little shed and now out and resting free for a while with Creasie. She laughed to herself. She looked out the window and he was out in the yard, standing by a rake and staring back through the window at her. A little chill ran in her. She went back to the stove and when she looked up again he was gone and the pile of leaves he'd raked lying on the ground. She slipped out the kitchen door and ran around the corner and didn't see him and kept on running, all the way around the house, Miss Birdie's head popping out a window she just passed and calling, -Creasie! Where are you running to?

-Ye'm, (she would explain after she had stopped, seen him raking way out in the front yard by the magnolia tree, big dry leaves clacking at the rake, and sneaked back into the kitchen, out of breath), I was just chasing an old stray cat out of this kitchen.

-A *cat*? she says. -What kind of cat?

-Ye'm, I on know, some stray. Some old orange thing, ears nubbed off.

-Orange! Miss Birdie says. -Now I saw an old gray cat slinking around here a while back. What's all these strays!

-Ye'm, he kind of gray.

Miss Birdie stops and gives her that look.

-Well now was it orange or was it gray? I declare, Creasie, sometimes I think you just make things up whole cloth.

-Ye'm, well I try to tell the truth, but you know them stray cats move pretty quick, like my colors blurs. I think maybe the lectric done messed with my visions.

The look on Miss Birdie's face then, just mystified, which was just as well, was what you ought to want in white folks, being colored.

Woodpile

EARL LOVED TO get into the Chrysler and head for the coast, Pascagoula, Maurier's fish camp on the river, take his boat out into the Sound and go for redfish and trout. Fishing was one thing he loved to do to relax. Take Frank along, nigger riding in the boat on the trailer behind the Chrysler. Quick son of a bitch got to where he could catch a Camel butt when Earl flicked it out the window and it zipped back in the slipstream. Frank'd catch it in one big palm and calm as you please take it and get almost half a smoke out of what was left, taking it between two fingers and smiling at him as he smoked it, looking at him as he watched in the rearview mirror as if to say, All right white man, it's your game but I can play it better than you, up yo ass, all right. So he got to where he would take him out on the boat too, in the mornings, Frank hung over from wherever he wandered off to the night before, some kind of coastal whore, probably white, the son of a bitch. He was a strange and sly one.

Junius said, -Why you want to hire that nigger to work around your place when I had provided a perfectly good electric nigger to do for you? Laughing.

-I wish you hadn't sold that thing, Papa.

-You couldn't rig it to rake leaves and mow the grass, I reckon. Wasn't doing nothing here but sitting in that shed. I'm disappointed in you.

-I'm not a mechanic. You want to give me an electric yard nigger, give me an electric yard nigger, not one rigged up to cut boards in half.

-No imagination, son. It's like the country, now. We can't come up with something new to do with all these niggers multiplying like rabbits, we better hurry up and send them all back to Africa, like they should've done after the Civil War.

-I don't think, Earl said, it was or is possible to load millions of niggers onto a hundred thousand boats and ship them all to Africa, contrary to popular belief.

-Well, we could've *tried*, Junius said. -Hitler wouldn't have ever gone to war with us, would've needed our advice on how to get rid of the Jews.

-Well you warm my heart, Papa, Earl said. -And after you naming one of your sons after a Jew businessman.

-You know I don't mean it, Junius said. -Old Levi was a good man, wasn't like some Jews, whereas the only good nigger I ever knew was that electric one you had out in your shed. Kept his mouth shut, didn't complain, worked when you plugged him in, stayed out of sight.

They were out in the backyard drinking lemonade.

-I tell you what, Earl said, things are going to have to change at some point. You had colored boys fighting in the war, fought for their country, came home and still just niggers, here. How you think that sat with them? I don't see the harm in treating colored people like human beings. I'm not saying treat them like they're white. But you treat people right and they'll treat you right, colored or white. Trash is trash, colored or white. You deal with good people, you get good results.

-I tell *you* what, they shouldn't have taken them in the army. Teaching niggers how to fight a war? That's crazy. Hell, they'll kill us all.

-Well I'm not sure I'd blame them. I was colored, I'd hang every white man I could get my hands on.

-See what I mean, Junius said.

-It'll all settle in, one of these days, Earl said. -It'll take a hell of a long time, but one day they will have their piece of the world, and my grandchildren or their children will be going to school with their grandchildren or great-grandchildren. And whites will be marrying colored. And everybody becoming some kind of light shade of brown. That's what it'll be one day.

-I think you have lost your mind.

-It's the law of nature. Things change slow but they always change. We got some shading going on already, have for a long time, and thanks if I may say so to many fine upstanding white people, present company not excluded.

-I don't have any nigger children running around.

-I'm sure you put on a rubber every time you visited the woodpile.

-Ease up, son, Junius said. -My woodpile days is over, I expect. I'll leave it to them boys delivering mail and newspapers to the quarters, such as that, getting their payment in the bedroom.

He drained his glass and rattled the ice in the bottom.

-How about getting up and getting your old papa another glass of lemonade.

-How about you call for one of them murderous niggers works for me to get it for you?

Junius said nothing, just held the glass toward Earl with an impassive, sweaty look on his face. Earl sighed, got up, and took the glass into the kitchen.

Creasie was standing at the stove stirring a pan of fried corn.

-Where's that lemonade, Creasie?

-Yes, sir, I put it back in the icebox. You want me to bring y'all some more?

-No, I'll get it.

He opened the refrigerator and got out the jug of lemonade and poured the glasses full. Dropped a couple of cubes of ice in, started back out.

-Mr. Earl, you want any more just holler, I'll bring it out to you.

-All right.

When he got back out to the lawn chairs, Junius wasn't there. He saw him lying in the shade of the oak tree over by the creek and walked over. Junius's hat was over his face, his breathing heavy. He sat down beside him and drank down his glass, sipped at Junius's. He saw Frank come out of the cabin then and go to the shed, get the fishing gear, and go to the car. Big buck grabbed the boat trailer handle with his bare hands and hauled it over to the car, hitched it, turned and waved at Earl sitting there. Bags already loaded into the car. Earl patted Junius on the arm and said, -All right, Papa, we're heading out. Get Birdie to drive you home if you don't want to take the train, now. Junius grunted, went on breathing heavy.

Frank was already sitting in the boat. Earl told everyone he made Frank sit back there, but truth was it was Frank's idea and he wouldn't budge from it. He liked it. Said come on up here, sit in the backseat. Thank you, sir, I like riding in the boat. All right then, Earl said, you hang on. I'm not taking it easy just because you're crazy enough to want to ride in an open boat on a trailer going seventy miles an hour. Yes, sir, I like a little danger, Frank said. Suit yourself, then, Earl said. Pissed him off, first time they drove down like that, and flicking his butt out the window was done in anger. He saw Frank dodge it and try to catch it at the same time. That made him grin. So he kept doing it. Third time, Frank caught it and smoked it the rest of the way down. After that, he rarely missed. Crazy son of a bitch had his own cigarettes, now, too.

Ann's car was already parked outside the cottage when they drove up to Maurier's camp, the little Mercury coupe he'd given her, driven up from the Tallahassee store, which he'd had her in about six months. He drove over to the landing, backed the boat in. Frank unhooked the cable and pulled the boat over to the dock while Earl parked under the trees across from the cottages and went on in, waving to Frank. Routine was Frank'd be there next morning at five o'clock to go out on the boat. Ann would sleep in most of the morning, work on her books for the Tallahassee store in the afternoon, when he'd come in from fishing. Then he'd leave the catch with Frank to clean and ice down and they'd go out to dinner. Last day, Maurier would set up his propane kettle and Frank'd deep-fry the weekend's catch and they'd all eat, Frank right there at the table with them. Even give him a beer. Ann liked her beer, and Earl wasn't one of those teetotalers cared if anybody else drank, as long as they weren't a drunk.

She was on the bed taking a nap in her clothes, pale yellow dress riding up over her knees and the toes of her stockings twisted from her shoes. Ceiling fan going full bore and blowing at a wisp of blond hair on her forehead, mouth just parted in sleep. Her eyes opened and without looking over at him, looking up into the fan blades, she said, -Hey.

-Hey, there.

He held back a second, watching her. Sensing her mood as if through air molecules in the room between them. She'd become tired of things being this way. Of only seeing him two or three times a month. He'd said, from the beginning, That's all you want to see of me, if you take my advice. That's about what I'm good for, when it comes to being pleasant company. Well then, she used to say, maybe you're not the company I need to keep. May be, he would say. But you know I can't leave Birdie, she can't take care of herself. Then she would pout awhile. For such a good-looking woman, she had a bad pout. Changed her whole appearance. Scared him a little bit. Her brooding light blue-green eyes had stopped him in his tracks when she'd come in the store the first time. Can I help you? he'd managed to say. You can give me a job, she said right back, just the hint of a smile. All right, he'd said, without hesitation. When can you start? Right this minute, if you like, she said. He'd thought about it, said, Why don't you start in the morning. But you can tell me your name now, if you want to. Ann Christensen, she said. All right, Ann, he said. I'm Earl. I know, she said. This is my store, he said. I know, she said. Stood there staring at each other a minute. Then she turned and walked out. Other girls hated her immediately, of course. Wasn't six months he got the chance to open the store in Tallahassee and made her manager, that solved that. Except that he found himself driving to the coast every weekend so he could spend them with her at Maurier's. By that time in love with her in a way he had not considered he was susceptible to. He'd never felt that way about a woman, before. Birdie had been cute, popular, and he realized he'd wanted to possess her, like a car or money. But just the presence of Ann had sucked something right out of him, left him spent and entirely open to something else. It made him feel vulnerable. Made him feel more alive. If he hadn't already pretty much set himself up by then he might not have given enough of a damn to do it, after that.

He loved it, being there with her. Watch her walk around the little efficiency as graceful a woman naked as God put on the earth, as Eve, he had to think, not an ounce of self-consciousness in her, and just naturally beautiful. Maurier had an old swimming pool out under the oak grove beside the river and she'd put on her pink striped swimsuit, a one-piece, and get onto the diving board and dive into the water and come up wringing her hair behind her neck, then shaking it gently out, resting her arms on the side of the pool, and looking at him.

She looked at him now with those eyes, and a salty gust from off the Sound seemed to nudge him toward her, and she said, Come here. And he did.

~

FRANK WAS SITTING in the boat at the dock next morning at five. Had the gear loaded, ice chest packed with ham and cheese sandwiches from Maurier's wife's kitchen, and bottles of Coca-Cola and ginger ale, crackers, and tins of sardines.

-You drive, Frank.

Frank primed the motor, pulled the cord, and got them going away from the dock. They bumped out through the gentle swells and about two miles out Earl raised his hand and Frank motored down and they dropped anchor.

-Going for trout, Mr. Earl?

Earl nodded. -No cover out here. There's a channel though.

He rigged his own line with a jig and a worm tail and began to cast.

-You can fish if you want to, Frank.

Always a pause after he spoke to Frank before Frank answered. Nothing you could call insolence, just shy of that, and just enough to establish some of his own purchase on the moment.

-Thank you, no sir. Just feel like sitting here today.

-All right.

Pause.

-I likes to fish but I don't really like it.

-You mean to eat it?

-Yes, sir. I grew up on the river and seemed like that's all we eat, fish.

-Well you eat it when we cook it up here.

-Yes, sir, I don't like to be rude. I mean I can eat it and like it all right every now and then but I don't hardly care for it no more.

He had one of those rusty sibilant voices, like a hoarse whisper, like he liked whiskey too much, but Earl hadn't ever seen him drink anything but beer, and he'd given him that. Sat there on the bench seat before the motor like a meditation in black, big squared-off head held at attention to something not here in the boat.

-What do you most like to eat?

Blink.

-Oh I like fresh vegetables, you know. And chicken. I love barbeque.

-Me, too, Earl said, reeling in and casting again, jigging the line. -You like, I'll get a rack of ribs and you can cook em up on the drum grill.

-Yes, sir, sure will.

-We used to keep pigs awhile, when I was a boy.

-Yes, sir, we did too till a flood come and drowned them. We didn't get no more after that.

-How old were you?

-I guess about nine, ten years old.

-And had to eat fish the rest of your life after that.

Rusty laugh.

-Yes, sir, near bout.

-I reckon I'd hate it too.

He cast. The swells made slurping sounds against the boat. Light coming up behind a gray cloud cover, darker below with silvery metallic openings. Gulls glided past angling their heads at them curiously. Laughing.

-I never liked hog-killing, he said. -All that mess. I wouldn't keep a pig now.

-No, sir, I didn't like it either. My papa had a gun, but he wouldn't use it on his hogs. He used a hammer.

-A hammer? How'd he do that, put them in a chute?

-No, sir, he just hit em with a hammer.

-I mean how'd he get up on them?

-He bait them with corn.

-Bait em? How you mean?

-First time I went out with him, he says to watch this. Got his old claw hammer in his right hand, hid behind his back, like. Got a palm full of feed corn in his other hand, going up to the hog and holding out that corn, saying, Here, pig. Hog watch him, saying, I don't know. Keep saying, Here, pig, walking up slow. Pig finally inch over there, you know. He trust him. Start nibbling the corn out his hand. That's when he brung the hammer around and hit him hard square in the forehead.

-I be damned.

-Yes, sir, laid him right out. Like to struck me hard as the pig, to see that. I was just a little old young un. I liked to watch them pigs.

-Probably one of them was your pet.

-No, sir, no pet. But I thought they was interesting, you know. They was like a family, playing all the time. Didn't fuss and fight, like we did. Just scooting around the pen, chasing each other, squealing. Not that old hog, I mean the young uns. Well, they strung up that hog by his heels, was going to bleed him. I snuck up there and look at him, his old tongue hanging out. Them corn kernels there still stuck to it.

-I be damned.

Frank laughed.

-Yes, sir, took me a while to trust my papa again, too, after that. He offer me a extra piece of gingerbread at Christmas, you know, I be looking for that hammer.

Earl looked at him, then laughed out loud.

-Where in the hell did you come from before you showed up at my place?

-South of here. Florida.

-Turpentine, then?

-Sir?

-You a turpentine worker?

-No, sir. My papa was, for a while. I just wander, do yard work. You know, like for you.

-You plan on staying around?

Frank said nothing for an extra beat, his face got solemn. Looking out over the Sound.

-Well, sir, I'd sure like to make me a little money.

Earl reeled in, set his rod down.

-Get me a sandwich and one of those Cokes.

Frank reached into the cooler and brought them out.

-Get yourself something.

They sat and ate for a minute, sipping the Cokes.

-What you got in mind?

Frank appeared to study the question for a while.

-Well, sir, you know how you get me to help out down to the store every now and then, up in the stockroom where you has your cot.

Earl stiffened a little at that. Let it go.

-Go on.

-Well, sir, I know how you cares for Miss Ann, and she off down there with that store in Tallahassee, and you having to travel down there all the time, and I don't mean to step in where I oughtn't but I know you worried about her, yes sir. And I thought maybe you put me to work down there for Miss Ann, make sure nobody gives her no trouble. I could work around the store, and keep up her yard same as I do yours here. I'm from Florida, now, Mr. Earl, I know how to get by in Florida.

-I can see you do.

Frank nodded.

-Yes, sir. Now, you know I wouldn't ever say anything about Miss Ann and yourself, not to nobody.

Earl lit a Camel and stared at him a minute.

-Don't recall asking if you would.

-No, sir. I'm just saying.

-You just saying.

-Yes, sir.

The boat rocked in the swells. It was quiet, occasional gull creak.

-Damned if you ain't about either the dumbest or the smartest black son of a bitch I ever knew. Didn't know better I'd think you were extorting me, here.

Frank shook his head and smiled.

-No, sir. Do what, now?

-Aw kiss my ass. Extortion. Blackmail, call it.

-No, sir, I ain't—no, sir, don't say that. Mr. Earl, I'm saying I *wouldn't* do that, now.

-Yeah, Earl said. -That's how they all do it.

Frank shook his head and gave the Mississippi Sound his grave look again.

-I don't know whether to knock you in the head with this anchor and throw you overboard or pay you a compliment, Earl said.

-No, sir. You don't have to do neither one.

The two men sat there looking at each other, boat rocking, clouds creeping overhead, gulls laughing and creaking, swells slopping against the bow.

-Well what about Creasie? She tells Birdie you two are married.

Frank drank the rest of his Coke, set the bottle in the boat floor beside his feet.

-Well, no sir, we're not married, not official. She's a good woman, now. I can tell she's set on making babies, though, and I figure she keep on trying she going to get it right one day.

-You want that?

-Mr. Earl, he said, I can't afford no babies, nobody knows that like you.

-I know it, Earl said. -I can't afford you to have no babies, either, know what I mean.

-Yes, sir. Frank smiled a wan smile. -I guess I just as soon Creasie didn't know nothing about it.

-Go like you came.

Frank nodded. -Yes, sir, I guess that's about it.

He sat there watching a gull while Earl finished his sandwich and drink and watched him. Earl felt like he'd never seen this joker before in his life, like he'd just winked into his boat there beside him out of the air. What am I thinking, he said to himself. Big son of a bitch could break *my* neck and take this boat to goddamn Cuba, if he wanted. But that's not what he wants. Just wants a better job. He shook his head and pitched the empty Coke bottle into the water.

-Cover, he said.

-Mr. Earl, Frank said.

-Yes, goddamnit.

-If you was to pay me a little more than what you paying me now, I think I could get by down there in Tallahassee, now. I wouldn't ask but I been there, and it cost more to get by.

-How much more then do you figure it costs to get by?

-Well, sir, I guess I'd be doing at least two, three times the work I do here, and quality work, too. And it cost more just ever way you look at it. Say fo' times what I make here I figure I can get by in Tallahassee, yes sir, that's about all it take.

Earl stared at him a minute, then looked away, speechless. In a little bit he reached over the bow and hauled up the anchor and laid it in the boat at his feet. Motioned with his arm for Frank to crank the motor, get them going. Frank hesitated, then nodded, turned slowly to the motor and gripped the pull cord. He held this station for a long few seconds, then gave it a snap pull and set it firing, phlegmatic, then a baritone pushing them up and out into the Sound.

~

A MAN COME into the store one day to take his order on Tweedies and says, -Say you know I was in Conway, Arkansas, the other day and saw this thing, man had a hardware store and out on the porch had this nigger dummy working an electric saw, and I stopped to see it. Said he got it from you. I said I was going to be calling on you this week, what a coincidence.

-What's the name of the store? Earl says.

-What?

-What's the name of the man's hardware store. I'm going to buy that nigger dummy back from him.

-What for? says the salesman. -What use you got for it in a women's shoe store?

-I'm not going to use him in my goddamn store. It's my dummy and I want it back. My father sold it without asking me.

-Well don't tell the man I told you where it was.

Drove up there the next Friday evening, arrived the next morning just as the man was opening his store and setting Oscar out on the porch along with a radial-arm saw and fixing his hand to the handle.

-Yes, sir, how can I hep you this morning? Earl standing there below the porch steps with his hands in his trousers pockets, tired and a Camel in his lips.

-That's my nigger you've got there, I'm afraid.

Man just straightened up and looked at him oddly.

-You from Mississippi?

-I am. My papa sold you this thing without asking me. I'd like to buy it back.

-Well, now, I don't know. This thing's pulled in a lot of business for me, here. Sides, this is what it was made for! Mr. Urquhart said you own a ladies' shoe store.

-Yes.

-Well, sir, not to be disrespectful, but I can't see you got much use for this fellow in a ladies' shoe store.

-Never mind why I want him back. I just said he was mine and was sold without my knowledge or permission. I understand you paid good money for him, now I'm offering to pay good money to get him back.

Man stood there blinking in the early sun for a minute, squinting at him. Hand on Oscar's arm as if to hold him back, to quiet him. Oscar grinning as ever in the morning light, as wide-eyed and oblivious as ever, ready to work if need be, ready to sit forever if need be, waiting in the dark on some shelf if need be. There and not there.

-Well, sir, the man said slowly. He's worth a lot more to me than what I paid for him, considering the business he brings in. I sell him back to you, I'm going to want to get me another one. First off, bound to cost more to get another one these days. Second, I wouldn't count on being able to find another one, if I was to try.

-What did you pay Papa for him?

He paused.

-I paid fifty dollars.

-I'll give you a hundred.

-Mr. Urquhart, this nigger's already made me at least five hundred dollars in business.

-I'll give you two hundred cash, then. You're not on the highway, here. You've already got all the new business from this thing you're going to get. It's just decoration now and I'm offering to make it seven hundred dollars you've made from him, which gives you a profit of something like twelve or thirteen hundred percent on your investment. I don't know about the hardware business, but in the shoe business we don't usually get returns like that.

Man stood there blinking.

-I don't have all day, Earl said, lighting another Camel. -I got to get back to Mississippi by this evening.

~

-WHAT DID YOU want to go and do that for? Birdie said.

-It belonged to me.

-Well we sure don't have any use for an old colored dummy you're going to let sit and rot out in the shed.

-It might be valuable one day.

-Well that's not like you, to say something like that. It's of no use to you now, and that's what I'd expect you to say about it.

-So it makes no sense.

-It doesn't seem to, to me.

-Well then all right it makes no sense. Humor me this once.

-For two hundred dollars? That takes a heap of humor, Earl.

-Humor me. If I want to keep an electric nigger dummy in my shed, then let me do it and leave me in peace. Some things a man does he can't explain and doesn't care to.

He went out to the car, reached into the backseat and pulled him out, hefted him limp and wooden onto his shoulder and carried him out to the shed and set him against the wall there while he unlocked the hasp on the door. When he'd opened the door, he walked in and struck his Zippo and looked around, saw the empty spot on the high shelf where he'd kept it before Junius sold it, clanked the Zippo shut. He went back out, hefted it back onto his shoulder, and took it into the shed and pushed it up onto the shelf. In the dim light he reached up to straighten the head on the shoulders, to rest the hands in the lap. He turned the feet so they pointed straight ahead where they hung there. Stood there to catch his breath, then light a smoke.

-What say, Oscar? he said, his eyes adjusting to the darkness in the shed so he could just see the black face with the white teeth, the painted whites of its eyes, in the glow of the cigarette. -Welcome home, you yellow pine son of a bitch.

He went inside and picked up the phone and dialed a number and Junius answered.

-Papa, I have that nigger dummy back out in my shed.

There was silence on the other end of the line.

-What'd you go and do that for?

-It wasn't yours to sell, that's what for.

-The hell it wasn't. I'm the one found it.

-And you gave it to me. What I still don't understand is why you all of a sudden up and stole it from me. You never gave me the money you got for it, by the way, and now I'm out two hundred dollars for it.

-Goddamn, son, I didn't pay but twenty!

-To hell with that. What did you get for it?

-I don't remember. Broke even, maybe.

-You're a liar, you got fifty, which means you made thirty dollars profit on my property, which means you owe me that plus another hundred and seventy dollars.

Junius scoffed. -I'm not responsible for your lack of common sense. And I'm telling you I think that thing is bad luck. You better get rid of it.

-I never knew you to be so superstitious. I'm keeping it, I don't give a damn if you like it or not. That's my electric or dummy or whatever nigger out there, and you keep your goddamn hands off of it, now. In fact, I'm locking it in there, so don't even think about stealing it again.

-Stealing! Goddamnit, I don't give a shit if you keep it or not, then. But if you ever bring that thing out in my presence I'll shoot the son of a bitch full of holes on the spot.

Junius hung up. Earl, laughing to himself, went back outside and lit up again. Stood there in the evening on what he'd made into a fine little fiefdom of his own in the flattened land, the brief plains between Mercury and rolling pine woods and farmland north, smoking, thinking it's not so bad old Earl you got a good woman for a wife and you got healthy children and a good business and another woman who loves you willing to take what's just her share, and here you got your own goddamn electric nigger out in the shed, to boot. Now what can you hold up to that, you old pig-eyed son of a bitch.

Wisdom

S HE COULDN'T HELP thinking that if they'd had babies, if they *could* have had babies, Frank might have stayed. Lord knows she'd tried, but nothing took. Began to seem like he was like a mule, some concoction of a beast not able to reproduce itself. But it settled in finally that it had to be her, and most likely something to do with the potion Aunt Vish had given her before, after Mr. Junius, to get rid of what he'd put in her.

One day she'd walked out into the untended pasture behind her cabin and sat down beneath a solitary oak in the middle of the field. There was a crow sitting in the top of the tree, started calling to another crow over in the woods. Crow was saying, What! What! Other crow comes back, What! What! Don't nobody know what, Creasie grumbled. A big rumble followed down in her belly, and she pressed it with her fingers, lay on her back. She put her hands on her breasts beneath the scratchy blouse she wore and pressed them, wondered if she'd ever nurse a child, nestle a child of her own into her bosom. The crow hopped down a few branches and cocked its head at her. He stretched his head up and called again to the other crow, other crow called back. Then he cocked his head at her again, said,

Rrraaack. She felt a muscle or something rise up beneath her hand and turn over, go back down.

Sunday she asked to have the afternoon off, told Frank she was going to visit her aunt, and caught a ride into town with Mr. Earl, who dropped her off near the ravine. He said he'd pick her up again at five. She watched him drive off, then walked on in. Down past the old Case house, down the dirt road, which turned into the steep trail down to the creekbed, and it was good to be back in with the trees and wild shrubs, all the viny green. She came to the narrow clearing where the old cabins were and went all the way to the end, to the last one nearest the creek. Aunt Vish was sitting on her front porch in a rocking chair with her eyes closed, rocking. When Creasie stopped at the base of the steps, Vish said, -I smell somebody works for white people.

-Just me, says Creasie.

-Mmm hmm, what you want now, girl.

-Nothing. Just want to ask you something.

Vish just kept on rocking. After a while she said, -I got all day but I don't know why you want to take it.

-I can't have no babies, looks like, Creasie said. -I been wondering about that potion.

-Mmm hmm, Vish says.

-What was that potion you give me?

-Did what you wanted.

-Yes'm. How good did it work?

-Did what you wanted.

-Ye'm. But what all did it do, besides that?

Vish opened her eyes, put the toes of her ragged old shoes onto the porch boards and leaned forward, looked at Creasie. She leaned to one side and spat snuff juice off into the dirt.

-Potion can't do but one thing at a time, she said then. -You want a remedy make a baby go away, that's what it gon do. You want one make the babies come, then that's another thing. Herb you taken might taken too good. That happen, I can't do nothing about it. Risk you take.

-You didn't tell me.

-Can't give a body *wisdom*, Vish said. -You get that on your own.

-Can you give me some of that baby-making potion, then?

Vish looked at her a minute, then nodded.

-I can give you whatever you want, child. What you gon give me?

-Ma'am?

-What you gon give me, child! You never give me nothing for that remedy.

Creasie didn't know what to say.

-I'm sorry, Aunt Vish. I thought, it being me—I didn't know I was supposed to pay you for it.

-Didn't know! What you think, I live on air? *You* getting paid, ain't you?

-Ye'm. I'm sorry. I can pay you now. I can pay you for the baby potion, too. Me and Frank wants some babies.

-Say he does too.

-He wouldn't mind. She only partly lied. Hadn't said anything to him about it.

-Vish sat back and stared at Creasie a long moment, saying nothing, then closed her eyes and rocked some more.

-I can give you anything you want, child, but I expect that potion done took too well with you. She opened her eyes and spat and looked at Creasie long and from afar again. -You bring me something from the white folks' house, I'll think on it, see if I can come up with something.

-What you want me to bring?

-Use your brain, child. You'll think up something old Vish can use.

Creasie stood there a minute, neither of them saying anything.

-I could use some new pots and pans, Vish said then.

-Yes'm. It might take a while.

-Like I said, I got time.

~

SO SHE WENT back to work. Made it seem like time was standing still. Time hung in the space between Frank's coming and Frank's going, she knew it would be just a patch of time that would disappear as if it never happened. Nothing but up in the early morning to cook for the Urquharts, then clean up and dust and wash clothes and cook again, dinner and supper, then make her way on back to her little cabin where Frank would be on the front porch smoking, his feet up on the rail, and waiting on her and a late supper for himself. He'd eat it out there, weather permitting, and then they'd go on into the cabin and to bed. She could see him getting bored, restless. He'd wake up in the middle of the night and she'd wake up at some point and see him sitting there beside the bedroom window, looking out. She loved the look of his body in the faint light from the window, just a shadow of the man, his shape, liked the way the memory of his shape stayed in her mind when she couldn't see him, perfect like that.

-Don't be sitting up, she said to him. -Come on back to bed, now.

-What is it? she said when he climbed back in silent and staring at the ceiling.

-Need something, he mumbled.

-I'll give you what you need.

After a minute,

-Need something, I don't know. I ain't got nothing.

-You got me.

-We ain't got nothing, woman.

She said nothing.

-I need to make me some money, one thing, he said.

-Well, who don't.

-I got some ideas.

-Like what.

-I don't know. Just ideas.

-We got a little money saved, she said.

-Nothing, he said. -I got more money in this tooth in the back of my head than you got stuffed in this mattress.

She'd every now and then take a pot of greens out to the cabin, kindly forget to bring it back next day, never the best pot, but one she'd used from way back in the cupboard, one Miss Birdie wouldn't miss. One old skillet with rust spots she scrubbed down real good, reseasoned, and made the bread in then set in the windowsill empty and slipped back to the house to take it out the window from the shrub bed late at night. These she took on this and that weekend out to Aunt Vish, who took the item, held it before her at arm's length to inspect it, nodded, set it down on the porch beside her. The Sunday afternoon she took the skillet out, she saw a twitch in the corner of Vish's mouth.

-That's better than the old one I got, she said, taking it and holding it in her lap to study it. She hefted it and set it back in her lap. -Bigger, too.

Then instead of setting the skillet down beside her feet she rocked a couple of times and launched herself feebly out of her chair with the skillet held before her and went into her cabin. Creasie, standing on the porch, heard her hard bare feet shuffling inside, heard the gentle clank of the skillet as she guessed Vish set it down on top of her stove. In a minute she came back out and handed Creasie a little snuff tin.

-Put just a pinch in a glass of tap water, pour just a little dash of vinegar in there, drink it first thing in the morning, she said. Seven days, she said. Don't do it no longer than seven days, now, you hear me?

-Yes, ma'am. Seven days.

She took it home, started the next morning, using some vinegar she'd brought over from the Urquhart house in a little jar. She
dipped water from the bucket of water she'd pumped at the well
beside her porch steps, opened the snuff tin, and sniffed first.
There was a light sandy-colored powder in there, like pale ground
mustard or something, had no odor she could make out. She
sneezed, blew her nose. Then took a pinch and dropped it into
the cup of water, poured about a teaspoon of vinegar in, and
drank it down. She stood there a minute, very still, but felt nothing but just a faint little ball of heartburn from the vinegar, which
subsided. Went on over to the house to work. Same thing next
morning, standing there, nothing. Same thing next morning.
Frank standing in the kitchen door watching her, said, -What
is that?

-Nothing, she said. -Just a remedy Aunt Vish give me.

-What's ailing you?

-Nothing much, she said, unable to look at him. -Just a little
ache in my bones.

Same thing the fourth day and the fifth. On the afternoon of
the sixth day she was on her hands and knees in Miss Birdie's
bathroom scrubbing the tile floor and up out of her before she
even knew she felt a thing funny came a quick gush of something
yellow with little streaks and spots of red. She felt something lower
down inside her then and quick got up onto the toilet, frightened
not only of what was happening but that Miss Birdie might come
back and see her sitting on her toilet and fire her right then and
there. Same as up top, a little gush then fell from her into the toilet, and she was afraid to even look at it, her eyes tearing up anyway. She quick wiped herself and flushed, and it was only that she
forgot to put the paper into the toilet and accidentally looked
down and saw it in her hand that she knew it was a dull dark dried-
blood brown, and she made a little cry and dropped it into the toi-

let, quickly cleaned up what she'd thrown up with toilet paper and then her scrubbing sponge, and wrung out the sponge in the tub, flushed the toilet, and scrubbed out the tub then.

-What's the matter with you? Miss Birdie said to her when she came through the kitchen on her way out to rinse the bucket at the faucet tap outside.

-No'm, she said, just feeling a little puny. I'll be all right.

Frank walked two miles and borrowed a pickup truck from Whit Caulder and drove her into town that night and waited in the truck while she walked down into the ravine and knocked on Vish's door. Vish came to the door with her coal oil lamp and cracked it, looked out, said nothing.

-I'm scared, Aunt Vish, she said. -That potion made me throw up, and blood like something came out me down there, too.

Vish said nothing, stood watching her with her head stuck just barely out the door, her eyes moving up and down her, like examining her feet and then her hands and then her face again.

-Best not take the rest, then, she said.

-Am I going to be all right? She was near tears, her voice tight.

Vish nodded after a moment.

-You be all right.

They stood there saying nothing. She was afraid to ask, then made herself.

-Is it going to work then?

Vish looked at her, her brow bunched up then, like she was mad. Then that look went away.

-Now what you think, girl?

Creasie stood there composing herself. No longer about to cry. Just feeling washed out.

-No, Vish said as she closed the door and went back inside, leaving her there on the porch. -You go home and rest awhile, if you can. Ain't going to be no babies.

The door closed to, and she heard the dry sound of Vish's feet shuffling off. She heard the tap tap at the truck's horn from Frank, waiting. He was leaning against the driver's side door when she came out of the trail, and he helped her into the passenger seat and climbed in and started it up, turned on the headlights.

-Well, what'd you get this time? he said.

-Hmmm? she said.

-What did you get from the crazy old woman this time?

She looked at him, a man who might as well be a stranger driving her somewhere, so unfamiliar he looked to her in the dark inside the truck at that moment, so strange the whole scene, him driving her somewhere, which he'd never done.

-The truth, she said then. -The truth is what I got this time.

Frank mumbled to himself as he pulled them into the road headed back out to the Urquharts'.

-Be crazy as that old witch yourself, you keep coming here, he said.

~

ONE EVENING SHE went back to the cabin and Frank wasn't there, and wasn't there the next day either. A little crazy with fear, and starting to panic, she burned meals and dropped a dish, Miss Birdie scolding, stood there looking at Creasie, shaking her head. Then mumbled something to herself and sat down at the table.

-You know Earl has gone and bought that old colored dummy back from whoever Mr. Urquhart sold it to and put it back out in the shed. Here we are scraping by, Earl putting everything he can back into the business and not even giving me enough to buy groceries half the time, and he up and pays somebody two hundred dollars for an old nigra dummy. It's crazy!

That afternoon she went out to the shed but it was locked. She could barely see, tears blurring her eyes. She put her lips to the little crack beside the hasp lock and whispered, -Frank? Nothing. But such a chilled breeze came out there against her lips it scared her. She went on back to the house and there was nothing there, no sound in there and no light. Bedding thrown off onto the floor, stuffing in the mattress hanging out, her little flour sack full of dollar bills gone. And on the kitchen table a gold tooth with a little blood at the root, and nothing else.

Blood

OUT AT THE lake in February to split some firewood, Earl remembered a day when he was maybe fourteen or fifteen, and like this raising an ax (in their backyard, then) for stovewood, some kind of old flivver goes by, and froze him like a statue. By God I'll have me one of those one day, and get the hell out of Dodge, he said to himself. Said to his father one day, If I had me a car, I'd be out on my own and you wouldn't have to worry about *me* anymore. Junius says, Let me tell you something, an automobile is like a woman and you'll be ready for one when you're ready for the other. I'm ready, Earl'd said. You're ready, Junius said. You're ready, you say. Let me tell you what you're ready for then. You're ready to be beholden to maintenance for the rest of your life. *Maintenance*, son. Once you got a woman or an automobile, you don't work for yourself anymore. You work for maintenance.

Now, in his fifty-fifth year, raising the ax above his head and thinking in that moment nothing but strike, split, you mother-fucker—angry then at he didn't know what, just everything—just at that moment it felt like his chest collapsed, everything in him, his entire weight and substance, compressed down within its walls, and an instant later ran up his arms and out into nothing.

Then he was on the ground. Knowing somehow he lay there beside the pile of split chunks he'd cut, his face in the iron-rich clay of a gouge a miss had made in the topsoil. Thinking why would this happen to me as I'm chopping a fucking piece of wood for the fire. It had always been the time he smote his enemies, with an ax to a piece of hickory or oak. It helped him to keep things in perspective, helped him remember not to choke every son of a bitch that just happened to piss him off.

You didn't fuck with an Urquhart is what Papa had always said. And that included whether you were family or not. The time he rode to town with him in the wagon and they came upon Aunt Phoebe and Uncle Thad coming the other way and stopped beside each other in the wide road. Junius and Uncle Thad were talking.

Aunt Phoebe said, -Not now, not with Earl in the wagon.

-I don't care, he can't talk to me like that, Uncle Thad said to her, but looking at Papa.

-I'll talk to you any way I like and when I like, Papa said. -And I'm telling you if you do it again I'll kill you.

-It's not your cross to bear, Junius, Aunt Phoebe said. -Come on, Thad, let's go. Hup, she said, and tried to take the reins from Uncle Thad and Uncle Thad hit her in the face with the ends of the reins, not hard but it scared Earl.

-Papa, he said.

Papa said nothing but locked the brake on their wagon, handed the reins to Earl, and started to get down when Aunt Phoebe screamed out her husband's name. Papa leapt sideways away from Uncle Thad off the wagon and Uncle Thad had a knife. He was down off their wagon now too and was holding the knife out in front of him toward Papa.

-Papa, he whispered.

-Tell him to put up the knife, Phoebe, Papa said. He said it quiet. -Tell him to put up the knife or I'll kill him now.

Aunt Phoebe had kept shouting Uncle Thad's name, and now she was screaming at him, Put up the knife, Put up the knife. Uncle Thad walked toward Papa and Papa pulled out the little pistol Earl knew he always carried in his jacket pocket and fired into Uncle Thad's chest. Both teams bucked and Earl held tight to theirs. Uncle Thad stumbled backwards against the wheel of their wagon and vomited red onto his shirt. Aunt Phoebe fell across the seat reaching down for him and when the reins fell from her hand their team bucked forward. Papa stepped aside out of their way and dropped his pistol in the road to catch Aunt Phoebe as she fell from the wagon seat. She fought from his grasp and ran to Uncle Thad lying in the road and fell down on him screaming his name. And then she was screaming at Papa, You killed him, You killed him.

Then Papa went away for a while to the penitentiary. Sundays, Mama took him, Rufus, Levi and little Merry on the train to see him. The engineer got to know them and let Earl ride up front and blow the whistle when they arrived. Papa's head was shorn and he wore baggy striped pajamas and would talk to them in a room with only a table and some hard-bottom chairs in it. He would hug Earl and the little ones and sometimes he would cry and they would all cry, too, except for Mama, who kept her face still and hard and would hardly speak until sometime the next day maybe after dinner and then she would be more like herself again and would come into Earl's room when he'd just fallen asleep and start talking to him. I hope you won't be like your papa, she'd say. I hope you won't carry on drinking, fighting, running with whores. I pray to God.

He didn't like the drinking, either. When Papa finally came home after two years he took it right up again. After all we did to get you out, Mama said. After all that, you haven't changed. He would do it at home, then, sitting in the chair on the porch drink-

138 / Brad Watson

ing straight from a bottle in his one pocket, the pistol back in the other like he'd never killed Uncle Thad with it. His friend the sheriff had given it back to him, said You might need it. He sold insurance then and made good money, never drank during the day, but at night. They never saw Aunt Phoebe anymore unless they went to Cuba in Alabama, where she'd gone to live with Uncle Thad's and Mama's family over there. Papa wouldn't go along. When they came home he'd say something ugly. Uncle Thad and Mama were brother and sister. Sometimes I think that's why he didn't like Thad, Mama said. Like he thought one of them had to be the family big shot. Your papa don't like nobody cutting his territory, business or pleasure or blood, none of it.

He, Earl, didn't like the drinking but what can a boy say about something like that. He fought other boys. Papa praised him for it, in word or gaze. Once when he fought after school in second grade he knocked the boy's front tooth out and brought it home and put it on his dresser. Mama wouldn't go into his room, told him to throw it away. Papa told her to leave him alone, she couldn't understand a boy's ways. They fought. He never hit her. That's why he argued with Uncle Thad, he told Earl. He hit Aunt Phoebe. Man hits a woman's no better than a dog, a sick weak dog, he said. He's a coward. Never be a coward, he said. Don't ever let anybody get away with crossing you, they'll never let you walk upright again.

Didn't need the lesson, it was in his blood. What it didn't do, like it did later with Levi and later with Papa, too, was turn to meanness. But just hot blood. Couldn't help it. Almost lost his job with the New York company that first time for catching a man up by his collar at lunch in the park one day. They'd gotten hot dogs from one of those vendors, taken them to the park, and the man said something about his accent. He had the man down on a pile of rocks and shoving a hot dog into his mouth before a New York cop pulled him off. Man said, No, I don't want to press charges, I'm going to have his job. I'll have his ass. He went for him again. No, let him go, the man said, I'll take care of that son of a bitch.

Well if the man had been smart enough to file an order he'd have had his ass, had his job, but went to complain and then didn't file an order and the manager says, Get your ass out of my office, you lying son of a bitch. Then calls Earl in and says Is it true, did you do that to him? And Earl says I'd do it again. Do it again, the manager says, and it will be your job. Just don't kick ass of anyone going to give us any real business.

He hit a man one time was trying to hire away his help, after he opened the store in Mercury. Found him in the barbershop getting a shave, towel on his face, couldn't see Earl come in. Snatched him out of the chair by the tie, dragged him out into the street like a leash dog and banged his head on the pavement a few times. Wanted to kill him, see his blood. You don't come around trying to steal my help, he told him. Cop had to pull him off again, but it was one of his buddies, Pinkie McGauley, had a laugh and sent the son of a bitch on his way. Yankee, anyway, trying to start up a cheap line in a store on Front Street and good riddance. He'd hit horses, mules, with his bare fists. Hit a nigger woman over the head with a high heel when she sassed him, didn't want her in the store in the first place then she says he's not fitting her right. Well he never hit anyone or anything didn't deserve it, just didn't have it in him to swallow an insult. Take it as you would, he was a man you didn't fuck with, like any Urquhart, but he wasn't mean. Just quick-tempered.

He could hold a grudge but not like Papa. Aunt Phoebe finally grew ill from her grieving, dying an early death, and calls for Papa to come over to see her on her deathbed in Cuba, and Mama badgers him with Bible verses till he finally consents to get dressed and go over there, of a Sunday afternoon. They're all there when Mama and Papa arrive, and Papa stands across the room. The others close to the bed. She's ashy pale, trembly weak, motions for him to come closer. He's got his hat in his hand, head cocked to one side like a fighter waiting for his opponent to get up after he's knocked him down. He steps closer to the bed, stands there, looking at her like he's studying her. No compassion in his hard blue eyes, just something like curiosity. That little cowlick of silver hair on the top of his balding head like a baby's first locks.

The old homeplace there, little more than an old dogtrot. Brown burnt-up cornstalks in the field beside, it's August and everybody's drenched with sweat and powdered with dust from the drive over, the highway nothing but gravel and the road from it just red clay dirt all dried. Everybody standing around in the heat and flies buzzing against the screens.

Aunt Phoebe's laid up on a stack of pillows.

-Well, he says after a minute, his voice kind of husky soft, I'm waiting. He looks again almost like what he is, her baby brother waiting on her word.

She has her speech prepared.

-I know I was wrong, she says. -I thought you didn't have to shoot Thad but I know he would have come at you with that knife. I know he wouldn't have stopped and you'd have had to shoot him anyway, and maybe gotten stabbed. But I couldn't forgive you for taking him away. I loved him too much. I let him beat me because I loved him. But I know that couldn't have gone on, either. Now I'm dying. I want to tell you I know you did it in self-defense, like you said to the judge. I'm sorry I didn't say so. I knew you wouldn't let little Earl into court. And I lied. I lied about the knife. But now I'm dying. I wanted to tell you how sorry I am for not telling it like it was and for you going to the penitentiary. I'm dying now and I need you to forgive me, Junius. Before I go to my maker.

Papa stands there a long time not saying anything. They're all straining their ears, sweat running into their earlobes, they let it stand, still. Aunt Phoebe has started to cry, not making a sound herself but the tears trickling down her chalky face.

Papa says, -You can rot in hell, for all I care, Phoebe. I'll never forgive you.

Aunt Phoebe's mouth then looked like it'd already been sewn shut by the undertaker, cinched in. Her eyes seemed smaller as if receding with her old soul. They watched him place his hat on his head, walk out without looking back. His own sister. Last time she ever saw him, nor would the closed lids of her dressed corpse deflect the light of his image, nor her shade darken his thoughts but for a flitting second as if seeking some sentimental purchase and, finding none, would it pass into scattered fields of those souls whose lives on earth had found nothing but unhappiness.

Poor Aunt Phoebe. Poor Aunt Phoebe, he'd often thought. I should have known seeing her grieve that no one in this family would ever sow much love in the family garden, what passed for love anyway being just a few unswept and moldered seeds at the base of an otherwise empty grain bin. A clutch of dry and twisted hearts. His love for Birdie was one thing, one move in the right direction, a grasp at goodness the closest thing to which he knew was his mother, poor God-ravaged grackle of a woman that she was, squawking scripture to ward off the terror of eternal fire. When Birdie balked at physical love it fired in him a muted, enraged despair, as if the demons in the old woman his mother had infected his bride somehow between the courtship and connubial bliss. Why, aside from his general greed, would his father have become the biggest pussyhound east of the Mississippi? Because the pussy at home was about as receptive as just that, might as well try to hold down the housecat by the nape of its neck and fuck it—that was his guess, anyway, given all signs and signals in the air all his growing up life.

Still, it was in the blood. Only one of them didn't cheat on his wife was Rufus, and that because he was a drunk half the time and a teetotaling holy roller the rest, and between being drunk on whiskey and drunk on Jesus he hadn't the time or the inclination for fucking around. Papa had set Rufus up in the barbershop years before. You never had to worry about Rufus being mean, that was for sure, only drunk. Earl always suspected he had a big heart and it was some kind of self-loathing kept Rufus such a gentle and ineffectual sap.

So he, Earl, would work hard and do well, finally set himself up in business, and extend a hand to Levi, helping to set him up with his own shoe store, too. Never mind competition, which was admittedly part of the plan, that with Levi as competition they could control things, keep a share each of different stock, swap around, lob customers back and forth between the stores like tennis balls. Never mind, of course, that Levi would order on the sly the same stock Earl was getting and offer it at lower prices, wouldn't put it out where Earl might see it but would sidle up to customers and happen to drop that he could get her this or that shoe a little cheaper than Earl, and sometimes that stock actually being Earl's own, which Levi would get out of Earl's store at night or Sunday mornings until Earl got wise and took away his key and slapped him around a little when he, Levi, called him, Earl, a liar.

Got into league with their sister Merry against him. Depended on Earl, the both of them, and the both of them hated him for it. Merry'd get drunk and drive around town shopping for dresses, purses, makeup, flowers, groceries, even whiskey and gasoline, and telling the merchants Send the bill to my brother Earl down at his store. He'd round up whatever hadn't been unwrapped or worn or drunk or eaten or shot through a carburetor and fired out the tail and take it back, make her pitiful cuckold husband R.W. pay for some, and would end up paying himself for the rest. Then she'd laugh at him over it. Say What do you care, you got plenty of money, nobody'd ever squeeze a nickel out of you Earl if they didn't steal it.

Your problem, he'd often said to her in private, is no man can satisfy you in bed so you just want to cut off every pair of swinging balls comes within your reach, but you can't have mine, you'll just have to be satisfied with R.W.'s hanging from your neck and all those johns' stuck somewhere in your craw but don't come looking to me for the piece of bread to help choke them down.

And Levi's problem he had no balls in the first place, and a brain about the size of a testicle itself. He'd ruined Earl's relationship with Maurier down at the fish camp in Pascagoula when he'd kidnapped that new salesgirl he lost his head over and then beaten her up when she tried to run off down the beach. When Earl found out he wired him there, LEVI STOP CAN'T BELIEVE YOU WOULD JEOPARDIZE ALL WORKED FOR TAKE SOME GIRL OFF BEAT HER UP STOP DO NOT LEAVE STOP I WILL BE THERE QUICK STOP EARL. Hauling ass through the blackleaved tunnel of 11 to 49, blowing the shutters off little towns along the way and down the flackity flackity 98 to the dirt road to Maurier's, dawn just breaking over the Sound, and busting into the cabin, their cabin, he even had to go and do that, and Levi there lying naked on the bed and the goddamn girl *tied up* in a little kitchen chair in the corner and screaming her head off, wearing just a powder-blue blouse and trying to hide herself with her legs. Maurier in right behind him yelling Cajun patois, took all he had in him not to simply beat the shit out of Levi right then and there—pointed, said, I'll deal with you later. Levi laughing, crying, couldn't tell which maybe both. Turned to Maurier, You shut up, too, I'll have them both out of here in thirty minutes. Don't never want to see him again! You'll never see either one of us again, goddamnit. Bon! Finee!

Fairly knocked and wrestled whining Levi into some clothes and shoved him onto a bus in town, gave the driver a ten, drove back to Maurier's, where he'd padlocked her in the room with the phone removed. Went to the office to pay the bill, Maurier in there fuming. Said, I got to make a phone call first. You pay for it! I'll pay for it goddamnit. Took out another ten-dollar bill and threw it onto his floor.

-Fred, is Pinkie there. Well where is he. Never mind. What time is it. Seven o'clock. All right. Tell him to be on the corner of 5th Street and 22nd Avenue at ten sharp. Wait on me if I'm not there, I'll be there around then. I'll make it worth it.

Put her in the front passenger seat she wasn't nothing then but a foul mouth on a couple of scratched-up skinny legs and a cigarette he kept burning in her waving hands, where in the hell did Levi find them, floored it after gaining 49 again and headed north. Took about three minutes before she began to realize something about the speed. Seventy, eighty, ninety, topped a hundred straight through Perkinston. Talking slowed, then she got real quiet. Damn near up on two wheels in the hard curve south of Wiggins, she screamed and grabbed the armrest and the dash. Up to then talky enough, You better get me a good job somewhere else is what you better do, I know about you and that woman in Tallahassee, your store down there, you get me something like that, you set me up somewhere or I'll have your asses, I'll get you son bitches thrown so deep in jail you won't never see the light of day I'll—

-You want to take everything I've got because of my fool brother, do you, Earl said. -Well you can take every goddamn thing he's got for all I care, but you threaten me and you got a whole nother problem, sister.

-You don't scare me.

-You offer this kind of arrangement to Levi he'll kill you and you know it, and you think you can just sit here and threaten me, then? Was looking at her and barely got back in his lane to miss a tractor trailer rig barreling by, foghorn blasting, woman screaming You'll kill us both!

-That may be, but if it happens, happens say in a car crash, won't nobody be the wiser, you'll be dead.

-Like you!

-I've lived a good life, made money, my family's secure. You're just a young woman, got your whole life ahead of you. You want to throw it all away like that?

She rips through a mindless wide-eyed recital of every cuss-word or phrase she knows, goddamn son of a bitch motherfucker dick pussy asshole shit piss cunt prick go to hell!, runs through them three or four times in a row, Earl thinking how most had to do with bodily functions, how little they strayed, two about condemnation, one comparison to a dog.

-Well I don't think that'll do it, he says. He doesn't slow up until just outside the city limits, coasts down the highway past the airport and the creosote plant, down 8th into town, turned down onto 22nd and stopped there at the corner of 5th. Sitting there engine idling, girl still breathing hard, staring straight ahead, steaming, finally and mercifully mute. Hands her five one-hundred-dollar bills in plain view.

-This ought to get you to another town and another job.

She grabs it.

-Don't you think you're done with me.

He nods to Pinkie standing at the lamppost in his uniform, twirling his nightstick, who tips his hat to Earl, the girl.

-Pinkie here just saw you take that and put it into your purse, he says. -Good friend of mine. He don't know just what this is. You could be a street whore, for all Pinkie knows. Wouldn't hurt my reputation much, but you wouldn't want it on your record. So we got a deal.

She spits a few choice ones, get out, slams the door, walks off. He laughs to himself, lights a Camel, waves to Pinkie, and drives out to the country to cool off awhile. Later over to Levi's house, Levi in the bedroom lying down, Rae sitting and smoking at the dining table, gives him a murderous look full of sloppy lipstick.

-Don't look at me, I just saved the damn fool son of a bitch.

-That's what I'm steamed about.

-Not if you knew what I saved him from.

-I know, all right.

Levi turns off the radio when he walks in, gives him a grin, nothing but an inch or two of tiny teeth bared on the perfectly round ball of his head.

-If you ever pull a stunt like that again Levi I'll kill you. You owe me five hundred dollars.

-For what.

-Never mind what. For saving your ass from picking cotton at Parchman for the next five years that's what.

-You give that whore five hundred dollars? Whistles. -You got a cigarette?

Never get that money, he knew, but easier to keep Levi straight if he owes you cash. The memory of it would last a year or two, anyway, things somewhat under control. Before Levi and Merry like bad children cooked up some other scheme to entertain themselves and torment him and Birdie.

Asked himself sometimes why in the hell he never left Birdie for Ann whom he loved and there's your answer: Might not have been much of a marriage but by God it was his family and a good one compared to anything he'd ever known, and be damned if he was going to give any of those godforsaken Urquharts the satisfaction of seeing him fail at anything.

Wanting to reach a hand out for the ax there in the graying film of his vision, not inches from his eye yet as if across some vast and light-bent field at the end of a long day, piecemeal light scattering the air like mercury from a broken thermometer skittling across the floor.

Habeas Corpus

As soon as Miss Birdie called from the hospital and said Mr. Earl had died out at the lake, Creasie went to her cabin, got her coat, and walked down the driveway to the road. She stood nestled into the leaves of the redtop bushes beside the highway and when she saw the yellow-orange school bus coming she stepped out and flagged it down. It was how she got into town and back on the occasional weekday she needed a ride. All the children raucous in the back so it was the only time she rode a bus and sat up front behind the driver and she liked it. The view was good, with the world swinging by so fast when he made his turns. But she hardly noticed, today. Every so often a little balled-up piece of school paper bounced off the back of her head to the wild chorus of delight behind her but she paid it no mind.

When he had delivered all the children to their homes, the bus driver drove back to town and let her off beside the road near the path down into the ravine. She didn't wave, as she normally did, when the bus drove off. She crossed the street and started down the trail. She hadn't realized she'd left her house shoes on, with the heels all flattened, until she got on the trail, with its roots and little dips and gopher holes, and so she shuffle-stepped slowly along it. Her feet cold in them now. A rabbit scooted a brown-and-white blur from the trail's edge across and into the brush on the other side and a gray squirrel barked at her from the low limb of an oak tree. And the winter birds everywhere, hardly singing but fluttering by so close as to breeze her face and sometimes squawking when they made a perch, or dipping away like on a bob string weaving down the trail ahead of her as it narrowed and the light grew gray and solemn blue through the deepening canopy of skeletal and veiny leafless great hardwoods and silent pines.

She went to her own cabin, which she'd painted green because she liked the color and the way it made the house almost invisible in green season when you were a ways off on the trail looking into the clearing at the bottom of the ravine. Inside, she shoved a few sticks from the trail into the stove, sprinkled them with some kerosene-soaked sawdust. When that was crackling she laid in a stick of stove wood and closed the door and sat beside the stove with her hands out, warming.

She got up and looked out her tiny kitchen window and could just see Vish's cabin in the gathering dusk, come early here in February. Was ending up a dreary afternoon after the sun peeking early on. No drizzle but the air in the woods turning so gray and damp as to almost seem like it. She stood there looking. Couldn't see anything for a long time and then a little light inside, just a flicker. She went back to the stove. Getting hungry. She got a sack of meal from the cupboard and poured some in a bowl. She got a dab of lard from a little bucket and put it in a skillet and put the skillet on top of the stove to heat. There was some water left in the water jug and she poured a little into the meal and stirred it. She took an egg from where it was wrapped in a soft rag in her handbag, cracked it into the bowl, and stirred that in. Would be better if she had some buttermilk but water would do. Just needed something on her stomach, for nerves as much as hunger.

When the lard in the pan started to smoke she gave the meal another stir and poured it in, hissing in the hot lard, watched it cook. She liked to make bread in the oven but didn't want to fool with that, and with no milk it'd be better browned on both sides and crispy. She'd made it thin. She watched it thicken and crack on top and then she turned it over with a spatula. The bottom was dark brown. She cooked it another few minutes and took the pan off the stove and set it on the table and cut out a piece to cool on a plate, and she ate it with a cup of water from the jug, chewing and washing down the dry bread with the water, and looking at the little flickering flame in Vish's cabin down the path. She saw something cross over inside and block out the flame for a second, then the flame again. She wiped her hands on a rag and took another drink of the water, closed the stove vents, and put her coat back on, looked out the window again, and then went out to the porch. It was getting pretty cold. She stepped carefully down the steps and into the path and walked toward Aunt Vish's cabin.

-Creasie! she'd heard him call, heard a clatter in the sink. He stuck his head into the pantry, mad. -I'll be back in an hour, so make up a fresh pot of coffee. That's the worst cup of coffee I ever tasted in my life.

-No, sir, Creasie said to herself now as she stepped up onto Vish's porch and lifted her knuckles to rap lightly on the old plank door. -I reckon it was worse that that.

~

AUNT VISH LOOKED made from a tough, blackened root in the flickering faint light from the coal oil lamp on the little shelf behind her. The cabin was hammered together of unplaned planks, burlap tacked to the walls for insulation tattered and torn here and there and stained. She held out a clean mason jar toward Creasie across the table. Her breath like smoke from her mouth when she spoke in the cold air.

-You put it in this. Tell young Mr. Parnell to put it in this.

-Yes'm, Creasie said. -What do I do with it after he give it to me?

Vish's bloodshot, jaundiced eyes watched her without movement. Outside it was quiet as inside, not a breeze rustling a
single dry leaf. Still February winter, maybe a drizzle drifting in,
maybe a patter on the dead leaves carpeting the trails. The woods
around there black as what you see when life goes out, before
whatever light in whatever world comes next shows itself, black
nothing, switches of branches and sticky spiderwebs like some
gauntlet between here and there.

-You keep it with you.

After a moment, Creasie nodded.

-Yes'm.

The old woman's hands lay on the table before her, two black
crooked claws, long yellow nails resting on the unfinished plank
top of the table. She showed what teeth she had then, one long
dark horse tooth in front, gaps between what seemed occasional
sharpened incisors here and there on back.

-Tell him what I told you to. Don't tell him who I am. He smart
enough, he'll know.

-Yes'm.

-Say Clint, helped his old papa, done told me about it. He'll
remember Clint, all right, used to help them out down there. Tell
him I know about the government, them bodies.

She nodded. She waited a minute, didn't want to say it. She
was afraid.

-Yes'm. What if he calls the police.

-If he smart, if he got any brains at all, child, he ain't going
to call no police. People find out what his daddy was mixed up
in, ain't going to be no more business for Grimes Funeral
Home.

She nodded, looking down.

-You go on. You never been here, now. I don't remember you, I don't know you. I'm just a crazy old nigger woman, you know what I mean?

She looked up. Old woman grinning at her with those snaggly black teeth. She grinned back, a little.

-Yes'm, she said. Everybody know that.

-That's right, the old woman said, raising her eyebrows and leaning back in the flickering yellow lamplight. -Everybody. Ha ha ha, she laughed then, her voice deep like a man's and quiet like she was laughing to herself, but those old bloody eyes never leaving her own.

Black Heart

PARNELL HAD JUST gone downstairs for a glass of milk when he heard a tap-tapping at the front door and when he looked out the side panes he saw a young colored woman standing there holding a jar in her hands. He saw her eyes cut over and see him looking. He sighed, opened the door enough to look out, as he was wearing his house robe and slippers. She stood there looking at him, mute and frightened it seemed.

-Yes? he said. -How may I help you, Miss?

-Yes, sir, Mr. Grimes, she said then. -I need to see you about Mr. Earl.

-Earl Urquhart?

-Yes, sir.

-Did you know Mr. Urquhart?

She stared at him, her eyes pools of something awful, he couldn't tell.

-Yes, sir.

-Well, what, did you work for Mr. Earl, then?

She didn't say anything for a moment, then she nodded.

-Yes, sir, she said, I worked for him, out at the house. I did. And Miss Birdie. Work in the house.

He looked at her, wondering what she was doing there. Maybe she wanted to view the corpse but didn't feel like she could come to the funeral, though black and white were always welcome at a funeral.

-The funeral isn't set till day after tomorrow, he said then. You could visit Mr. Earl then. I'm afraid he's not been prepared for viewing, just yet.

-Yes, sir, she said, and stood there.

-I was just going to bed, Parnell said.

-Yes, sir, she said, I didn't want to see Mr. Earl. I needed to get something from him.

Parnell thought, What in the world. He saw the jar in her hands then.

-What do you have in the jar, there?

-It's a empty jar, the woman said.

-I can see that, Parnell said. Thinking, what? Some piece of jewelry or something? Did she think Earl Urquhart owed her money and come now to collect it in what looked like an empty preserves jar? Colored people. You couldn't figure them.

-It's late. What did you say your name was?

-Creasie Anderson, she said. -I keep house for Mr. Earl and Miss Birdie.

-Well, Creasie, why don't you come back in two days and attend the funeral, I'm sure that's what Miss Birdie would want.

The woman stood there, didn't move, just staring at him with those eyes. He was about to shut the door when she spoke again.

-She say to tell you she knows about the government bodies. She said to tell you she knows old Clint what helped your papa sell them bodies to the government, and if I said that to you that you would let me in.

Parnell lost his hearing there for a long moment, and his vision seemed to tunnel down to a small round area within which this strange little brown woman with a kerchief on her head stood on the home's veranda. Then through the roaring he heard something plaintive.

-What are you talking about? he said, though he was whispering now, without even thinking he needed to whisper, some automatic response to alarm. -Old Clint who used to work here? *Who* said?

He heard something again. Selena's voice, from up at the top of the stairs, out of sight.

-Parnell, what is it?

He stepped back and motioned the woman to come in, and put a finger to his lips.

-Nothing, my darling, he called up to Selena, his voice sounding strange in his ringing ears.

-Parnell? Are you coming up? Selena's voice carried like the quavery notes of some strange wind instrument down the stairs. -Come up to see me?

-Wait for me, Selena, he called, shooing the colored woman ahead of him down the hallway toward the door to the basement stairs. -I'll be up soon, sweetheart.

-I'll be waiting on you, Selena's voice floated down, playful now, enticing.

He whispered to the colored woman when they reached the door to the basement stairs.

-Shhh, now. We can talk down here.

He watched the woman go slowly down the narrow stairway, holding to the rail, and tried to gather what she was saying into his brain. After his father had died, Parnell had been going through his papers when he saw a packet of official-looking letters, unmarked as to their origin. They were cryptic but seemed to suggest his father was involved in a project of some sort and that this involved those people and maybe more he didn't know of who'd disappeared from the home but whose funerals had gone on as planned. And then one evening about a year after his father died another strange man came calling on his father, and when Parnell informed the man his father had died an unexpected death, along with his mother, the man nodded and stood there a while.

-Did your father tell you anything about activities on his part to assist the federal government, sir, in a study of some sort?

-No, Parnell said after a pause.

-He did not inform you in any way of his cooperation with a very important government project involving matters of national security, sir?

-No, sir, Parnell said, his heart racing. -Perhaps you can inform me, sir.

The man looked at him. Then he looked him slowly up and down, as if appraising him. Then the man said, -I'm sorry for your father's untimely death, Mr. Grimes. Then he turned and walked away and got into a black car with plain hubcaps across the street and drove away.

For a while Parnell had been convinced that the government had something to do with his parents' death. That whatever his father was involved in must have endangered him, he must have known something he wasn't supposed to know, and so some strange espionage-like death was concocted for him. And for a long time after that he had worried that they believed he knew something and would one day be coming for him. But he never heard from them again. His mind was now reeling with the absurdity of the whole business now coming up again in the form of this dumpy little auntie standing there beside him at the empty preparation table, still in her old ragged coat, holding the jar in her two hands in front of her and just waiting.

-Miss V—and she stopped. -She say—

-Who is this *she?* Parnell interrupted her. He heard a tremulous quality in his own voice and realized he was beginning to perspire.

-Say we got to have the poor man's heart, she said then, not looking at him.

-What? Who's heart? Earl Urquhart's heart? You are telling me you want this man's heart? To put in that *jar* there?

Woman just nodded. She looks worse scared than I do, Parnell thought.

-This is insane! he almost shouted. He started to take her by the arm and rush her out the back door then, but she said again,

-She say to tell you old Clint know about your papa and giving the government them bodies. She say we got to have Mr. Earl's heart in this here jar or she going to tell about it.

-*Who* says? he fairly hissed, throwing his arms up in the air.

-Mr. Grimes, I can't say! she said, looking at him now and he could see tears in her eyes now, beginning to run down her big cheeks.

A thought tickled up to the front of his brain as if released from some little air bubble in the back of it somewhere. That this woman was an emissary of Birdie Urquhart. This was the man's widow asking him to give her maid her husband's heart in a goddamn mason jar, for God's sake. Earlier that evening a drunken woman had telephoned him, said she was Earl Urquhart's sister, and that she wanted him to do an *autopsy* (she'd ripped out the word in her slurring speech) on the man because in fact he'd been *murdered* (ripping that one out, too). He'd hung up on her, thinking it a vicious, foolish prank. And now a chill settled into his blood. Mrs. Birdie Urquhart. He felt a strange and ridiculous momentary sense of relief that maybe this actually had nothing to do with his father and the bodies but it was too confusing and his thoughts wheeled into chaos again.

My God, he thought then. This woman he'd worshiped from afar for much of his life, who looked like the movie stars he'd idolized as a child, who seemed some sort of essence of feminine allure to Parnell, about whom he'd fantasized in the earliest mixings of his contorted desire.

Standing there in the dim room lit by the auxiliary lamp in the corner looking at this frightened colored maid he felt a calm move through him as if he'd been administered a drug. It was the calm of the man who has resigned himself to a terrible turn of events in his life, say a murderer of some sort, whose deed is done and he resigns himself to the way it is and does not acclimate his mind to the anxieties of the lawful majority. He let go of the colored woman's arm then and went over to the locker, opened it, and wheeled the gurney with Earl Urquhart's body on it out, and turned the overhead lamp on and pulled back the sheet from his stricken face. He heard the woman catch her breath.

-You might want to wait outside, he said. -This won't be pretty.

She stood there like an idiot, apparently unable to move.

-Suit yourself, then, he said.

He got out the scalpel and the saw and the spreader from the chest where they were stored, where his father had stored them since Parnell was a child, and went to work. When he'd opened him up, he took the separator, set it in place, then cranked it open. Adjusted his lamp. Then the second chill of the evening hit him, this one worse than the first, for the man's heart was as black as if it'd been skewered and turned on a spit over a fire. Parnell wondered for a moment if a bolt of lightning could have shot down and pierced straight to this man's heart, entering and leaving it clean as a blade of light and blasting nothing else. Hardly thinking, he quickly sliced a small section from one wall and concealed it on the other side of the corpse, between the arm and the ribcage. He paused and looked up at the woman. She was staring into the dead man's chest.

-Look like some kind of buirnt root in there, she said.

-Open the jar, he said to her, all cool and formality again now. He felt possessed of a strange calm, as if resolving this weird issue for this woman would resolve more than he could understand. -You might want to look away, here. Plenty of time, I suppose, for you to see what is in here when you are on the way back home.

She stared at him with her baleful, frightened eyes and without looking slowly unscrewed the lid to the mason jar and held it tentatively out in front of her, and then she turned her head to look away at the stairwell leading out.

-You'll be going out the back door, Parnell said as he leaned in with the scalpel and a pair of tongs.

~

THE WHOLE ORDEAL had taken only a half hour and now he was washed up and trudging in a horrified daze back up the stairs to their living quarters. He was muttering a prayer to himself, my God forgive me and mine own for all our sins and our wretched natures. When he reached the top of the stairs he just did catch a glimpse of a pair of bare feet and legs sprawled invitingly from the door of the guest room and for the third time in less than an hour, he felt a shock and a chill—then he calmed, almost smiled to himself, and began unbuttoning his shirt as he approached the supine form of his sweet bride there, just her nightie top on and her arms flung over her head. Again, a cool sweat broke on his broad forehead.

-I'm coming, my darling, he whispered, don't go.

~

THE FORENSIC PATHOLOGIST from Jackson called him two days later, just after Earl's funeral, having examined the sample of Earl's heart Parnell had sent him via one of his helpers on the day following Creasie's visit. After the usual civilities, the pathologist asked in a somewhat incredulous manner just what in the world that man had been up to in his days. Parnell took a long pause, then informed the doctor that his family had taken care of Mr. Urquhart's father and his grandfather, as well, and that among the Grimes family, in a professional sense, the Urquharts were known as the Blackhearts, for the propensity toward this condition, for which Parnell had no explanation.

He said to the pathologist, -So you reached no conclusion, yourself, based on lab tests?

-Afraid not, the pathologist said. -It could be a damned interesting study, though. I'm tempted to come over and take a look at this situation myself.

He had a voice like a big man speaking with his cheeks full of cornpone, rich and congested and mealy. Strong and suspicious.

-It may involve negro occult matters, I'm afraid, Parnell said. -I'm not sure it would be something we could understand.

-Well if you are inclined to write up what all you know about it, I'd be interested to read such a document, the pathologist said.

-Personally I would like to put it to rest, Parnell said. -This family and their indecent ways and their dangerous and self-destructive habits have been a blight on this community. I would not relish the publication of any sort of record which might also blemish the reputation of the community by association.

-Well, the pathologist said after a moment. -Thank you for the enlightenment, Mr. Grimes. I'm afraid there's nothing concrete this office can truly contribute to your understanding of what led to this man's death. He paused. -Should you see any lateral evidence of this sort of thing, however, I'd be obliged if you would let me know so that I could take a peek, so to speak, at—ah—such goings-on.

-I will do that, Parnell said. -Good day to you, sir, he said, and they hung up.

Finus Inquisitus

LATER ON THE afternoon he'd seen Birdie outside Schoenhof's, Finus got into his pickup and drove out into the country, taking little back roads in a meandering way around the circumference of Mercury, until at dusk he was rolling slowly past Birdie and Earl's house on the highway. The lights were on in the kitchen and den, dark everywhere else. He slowed and turned down the road that ran between their house and the junk-yard Earl's son-in-law ran with his father and peered into the darkened three-car garage to see if Earl's car was there. He'd be somewhat outside of propriety to drop in and say hello if Earl wasn't home. He could see at least one car there. And then he saw the grainy shadowed figure standing in the driveway. He had to turn in, then, for to pass on by in that manner would be too odd. He pulled up beside the figure, Earl, who was just standing there smoking in the last light. Finus shut the engine.

-Finus, Earl said, offering him a cigarette. Finus took it, lit up. Earl looked up as if to check for an early moon, and the men didn't say anything for a minute, smoking in silence.

Earl looked at him, took a last drag, and flicked the cigarette butt into the yard.

-Been a while. How'd you like Tuscaloosa?

-Never did feel quite like home, Finus said.

Earl nodded. -I never did get to tell you how sorry I was about your son.

-Well, Finus said. -That's all right.

-I'm sorry about Merry, too, Earl said, all the trouble that caused. But you know as well as I do there's no controlling that bitch.

-Ancient history, Finus said.

-Well, Earl said, and nodded. He gave Finus a faint smile. -You lost your boy. Can't get a divorce, so I hear. You've nothing left to lose but your business, now that it's all in your hands. May as well just work hard and play the field.

Finus laughed. No doubt about it, Earl looked like a movie star, handsome and confident in his manner. No wonder he had his reputation with the women. But even now he couldn't help thinking what an odd match he was for Birdie Wells.

-I reckon I could get a divorce, if I wanted to pay the price, Finus said. He put on his best rueful smile. -I was just driving around, thinking, thought I'd say hello.

Earl nodded, looking at him, then turned away toward his house, where Finus could see Birdie's stockinged legs through the den screen door as she sat in a chair, maybe reading from the lamp glow that bathed them.

-We'll see you around, Earl said over his shoulder.

-Right, Finus said. -I'll see you.

~

TWO WEEKS LATER, word came from a friend of Birdie's that Earl had dropped dead of a heart attack while out splitting fire-wood at his lake. When Earl didn't come home two hours after leaving, Birdie had driven out to check on him and found him on the ground next to a pile of cordwood he'd split, one hand still on the ax, his eyes open. She'd pulled him into her car by herself and driven him to the hospital, way too late. Parnell Grimes judged it cardiac arrest, and there was no inquiry.

That evening, Finus dressed and went out to Birdie's house. Earl wouldn't be ready at the funeral home till the next day. Finus knew Parnell never got them ready the same day if they came in after noon – he was a perfectionist.

Birdie was in her den, with visitors in there and the kitchen, a few scattered into the living room and sunporch. The visitors served themselves from a large percolator on the kitchen counter and ate baked goods from the kitchen table. Creasie was nowhere to be seen.

After Finus had been there a half hour, Earl's brother Levi and his wife, Rae, and Merry came in, obviously drunk. Merry wore the requisite black, but around her neck along with a string of pearls lay some kind of fur stole. On her head was a bright shiny red hat that seemed made from the skin of some large exotic bird, half a dozen blue feathers askew from the crown, bedraggled, as if she'd just killed, skinned, and partially plucked the creature out in the yard and stretched it onto her skull still steaming from lifeblood. She looked over at Finus and closed her eyes slowly, let an odd smile slip across her lips, then opened her eyes and batted them once at him. He couldn't help but wonder where Avis was at that moment, since he'd seen her car parked outside. Just then Merry murmured something to Levi, who gave her a look like he'd just swallowed his tongue and wanted to say something but just shook his head. Merry looked back up at Finus then and said, loudly enough for everyone in the room to hear, -Well I'm surprised you're here, Finus. Being the disgruntled lover and all.

He was confused, at first, felt himself blush that she would joke about their old affair in public, but then he realized from the look she was giving Birdie that she meant *Birdie*, as in Finus and Birdie. Levi still hadn't spoken, still didn't look like he could. Birdie turned paler than she had been. Finus stood in the center of the room like some stiff ridiculous totem. Levi took Merry's elbow and tried to pull her toward the door, whispering something to her, but Merry yanked her arm free and turned back to Birdie. Birdie looked up at her, horrified.

-I don't know how you can sit there and play the grieving widow, Merry said. -*Sweet little Birdie,* she mocked her. -Well you don't fool me.

-Merry, please, Birdie said, don't do this.

-Do what, honey, tell the truth? Everybody thinks she is so-o-o innocent, she said loudly then, sweeping her arm around the room, almost losing the ridiculous hat from her head. It seemed the entire house had fallen silent, everyone in the den and in the other rooms, too. -Well, she went on—but Finus had heard enough and if Levi couldn't handle her he would. He stepped over, took her by the upper arm, and hustled her through the kitchen and out into the driveway.

Outside, she twisted from his grip and swung her purse at him.
-What the hell, Merry.
-She *killed* him, is what, Merry said, pushing her hair back out of her eyes and spitting onto the sidewalk. She wiped her mouth with the back of her hand, smearing bright red lipstick on her pale skin.

-Jesus Christ, Finus said, are you insane? You couldn't be that drunk.

-I don't know *how*, she said, but my brother Earl was healthy as a horse and did not just keel over from a heart attack. Wasn't enough she lived like a little queen out here, having her every whim, new cars, new clothes, a goddamn nigger maid to do all her work, this pampered little goddamn thing, but everybody knew Earl was fucking every girl came through his store, and everybody knew he fell in love with Ann after she went to work there, and everybody knew he set Ann up in the Tallahassee store so he could go down and be with her, and Birdie knew he was going to leave her for Ann and if you don't think that's enough motive for a woman to kill her husband you're a bigger idiot of a half-ass small-town newspaper man than I took you for.

She realized she'd locked herself out of her car, took off one of the expensive high-heel shoes Earl no doubt had given her gratis from his store, and smashed the heel into the driver's window shattering it. She tossed the fur stole onto the seat over the glass, climbed in, cranked up, and peeled out of yard. Finus heard something behind him then, and Avis walked up in the shadows, though he could make out the ironic smile on her face. She nodded to Merry's car hurtling away.

-Too bad you two didn't work out. You deserve each other.

Finus ignored her and went back in to apologize to Birdie for his part in the scene, even though that'd been ending it. He heard Avis's heels clicking down the driveway toward her car.

THE NEXT DAY, Finus went back to the funeral home to pay Parnell Grimes, county coroner and funeral director at the home, a semiofficial visit.

The old Victorian mansion Parnell used for a home and business stood on the west side of downtown near the library. Inside, Finus could smell nothing of the large bouquets and wheels of flowers standing in the foyer and parlors, but only (perhaps in his mind) the faint and pervasive odor of the chemicals of the trade, something like and not like formaldehyde, and sitting across from Parnell Grimes in his back office, looking at the soft little pudgy fellow he was, his pinkness, he couldn't help but entertain the morbid fantasy that a strange ancient secret funerary chemical ran in Parnell's veins in lieu of blood. He seemed distracted, shuffling papers on his desk, glancing up at Finus with a nervous smile, asked what he could do for him. With his smoothness, his balding slicked-down head, and his tight black suit, he looked a little penguinish standing there, to Finus.

-You'll have to forgive me, Parnell said. -Busy day. As always!

-No problem, Finus said. -Take your time.

-Um hmm, um hmm, Parnell said, shuffling his papers, raising his eyebrows and nodding, checking a drawer for something, shutting it. Then stopped all his fidgety activity, placed his pudgy little hands on the desk in front of him, and looked at Finus, eyebrows in a question mark. His child-size hands were almost translucent, made Finus shiver a little at the thought of them handling the dead—or him, dead. And within that cartoonish gathering of flesh blinked those deep-set and absurdly pretty eyes, like a movie idol's, so anomalous as to shock one upon first noticing.

-Well, I was just passing by, really, Finus said. He put his hands in his pockets, jingled his change, smiled at Parnell. -Any new customers today?

-I'm afraid so, Parnell said. -Mrs. Terhune, from Southside.

-The tamale lady?

Parnell nodded.

-I'll miss them, Finus said. -Used to buy them by the sackful.

-Selena will, too, Parnell said, referring to his wife, who lived with him there in the home. -She loves tamales.

-Mmm hmm, Finus said. -Say, Parnell, when I called yesterday you said Earl Urquhart died of a heart attack.

Parnell stood somewhat at attention, his head cocked in question. -Yes?

-Well, I was just rechecking that. Just wondering, no real reason, if there was anything odd there, anything that might have suggested any other cause.

Parnell kept his odd, penguinish pose.

-No real reason, Finus said, just that he seemed so healthy, you know, just talked to him the other day. He shook his head. -Just goes to show.

Parnell, after a beat, nodded as if the pose had been prelude to some odd penguin mating dance.

-Yes, yes it does. You never know. Well, no, Mr. Bates, no sign, no reason to think anything other than cardiac arrest, as far as I could tell. I suppose it could have been a stroke.

-Hmm, yeah, Finus said.

The men stood there awkwardly a moment more.

-So, Finus said. -Well, Mrs. Terhune?

-Heart, Parnell said, doing the nod again.

-Umm hmm, Finus said. -Guess she probably ate a lot of her own fare.

After a beat, both men laughed a little awkwardly, though quietly.

-Well, I won't keep you, Finus said. -I know you're busy.

Parnell's eyebrows jumped again and he shrugged his narrow little shoulders in the too-small black suit. He nodded.

-Yes, three funerals today, as I'm sure you know, Parnell said. -Sorry to be so distracted, Mr. Bates. He gave a nervous little laugh. -I'm terminally disorganized.

-Terminally, Finus said, and gave a little laugh of his own.

-Yes, oh, ha ha! Parnell said, standing up and starting to offer his hand, then withdrawing it as instead he came around the desk to usher Finus on out. -Well good to see you, Mr. Bates, sorry I couldn't be more help.

-No, Finus said. -Just obligatory, newspaper business you know.

-Yes, Parnell said, already somewhere else, showing Finus to the door, and seeming already away from there into another room as Finus stepped out the door and said goodbye.

-Yes, Parnell said, thank you now, give my best to Mrs. Bates.

Though everyone in Mercury who knew Finus and Avis knew they'd been separated for years, a terminal separation, as it were. Well he was an odd one, Parnell.

Finus made his way on down the sidewalk in the cold gray of the afternoon. It was February. Earl's wake tonight, services tomorrow, time would roll on. God help him, but he was thinking mourning period. He'd be visiting Birdie every now and then in between. Come late spring, he figured, all this would have pretty much died down. By then, it might be proper enough to propose that his visits take on a different tone. In the meantime, he'd check in on her every now and then to make sure she was doing okay.

~

BUT WHEN HE called her the next week she was upset. Wouldn't say why at first, then finally told him she'd received two letters, unsigned, with no return address. The text of the letters was made from cut-out magazine headline words, odd sizes, accusing her of poisoning Earl, and threatening to have his body exhumed for an autopsy.

-It's Levi and Merry, who else? Birdie said. -Finus, they have hated me and tormented me from day one, always jealous of me, jealous of Earl. And you should've seen them in the executor's office the other day. They stood up after Earl's will was read and said Earl would never have left them out, that something was funny, they were going to sue me, and just up and walked out. Hubert Cawthon called me and said they'd tried to get an order to dig Earl up, so I know it's them.

Finus called Cawthon, the district attorney, and Cawthon's assistant DA. Spud Meriwether confirmed, off the record, that Merry and Levi had indeed sought the order.

-Hell, Spud said, if anybody poisoned Earl Urquhart I'd think it his sister. Woman's crazy. Besides, Parnell Grimes said he sent a sample from Earl's heart to the state lab and came back negative.

-Is that right, Finus said, wondering why Parnell hadn't mentioned this to him. -No poison, then?

-I reckon that's what negative means, Spud said.

Finus knew from the grapevine that Spud had been one of Merry's victims, too, only unlike Finus (apparently an exception) Spud had been stuck for a life insurance policy before getting out of his affair.

He went to see Birdie that afternoon. Creasie met him at the door, nodded and hardly spoke, disappeared into the back somewhere. He and Birdie sat in the den. He asked her if she wanted him to help her with a lawyer or anything.

-This is harassment and slander, at best, he said.

-No, I'm just going to ignore them, she said. She sat in a stuffed rocking chair in the corner, fiddling with a silk handkerchief and looking out the window on the long front yard. -I don't want any more trouble.

-They're making it, not you.

-I'm not going to give them the satisfaction.

-Well, you let me know if you change your mind.

-All right.

She still looked out the window. Her hair was down, and beautiful. Her face was lined and puffy with the strain of everything. Her hands were slim and still pretty. The pale blue of her eyes in the afternoon light, absorbing the color of her pale blue dress. It was a still moment in the small room, steam heat ticking in the radiator against the wall. Through the door to the foyer he could see beyond to the big living room, cold marble fireplace with the big mirror over it, mute grand piano black in the corner like a museum piece. Here she was, a duchess set up in her little estate, the duke now dead at an early age, wondering what she was going to do with the rest of her life.

He wanted to ask her about Ann, Earl's girlfriend down in Florida. Not sure why he wanted to ask about that, then.

-Birdie, he finally said though. -I know Earl hurt you. Ran around on you.

She said nothing.

-Do you want to talk about it? All that?

-You're one to talk, she said. -You and Merry.

She was looking out the window. He shut up then, and they sat awhile in silence. Then Birdie opened a drawer in the little lamp table beside her and pulled out a letter in an envelope and handed it to him. It was addressed to Birdie, no return address. The postmark was back in September. There was another envelope inside, addressed to Earl at the shoe store, with a Tallahassee postmark from the same month. A letter inside it. He looked up at Birdie.

-Go ahead and read it, she said.

It was a letter written in what looked to Finus like a woman's handwriting. The salutation wasn't to Earl, was just a familiar *Hey*, followed by epistolary smalltalk, as well as some discussion of business. He looked up at Birdie again.

-It's from Ann Christensen, who runs the Tallahassee store, she said. -Go on.

Finus hesitated. -Was she there, at the funeral, then?

-She had the decency to hang back, but she was there.

Page two became personal again. It was a love letter, finally. She missed him. She hated not seeing him more than once a week, twice at best, but often only once or twice a month. She cherished their time on the Mississippi coast. She ached for him whenever they would part, after those times. She didn't even *want* to love someone as much as she loved him.

Do you think, she wrote finally, *that Birdie would be all right if you did in fact leave? I want so much for us to be together, but I don't want you to be miserable because of it. I don't want us ruined by your guilt and fear and worry over her. Sometimes I get so jealous that you feel so protective of her, so fearful of her dependence on you. Wouldn't she be all right, in that house, with Creasie there to help her out, and all her biddy friends? I feel terrible urging you to keep thinking about this, I don't like to think of myself as a homewrecker. But your children are grown and gone. They and your grandchildren could come to see us down here. We could run the businesses from here. Or hell, sell the Mercury store, let's open another one in Mobile or Jacksonville. I'm sorry. I can't help wishing for what I think is right, in spite of the fact that you are married. It's me you love, we both know that. We should be together. I try not to think about it like this. I can't help it. I love you. —Ann*

Birdie was looking out the window at the day, a blustery wind blowing in a front, clouds sailing above the bare oak limbs in the front yard, bright blue between them. It had enlivened Finus, coming out. Now he felt they were in a muffled cocoon, buffeted by the wind and isolated from all that had made him feel good in it, before.

-Do you think he was going to leave you? he said. -*Did* you?

She shrugged, after thinking for a moment.

-I always said he'd never leave me for anyone he just slept with, she said, pulling at a loose thread on her skirt.

-But this wasn't just that, Finus said.

She shook her head.

-I knew that, anyway.

They were quiet a while.

-It had to be Merry sent me that letter, Birdie said. -Stole it from Earl's office and mailed it to me just for meanness. Meanness to him or to me, I don't know. Both, I guess. I think he knew I had it, what had happened. He was nervous and irritable about it. But he wouldn't ask.

-You didn't say anything to him.

She shook her head.

-I didn't want to make a fuss about it. She looked up. -Well what difference would it have made, anyway, Finus?

-Maybe make him face up to what he was doing—

-And maybe decide to leave me. I didn't ever think he would, he knew I couldn't get by on my own. I've never worked, just been a housewife and a mother. Never went past the eighth grade. What would I do for a living?

Finus said nothing.

-I'm going to ask Edsel and his family to move in with me out here, I think, she said. -Just to have somebody around, and my grandchildren. They don't have a house yet, and this one's so big. Maybe they'd be happy here for a while.

-That sounds like a good idea.

He could still see her, a young girl naked in the woods, turning like a wheel in the light slanting through riverside trees. Looked at her feet now in the new slight slippers from Earl's store and remembered her short plump girl's feet flung up and over, how they made a *ka-thump* sound upon landing on the ground, the little muff of hair diaphanous in light from the leafy boughs behind her. He flushed with physical pleasure and a lamentable sense of loss. He wanted to go over, kiss her on the cheek. Felt as if he could not keep himself from doing it, in any case. But then he heard a whistling sound from the kettle, and Creasie pushed through the swinging door from the dining room to the kitchen. In a minute she came into the room carrying teacups steaming on little fragile saucers, no tray, just one saucer tilted in each hand, Lipton labeled tea strings hanging over the cup rims, a look on her face as if she were in some distant thought, had arrived in the room almost by luck, the kerchief on her head a comical nod to some old type though she was still a young woman, this belied too by the lump of dip pooching out her lower lip.

-Thank you, Creasie, Birdie said, her voice a little wavery.

-Yes'm, Creasie said, and ambled out of the room on, Finus just then noticed, a pair of pink-bottom, slightly squashed-down splayed bare brown feet.

~

IT WAS ON one afternoon while they were fishing for bream on a bed stinking of roe that he felt silently overwhelmed with a sense of urgency, that whether or not he understood what he'd felt for this woman now and at various times in the past he had to make a move, had to leap into something in order to understand the very element in which he existed, to understand his own mind.

He looked at her. Just a little plump with her fifty-four years, hair still dark brown and long, in a braid this day, a few gray strands, a little fleshier in the cheeks, but still pretty. The same impertinent mouth, the gapped teeth. Easy laugh. She saw him looking.

-What? she said.

-Do you know, Birdie, he said, I've seen you naked.

-What?

-A long time ago, the day you fell into the river during the picnic at the Methodist retreat. I was in the bushes when you and Avis came down the path to change you.

She colored. -Well what am I supposed to say to that?

-I don't know. Something happened to me that day, watching you. Avis saw me in there.

-Well what were you doing there? Just spying?

-Yes, but not on purpose. I'd gotten sick, went away from the camp, and y'all just happened along.

-You should have said something before I took my clothes off.

-I didn't have time. I didn't know what y'all were up to. Well I *couldn't*, I had my own pants around my ankles. But what I

174 / Brad Watson

wanted to say, you put a spell on me that day. It's like it's never
worn off, all these years.

Just saying those words released something in him, a prickling,
blood pressure up, compromised vision.

-What kind of spell?

-That's what I'd like to know. I was stricken. Smitten, maybe,
but stronger than that. I wanted you, somehow. I was so mad you
decided to marry Earl.

She laughed, half dismissal and half embarrassment. She lifted
her line from the water, examined the worm on the hook, and
lowered it in again.

They sat in uncomfortable silence for a while.

-I don't have to remind you that you're still a married man. I
probably shouldn't even be out here fishing with you, come to
think of it. Sometimes I forget you and Avis are still married.

Finus snorted. -Wish I could. No, sometimes I *do*. But only for
a moment or two at a time.

-Listen, Finus. Oh, I don't even like to throw my mind back so
far. But you were right way back when you said I wasn't ready to
get married, too young. And so much of my life went into it. I just
want to be alone, live with Edsel and his family awhile, as long as
they want to stay with me at the house. I'm just tired, I feel worn
out. Like I've had the life drained out of me. I know I'm not real
old but I *feel* old. You're a good man. You had a bad marriage, I
know. I did too in some ways, but it was good in others. If you
want to try to convince Avis to give you a divorce, well go ahead,
I think it's best anyway. But *I* don't want to run right into something else again. I've lived a whole life already, seems like. I may
have more in me but not right now. Maybe not ever. I just want
to rest. All this mess has just exhausted me.

-I'm not talking about marrying. He laughed. -I don't really
know what I want, Birdie.

-So what else is new? she said, but gentle, mocking him.

-Finus, she said after a bit, you and I are friends and I like it that way, always have. Even if you have seen me without my clothes on.

And she laughed, then, to think of it, and the sight and sound of it released a flood of feeling that was deeper than the old surge of sexual desire, though he felt a stir of that, too. How much he was drawing upon that indelible image he could not know. It didn't matter.

-I love you, Birdie. Always have, from the first time I saw you, I believe.

-You don't mean that any more than you did the last time you said it.

But she remembered that he had once said it, a long time ago. He took note of that.

Obits

AS FINUS GREW older, obituaries came to make up a goodly portion of the *Comet*, which was nearing the end of its arcing streak as was its body of readers. Often he was asked to write the obits for people not necessarily from Mercury though well known throughout the county because he made an attempt to tell something notable, or even simply funny or unusual, about that person's life. Your average obituary was a disgrace in its sterility. Nor could he stand the notion of families writing their own, which some papers were allowing now. He could just imagine the tears and flapdoodle from those pens, along with a host of the awfulest verse. He should know. Some still had the audacity to ask him to print their own words, whereupon he'd tell them to take it to one of those papers that made you pay for obit space. His newspaper wasn't the community wailing wall. You couldn't convince a body anymore that there was integrity in the use of the language.

In the awkward days following Earl's death, he wrote his obituary with some restraint, given his anger about what Levi and Merry were up to then.

EARL LEROY URQUHART, 55

- He built a sound business and his own small wealth from little more than grit, savvy, long hours, and professional integrity.
- He loved nothing more than taking his skiff to Pascagoula to fish for trout, redfish, Sound cats, and tarpon.
- He once hit a negro woman on the head with a high-heel shoe, in his store, for some impertinence.

Earl Urquhart, prominent Mercury businessman, died last Friday while splitting firewood out at his lake north of Mercury. He was 55 years old. Coroner Parnell Grimes gives as cause of death a heart attack. An autopsy was requested by members of his family. There was no evidence, Grimes said, of foul play.

Mr. Urquhart was born in Cuba, Alabama, but his family soon moved to Mississippi and he grew up in Union. The Urquharts moved to Mercury in 1915. Soon after, Mr. Urquhart met Birdie Wells, and wasted little time in courting her and persuading her to marry him, though she was just sixteen years old at the time. Mr. Urquhart was already a successful businessman by that time, and soon was managing a chain of shoe stores in the south for a New York manufacturing firm.

Mr. Urquhart worked in New York for a while, opening new stores for his company. In 1928, after a series of different assignments which took him to cities such as Baltimore, Cincinnati, Memphis, and Atlanta, he opened his own store in Mercury and settled there with his growing family. Through shrewd business practices and a conservative approach to marketing, he managed to keep his store through the Depression years. He opened another store in Tallahassee, Florida, in 1950. He owned partial interest in a shoe store run by his brother, Levi Urquhart, also in Mercury.

Mr. Urquhart was known as an honest man who worked hard and treated all fairly. He never drank, people like to point out. My impression was he wasn't proud of it so much as just not interested in liquor. He loved fishing, and often traveled to the coast to fish in the Mississippi Sound off Pascagoula and Biloxi in his own boat. He also owned a piece of land around a small lake just outside of Mercury, where he kept a couple of horses.

He was an emotional man and it was not unheard of for Mr. Urquhart to engage in quick bouts of fisticuffs on occasion, if insulted or if he perceived it to be the case. Most men treated him with respect, accordingly.

He is survived by his widow, Birdie Wells Urquhart, his daughter, Ruthie Mosby, his son, Edsel, and three grandchildren. Services were held at Grimes Funeral Home, with interment at Magnolia Cemetery.

LATER FINUS WROTE about the death of Birdie's daughter, Ruthie, when she succumbed to cancer in her early fifties. And about her son, Edsel, of a heart attack at the age of forty-eight (striking something of a blow to those who still entertained the thought that Earl's similar death, at fifty-five, was suspicious). And he wrote a heartfelt one about the death of Birdie's grandson, Robert, in an automobile accident at the age of twenty-two.

ROBERT EDSEL URQUHART, 22

· When he was only five years old, he wandered into the woods near his family's home and was lost—so everyone thought— until nightfall, when searchers saw the light of a fire. Reaching that spot, they found little Robert, pellet gun by his side, roasting a young squirrel over a campfire. A little lean-to he'd constructed sheltered him from the elements. He invited everyone to sit down and join him for supper.

- He was a precocious child in other ways, as the family story goes that he could stand on the transmission hump on the car's back-seat floorboard and name the make and model of every car headed their way before it got to within a hundred yards.
- But he definitely seemed more at home in the woods, and there wasn't a plant or animal he didn't know by name and habitat, simply by first-hand observation. This, in a time when the big woods had already begun to disappear in the south, and there was something of the boy that seemed not of his time, and something that seemed to project a quiet awareness of this. He would have spent every waking minute in the woods, had his family allowed it—they almost wish they had, now.

Robert Edsel Urquhart, 22, died in a car wreck on Langtree Road last Saturday night. He was looking for a boy who had insulted his girlfriend—boy was a friend of his —not to fight him, but just to ask him to be civil and apologize. As he and his girlfriend and two other young people headed in Robert's car up Langtree Road, another car came speeding around the sharp turn near the entrance to Ludlum's Woods, left the ground, and hit Robert's Jeep head-on. Somehow, no one else was seriously injured. Robert died instantly in the collision.

It was typical of the young man to try to settle a dispute between two angry people. He had a hot temper himself, but it was superseded by a kind disposition and a desire for everyone around him to get along. His grandmother, Mrs. Birdie Urquhart, never made any bones about the fact that Robert was her favorite grandchild—and I have permission and even the blessing of Mrs. Urquhart's other two grandchildren to make that statement.

Mrs. Urquhart once told me that Robert was the only child she'd ever known, other than herself, who took to nature as if he were truly at home in it. When she told him the name of a tree, or bush, or bird, he would remember it. She said a bird once lit on his shoulder as they stood still in a thicket watching another bird, and the boy, though only five years old, knew to be still and not make a sound until the bird had flown off on his own. She said to him, Do you know what kind of bird that was on your shoulder? He said, Yes, but then wouldn't tell her what kind of bird he thought it had been. Later that afternoon she asked him again, and he said, I know what kind of bird it was. Was it a finch? He wouldn't answer. Was it a sparrow? He wouldn't answer. At supper she told the story to the others, and said, I know you know what kind of bird it was, Robert, so why won't you tell us? And Robert considered this a minute and then said, If I told you, a bird would never land on my shoulder ever again.

He is survived by his mother and father, Edsel and Janie Urquhart, his grandmother, Mrs. Birdie Urquhart, and his maternal aunts and uncles. Pallbearers are his uncles Tom, Bernard, and Rupert Williams, and the deacons of the United Methodist Church.

One morning in late February '77, suffering the gray chill of a drizzling front that seemed to swell his aching bones, Finus rose and went down to the *Comet* office before coffee, before the radio station, and began typing what he'd composed in his head during the night.

AVIS CROSSWEATHERLY BATES, 76

- She was a basketball star in her little country school up in Kemper, and went on to play for Ole Miss, where she majored in education. Became a teacher and taught in the Mercury public schools for forty years.

- She once had her husband (yours truly) thrown in jail for missing a child support payment, and then had him thrown out when his buddies down there left him in charge of the keys.
- Most famous quotation: When told that her estranged husband (still yours truly) might have a brain tumor (false, rumor), she is reported to have replied, -As if he ever had a brain.

Avis Crossweatherly Bates died last night, bitter and twisted in her body by the disappointments in her life, her heart. Her father was a hard man, and possessive, he loved her so much. Saw her as everything he hadn't been able to be or do, and what a burden that was. Because the school's girl's basketball team wore these cute little skirts to play in, he followed the bus to every game, never let her out of his sight, ever, she never made a move his stern bony countenance wasn't hovering over as if from a cloud at her shoulder, like an angry God.

After college, she taught history at the high school, and used to remind yours truly, whenever he got too full of himself, that no one through history remembered the lowly scribes but by the quality of their words, and that he was after all just a small-time hack. This was about as true as words could be.

Well, you can imagine. You fight your way into town from a hardscrabble cattle farm way up in the sticks, fight your way through college on an athletic scholarship in the days when (especially for women) that didn't amount to more than room and board, fight for your independence every step of the way, get the man you want, and it all turns to manure, after all. Marriage, a tough business. It wasn't happy for Miss Avis, that's for sure. Yours truly had no small role in that. And yours truly was never forgiven. Add that to the list, as there's plenty yours truly has never forgiven himself for, too. We tell ourselves, after they're gone, I should have been a better father, husband, friend, brother, sister, daughter, son. But truth is most of us do

the best we can, just have a hard time accepting our limitations—
accepting that we dealt with things according to our best lights and
capacities for dealing. Disappointments flock to us like crows and
mock us from their perches on buildings or the flimsy swaying tips
of pines, or flying over, a glimpse of black wing and parted beak, or
in dreams, caustic, ephemeral. You love someone, you hate them.
The major crime, as has been said: indifference. The two-headed
monster, love and hate, accompanies our halcyon days. Much love
to Miss Avis, my estranged embittered bride. I ask her forgiveness for
all inadequacies and wrongs. May she rest in peace.

Survivor: Finus Ulysses Bates, husband.

He'd wanted to add long-suffering after his name, but thought
better of it. Let her have the last harsh words. On her deathbed,
he'd been there, holding her hand. She'd looked at him, her red-
rimmed eyes brimming with tears. -You ruined my life, she said in
her strained and halting voice. He'd only nodded, squeezed and
patted her hand. And later that night, she'd passed on. That was
just Avis, she'd needed to say it. He never for a moment thought
that, in her heart, she believed it was all that simple.

11

Her Remembrance of
Awakened Birds

CARS CLACKITY-CLACKING by out on the old high-
way, tires slapping the tar dividers, always put her to sleep, and
Earl, it would wake him up in the middle of the night, he'd have
to get up and go in the kitchen, make a pot of coffee and smoke
before coming back to bed. His heart racing. The man had to be
going all-out even sleeping, when he could sleep. It was all that,
killed him. They could say all they wanted about her but it was
that what killed him, cigarettes and no rest and womanizing, and
work all the time, and just that temper, all pent up and not
enough chances to steam it out. She gave him every chance she
could and then some, let him rant and rave all he wanted, but it
wasn't enough. The man had plenty of poison in his own glands,
keeping that backed up in him for want of putting it into her, but
it just wasn't in her to do that all the time, rutting away like he
wanted, and she reckoned he didn't let it build up too much, with
Ann and all the girls at the store as wanton and willing vessels.

The old mockingbird with the nest in the camellia was singing
in through the window screen again. She'd had Finus's radio
show on earlier though she missed whatever he'd said about her,
he'd said he was going to say something and she'd said not to tell

people she was out here about to die, they'd come and wear her out visiting and kill her for sure, and she didn't want to go that way, with people all around gawking. But when she turned on the radio and heard Finus that bird was out there, cocking his head, and when she turned him off in a little bit sounded like the bird was mocking Finus, singing a waw-waw-waw song made her laugh out loud, it had to be Finus's old sawing drawl he was after. She wondered sometimes if that crazy bird wasn't mocking her, nobody knew better than she did how she yammered on, when she was feeling good anyway, when she was on the telephone, talk talk talk, and suddenly in the middle of yapping-on hear that bird trilling some loud funny song didn't sound like any other bird, and she'd think My lands, that's me!

Now there he was, bouncing on that little camellia branch and cocking his head in and making some rrrack! rickety sound like a crow.

Out back of the house the old junk cars from her son-in-law's junklot across the road had accumulated over the years, spreading into her back lot where there was once just the little field laced with honeysuckle and hanging oak boughs and Creasie's cabin— now fallen in on itself and vines—gathering like the empty husks of giant cicadas, all through the ruined apple orchard. She used to make the best pies of those tart green and brown speckled apples. She couldn't look out the window on the east side of the house or go in the backyard without seeing all those empty rusted car bodies sitting there. Like a joke on Earl, who had loved the automobile second only to other women.

-I don't mean anything by that, now, your papa was so good to me and took care of me all these years, and had to live with me to boot, but you know it's the truth!

Her granddaughter said nothing, but her chin jutted out a little more and she looked away. That Mosby chin, like pictures you

see of those old kings and such that inbred so much, though she
didn't think that'd been the case with the Mosbys, just bad luck.
They say you're attracted to yourself in your mate. You'd think
they'd not liked the chin so much, though. Ruthie'd had a normal
chin, but this child had come down through her Papa's line.
Edsel's boy Robert had looked more like the Urquharts, before
he'd died in the car wreck. He'd be grown now like Laura, here,
if he'd lived.

Her granddaughter sighed.

-I've got to take Lindy to dance lessons and Chaz to baseball
practice, and Dan's on the road again. I probably won't be back
by today but I can check in around dinner to make sure everything's okay.

-No, hon, Creasie's got some peas and greens and we'll just eat
vegetables. I don't have an appetite, anyway. She coughed dryly
into a tissue. -I got some cream in the freezer, maybe I'll just eat
some of that later, to settle my stomach.

-Okay, her granddaughter said with another sigh, and kind of,
it seemed to Birdie, huffed in a tired way out of the room.

~

ONE LATE AFTERNOON at Pappy and Mamaw's house, she
was just about seven years old, she and Lucy'd been sent over to stay
with them, and Pappy took her out into his garden. Gardening was
his passion, then, and his garden was lush and beautiful. It was
dusk. The light faintly blue, and graying. Pappy had taught her the
names of the flowering bushes, the pink camellias and wild azaleas
with their yellow blooms, his roses and on down the little slope in
back the tall sunflowers like Uncle Will would grow himself one
day. Pappy knelt down beside her. Little Lucy was in the house
asleep. And in the light becoming so faint she was afraid they were
disappearing into it, like with the lessening vision they would both just
sift into the gray and disappear, so she gripped his empty coat sleeve

with her small hand, the thin wool fabric weightless between her fingers where he'd lost his arm in the war. His long white beard and hair looked silver and luminous in the spare light. He covered her hand with his own and said softly, -Listen, Birdie, can you tell it's something special? She looked at him, afraid. He whispered, -Something has happened. Can you tell?

-Yes, she whispered.

If she held on tight to Pappy she would not disappear without him, he would be with her there, where they went.

Pappy said, -It's a miracle has happened, Birdie.

She looked at him. In the disappearing light he was becoming darker, a shade lingering here on the earth. Within the soft glow of his beard and hair she could barely see his pale eyes.

Pappy said, -Your mama has given us a new little girl. When you get back to your house you'll see. And then, as her eyes became used to the darkening light, she could see him, like a child himself, somehow changed.

And that was when Pud had been born. In the last wisp of light from behind the trees they had walked holding hands back into the lamplit house and stood over little Lucy asleep in the middle of Pappy and Mamaw's bed and looked at her sleeping face.

-Another beautiful child in the world, like little Lucy here, but just a *tiny* baby, brand-new, Pappy said, and he stroked Birdie's hair. -In the morning, we'll all go see her.

She was so happy he had not gone away, the world had not ended in the beautiful moment in the garden, that she began to cry. He held her in his arms, shushing her, and took her into the kitchen, where Mamaw fussed over her and fussed at Pappy for telling her stories and scaring her so. The way he'd point to a plant and say, This here's hemlock, what they used to do away with their enemies in Shakespeare's day and so on. I ever get sick and out of my mind, you bring it to me, in a little tea.

Rrraaack! Mockingbird squawking at her again.

-Sing like the songbirds, that's what you're supposed to do.

The bird cocked his head.

-Go on!

Ooodle oo! Mocking her again.

Pud was so funny, when they was little girls, once learned the f-word and went around saying it when the grown-ups weren't there, till one morning when she'd waked up at dawn and was all by herself in the wide-awake world she heard this old crow cawing outside the window, sounded like he was saying *fuck! fuck!*, and it scared her so she ran into Mama and Papa's room crying, -I'll never say it again!

~

PEOPLE DIDN'T KNOW what she'd lived through in her life—if Finus Bates was to write the truth in her obituary it'd be an outrage. She told him once, said, I have suffered pain, insult, treachery, I guess nothing'll kill you till the Lord gets set to take you. Finus said, Well some say you're left here for a purpose, and she said, Well I wish He'd let me know just what that is so I can do it and hurry up and go. And Finus just laughed and said, Well you know I don't believe such junk anyway. Well I do, she said, or I did, anyway. I don't know why I'm still here, anymore, I feel so bad.

That Levi. The night Earl had the attack, before he died, Levi was to pick up some five hundred dollars in shoes in Memphis and bring them down to the Mercury store, and they never did get delivered. Already paid for. Birdie was at the Auxiliary weeks later, saw Hettie Martin wearing a pair of their shoes and said, Oh, you're wearing some of our shoes, and she says, Yes, Levi sold them to me, said he was helping y'all out. But they never saw any of that money, Levi just took advantage of all the confusion and stole them. Then turned around to the executor and said, I know Earl! I know Birdie! Lawyer said I don't care what you say, Levi,

Earl had a son, you are not named in this will. Then the cut-out letters start, they're going to dig Earl up and do an autopsy, on and on. Oh, it was terrible.

Merry was the worst of the lot in a way but she never really expected any money out of Earl after he'd died. Levi was greedy but with Merry it was more about mischief and mean practical jokes. She got mad at Earl one time and went down to the florist and sent bunches of flowers to this friend and that, in the hospital and here and there, and said just send the bill to Earl Urquhart, my brother. Earl said Goddamn, R.W., I'm not going to pay for that! And R.W. said I know it Earl, I'll pay for it.

He was the sweetest man, R.W was, and Merry did him so wrong. That time he was laid up in the hospital, and said, Well, one thing I know, Merry'd never cheat on me. Well. He was a good man, and made good money selling insurance, made the million-dollar club every year. But didn't have a clue. He never did know about the time Mr. Grant who had the appliance store downtown come by one day when Earl was out of town, said to Birdie, -Mrs. Urquhart I hate to talk to you about this but I got to talk to somebody, and I thought it might be better if you told Earl about it. I figure he might know how to handle it, but if I tell him he'd just get mad.

Well she, Merry, had been running around with his partner, Mr. Ethridge, and Mr. Grant says, Mrs. Urquhart, he's leaving money underneath the carpet there at the store for her, where she can come in and act like she's browsing—browsing washing machines, now!—and reach down like to scratch her heel and get that money. She's said if he don't, she said, I'll go to your front door and tell your wife what you done.

Not to mention what she did to Finus, all that mess.

-Now, I'm telling you, Birdie told Claudevelyn Peacock, who'd come by early that morning with a chicken and rice casserole and given it to Creasie in the kitchen and come on back to her bedroom, I'm telling you, you may not remember but now Merry was a beautiful woman. She could've been a movie star, I mean she really could.

-Oh, I know it, I remember her, she used to scare me the way she'd just look at you, Claudevelyn said, leaning forward with her hands on her flabby knees. She'd done something to her hair, Birdie thought, or maybe hadn't done anything, or tried and couldn't, anyway it was standing up like she'd put a little box on her head and slept in it. Had a good color, though, strong salt-and-pepper, her own hadn't been anything but pure gray since her sixties.

-That's right, like old Jane Russell, kind of, just a sexpot.

-Oh, yeah, honey, Claudevelyn said. She leaned back in the chair beside the bed and sucked her teeth and looked off like her mind was wandering to something. -Land, yes, she said.

She woke up at some point, Claudevelyn gone.

Earl said one day, I don't see—she told him about Mr. Ethridge the night after Mr. Grant came by, and he said Why didn't you tell me sooner? and she said I just couldn't—but Earl said, I don't see what people see in her. Well, she was just charming as she could be, kept her hair long and was pretty. But you know what Earl said about her, said her breath smelled terrible, he said I don't see how anybody could kiss her, her breath smells just like s-h-i-t. And it did. You could walk into the room and you could smell Merry's breath. Birdie didn't know why it was and couldn't see herself how anybody stood it, she couldn't ever stand to smell bad breath. It comes through your gums and they can be treated. Earl's breath never did smell like that, he smelled so much like cigarettes. But then he had his own problem, with the stinky feet. She'd been with Earl when he'd be opening new stores and wouldn't take his shoes off for two or three days, then come home and his feet smelled like, oh, something awful— she'd pick up his shoes and set them outside, she couldn't stand it. They finally quit smelling that way, but you keep your shoes on for days like that and your feet smell—well you don't know how bad they can smell.

Well she never thought life would be so full of meanness and disappointment. She hadn't been prepared for it.

They'd had the best time at night, when she was a little girl. The house had a big room with a fireplace, and they'd all get in a circle around that fireplace. And Uncle Will was an old bachelor, he'd come down, he lived just a hop and a skip down the road, just a garden between, when you looked you saw the big bright yellow faces of sunflowers looking back. He'd come walking down through the sunflower stalks, singing, and she and Lucy and Pud would play tricks on him all afternoon. One time put some water up over the door and it spilled on him. And put pins in the chair cushion, he'd sit on it. He was one of those old grouches, wouldn't want to laugh: Ain't you got no better sense than to do things like that? But you could see how he was tickled about it.

The neighbors had an old white horse named George stayed out in the pasture, and when she'd wake up in the morning sometimes she could look out in the field, sun just up, and see George out there and somehow it made her feel good. She couldn't remember what happened to him, they must have sold him. She took to a baby goat Papa had and went out to the barn with Papa one day and he got angry and had a hammer in his hand and he slung it, didn't even know the poor thing was standing there, and the little goat just fell over dead. Hit him in the head. They didn't even dress it out. It wasn't a pet or anything but it made everybody sad. Once she got up onto George and rode him out into the pasture and he went under a tree and nearly knocked her off. She was always scared of a horse after that. Earl wanted to get all of them a horse. Well he did have one—a beautiful mare—there was a way you'd pull her and she'd rare, and she'd rare up with the kids, and scare her to death. And Earl was going to break that horse. It's a wonder he didn't have a stroke over there one day. He got so mad at that horse he led her out into the lake up in the woods behind the house, that horse had to hold her head way up, Earl was just going to drown her. That's how he was then. Why in the world he didn't have a stroke right then, his face was so red.

He had a temper like a lion! But he'd get over it.

She could hear a gentle swishing in the trees. Could be rain, coming.

When they'd go out to that lake Edsel and Janie's little Robert would say, wasn't but about three, -Su-u-re is a lot of *horse* grunt around here. A little boy then, now long gone in the car wreck. What was the good in her living so long, when such things happen to young people? It just wasn't right your children and even grandchildren should die before you. Finus would know about that.

She couldn't hear. She'd heard thunder last night, oh, it was so loud one time. It's funny about hearing, the way it goes. She finally got her hearing aid to work right, got it to squeak, but that lady down at the nursing home said she just took hers out, said she'd heard enough already. Earl used to sell that woman shoes, and she never would listen, and he just quit selling to her, he said he'd rather not have her business than to misfit her.

She knew he opened that store down in Tallahassee so he could be with Ann, she knew that.

-Miss Bird?

Old Creasie sticking her black head in the door.

-No, I'm all right, now just go on!

Merry even wrote that book, nobody would publish it, all about the family, and made Birdie out to be someone who pretended to be dumb but was really devious. Well she might have let them think she was dumb, but she wasn't devious, she just wasn't going to have all that fussing and fighting, the Urquharts did enough of that among themselves. And Earl knew she knew what was going on. Every now and then he'd come to her crying, You're the best woman in the world! No woman'd put up with me but you! Things like that. Crying. I'll never do it again! She didn't say anything much, but naturally it killed something in you. She loved him but she didn't respect him too much.

You know the first train that come through up there where Earl was born, where they lived when he was a boy, said it scared him so bad he run in and got under the bed. He used to tell the story. Little boy, he was. He was born in 1899. Maybe they'd all been different if the times had been different. These days nobody thought anything about sex, but back then it wasn't so common, so maybe those Urquharts were just ahead of their time that way. Except with them it was more like couldn't think of anything but sex. Peggy one time, she was Levi's oldest daughter, and she told her mama, Rae, never will forget, she said old Junius Urquhart felt up under her dress. The idea of such a thing, and his own granddaughter, too. And the old man said, Aw, she's just lying. But Birdie knew now it was true because just about three weeks before Ruthie died she told Birdie and Pud that he did her the same way when she was a little girl. Birdie said, Why didn't you tell us before now? Said, *Ruthie, that's ruined your life and you hadn't ever told us anything about it.*

Now that old man could have done well by his family if he'd wanted to. He was a good insurance man, but all he cared about was chasing women. One time he put Edsel on his lap and was talking to him, before Edsel knew it big tears was rolling down his grandfather's face, and Edsel was a sensitive child, you know, and he started crying too before you know it, and he says, What's wrong, Grampaw? And old Junius says, Son, nothing's wrong, that has sold me more insurance than anything in the world. That's what he'd do, you know, in the Depression. Go into people's houses and when they wouldn't buy insurance he'd start to cry, say That's all right, he knew times was tough, he could hardly feed his own family, he never knew when they'd be out on the street, and so on, and they'd buy a little bit. He worked hard, but he wasn't honest.

My lands they was all bad, Earl too, but she held her head up and acted like she didn't know a thing in the world because listen she knew that she could not work and make a living, she'd married too young and was spoiled, and she knew Earl would never marry anybody he just slept with, so she let it go. She knew he respected her, in spite of everything. And everybody depended on Earl, everybody looked up to him, never dreamed he'd die as young as he did, just fifty-five years old. And when he died everybody just fell apart. She'd lived almost as long without him as she ever did with him, and got by all right. But Pud's death like to killed her. And Lucy going like that, on the stairs in her home, and nobody there. And losing Ruthie and Earl and then Robert. Well it wasn't fair she should have to live through all that, she should have gone before any of them except Earl.

None of the Wells girls turned out well in married life, she guessed, well Pud did but Lucy didn't. She was so beautiful, Lucy, nothing but a set of big brown eyes in a little birdlike face, and married that silly man couldn't let go of his mama and then had to just divorce him, and then married that old goat, wasn't nothing but a servant to him, he wouldn't take her anywhere. Birdie felt so sorry for her. Pud's Anton was a good man but he was as crazy as she was, always clacking his teeth out like a cash drawer, the kids just loved it.

There was that mockingbird come back and looking in. If he had any sense he wouldn't build in the camellia, he'd build in one of the trees in the yard. She loved to climb trees when she was a little girl but once she got up there she'd be too scared to climb down. Never would forget, climbed up in the loft one time and couldn't get down, and stayed there and worked her stomach till she nearly bled, she was so scared. Always scared of heights but couldn't help but climb up. Just a birdbrain, she guessed, reason they named her Birdie.

The mockingbird went into his repertoire, so loud it sounded right in her ear.

Sometimes she liked to think she could have poisoned Earl like Levi and Rae said. It was so ridiculous, she liked to think she could have done it. She'd thought she was losing her mind there for a while, would go into the spice cabinet pulling out little spice tins, sniffing, thinking, Did I do something I didn't even know? She had for a while put boiled sassafras water in his coffee because there was a doctor in Huntsville who'd said it countered the bad effects of tobacco. But she'd stopped because Earl said it tasted so bad. But could it have done some damage before she stopped? It froze her to think so. Levi and Merry had it like some old detective story, like she'd made him scrambled eggs one morning and sprinkled arsenic or—what was it Pappy had in his garden? hemlock—into it, and he'd gobbled it up, gone out and got into the pickup and over to the lake, down to the woodpile to chop some wood, the old mare snuffling up to him wanting some sugar, and fell out, spooking the horse so it ran off across the dam and into the woods. She liked to think sometimes she could have done that, not because she hated him or wanted him to die but just because it'd surprise everybody so, the ones with any sense, who weren't crazy, it'd be so contrary to their notions about little old Birdie—Merry might have said she was devious but get right down to it she thought she was a birdbrain, too. It's been so many years since all that, she couldn't even be sure to tell you the truth herself that maybe she didn't.

Mockingbird was so loud she couldn't even see, like she was passing through that song into nothing.

Finus Querulous

THAT MORNING, FINUS had steered his old Chevy pickup into the long driveway, two parallel curving shaded wheelpaths of cracked concrete ruptured here and there by the roots of thick tall oaks, and parked beside the old pumphouse beyond which now leaned the stacked empty carapaces of gutted ancient automobiles. They filled the once grassed little meadow between the house and old Creasie's cabin at the back edge of Earl's property. But since his death these discarded wrecks had been hauled here for storage from Birdie's son-in-law's junkyard across the side road. It was something probably would have driven Earl Urquhart into a rage, him a man so in love with glamorous cars that he'd bought new every year, always paying cash. He'd had him a nice little estate out here, Finus thought as he helped his old collie, Mike, down from the passenger side and together they walked around the house back into the front yard to the main entrance.

He'd held the railing to the broad covered stoop and climbed the old Mexican tile steps, rung the buzzer. Another car went by out on the old highway, its tires slapping a regular rhythm on the tar dividers. In a minute the door to Birdie's house opened to reveal Creasie, bent over a little. She looked up at him, then cast a scant eye down at Mike, then stood back and held the door open. -Come on in, she said, shooing them, as if they were both old dogs late for a feeding. -She don't want no company but I imagine she'll see you. She said the other day she wanted to talk to you. He passed Creasie and nodded down to her, her appraising eye cast up at him, and he took in her old dress cinched up beneath her baggish bosoms and ending at the SlimJim presence of her scrawny shins. Her feet in dilapidated Keds like tattered skiffs with big dusky bunions thrust out either starboard prow.

-Hello, Creasie, he said, to force a greeting.

-Mr. Finus.

-She in the den?

-She in the back laying down, Creasie said, already headed that way. -I'll go see if she's awake.

He followed her as far as the living room and stopped while Mike wearily followed Creasie on back. The room contained, as if sealed there, the chilled stale odor of a neglected museum dedicated to the finer middle-class living room in the 1940s. Heavy furniture with thick and gnarled wooden protrusions like mummified hands at the ends of the armrests, no give he knew to the cushions beneath fabric developing the sheen of old clothing mothballed for years, springs as hard as the springs on the rear axle of his truck. A grand piano at one end of the room gave his peripheral vision the image of a reconstructed stegosaurus. The gas logs in the fireplace, artificial hickory, not fired in twenty years. Then Creasie's rag head popped into the far doorway and beckoned. He started across the living room, passed Creasie going the other way and listing slightly to one side, drifting back toward her kitchen.

Birdie was more drawn than before and pale, as people whose hearts are failing are, skin seeming thinner and papery, and her pale blue eyes were rheumy, though he could still see in them the innocent mischief that was her nature. She laughed.

-Mike's already made himself at home.

The old dog had lain down beside the window, and looked with his eyes over at Finus coming in as if to say what kept you?

-You look all right, Birdie. You still look yourself.

This was true if qualified by age and illness. She was puffy with the fluid around her heart. Her hair was long and clean, silver and resting across her shoulder as she sat up against the pillows. Still the small impertinent mouth and gapped teeth. But her eyes were rheumy behind the wire-framed glasses, her hands bent and all spotted up, nails long and yellow, she'd been cared for but couldn't really care for herself, the details showed.

-I'm not sure I ever wanted just to look myself, she said, and laughed a little.

Her bedroom was pleasant and even fairly cool, though the day was hot, late July. It was at the northeast corner of the house, and there were windows on the north and east walls, and outside the windows there were blooming azaleas, and out in the oak-shaded yard beyond there were dogwoods that in March had been solid white with blossoms, now pale-barked and leafy green. Birds flew from the dogwoods and the oaks nearer the creek at the border of the property and flitted into the azaleas, you could hear them pecking at its mulch below. A mockingbird sat somewhere nearby out of sight but not out of mind, belting a repertoire. Finus liked to imagine the phrases the birds were going through: ohmygod-helpme! ohmygodhelpme!, dearme dearme dearme, lookahere! lookahere!, boogedieboogedieboogedie, therewego therewego therewego, who, me? who, me?, stick close! stick close! stick close! stick close!, I don't know. I don't know. I don't know. Some mornings he woke up and heard the Eurasian collared doves call-ing, a big Old World bird new to Florida and spreading north fast, their voices hoarse like young roosters crowing, What world is this? What world is this?

The sun lay full-bore upon the north meadow beyond but here broke through the oak boughs only in bright angled blades to the sparse and spotty lawn grass.

-This old house, Birdie said. -I don't like being out here alone at night, but I don't reckon I'll have to be much longer. I mean, Creasie's here but she just goes back in her room after supper and it's like being alone. Oh, I tell you, Finus, I feel so weak. I wish I could just go ahead and die.

Finus said nothing and kept his face neutral.

-Tell me again what happened at the home, he said.

-Oh, well, I reckon I died and came back.

-You said that. But, now—you mean all the way out?

-I tell you, Finus, after Pud died, it just like to killed me. It ain't right. She was ten years younger than me. And then Edsel and Ruthie. She stopped and her face went blank as if she'd forgotten what she was talking about. But she hadn't. Just at a momentary loss for words. -And I said to myself I'm just not going to stay around any longer, it's just not right, everybody dying but me. I believe I just started to shut down. She fiddled with a tissue at her nose. She looked up. -Well I *believe* I died. I was going so peaceful, just like I'd always hoped I would, and it felt so restful, and then something started happening and I woke up with all them standing over me and tubes sticking in me everywhere. Choking—it was awful! I was so mad! And now here I am, just miserable. You tell me what good's in that. I told them just to go to the devil, I was going home. Laura and Joe said they'd hire a nurse but I told them I didn't want it, just let Creasie tend to me best she can.

The outburst winded her and she rested a few minutes, breathing hard and deep and slow. -I reckon they think I'm being hardheaded.

I don't want it to be hard on them. But I don't want some nurse out here pestering me. I just want to go ahead and die.

-Well, Finus said, sitting in the chair beside the bed and lifting his own glasses to rub at his eyes and the skulled skin loose around them, then replacing the glasses to refocus on her. -Sometimes I think that old saying, One foot in the grave, is almost literal, you know. I mean sometimes you feel like you can almost see into it, like there's a period there when you're a little of both, the living and the dead. That's dying.

Birdie just looked at him blankly a moment, and laughed.

-You're a crazy old coot.

He got her a glass of water from the bathroom tap and she drank from it. Her nails needed cleaning pretty bad. He wanted to go get some tissue and a nail cleaner and take her hand and help her with them, but such tenderness would embarrass her, he knew. He took the glass from her hand when she'd sipped and set it on the little table beside her bed and sat back down. It was true she was left all alone. Her grandchildren took good care of her but you didn't like to wear out the young, didn't feel worth it, not if you had Birdie's temperament anyway.

-I just remembered a dream I had last night, he said to her then.

-Do you believe in dreams? She turned her head on the pillow to look at him.

-Well I think they come from the waking life. People used to think they came from the gods, or God. He waved a hand at the thought.

-I never could remember my dreams, there'd be just a little flicker of it when I woke up, then gone, she said.

-Well this one just now came back to me, because of your telling what happened to you at the home. All right. In this dream I was a young man again, and strong as I could be, it felt fine. And every night—in the dream, I mean—my spirit would go out of my body and fly around the world, seeing all kinds of things. I might go way over to China in the old days, before there were any Western people there, you know. Or I might be in the body of a sea turtle, swimming deep in the Gulf. And while I was gone out of my body I had this dog who would guard it.

-You never had a dog till you got old Mike, did you?

-No, I never had a little dog of my own when I was a boy, Finus said. -I don't know why. Avis didn't like dogs, is why I didn't have one as an adult, I mean older. But I don't remember why I never had one as a boy. My papa had a dog, some kind of old black-and-white dog. And we were friends, but he wasn't really my dog. Anyway, I had this dog in the dream, guarding over me lying there, and I can't remember what he looked like. He was a talking dog, I guess.

Birdie said, -You're making all this up.

-I was out spriting around and this dog got restless one night and went out wandering, and some people came and found my body and thought me dead and took it off and buried it, so when I came back the next morning I had nowhere to go, and I had to find a body to go back into or my spirit would die. And I looked around and I saw the dog coming home, but when he saw me he ran off, and I saw a horse, but he shied and ran off, too. Then I saw this old, old man lying out in the high grass in the field where the horse stayed. He was so tired he was about to die, and the sun was about to come up over the treeline and so I quick went into his body and was safe. And then I woke up.

Birdie looked at him blankly a moment.

-That's how I got so old, Finus said.

-Aw, now, you read that somewhere, she said, and laughed. -I know you. Well Finus it's good to see you, but you know I told you to say on your show that I didn't want any company. They say it's all this fluid around my heart that's making me feel so bad. It's just so hard to breathe.

Finus nodded. -I thought I'd come out just for a minute, I don't want to wear you out.

-I guess I look as bad as I feel.

-Naw.

She did look miserable and tired. He couldn't trouble her anymore.

He stared at her a long while.

-That time at the Potato Ball when you said you wanted me to run away with you, I thought you were serious, she said. -If I'd a been Pud, I'd a made you do it! She laughed again, and coughed.

-Well, he said after a bit, if I'd a been Pud's Anton, I reckon I would've done it, too. But I was a shy boy, kind of. I sure was smitten, that's true.

-Well, I reckon it wouldn't have been any crazier than doing what we did do.

-Ha, he said. -I guess that's the truth.

They looked at each other. He tried to imagine what it would have been like, to have had a whole life with her as his mate. Seemed like something that would've had to happen in a separate universe or something. Maybe it had.

-I should've done it, Birdie. I should've run off with you. I was a coward, I chickened out. It's the most disappointing thing I ever did in my life. I'm still ashamed of it.

-Aw, now, don't be, she said, dismissive. -Finus, I tell you, I don't think I could've lived with you. I mean I probably would have, since I lived with Earl and never left him, but I don't think I'd have been happy with you.

-Why not?

-Well Earl was hot-tempered and he run around on me, and I don't think you'd have done that, even with Merry, if you'd been married to me. But you've always been so gloomy. Even back then. I think I would've just lost patience with you, being so glum all the time. One thing you could say about Earl, he had a temper but he wasn't gloomy. He was cheerful enough.

-Maybe I was gloomy because I didn't get you. He grinned at her.

-Aw, fiddle, she said. -You were gloomy when we was just boys and girls. I remember I used to tell you to *cheer up*.

-I don't remember that.

-Well I did. And you would always say, What's to be so cheerful about? And I'd say, Well life! Can't you just appreciate how everything's so pretty and life can be so much fun?

-And what would I say to that?

-Oh, I don't know. I don't remember. I just remember you were a sweet boy, but just as gloomy as you could be. I said one time I think, I'd never marry Finus Bates, he's so gloomy.

-You didn't.

-Well, maybe I did. She laughed. -I don't remember! My lands, that seems like another lifetime, it was so long ago.

-I guess it was, he said.

-Gloomy, just like that! she said, and laughed again. -Now, look, why don't you stay and eat dinner? I'm not real hungry, myself, and I know Creasie has plenty to eat.

-Listen, I'm not gloomy, I'm just introspective. How can you say we wouldn't have been a good couple just because I was a little moody?

-Now don't get upset, she said.

He heard the slappity sound of another car's tires out on the highway, passing by.

-Say what you want though, Finus, but you are gloomy.

A mockingbird flew up to the window screen with the sound of ruffled skirts being tossed. It perched on the sill, cocked its eye at him. Startled him. He eyed it back. Thought for a moment he recognized something in its hard beady glare. The bird parted its beak as if to speak.

-Shoo, he said, half rising and making a shooing motion with his hands. The bird flew off. Mike lifted his old hoary head from the floor beside the dressing table.

-What was that? Birdie said. -That crazy mockingbird?

Finus looked at her. He'd forgotten for a second just where he was, forgotten she was even in the room.

-What does it matter now, anyway?

-See what I mean?

He caught sight in the corner of his eye now another face, looking round the doorjamb, a faded blue kerchief knotted above the brow.

-You better rest up, Creasie said to Birdie, unless you want to pass on in front of Mr. Finus.

Birdie flicked at her with a hand.

-Mm hmm, Creasie said, retreating. -Dinner be ready directly.

Meaning lunch, of course, and Finus could smell Creasie's unmatchable cornbread muffins and pots of greens and peas with okra and it made him suddenly hungry enough to stay if anyone asked.

-Stay and eat dinner, now, Birdie said.

He skitched his cheek at Mike to wake him.

-I'll run on, he said. -No need for you to get dressed. And he leaned over and gave her a kiss on the cheek, her skin soft and malleable as a plucked dove's, and squeezed her cold thinning hand, and her eyes had already fallen aside in a half-focused gaze of distraction as he showed himself out.

Finus Uxorious

AT THE BRIGHT blurred window there was a shape, and a sound like pecking on glass. Finus reached to the bedside table for his spectacles, put them on, but the shape was just a flitting shadow, gone, maybe just a figment of his now cluttered and wayward imagination. He cast a cautious, sidelong glance at the stuffed chair in the corner of the room: his dead wife Avis was no longer there. She'd been there the night before as he lay in bed waiting for sleep, just sitting there looking at him with the stony gaze of the indignant dead, saying nothing but refusing his silent demands that she go away.

He hadn't slept too well. Creasie's call in the afternoon, day before, had set off all his memories about Birdie, now she was gone. -Miss Birdie's passed on, was all she'd said.

After a moment, he said, -You okay, then?

-Yes, sir. I'm all right.

-I'll take care of it then. You wait there with her.

-Yes, sir. I ain't got nowhere else to go.

He had called Parnell Grimes, let him take care of it. No need to go back out, see her like that. He'd have his last memory of her, alive.

He wondered now if he'd have some sort of Birdie vision, now that she was gone.

He lowered his feet from the bed to the floor beside the sleeping head of ancient Mike, scratched the dog's head, and shuffled into the bathroom. He stood over the toilet and made water, a pretty good stream, better since he'd been taking the saw palmetto. He looked into the mirror, gave himself a little upper body massage. A spry eighty-nine, he suffered the loose skin of the aged, as if it had been removed from someone larger, stretched and dried, then pulled over his old meat and bones like bad taxidermy. There was nothing to do but accept he was very old. He still walked every day, some days did a few half-push-ups and stomach crunches, and he gave up beer, it gave him such gas. Now he drank only bourbon and gin, and that in moderation. He could only be thankful. He easily passed for seventy-something. Most his age were long gone to the boneyard.

In the kitchen he poured himself a cup of coffee from the automatic coffeemaker he'd set to make coffee by itself every morning at four fifty-five. Outside the window over the sink, the courthouse lawn and the tall Confederate monument and the white concrete courthouse itself were just touched with the slanting yellow light cutting over the bluff to the southeast of town. Finus tasted the dark, bitter coffee and touched his fingertips to the window glass, already warm at this hour in late May. He heard clicking old claws and Mike walked stiffly into the kitchen and leaned his head against Finus's leg, stood there wearily.

-Good old Mike, Finus said. -You still tired? Dreaming them squirrel dreams? Wear you out, old boy.

The dog was fifteen years old, which made him even older than Finus in dog years.

Finus took his coffee to the bedroom and sat on the edge of his bed and let his parts hang over the edge of the mattress. His sac sagged like an old bull's, and he wore his britches a little low on the hips to make plenty of room for his equipment, whose function now was mostly to get in the way of crossing his legs. Inside his apartment in the Moses Building above the offices of the *Comet*, he often went naked in the mornings and after evening baths, as clothes were so restrictive and there was too much cinching up of critical parts. He had few visitors, none of them women. The triangular Moses Building wedged itself into the convergence of two streets leading to the civic enclave of the courthouse, its annex containing the sheriff's department and the food stamps office, an abandoned highrise parking lot that had failed in the seventies, and a row of shops trying in a desperately futile way to help revive downtown in the wake of the mall one mile south. The mall had been failing in its own hapless and inane fashion since its construction, also in the seventies, the decade during which it seemed to Finus that the entire country had seen a failure in terms of morals, economy, politics, and fashion.

At his age he was by some sort of osmosis as venerable in this town as the passing century itself, and was sometimes hailed on the sidewalk: Hey, Mr. Bates! What's the word, Finus! Slow down, there, Mr. Bates, you're moving too fast! And such foolishness as that. Finus bathed in it. There was nothing, he had once observed in his obituary for Adolphus William Spinks, a well-loved and longtime mayor, like local fame. It put the national and international variety to shame.

A watering in his saliva glands sent him shuffling to the kitchen for another cup and his daily ration of gin-soaked raisins, an arthritis preventive he thought maybe he'd picked up from Paul Harvey, though he wasn't sure. For all he knew, they were keeping him alive. He dipped his fingers into the jar and rolled or plucked out exactly nine and dropped them into his mouth, chewing while he rinsed his fingers, and then poured another cup of coffee. If that didn't keep the arthritis away, he'd help it out with a little Bombay on the rocks later on. Mike lay on the kitchen floor now, and breathed heavily when Finus came in, as if he found all this activity tiresome.

He sipped the coffee on the way back to the bathroom, set the cup down on the sink's edge, and sat down on the cool toilet seat, which made his pecker draw up like a catalpa worm. He set his feet apart on the cool tiles, hands on his knees like half of a serious discussion, and stared at the blank opposite wall, the nubble of plaster covered by a coat of glossy blue enamel paint. He waited. He ran a hand through through the thick white hair on his head, secure in the knowledge he'd take it to the grave, they were his immortal hairs, always warned Ivyloy to use his Kryptonite scissors on them, didn't want to dull or break the blade.

-I'll use the ones you brought back from Mars, Ivyloy once said.

-That'll do.

Finus detected now the smallest, most insidious of movement. He closed his eyes. What an ungodly business, a man should be afeared like Adam, terrified of this body our garden that contains the seeds of our own demise, slow and cruel deterioration from God's own image—whatever that was or had been he was sure we were not made in it anymore. Not just the aged. Why did Genesis never once mention shit? Or did it? Finus reached his arm back and flushed, the old toilet roaring like a waterfall. He remembered his first indoor toilet, when they'd moved into town. He'd run down the stairs to see where it all dashed out, looked into all the rooms, expecting disaster, but they were pristine. That had to have changed the mental parameters of the human race, there. No doubt one reason primitives were nomadic was because they so befouled a place they had to move on, but no more—it all just disappeared. Now he pulled off a great pile of tissue to make a wad. Are you a folder or a wadder? he'd once said to a man he didn't respect. The man hesitated. That's what I thought, Finus said, and turned away with a dismissing wave. You had to let a man know when he wasn't acting right. Finus's friend and physician Orin Heath had once said, -Well Finus, you'll live as long as a sea tortoise if you can still take a good crap every day.

-That's my former life, Finus said. I know every inch of the Gulf of Mexico.

-You're deep all right, said Orin, it's deep around you, considering the subject.

-I know where the treasure is, down there on the old pirate beach, Finus said.

-I bet you do.

Finus whacked the toilet handle again and stood up. Done and hardly a stink. He took his cup back out to the bedroom, stepped carefully into a pair of boxers, and opened the dresser drawer containing his pants, all cotton khaki slacks cleaned and pressed at the One Hour Martinizing. He pulled on a pair, then selected a white Oxford short-sleeve shirt from the next drawer and angled his longish arms into the sleeves.

So he'd have to write two obits, today. Parnell told him, when he'd called about Birdie, that Midfield Wagner had passed on, too.

He finished dressing, turned off the radio, went into the living room and picked up the phone and called Parnell Grimes at the funeral home for a couple of details about Midfield and Birdie, then coaxed Mike downstairs for a little walk to the courthouse lawn across the street to do his business, then praised him up the steps again. The dog made his way back to the bedroom for a long siesta. In the kitchen Finus filled Mike's water bowl, shook out a few chunks of food from the sack, then poured himself a third cup of coffee, which he drank standing at the sink. He set the empty cup down in the sink, navigated the stairwell down to the street, and went out into the morning air. He allowed himself a glance at his reflection in the plate-glass windows of Ivyloy's barbershop, dust motes suspended in the slant rays reaching the chair and around the glass jars of tonic and oil. He'd forgotten to shave or comb his hair and his reflection showed him to look a little seedy. He stopped and took a look, ran his hand over his bristly face and over the top of his head. Maybe he'd stop back in at Ivyloy's before dinner and get a shave, a nice hot towel on his face. A good way to relax after writing a few things up in the morning.

He remembered the first time he'd seen Birdie. Small child astride a big short-haired dog that carried her slowly down a stretch of narrow beach along a peninsula that jutted into Mobile Bay, following an old spotted gray horse that clopped along in the sand, head down as if pondering. In the afternoon sun they made a picture both forlorn and comical. Where had she been going, a little girl astride a hound and following a downtrodden dray? He hadn't called out to ask. It was beatific, the way he remembered it now.

His family had been vacationing down in the old Henrietta Hotel on the Alabama coast. The day was bright and clear but blustery. By noon the sky turned gray and low, and soon took on a weird, greenish glow. He stood on the deck with his mother and father and grandfather while they looked at it and murmured to one another about it. By early evening the wind was blowing hard and then sometime in the night he was taken from his bed wrapped in a blanket and put into the back of a wagon with other people from the hotel and they traveled down the old road to the army fort at the end of the peninsula. There they were taken into the huge vaulted munitions rooms deep within the fortress walls where they and the Commandant and a group of soldiers sat around a wood stove, the soldiers and his parents and grandfather drinking coffee and talking while the wind howled. Finus fell asleep again with his head in his mother's lap in a little brick recess in the wall on which there had been piled soft blankets, and the wind howled him sweetly into dreams he forgot as soon as he woke the next morning.

It was a watery world around the fort, as he could see through still pelting raindrops from the high parapet where his grandfather took him to see. The marsh east of the fort was lapped with little waves, tips of tall sea oats just visible above them and the sky a gray soapy foam. Pines to the south and farther east waist deep in brown water, the clumped tops of the scrub oaks just showing. A group of officers in their ranger hats stood a few feet away from them, looking through binoculars to the east and pointing and talking.

When they went out in the long rowboats to look for survivors in the bar pilot village a few miles east of the fort, his father and grandfather let him go along. He sat beside his grandfather in the prow of the boat in which the Commandant sat with his father in the rear as two soldiers manned the oars. They launched at the marsh's edge, and rowed between the pines and around the clumps of scrub oak tops, in the lapping brown water and debris from broken limbs and here there the strange item, a floating washtub or wooden ladle, a well bucket, a floating length of swollen rope. An old steel gray and rusted buoy rocked against the side of a high dune as they neared the village. A sopped and piti- ful rag doll, face-up and bobbing. Finus wanted to reach for it, but did not. The others seemed to glance at it and look away.

When they reached a place from which they could see the bay out beyond the battered piney dunes the boats slowed for a minute as the Commandant directed them to spread apart and search for survivors. One boat of soldiers headed out into the bay for the other side, where someone had seen something through the binoculars in the far trees. Another struck out farther east, to cut into the sluiced gaps of a flooded tall and broken pine forest, their tops cracked and splayed and gleaming yellow-white wounds luminous in the gray air. The boat with Finus in it turned to go straight inland at the village site, and they had not gone far when there was an exclamation from the Commandant, who stood up in the boat and hailed someone. Finus looked. A man on a ragged grass and sandy knoll stood up and gazed at them as if they were an apparition, and for a moment he seemed one himself, then he raised one arm in silent reply. And then sank to his knees.

-What are they doing out here, Pawpaw? Finus said quietly to his grandfather.

His grandfather, watching the man, said, -They live out here. Or did.

-Where are their houses?

There were no structures at all in this place, and mostly water, and little ground showing at all but for this knoll, and further on another two like it, where now other figures stood and hollered at them, waving their arms.

-Gone, his grandfather said. -The hurricane has washed them away. Out into the bay, maybe.

They took in the man on the first knoll and with him those left in his family, a woman and child and a man about the woman's age. The man who'd stood first was older, with a long white beard, and had raised one arm when he'd seen them because it was all he had, his other sleeve wet and pinned upon itself higher up.

He said, -An angel of the Lord sent you to come find us here. We thought we were lost. Some were, he said. His voice was high and soft and trembling.

In the seat just behind Finus and his grandfather in the prow, on the bench between them and the two soldiers rowing, was the little girl he'd seen on the dog. She sat in the woman's lap wrapped in a dry army blanket and staring at Finus with large, close-set watery blue eyes and a tiny mouth like the chirp of a bird.

-What's her name? Finus said to no one in particular.

The girl turned her face and buried it in her mother's chest. Her mother patted her and looked at Finus.

-Her name is Birdie, the woman said. -She's my little girl.

-I'm Finus Bates, Finus said. -Were you out all night in that storm?

The woman said nothing but tears welled in her eyes and the man beside her put his arm around her and patted her shoulder.

-Shh, Finus, his grandfather said then, for he was near to crying, too, just seeing this and feeling for them in a way that surprised him, so suddenly, he just wanted to bawl.

The old man with the long white beard said, -It was the hand of God brought this storm, to punish us. This was a paradise, he said to the Commandant, his voice rising. -This was our Eden. Now we're driven out, for our sins.

-Yes, sir, the Commandant said. -You're safe now. We'll have you all safe in the fort very soon.

-Where's your dog? Finus said then to the girl, who yanked her head from her mother's bosom and stared at him wide-eyed and then screwed her own face up tight and began to cry herself, as did Finus when the girl's mother glared at him so.

-Pull, gentlemen, the Commandant said to the soldiers manning the oars. -We have more work to do when we've taken these few to safety.

They would find the dog, on the way back to the fort, barking with hopeless energy on a treeless nub of wet sand some ways to the west, and pick him up, and the girl hugged him to her tightly until they arrived at the fort and her mother coaxed her arms from around it until they could get inside, whereupon the girl sat in a corner in one of the munitions rooms and held the dog tight and would not let go, every time Finus peeked in around the corner she was there, holding the dog like it was a huge impassive furry child that only she had the power to comfort.

In the years after the storm, Birdie's grandfather moved them to Mercury, where he'd received succor long ago on his way home from the Civil War, and where Finus's grandfather had told him he and his kin would also befriend him. Finus played with her when they went to visit. He and Birdie roamed in her grandfather's garden, among the bougainvillea, azaleas, and deeply sweet-scented gardenias, down the hill behind their house into the woods where they would roll little balls of sweetgum sap onto their fingers and chew it delicately between their top and bottom front teeth. Birdie's two front teeth were gapped, which gave him a strange stirring in his heart. But she was no more claimable then for sappy loving sentiment than she ever would be, and would always deflect his attempts to moon. *Uxorious* was a word he later learned and would apply. She had a face, it seemed to him, that was unreal somehow, as perfectly unreal as a doll's yet with the capacity to open, become human in an instant, and suck him in unawares. Her chattering banter would cease and she would be vacant, not unlike someone having a mild epileptic seizure. As if she'd been grazed by a fleeting memory and her mind had gone out with it for a ways. And then, her mind coming back to the moment, she would turn her eyes to him and before he could gather his far-flung self again she had drawn him into her like some stronger, brighter heavenly body. He was possessed, almost, something essential in him trapped in her, trapped but not entirely uncomfortable. He could never quite reconcile her real presence with what her presence suggested to him, and it kept him not only enchanted but also confused in some deep sense he couldn't grasp. More than one evening after a visit he wished he could convince his father to drive them back out to the Wells house, so he could see she was still there and had not vanished, that he hadn't only imagined or daydreamed the day. This was not her fault. To her mind, as far as he could tell, she was as normal as the next girl. It was all in Finus, this sense of her. He had no idea what to say to her. When he looked into a mirror, it was if he saw nothing there.

She would point out the trees and flowering shrubs and tell him their names, taught to her by her grandfather. The shapes of their leaves and of their branching were for her the fundamental shapes in the world, what could be more beautiful, as God knew what shapes by which our minds arranged themselves, by which our imaginations are arranged. And he would name with her the songbirds he heard calling and could identify that way, his own grandfather's gift to him, those flitting shapes like darting shadows or figments of the spirit.

Like all early childhood friends they drifted apart with different schools and new friends, though their families attended the same church and later they attended school together, too. But he wouldn't be touched again by that sense of her, as if his spell had been suspended, until her cartwheel. In an instant, and unexpected, it would happen again. Years later, off to college, he would write an essay in his English class, ostensibly on a couple of English poets. He would describe a hypothetical situation in which a young man is watching a young woman across a large crowded room, such as at a ball or dance. The young man's hands are shaking. He has seen her walk into the hall that evening and a great roaring has begun in his ears and receded into the back of his head. His vision has tunneled down as if he is about to faint. He sees two little images of her before him, tiny as if in a miniature painting on his corneas. He later decides that every bit of his blood had rushed to his heart, and that there could not be a more powerful sign of love than your almost dying in the presence of it, than it being so powerful it could kill you. His transformation is complete. This phenomenon, Finus realized when he was forced to read things like *Astrophel and Stella* and Shakespeare's sonnets, was a thing from the past, a different world, when people really did die of love. Maybe because it was just harder to end up with the one you loved back then, because of stricter rules and harder circumstances in general. But also maybe because love was more real to them then, when there were fewer things you could use to distract yourself from something so frightening and strange. That's the modern habit, he wrote in his paper, the fear of love has become so ingrained in our character that we no longer even recognize love, in the same way that we shy away from the recognition of evil, for fear it will consume us with its terrible and inexplicable attraction. The professor wrote back, Mr. Bates, other than a suggestion to find a more powerful and graceful word than *inexplicable*, your essay is remarkable, and I should only hope that you are able to complete your studies at the university before whatever it is that threatens to consume you does so and ruins your academic career.

He looked up. Someone had hailed. A figure hardly more than a nebulous collection of white light, somehow on the courthouse lawn, though he could tell it was his boy, Eric, dead now almost fifty years. He wanted to call out, My darling son, my boy! and stood there a moment fixated in the vision of the moment. How was it he was seeing the boy at this time of the morning, when usually he only sensed his presence in distorted slips of air that revealed, like thin and vertical flaws in a lens, the always nearby regions of the dead? He waved back, his heart turning over in love and sadness. Closed his defective eye, damaged by a pellet of birdshot in 1918, and the boy dissolved back into the air.

PARNELL GRIMES, NOW county coroner as well as owner of Grimes Funeral Home, leaned over the stainless-steel preparation table and gripped the edges of the starched white sheet with his plump, short, pink fingers and pulled it away from Birdie Urquhart's face. Even at this great age and dead she had a lovely face—a fact often more obvious in death, with the very old, since their stricken, weary, saddened, impish, or disengaged eyes distracted one from their essential features.

For a long time now he had believed that he and Miss Birdie were partners in the context of their secret crimes, he and Miss Birdie, each the perpetrator of some strange and solitary criminal act that no one would ever know about—or so she must have believed, for only he knew of both his and hers and he would never tell of either. But it was knowing of hers that made the bond, for him.

Miss Birdie's face was classically oval-shaped with a good nose—straight, medium-length, none of the bulbousness of some old noses. She'd always had beautiful hair and kept it long, combed up in a bun or even in braids coiled at the back of her head, but now it had been let down and it lay white and fragile and across her bare left shoulder. He pulled the sheet away from her breast, hips, and legs, and looked upon her naked corpse, discolored around the edges of her buttocks and the backs of her arms and calves. As with many he tended, her skin had smoothed like a baby's, its wrinkles fleshed with death's gentle swelling, and had the seeming translucence of those white dead not sallow with tobacco smoking or racial complexity. He used to watch her when he was a boy and she was, he guessed, in her middle thirties, at the old Mercury Park pool. He'd owned a Kodak then and was known for going around taking pictures, all black and white, of course. One he'd taken was of several regulars there at the pool in the forties, a photo in which Miss Birdie's image seemed luminous tissue among the shaded, shrunken features of the others. Next to Miss Birdie, they seemed corpses already, no more to Parnell's practiced eye than fleshed skulls drying in their gradual and imminent declension toward the grave. Somehow the hard light of that day fell softly upon Miss Birdie and did not cast the sharp, cadaverous shadows it cast upon the others. They, the others, would preclude the creative process behind his art, which after all required a model, a ghostly ideal lingering vaguely in their faces. He used to watch Miss Birdie, her beauty reminiscent of the early movie stars', unable to keep himself from fantasizing that she would depart the world early in some nondisfiguring accident, without the usual markings and poolings. And that he would be allowed to gaze upon her.

He felt for a moment a vague stirring of the old desire, but long ago he had vowed he would never again betray his calling. Was not a man in Parnell Grimes's profession indeed a priest, a medium, the only one allowed to gaze upon the naked flesh of those whose bodies would not be seen again until they arose into the kingdom of heaven?

This analogy had not actually been his own. It was the inspiration of Selena Oswald, who would become his wife. Selena had given him the gift of redemption, so that he could live his life with some sort of hope for his confused and deeply stained soul. And it was the corpse of Miss Birdie here now before him that caused her, Selena, to swell again into the void she'd left inside him since she'd died.

He had thought perhaps he would never marry, would be like a suffering, perverted priest with many imaginary wives, the poor and vulnerable, old and young, ugly and beautiful, all lovely in God's eyes, all returning to clay in his hands. But when he met Selena, then just twelve to his eighteen, he had lusted after her with the fervor that only a young man who believed he knew an exquisite corpse in the making could lust.

He had first seen and met her when he and his father had the unhappy occasion to prepare her mother, Mrs. Medina Oswald, for viewing and burial. The woman, only thirty-nine and known to be a vigorous Primitive Baptist, had died of a coronary, an hereditary ailment, her heart greatly enlarged. Parnell in his youth considered that her flaw most likely was the too-great love she exercised for her husband and children. Solemnly with his father he greeted them for the viewing: Mr. Oswald, a mailman bewildered by this unhappy event; his son James, a tall young deputy sheriff with the slow and solid look of a laborer; and then Selena. When he held out his hand toward her long, slim, pale one she did not move, and he looked up into her eyes and was shocked and even afraid. This twelve-year-old girl may as well have pierced his breast with a spear and held him before her as he died. Her gaze was not one of fearfulness or repulsion or anger, nor was it liquid with the more common helpless grief of the mourner. It was lucid. He sensed that in his own eyes she sought something no one had ever had the courage or audacity to seek before: the vision of her beloved as she was last, before the preparation, in the great nakedness of death, between the dying and the viewing. She looked down at Parnell's hand, held oddly open before her, as if she understood something of the intimacy of his art, understood the nature of the intimacy he had experienced with her mother—and then she took it into her own flawless hand, sending a mild current through his arm. He believed she understood his secret, that which he'd hidden even from his father (who approached his craft with all the reverence of a taxidermist). She was on to him, instinctively, although she did not yet understand what she knew.

He courted her with patience, first befriending her brother James, and seeing her whenever he joined James at their house in the early mornings after cruising with James on the sheriff's department's graveyard shift, which is what they always called it whenever Parnell rode along. He learned much about police work, which would lead to his running for coroner and winning, but he learned even more about Selena, who would appear in the mornings, sleepy-eyed, one who did not especially like to rise, carrying her books in one of her father's old and worn leather mailbags and dropping it beside the kitchen door so that she would not forget it on her sleepy way out. From the corner of his eye Parnell watched her, a tabby kitten named Rosebud in her lap, as she pushed her grits around and cut her fried egg as if it were of no more interest to her than a shingle. Then she would dutifully eat it all, without relish. Parnell knew that a woman with little interest in food beyond what was necessary for sustenance would age gracefully. And though slim the girl had hardly a visible bone about her, no hard and jutting cheekbones or brows or chin. Her nose, though straight, was small and unobtrusive. Her eyes neither bulged nor seemed so sunken as to suggest the specter of sockets. She would be beautiful until the end. He would never have to gaze upon her as bones and skin and a sac of dying organs wheezing, rotting even as she sat across from him at the breakfast

table, still wearing the drawn and cracked deathmask of her desiccated facial cream. She would no more dry up than an apple
never plucked from the tree, until it fell into the grass and reen-
tered the soil discreetly in its swift and natural collapse from
within, its skin retaining to the end its general dignity. She drank
her milk like an athlete, though, and would eat her egg, eventu-
ally, and after some time would bid them farewell, saying, -G'bye,
Jim, g'bye, Rosebud, g'bye, Mr. Parnell, her father having been
gone since five o'clock to the post office.

When she turned fifteen he began to strike up conversations
with her whenever they were alone in the kitchen or the living
room or on the Oswalds' front porch. Then he began to invite her
on walks down to the drugstore or to the park just beyond. And it
was there, one day, she admitted that his continued presence in
their home had allowed her to move gradually beyond her grief
over her mother, and finally to imagine those who daily lay before
him to be embalmed.

-Embalmed, she said to him. -Parnell (for she'd stopped
calling him Mr., which he missed in a way), that word had always
horrified me. But the more you were around, I started to think
about it in another way, thinking about the word *balm* in the middle of it. I started to think that you see it as soothing the body, in
a way.

Parnell's heart surged. They were sitting on a bench beneath a
broad water oak in the park, she on one end and he on the other. He
was the most ordinary-looking of men, shaped something like a
cheap cigar, small hands and feet, beginning to bald. But though his
face, neither round nor slim, had no distinguishing features, it was
saved by his eyes, which were mysteriously handsome—it was as if
Errol Flynn had stepped up behind a cardboard cutout of Parnell
and put his eyes behind the empty eyeholes. And women had often
been arrested, just for a moment, upon gazing at Parnell, until they

remembered where they were and who they were talking to, and pulled themselves back into the world, looking upon Parnell Grimes, mortician, and they determined that his captivating eyes were merely another manifestation of his strangeness and even perhaps part of what made him creepy.

And now Selena looked into them. She had known him long enough, had become accustomed to him, so that as will happen she saw his eyes moreso than she saw the rest of him.

-Yes, he said. -*Embalmed* is a beautiful word. What it really means is to preserve the memory of the beloved, to cherish the memory. It is not distasteful to me.

-Parnell, she said, what does one look like when you get it?

He paused. He knew exactly her dilemma as she gazed at him, her heart filled with morbid curiosity, her mind with the budding intelligence of a girl near marrying age—she was sixteen now. How could he answer so as to maintain an element of each in her, to open her imagination to his art in a way that he must have in a lifelong companion? Were he to wed a woman who would take the conventional view she would soon shudder and shun him as she would the idea of her own mortality when such awareness descended upon her. He would marry only one who understood the beauty of death's role in the world and, beyond that, the strange and inviolable beauty of the dead themselves.

Oh, he could tell her some horrible things. Of breaking jaws to fix gaping mouths into beatific smiles. How one must cement the eyelids down to keep them from popping open as the loved ones gazed upon them one last time. Of embalming fluid seepage. Of how Mrs. Vogel's skin began to turn green. Of the time he helped his father to sew up and sew on the head of Mr. Fondelet, which had been removed somewhat raggedly by his disker. Of how her own mother's face was hardened into such a grimace from her painful death his father'd had to pry it into a more relaxed expression and keep it there by inserting three steel rods. But these things were immaterial, in Parnell's view. What mattered was the presentation, the viewing of the final restoration. The body was no longer important, in itself. In truth, it was the ravaged memory of the bereaved that Parnell restored.

He tried to take her hand, but she shrank and pulled it away.

-Selena, he said after a moment, holding her uncertain eyes with his own gaze. He chose his words carefully. -I know you might think me strange. But when I go into the preparation room and take my first look at the beloved, I feel the most soothing kind of peacefulness flow into my heart.

He felt her relax her resistance then, after a moment.

-I don't think it's strange, Parnell, she said, looking calmly and frankly right back at him now. -Shouldn't we feel at peace around the dead? It seems to me like they prepare the way for us, in their brief presence with us, I mean. In our minds.

Parnell was astounded and, for a moment, speechless.

-You're too young to be so wise, he said.

Her expression, as she considered this, was inscrutable. She looked away.

-I have always had, she said, a certain understanding of things. For a while, I felt very close to God.

He leaned forward and took her hand.

-Selena, my calling is almost religious, to me. When I see the dead lying alone and unadorned on my preparation table, they look to me like they are God's children once again. To me they are as beautiful as babies, and it is my privilege to place them, like the midwife, into God's hands.

He had the soft but commanding voice of a gentle preacher, Parnell did—not unlike her own late mother's, she said to him once—and Selena's face had opened as if hearing him read from the scripture.

They married the day after her graduation from the high school, and rented a little cottage far out the peninsula down at the Gulf, not far from the old fort. Since it was already hot they would emerge only in the late afternoon or early evening to play in the surf or to hunt for sea turtle nests in the dunes. Later they ate shrimp and fish they bought from a little seafood plant on the bay and cooked in the cottage's tiny kitchen. She didn't know much about cooking, Selena, not being one who much cared about food. But the first evening, she seemed proud as she set the steaming plate of boiled shrimp between them on the dining table and took her seat. They'd been on the beach all afternoon and were still in their bathing suits, and as she placed the meat of a large shrimp between her teeth and bit into it, its juice spurted toward Parnell. Startled, she laughed with her mouth open, holding the other half of the steaming shrimp between her thumb and middle finger. Parnell stood up from his chair. She watched him, waiting, then dropped the shrimp gently onto her plate. They engaged in a slow precoital tango toward the daybed in the living room. Their fingers clutched skin still sticky and gritty from the afternoon on the beach, still pale beyond the possibility of tanning, blushed with sun and red-rimmed about the edges of their suits. Parnell, in love, his mind on fire with love as if he'd inhaled some powerful essence of it from Selena's pores, nevertheless sensed an irritating hesitation deep in his blood. A gray fear began to gather behind his eyes like iron filings. He closed his eyelids and attempted to pray as he normally only pretended to pray. As he did he felt Selena change somehow, and fearing he'd ruined the moment with her he opened his eyes and pulled back to find her looking at him in a way that nearly froze him. It was the same look she'd locked upon him the first time they met, at her mother's funeral, when she had first divined his secret. And now he felt something happening in her. He felt it in his fingertips against her sunwarmed skin, now cooling. He felt the very character of her tissue begin to evolve against him, and he was afraid.

A word escaped her lips as little more than a breath: -Parnell, she said, her lips barely moving. Her eyes no longer penetrated him, but softened in focus and seemed to drift away.

-What is it? Parnell whispered in return.

-Parnell, she said, I want to pretend.

-Pretend what? he said, his voice scarcely more than the last little bit of a breath to empty the lungs.

She made an absent gesture with her hand, turning it outward, palm up, as if to receive a coin, or a key.

-Pretend I am more beautiful than alive.

When his pounding heart subsided enough to allow it, he held her by the arms and laid her down upon the daybed. She looked at him again in that absent way, then tilted her head back onto the mattress, her mouth parted. She whispered again, -Parnell. And she said something else, too faint to be heard. Hands upon her cheeks, growing cold, he leaned down to her lips. He laid his ear just barely against them. -Parnell, he heard her whisper again, something's wrong.

He knelt and grasped her by the arms again, and believed he could feel something in her beginning to slow and thicken, heard a gentle rasping deep in her throat. The shadow of her dusky blood crept into tender crescents below her eyes. The delicate fibers in her cornea quivered, and in her dark pupils the tiny reflected image of Parnell's face seemed to dissipate and disappear.

-Parnell, she whispered, barely audible, save me.

Then she lay still, eyes upon the ceiling. The cottage timbers shuddered in the gusts off the Gulf. Parnell rested his head upon her breast. He could hear the crushing sound as breakers collapsed against the beach. -Parnell, she whispered again, don't be ashamed. Take me, like you want to do. Parnell began to tremble. He knelt before her on the daybed, and pulled apart her cool and sticky, lovely white legs. In a moment he groaned as heat flushed through him. He gave in and fell upon her. Her breath huffed out as from a cushion, her arms lay rigid at her sides, her head arched away as if in the throes of some horrible death, eyes turned to look unseeing out the Florida windows, lovely mouth opening in dry exhaustion. Parnell crushed his lips to hers, the ripe taste of shrimp still upon them. He squeezed her small and lolling breasts to his chest. And slowly she began to change again, her whisper taking voice again, love literally coming alive beneath him. He heard himself saying her name, his voice deep and crusty as a troll's, and she responded with a cry that shot into his spine. Blood slammed at the ends of his fingers and toes. He was momentarily blinded. She gripped him with her heels and nails and he felt as if there were no longer any bed beneath them, and a roaring in his ears became their own sobs. She clasped him to her. She knew then, she would tell him one day, that he had unbound her from the tyrannies of grief and fear. Those who would embrace the beautiful dead are most open to the living, have nothing to fear, neither loss nor oblivion. The world was flesh and blood and bone, and through the blessed privilege of sensual touch lay contact with the spiritual world. The air is adrift with what presences are left behind, which find new forms in the living, in those who are most open and alive themselves, not slaves to ignorance and fear. In this world, Parnell had given her that. But in his secret heart Parnell knew, and he would always believe Selena knew, that it was Selena who had saved Parnell.

Selena in Ecstasy

WHEN SHE WAS a child listening to her mother's sermons she came to realize the possibility of the divine in an ordinary life, this miracle that had occurred with Our Lord Jesus Christ was as much chance and the openness of one's divine nature to the miracle as it was the big finger of God pointing out he or she. *We do not choose God*, her mother had boomed from the pulpit over and over. *God chooses us.* Our choice, she always said, was to be open to God or to close our hearts forever and ever. Her mother was obsessed with death. She always said she couldn't wait to go to the other side, to be in heaven. Such words had so frightened Selena that her own obsession with death took a hard turn toward salvation and the only way to guarantee that was to be the agent of it herself. She drew pictures of heaven in her first-grade class, and all the angels were her mother. God was a very old man with wild hair that hid his eyes, and a fierce beard that hid his features, and in his hand he held a long-handled scythe. Beside him stood a smaller figure with jet-black hair and a little wand of her own. And who is that? her teacher asked brightly. That's me. Really? the teacher said brightly as before. Why are you standing next to God, hon? I am standing at the right hand of God the Father Almighty, Maker of Heaven and Earth, Selena said. The Christ Selena, who died for your sins. You're not dead, though, honey, the teacher said. And Selena hon, it's the angel of death that carries the scythe, her teacher said. Not God. God *is* the angel of death, Selena replied. Selena the Christ is the life everlasting. *Selena is a very wise child*, her teacher wrote home in a note, *but with somewhat disturbing notions. Perhaps she has been exposed to ideas which she is not yet equipped to handle.*

She did not see God as evil, but indifferent to the kinds of things that so grieved human beings. He was above all that, and so she strove to be more like God in this way, and this made her an aloof child, difficult to reach or decipher emotionally. At twelve she knew from the scriptures it was time to shoulder the burden to which she had opened her infinite heart. It was in the evening, very late, in her bed. She rose to her knees in the moon-light soft on her bedcovers and asked God to take her then and to use her to His ends, and a flood of emotion washed through her as she had not felt in her life to that point. She wept a long time, wept herself into exhaustion, and then it was that the spirit entered her and gained a hold.

There were miracles she performed, in her own quiet way. She could make her teacher call on her for an answer, if she wanted her to. And if she wanted to be passed over, she could control that, too. It was a simple matter of will, and something she did through her eyes, which were large and such a dark brown as to appear almost solid black globes of softened glass. If she wanted into a group of other children who were occupied with something, she approached them and they parted to let her in. And if she was not interested, she was invisible, they never even sensed she was near. She could arrest animals with her eyes, as well, and keep them from approaching or slinking away. Her cat, Rosebud, understood her every mulling thought, and watched her as she would an object of prey, but one beyond her powers to prey upon, and therefore a kind of god. She did not worship, though, being a cat. She expected to be worshiped herself, Rosebud did, and so was always unsatisfied. But when Selena touched her on the top of her head between her ears, she gently closed her eyes and was absolved of her envy and felt content, for a brief while anyway, to be just a cat. Other things she could do were make birds fly from a bush without herself making a sound or a move, turn bad dogs away tails tucked, shut up talkative grown-ups who got on her nerves, and if she really wanted to and it was something she rarely did, knowing it would be an abuse if she did it too often, she could change the weather. But more often she merely willed weather to stay as it was, since she liked most kinds of it, rain and storms as well as sunny days and clear nights. She could make a tree die, if she thought it was a bad tree, though this was rare. She could make other people, the whole town, sleep later in the morning, if she wished. If she was sleepy and didn't want to get up for school, she could do this, and when she finally dragged herself to the schoolhouse, her father's old postal bag stuffed with her books slung over her shoulder, the others would be just arriving, too, all sleepy and draggy, including the teachers, who yawned and slurped from cup after cup of coffee, and declared they just couldn't wake up this morning to save their lives. She could simply slow things down. And sometimes she did. Riding in the backseat of their old black lurching car to church she could tell there were fewer cars on the road, the people inside looking sleepy and tired, and there were fewer people in the church itself, and her mother had to work extra hard at her sermon to keep them awake and responding with Amens and nods of the head that weren't noddings-off. When Selena noticed that, and before the collection plate was passed, she willed them to wake up a little bit, and they would. At home she scaled herself back. For some time she wasn't sure if she wanted her mother to know her secret or not. She realized she might not be believed, and that her mother might think it a sacrilege that she even would think such a thing.

When her mother fell to her early death Selena at first believed she had been horribly wrong, deluded in her sense of herself, but in prayer that day and following she came to understand she had seen this about to occur, had felt its presence in the hand her mother used to stroke her head as she lay falling asleep in bed in recent evenings. And if she were not some kind of Christ, a notion that had begun to slip from her presence of mind after all in the way that the awareness of breathing slips away from those who have their health, that was okay. It was not necessary to save the world or mankind in order to practice her obsessions.

She knew Parnell to be someone in touch with God, in his own way, a person through whose hands people passed on their way to God. She saw him as an instrument whose own powers he didn't understand, and therefore an innocent. He was the last person to see her mother in her natural earthly form, before the preparation for burial and the soothing of the living souls. When she held his hand there in the funeral parlor she could first feel its presence and then she could see the divine glow in him as a faint blue aura about his oddly beautiful body. She could see something soulful in him that had come, she knew, from his having been so intimate with so much death. He had his hands on death, and wasn't afraid. He understood something about it that other people did not. After they married, when people were brought into the funeral home to be embalmed and buried, she absolved them all of all their sins, quietly, to herself. They would all enter heaven, to keep her mother company, and she would send them all with a message, that when her work on earth was done she would join her in paradise.

~

SHE KNEW OF Parnell's sickness, something she had divined anyway, through various things he said to her which first implied it
and later confirmed it for her in the months of their courtship.
When she had first taken his hand in the funeral parlor she had
sensed something strong in terms of his relation to the dead, but
had not included sexual passion in what she sensed until he told
her of the girl who'd been in the farming accident and how she
had changed him. A general anxiety had to that point given him
such problems he thought they would undermine his chosen
career: sweaty palms, a nervous pallor, a popeyed uncertainty in
his speech. His father barred him from working the parlors. This
continued until one day when the body of a girl in his high school
class, mortally wounded in a hay baling accident, was brought
from the hospital to the Grimes embalming table—naked, flayed,
pale, and cold. Her child's face mauled by indifferent machinery.
It had been a face, Parnell recalled, upon which none of her peers'
eyes had rested in admiration. She'd been as plain, even homely,
as a day-old drop biscuit. And now he looked upon her remains
(beyond the corruption of his confused imagination, Selena would
come to understand), disfigured with slices and gashes from the
baler, and he saw beyond them more clearly than anyone had ever
been able to see just what her perfection had been, and realized
that he loved her and mourned her loss. That day, he began to
understand something of his mission, and the experience was lib-
erating. His grief filled him with a bouyant joy, and immediately
he arrived at a deeper understanding of all that he'd felt and feared.
Later, when they had no such secrets between them, after he had
further confessed the nature of these fears, telling her what
had happened with the Littleton girl, she comforted him, absolved
him. Together they giggled like children over the fact that the mes-
senger of such a mission had been unspeakable lust.

From the time they married and she moved into the second floor of the funeral home with Parnell, this place that had been his lonely habitation since his parents had died when he was only sixteen, when he had taken over the business at that young age and done quite well with it, she had felt more at home than she had since the day her mother died. Her own home, since then, had been such a lonely place, even with her father and brother living there with her. She had felt more comforted by her cat, Rosebud, than she had with her family, though they loved her and she loved them. The cat, Rosebud, had a way of looking at her that was so unguarded, so frankly a look into who she really was and what she felt, that she knew no living human being could match it. And the week she'd been at the Gulf with Parnell on their honeymoon, Rosebud had disappeared, and she knew this was because Rosebud's role in her life had come to an end. That her life with Parnell in the funeral home would now supplant it in ways she would come to understand. So she grieved for Rosebud, but not unconsolably.

In only that first week she had asked Parnell to let her assist him in the embalming downstairs in the basement. He hesitated only a moment, and then she could see settle into his features the knowledge that this was her destiny as much as it was his own. He gave his regular assistant, Mr. Peach, a two-week vacation, and she worked with him on every body that came to the home during that time. The greater her experience at handling the dead, the greater her desire for communion with them.

It had been entirely a risk, an experiment, that first time she had drifted herself to near-death to be revived by Parnell on their honeymoon. As a child, and soon after her mother's death, she'd discovered the ability quite on her own. She'd walked away from the house on a cool and overcast day when low gray clouds carried over with a breeze from the front that pushed them. She walked to an old pecan grove a couple of blocks away and lay down in the tall grass that had grown up around them, an old crop of nuts from the now sterile trees knobby on the earth beneath her back and legs. She could see the clouds pass as if through the gnarled and flay-barked limbs and ragged narrow leaves of the pecans. She closed her eyes and pushed herself in her mind toward where her mother had gone. She saw a nebulous blue glow aswirl in the spot just between her closed eyes and put her concentration into it. And passed into it and through it. She felt herself traveling somehow in this direction, not through the limbs of the trees and the billowy clouds above them but beyond them in some other-dimensional way. As if sucked in upon herself the weight of her body seemed released, she herself was weightless. She traveled as if flying in a dream but without the sense of moving through the world, or of there even being a world. Through time, perhaps, but not thinking that, either. And after some time of very swift but relative travel in this way she slowed, something like slowing, or came into herself, what that was she couldn't say, and seemed to float there, and had the sense she was waiting. Some harmonious and distant, untrace-able musical sound. And she began to fill with a kind of happiness. She was content to be just there, and was not disturbed for a time with the expectation of there being anything else. But something began to nudge its way into this state, and gradually she became aware of it as a presence, and something physical in the world, and there was a heaviness on her as well as a warm wetness about her face. She opened her eyes. There sat Rosebud two inches from her eyes, sitting on her chest, licking her face. Rosebud mewed, a question, *Mggrrrow?* As her sense of being in the world again curled into her body, she roused, petted Rosebud. How did you follow me way down here? she said. Rosebud wound her way around her legs, her tail straight up, stopped and looked up at her words. They walked back home together.

In time, with Parnell, she began to love thinking of the new places and the new ways. At first she had merely lain in their bed waiting for Parnell to come upstairs to find her there, to speak to her as he removed his business clothes, to stop and turn his head slightly toward her when she did not respond, to creep over and touch her here and there. And she was in that state she had somehow perfected, of being there but not there, in her body but out of it too, somehow breathing though her lungs all but still, all but dormant, and she seemed to see him through her closed lids, which in those moments seemed to her as thin a membrane as the protective covering on the eye of a fish, she could see right through them, the image before her pulsing almost imperceptibly behind the tiny, spidery veins.

But this gave way soon enough to other places. The supply closet off the main hallway. In a plush chair in one of the parlors, Parnell having to pull her lifeless body from the chair onto the carpeted floor. Collapsed into a heap on the kitchen floor, half a sandwich left on her plate at the table. Once, in the little hedged bit of private yard they kept behind the home. And finally on the preparation table itself, surprising Parnell there as he came in tugging on a pair of surgical gloves, only a miracle he hadn't brought a policeman or distant relative of the deceased in there, of the one who lay under the sheet just feet away from Selena's supine, naked, chilled but latently vital form.

They rarely went through the long elaborate playing out of the game, after the honeymoon, as it was Parnell's genuine fear that had led to it that time, and he was no real actor, Parnell. Which is not to say he had no imagination. For when he stood over her and she didn't respond, though he knew she was only playing again, his imagination soon took him to the time and place when this would be no game, when he would be speaking to a Selena who would never respond, and it filled him again with the old grief and lust.

This was her understanding, and she understood Parnell. She understood perhaps better than Parnell himself his attraction to the dead. She had known the first time she looked into his eyes that he was less fearful around the dead than around the living. What threat the living presented to him she wasn't quite sure, at the time, but she came to understand even that. It was that he and the dead shared the same secret, which was that the fearful illusion of mortality—and immortality, as well—is lifted like a veil to reveal something simpler and more profound, without fear. Only the dead see one another, and themselves, for what they truly were, or are. The terrifying idea of time did not apply at all.

What was it, the evening she went on her way, not to return? Parnell had stepped outside to get something he'd left in the car. She had stepped out of her dress and was walking about upstairs in her slip, barefoot, cooling off. She went into the bathroom, the soles of her feet cool on the bare blue tiles there. It felt so good. She lay down, the coolness of the tiles pressing through the silky thin material of the slip. She placed the palms of her hands down on them, too, pressed the back of her neck against them. It felt wonderful. A breeze from the ceiling fan in the hallway wafted in and over her, lifting a tuck of the slip from one of her knees. She knew Parnell would be up in a second, and she couldn't resist letting herself go. She closed her eyes, she found the blue swirling light in the darkness in the center of her forehead. She drifted deliciously. Delicious the last thought of that peace and of the stirring excitement of finding him on her, in her, as she came back to the world. She was weightless and moving swiftly toward the place of stillness. There she lay, in a kind of heaven, while in another, heavier, more burdensome world her love made his way to and from the drugstore to retrieve the package he'd thought he'd left in the car, to where the body of his beloved Selena awaited him, serene and beautiful in her slight undergarments, her lovely feet bare and clean, her palms down on the blue tile floor.

Finus Homerus

A N EMPTY STOMACH always sharpened his sadness. He leaned himself on down the sidewalk in the brimming morning, light like a bubble to the range of his vision in the air. So stunning now he stopped, to take it all in. Mercury lay nestled into the vale below the piney ridge to the south. It was the ridge over which the 1906 cyclone had skipped and fallen down onto Front Street, blasting to splinters and rubble what had been built since Sherman's March, when the town's first buildings had all been burned to the ground. After the cyclone the town had been rebuilt again with brick and stone into a thriving city in the twenties, its apogee, after which the railroad industry had abandoned it for Birmingham, where there was steel. Never enough gumption and guts in this town to sustain much strength. Throughout the century it hung on by its fingernails. And now downtown lay in a gauzy summer morning haze, and somehow its sleepy survival filled Finus with a kind of saddened joy.

There had been lately some occasional things envisioned, rare but distinctive, so that he had to wonder if he wasn't himself walking along so close to the edge of another dimension, like a man half in the mirror, half out. The week before, he'd been standing there in the *Comet* office talking to Maxine Thornton,

238 / Brad Watson

a big redhead who'd been a real looker in her day, Miss Mercury and all, even though she was on the heavy side, went all the way to the state beauty pageant, and all on account of having a most beautiful, ICBM bustline. She lost at state, came home, went to work in the chamber of commerce office, took on a walking regimen, marching around town in the hours between dawn and the start of the working day, gradually diminished in size to something like petite. But the boobs were a casualty of her fitness plan, much to the chagrin of old farts who liked to watch her flapping along in pink walking togs. So, standing in his office talking to Maxine Thornton, his assistant Lovie out to lunch, Finus was listening to Maxine talk about an ad for the upcoming Business Fair when she pulled out her left bosom and held it cradled there in her hand, big brown nipple bold as an eyeball staring right at him. Finus snatched off his glasses, closed his bad eye, no boob. -Well, what? Maxine said, coylike. Finus told Ivyloy about it later on, still in a daze.

-Well, I liked her better heavy, myself, Ivyloy said. -Now *that*'d been a bo*zoom*.

~

HE MADE HIS way to the Dreyfus Building, watched his reflection in the polished gold doors of the old elevator, rode it to the fifteenth floor, nodded his hello to Floyd, the sleepy engineer, settled in. Played "The Star Spangled Banner" to help wake everybody up.

-Good morning in the a.m., each and every one of you, and it's a fine morning, if a little sad by my lights.

-Midfield Wagner, farmer and carpenter, passed on last night. I'll tell you a little about old Midfield, wasn't really all that old. And Birdie Wells Urquhart. One of my oldest and closest friends. Companion. I need to spend a little time talking about Birdie, if y'all don't mind.

First he would tell about Midfield, in order to (though he wouldn't say so) get it out of the way. He would tell about Midfield's life. Twenty-two years at the Steam Feed Works, twenty before that with the telephone company, Named Midfield because of where he was born, while his mama was out picking ears of Silver Queen. Raised on the farm the family lost in the Depression. Started out stringing wire from here to India Beach while they were still digging the Intracoastal Waterway down on the coast. Caught malaria when he was only twenty-five, camping out in the swamps and digging pole holes, and recovered from it though many had died. He lived to suffer a stroke last night while out back feeding his dogs.

He said when and where the services would be, moved on to other business, news items about the day. He was saving Birdie for last.

He told about some of the high points of her life, including physical ailments she overcame such as colon polyps and gallstones in her forties, hysterectomy somewhere along in there, thought she was going to die of infection, didn't. Told about being widowed at fifty-four, living the rest of her life in that condition. Didn't go into the unpleasantness with Earl's family. He wound around back to her early years. He told the story of how he first met her, down in the little fishing village where she lived before her family moved to Mercury, the village wiped out in a hurricane, the same one that would move inland and spawn the tornado that wiped out most of Front Street in Mercury, 1906. How she made a life up here after that. How the vision of her as he'd known her young was what endured, for him.

He'd talked for two hours, mostly about her. Floyd the engineer tapped on the glass. Finus looked up, nodded, signed off. Took the elevator down and walked back into the air, onto the street, the morning traffic chuffing by, idling at lights. Amazing, he was still somehow alive.

And Finus, because he was ravenous now, thought he'd stop at Schoenhof's and treat himself to a rare breakfast of biscuits, bacon, and eggs before going in to work at the *Comet*.

~

HE MADE HIS way down past the two remaining banks, Citizens and Peoples, past the Feinberg's fading clothing store, and into Schoenhof's. Shorty hailed him from behind the counter and he took a stool, leaned backwards for a moment to check out the back room where just one couple sat drinking coffee beside the stuffed mule in the corner. The mule belonged to the original owner. Was said to have been sired by him with the old mare he lived with until his wife could join him from Arkansas. Said it looked like his wife. Well that don't make sense. I know it. He ordered two eggs over medium with grits, whole wheat toast, and just two slices of streak-o-lean as Shorty stood with his square head—trimmed in a piece of Ivyloy's most serious work, skin-tight on the sides and bristly black on top—thrown back, gazing at the ceiling. Then Shorty jerked into action.

-I got your eggs over medium, freshest eggs to ever touch a tooth, and here's some hot coffee. He plunked a steaming cup before Finus and disappeared through the swinging doors to the kitchen. In five minutes he was back with a hot plate and clattered it down.

-See you got to write two today, Mr. Bates, he said.

Finus nodded. -Miss Birdie, he said.

-A fine woman, Shorty said with a grim snap of his head. -I remember Mr. Earl, used to come in here every morning before opening up his store. Hell of a gentleman. Finus nodded, studying his glistening eggs. Shorty shook out the white linen napkin he carried at all times and folded it back over his arm. -Hello, Mr. Mayor!

he sang out then, and in a second Pearly Millens took the stool next to Finus.

-Morning, Finus said.

-Finus.

Shorty slid a cup of coffee before the mayor, who nodded, waved off anything else. Pearly brought the cup to his broad, red mouth, his flabby lips divining the steaming coffee like a horse's lips seeking sugar in a palm, though his winged eyebrows, bony hooked nose, and bald head made him look more like a plucked owl. Finus turned his attention to his breakfast. He pricked the eggs with the tine of his fork and watched orange yolk trickle out onto the white. He cut a piece of the white and dipped it into the yolk and ate it with a bite of bacon and a bite of toast. Its deliciousness spread through him. He was lost in it for a long moment, eyes watering.

-What you into today? Pearly said.

-Not much, Finus said. -Got to write Birdie Urquhart's obituary. She was my childhood sweetheart.

-So I heard you say on the radio this morning, Pearly said. -I didn't know her too well, myself. Now I knew her son, Edsel. Did he die?

Finus nodded. -Down in Laurel. Bad heart, like his papa.

-I remember his papa Mr. Earl, now, Pearly said. -Sort of a distinguished old fellow.

Finus snorted. -Old. Didn't live to be but fifty-five.

Pearly looked at him in astonishment, himself being sixty-two.

-Time does move on, he said after a moment.

Finus grunted, sipped his coffee.

-Rumor had it, as I recall, she did old Earl in herself, way back then, some kind of poison or something, Pearly murmured, sipping his own.

Finus slowly turned on his stool and stared at Pearly.

-Say what, now?

-I didn't say it, I said *people* said it, back then. He looked sideways at Finus, then dropped his pop eyes back down to the coffee cup, mumbled, -Anything to it?

Finus glared at him a moment longer, then ate in near-silence, the light clattering of his fork against china, the gentle slurp of Pearly at his coffee. He swiped the plate with a wedge of toast, washed it down.

Pearly said, -Did they do an autopsy on him, then, on Mr. Earl?

Finus took up his napkin, wiped his lips hard, tossed it onto the counter next to his plate.

-Politicians can't afford to be rumor mongers, Pearly, he said then, pulling out a five and dropping it onto the napkin. -Your realities are sordid enough. Mind your own business. Or the town's, for a change.

Pearly looked back at him, winged eyebrows in flight.

-I'm going on, Finus said. -See you at the council meeting tomorrow night.

-You can skip this one, Pearly said.

-That's when you'd pass a pay raise, Finus said, and walked out.

At the *Comet* building he opened the door and went on in. Lovie was there with the Mr. Coffee gurgling, typing the community columns. With her big pink ears she looked like a silver-haired elf.

-Who you got, Lovie?

-Spider Creek, she said in her hoarse quaver. She didn't look up, focused on the computer screen. She'd wanted a computer since 1985 but Finus hadn't given in until last year.

-What's on Mrs. Chambliss's mind?

-She's down in the back and did all her snooping by phone this week. It's a long one.

-She knows I cut her off at twenty-one inches.

-I guess we'll see about that.

-I'm not giving in again. Twenty-one inches of Spider Creek is about all we need.

-I guess we'll see.

The newspaper's office was one large room that had been a tack and hardware store on the west edge of town in the early 1900s. The old press was in the back room, looking like some complex medieval torture machine for removing the bones by stages and flattening the body into figures for a ghastly tapestry.

He sat down in his own old wooden swivel armchair and made a couple of phone calls, then faced the heavy Underwood desktop manual he'd used since 1935, inserted a clean sheet of paper, and whacked out an obit on Midfield.

MIDFIELD WAGNER, 68

- He once took two of his laying hens to the top of a water tower to show his boys that they could fly a little bit, but instead of gliding to the ground as expected the hens, apparently inspired by the view, caught a thermal and floated all the way across the creek into Claxton Swamp and were never seen again. Now wild, mischievous chickens are among the most mysterious of creatures in that low tangly stinking place, and their presence is suspected of being the resource fueling the resurgence of the swamp's alligator population.

- He worked twenty-two years at the Steam Feed Works and could do any job in the foundry, from casting to repairing machinery, spent twenty years before that with the telephone company, and in spite of what some say about his lifestyle he never missed a day of work with either concern in all that time except for one week when what we'd now call a microburst blew his barn down in 1976 and he reconstructed the whole thing from broken timbers

and splayed lumber and bent tin, so that the result looked like
the same barn been out on a three-day drunk, and some said that
was fitting, anyway.

· Although not a churchgoer himself he helped construct out of
the kindness of his heart every one of the seven churches built in
this area between 1963 and 1987. His wife was a Pentecostal but
a gentle one, and he never succumbed, himself, to that spirit.

Midfield Wagner of Booker's Creek Community died Sunday
night about 9:30 as he was feeding his dogs in the pen out back of
his house, or at least that's when he had what was apparently a
heart attack and fell down in the pen. He went out back with the
dog food, his wife Althena heard the tinkling of the pellets into
their pails, and then a funny sound. She went out there and that's
when she found him, the dogs kind of looking back and forth
between him and the food in their pails.

He had been despondent for some time following the death of
their older son and the boy's two preschool children in an automobile accident on 45 South, headed to the beach for vacation.
He was 68.

Midfield was raised in Booker's Creek and served in the Air
Force during the Korean War as an aircraft engine mechanic. He
worked on P-51 Mustangs, which most people don't know carried
at least as much of the load in that conflict as the famed Sabre Jet.

When he returned home after the war he married Althena "Al"
Curry and after a honeymoon at the Gulf they settled into a
mobile home back on his parents' property. When his dad passed
away they moved into the old farmhouse with his mother, and she
died in 1971. Midfield will be buried beside his parents in the oak
grove on their property, beside the creek.

He farmed some ten acres of the land on his family place and
kept cows on the other 40, and his wife said he'd planned to give

up the cows and plant pine seedlings, which she may do now that he's gone.

Visitation and service will be at Grimes Funeral Home, the service starting at 3:00 Wednesday, and proceeding afterwards to Magnolia Cemetery. Honorary pallbearers are the workers in the works foundry. Pallbearers are James Troy, Lucky Williamson, Egstrom Anderson, Ralph Svoboda, Ted Melancon, and Barclay Teague.

Finus rolled the sheet out of the Underwood and underlined a couple of things he wasn't sure of in pencil. He made some calls, to Midfield's relatives and friends, made a couple of corrections, and laid the obit in the copy box on the corner of his desk, on top of the three others he'd written since Friday for Wednesday's edition.

He looked up. Lovie was standing next to his desk, looking through her bifocals at the pages he'd done.

-Ha, she said, that chicken story. Jeepers, I remember my ma used to wring a chicken's neck, just like that.

She made a little flick of her slim speckled wrist.

-Say that was in Indiana, Lovie?

She looked at him a second, mouth cocked.

-Michigan.

-Oh, yeah.

Jeepers, she'd said, one of her words. Rubbing his stubble, Finus considered Lovie, her fading Michigan twang now warbled into some kind of new American generic fostered by television and a misplaced embarrassment over accents in general, a psychological and self-imposed diaspora of the regional self.

-I've still got to write up Birdie, he said.

-Ah, poor thing.

She'd come down, Lovie had, in tow with her retiring husband in '78. He was a salesman of nuts, the metal kind, nuts and bolts, a fisherman whose prize catches on their weekend trips to the coast she still displayed on her desk in the pastels of washed-out Polaroids. Why had they stopped here, in Mercury? Something to do with a cousin or elderly aunt, he thought he recalled. He favored one photo, with Lovie hoisting a huge red snapper, a little strip of flesh showing between her shorts and tied-up shirttail, her browned and more youthful feet beside a line of two-to-four-pounders laid out in the sand, invisible tiny fishteeth bared to the hostile air at her toes. He could have loved her, then. Anyone could've. His tender expression seemed to puzzle her, though.

-What? she said.

-You inspire me, Lovie.

-And just what does that mean? her voice querulous as a parrot's.

Finus just looked at her, smiling. She gave him her admonishing look and half-hobbled back over to her computer and began tappity-tapping the keys.

Finus bent again to his more formidable machine.

Birdie Wells Urquhart, 88

- She was born in a little fishing village on the Alabama Gulf coast, but moved here with her family after the storm of 1906 wiped out most of the homes, and most of the people there, too.

- Her favorite story about herself was that she once threw a shoe at her sister Pud to make Pud stop snoring. Funny she'd marry a man who threw shoes out his shoe store at fleeing women who'd argued with him about their shoe size. The shoes he (her husband, Earl) threw were the size the women wanted: too small. Say all you want, good or bad, about Earl Urquhart, but Birdie never wore a shoe that wasn't right for her foot, nor any customer at the Vanity Boot Shop, either.

• Along with her two sisters, she once drove three hundred miles in a day chasing Earl from town to town as he made business calls, just missing him, and then got in trouble with him later because there wasn't any supper ready when he got home—just ahead of them. They hadn't wanted him for any special reason. Just a whim that got out of hand.

Berthalyn ("Birdie") Isabella Wells Urquhart died Sunday at home in her bed of apparent heart failure. She was 88. She was born on the Gulf coast and grew up in Mercury, married Earl Urquhart when she was sixteen years old and raised two children who died before she could, having lived thirty-something years a widow.

Birdie was much loved in this community and for many years helped out as a Pink Lady at the hospitals. The Pink Ladies, mostly retired housewives, wore pink outfits and helped to comfort the sick and dying. She was a good storyteller, professing ignorance but possessed of a great deal of wisdom born of long experience. Though she lived out the second half of her life in relative peace and quiet, her years with the Urquhart family after her husband's death in 1955 were somewhat tumultuous, the subject of much local gossip. She once said she guessed the only way to finally get along with your in-laws is to outlive them. Which she did.

Survivors include two grandchildren, five great-grandchildren, several nieces and nephews, and many many good friends and admirers.

Scratching his beard stubble he pulled the obit from the platen and read it over, thinking. He knew he wouldn't stop at that. Pretty dull. If he'd been a poet, maybe, he could have written a poem and said what was in his memory concerning her. A brief epic. If he were a novelist he could tell her story. But he was an old man with a rambling imagination, a spotty if distinct memory. He wandered over to Lovie's desk where she clickety-clacked away, picked up the raw copy of the Spider Creek News, drew a line in pencil about where he figured twenty-one inches would stop, and put it back down on Lovie's desk.

-That's all, he said to Lovie, cut it there.

If not Johnette Chambliss could go on for columns with the running diary of her amazingly mundane week. Went to see my sister over in Bay Springs, she was having a time with her new washing machine, which was whirling catywampus, enjoyed our visit very much. The girls choir sang in the church Sunday morning, they sang three hymns including my favorite, we enjoyed the services very much as well. The drive home was really beautiful, the Lord had spread his grace upon the countryside, and we enjoyed the drive home through its splendor very much. I was down in the back, but managed to get Shelley Jean to drive me to see Coretta Mayfield who has been suffering so with her spider bite. Ankle still swole up big as a man's neck and all purple like. But she was in good spirits, and served us coffee and a delicious angelfood cake from IGA and we ended up enjoying our visit very much and it seemed like Coretta did, too. There wasn't a thing in the world Johnette and her sister or daughter or semi-comatose husband Fleck didn't enjoy very much, be it the simple pleasures of rocking on the porch or sitting around the space heater drinking coffee and gossiping, commiserating with others ailing or lame, or the sublime pleasure of laying somebody to rest, for that grief given lip service and noted in tones reverent enough it was on to the food laid out later and to the passel of flowers bunched around the grave which were quite beautiful and the words said over the corpse plowed satinly into its coffin and maybe even a brief hymn sung by the mourners around the tent, which was beautiful and which we all enjoyed it all very much. For no doubt not to enjoy anything on God's earth ultimately would be an affront to the Lord, cast confusion across the waters and among the peaks. Why yes Johnette we enjoyed your article this week very much.

He went back to his desk and put another sheet in the Underwood and started in.

But to take another angle. Or addendum:

She was a woman to whom nothing much happened in life except that she got married (too young), was widowed (at fifty-four, too young), had a couple of children who died (not young, but before her, so too young there too), who spent some thirty-five years of widowhood doing a little charity work but mostly just helping out with grandchildren, doing a little canning, making an astonishingly sweet and delicious tub of homemade ice cream, and visiting her two sisters until they died (at good old ages, though Pud went a little too young, and both too young by Birdie's lights, as she was the oldest of the three). Whose sole aberration in the long line of her life should not have been her mean-as-snakes, crazy-as-loons in-laws accusing her of poisoning her husband, harassing her with missives collaged of cut-out letters from trashy magazines, which threatened among other things to have her deceased husband exhumed for an autopsy.

Imagine this for yourself. You marry a strong-willed man mostly because he is so strong-willed you can't resist. You live nearly forty years with him, bear him two children, bear his somewhat difficult ways, make him a home, put up with his somewhat insane family, only to have him die on you before the age of sixty, and then these insane in-laws descend upon you with vengeance born of their not receiving any money from your husband in his will, and accuse you of murdering the man—for which reasons it is never really made clear, for which motive is never established by anyone, for which advantage does not exist. One such cut out letter says, Someone we know has murdered someone—POISON—and made it look like a natural death. Beware. THE TRUTH WILL OUT.

Imagine it in letters of motley colors, odd sizes.

Many of us old-timers know all about that business. But let us set the record straight. The story survives in this case because the charges were absurd, groundless—just as it would survive if it were true because of its truth—and were never taken seriously by the legal authorities, including the coroner at that time, as now, a then-youthful Parnell Grimes. And no one else ever took them seriously, either, not Miss Birdie's in-laws who made them, not the old sick folks in the hospital who would joke with her when she came by as a Pink Lady, saying, -You ain't going to p'ison me, now, are ye? and laugh like the wheezing geezers they were. She'd laugh right with them. And it was only out of her complete lack of desire for any sort of vengeance and great desire only for peace and quiet that Miss Birdie did not have her in-laws charged with slander.

There were many things that could not be said publicly and certainly not written about this odd and unfortunate moment in the long life of Birdie Wells Urquhart, but now that she is gone, and now that I am old enough not to care, things can be said. Because unlike her I don't give a nether hoot about what other people think, including any descendants of the Urquharts.

He yanked the page out of the typewriter and slapped it face-down in his tray.

-Well what's got into your craw? he heard Lovie say from her computer, eyes on the screen.

-I can't get a handle on it just yet. Think I'll walk over to Ivy-loy's for a shave.

-You could use one, Lovie said.

He looked at her a long moment, coming back to himself.

-Did you get breakfast, Lovie? Want me to pick you up a bite to eat?

Lovie patted a crinkled lump of foil on the desk beside her machine.

-I brought a sandwich, she said.

-What kind?

-Beg your pardon?

-What kind of sandwich.

She looked up at him with an expression as if he'd asked her the color of her dead husband's eyes.

-Turkey, she said finally.

Finus considered this as if she'd said something of grave import.

-All right.

-You're a queer one, she muttered to herself just loud enough for him to hear as he went out the door.

Through the Mockingbird

IN THE MOMENT just the other side of the mockingbird she drifted down the trail through the woods to the low and damp place where the little cabins sat like crooked tales of those who had once lived there in their way.

She knew she was in the ravine, a place she'd never seen except from the lip of it, and far back from that, from the car. It'd been like a hades the edge of which she was too scared to approach. Here was a little, old old house, a little bitty frame house with faded green shutters and porch that leaned away and down and had two old green wooden rockers on it.

I like green, Creasie said. Then she said, Nobody much lives down here anymore.

Inside the walls were papered with the funnies and looking close she could see one date was July 27, 1947—that would have been her funnies. So every Sunday paper Creasie took home ended up here on the walls, she thought some of them might have ended up in the outhouse. Maybe so. There was no natural color left to the funnies on the wall, they just glowed with their color again when she drew close to see them. Get out of my sight! Mr. Jiggs cried to his frumpy wife, Maggie. Oh, she used to like that one.

She said, I want you to forgive me, Creasie.

Creasie stood looking confused near the cabin's door, her arms at her side, a look like a blind woman's on her face, seeing nothing.

What for, Miss Birdie?

Well, I don't know. I done the best for you I could. I guess for being white, and you black.

Nobody couldn't help that, Creasie said.

I guess not. I know I was hard on you sometimes.

Well. Yes'm. She laughed uneasily. We done what we could.

Well, still.

All right, then, I forgive you, Creasie said. You can forgive me, too.

What for?

I don't know, Creasie said. I can't say.

Well, Birdie said, seeming distracted. All right then, I forgive you. And at that moment she diffused so thoroughly into the air her presence in this space was but a mote that Creasie could no longer see.

Creasie blinked her eyes, readjusting her sight to the dim light in the pantry. She cleared her throat. She was in the pantry in Miss Birdie's house, still waiting on the ambulance. Her coffee'd gone cold. She looked at the cup in her hand. The hair on the back of her neck bristled up.

-For hatin you, she whispered.

~

SHE WALKED THROUGH the shorn corn stumps and furrows though mud would not cling to her long, thin, translucent feet. Out in the flat farmland, it was as if the earth were small, a ball no more than oh a hundred miles or so around, you could see the curve of the land so clearly, but surely she could not travel it round since she had never been around it in life and no spirit would travel into unknown lands where surely she would dissipate into the scattered bleak and deluded imaginations of a million strange and unknown souls, what hell those foreign tongues surrounding her, like some old madhouse from the days when they kept them in chains as if possessed by evil spirits. And such it would have seemed, to her. She would walk the lands she knew when awake.

She topped the little rise in the field and the homes of those who'd built out toward them north from town began to appear, drifting beneath her as if clouds skimming the surface of the earth. Ludlum's barn with the fading paint on it, See Rock City, as if anyone around here knew what that was anymore. Skirting town and over the little subdivisions with toy houses and the graveyards, large and spread-out neatly, and some so forgotten and neglected they were just a faint and luminescent greenish glow through the brambly growth that had overtaken them. She skimmed up the tended grass plots to where she'd lain Earl more than thirty years before. And then she was there before his grave without another second having passed and she spoke to him.

Earl, it's me, Birdie.

Only a murmuring from within. The particles of the earth hummed and spread apart like sand on vibrating glass so she could see him as through a grainy television screen. His old moldered body shivered, mushroomy eyelids blinked once or twice, a mossy old bone-stretched mummy he was, mustache grown long and flowing down into his armpits. His hands lay on his stitched and blackened chest. He coughed.

That's what you get for all that smoking, she said. Otherwise you'd be up and about like me, maybe moved on.

But then, she thought, I'd a had to put up with you all those years.

Wasn't the smoking, he said. How can you say that? Look what's happened here. He ran his withered fingers over the stitching on his chest.

Well it looks awful. I never knew they cut you open.

Worse than that, Earl said.

What are you saying?

I felt fine, leaving the house. Driving out to the lake I felt a tingling spread down into my chest, like when your arm or leg has gone to sleep. Got to the woodpile, started splitting some chunks, raised up for a chop, had the ax in the air, felt something let go, felt like, and just kept on going up, with the ax, all the way.

Well ain't that the way it happens? she said. I come through a birdsong.

I felt my heart, though. Squeezed like to field-dress a rabbit. It turned to a little ball of fire in my chest.

In another hand he then held his liver for her to see, a hard flat stone likened to the head of a caveman's club, and colorless.

And here's my kidneys, he said, reaching into his side and removing a couple of little withered yellow beans.

All that coffee, Birdie said.

They were silent a moment. He seemed to squint through the lacy growth on his eyes.

You were the prettiest thing, he said, it's just a shame. We weren't suited, were we.

I know I was pretty, but I was too young. I didn't want to get married. You all ganged up on me cause Papa thought it best. But I should have said no. It wasn't your fault.

Oh, well.

I'm going on, Earl.

Earl lifted his gnarled and blackened lungs.

Could you take these, they lay so heavy on me now.

She turned away. The soil sifted together again, and the grass snakelike intertwined, and she moved over the silent graveyard, once again all in the present air.

~

EVEN SO, GUILT gave way to the stench of his cursed feet, curling back through some root or worm or aggregating grit so that Earl recalled and relived a moment insignificant in the long thin line of his brief life, a line that focused and broadened into the Brooklyn Bridge, in the middle of which he stood beside the tower smoking a Camel and fanning himself with a copy of the *Herald* beneath the lantern hanging from the tower. One thing you'd think about being up north is at least it'd be cooler, but no. Hot and humid, and not a breeze but the occasional stinker full of exhaust and rotten trash. He wriggled his toes inside his socks, felt a little grimy. All that stone and macadam.

He smelled the woman before he saw her, smelled her not so much over as through the smoke of his cigarette, and cut his eyes to see her sashaying, the very word, toward him, a scissoring walk, one leg crossing over the other as it landed, well he'd see how that worked in another territory. She was wearing a Tweedie, a perfect fit on her size six and a half, but only because he'd fit her, as she'd be wearing a six were it not for him, and not nearly so happy to be sashaying across the bridge in them as she was right now. A woman with a roomy shoe is a woman with happy feet, and a woman with happy feet is a happy woman, a woman who has learned how to curl her toes outward instead of inward. Squeeze a woman's foot when you're fitting her shoe and, if she's game, you're her man, simple as that, unless you're some kind of toad, and even then you'd have more of a shot than most men. It was the blessing and the curse of the business, for sure, but he was trying to make the best of it. He had license, anyway. A man whose wife gave it to him on the average of once or twice a year at best, and looking like it would only get worse, had plenty of license in his book.

The six-and-a-half had come into the store on his last day there so wouldn't she be some kind of reward? He saw it that way, and it was like she did too. On Monday he'd be some thirteen blocks away, opening another store, getting it going, two more stores and he would get the hell out of New York and back home for a while, but that'd be another two months. It would take at least eight women to get him through eight more weeks in New York. Some men loved New York but you could have it, have the stinking sewers and screaming subways and yapping yankees, most of them ugly as mongrel dogs. Sounded like a waddling flock of honking geese when they spoke. Birdie said she wished he'd take her and Ruthie up to be with him when he had to be away so long but he'd said he wouldn't take them to that place to live for a million dollars a year, and meant it, and not because of the strange pussy, he could get that her along or no. But what man would bring his family to live in such a place had they not been condemned to it from the beginning? Best stay home where you can still smell something other than piss on flagstone when you step out the door in the morning, he'd said.

Of course Brooklyn wasn't so bad in that way. The problem with Brooklyn was it was a foreign country. We couldn't live there, he said, we speak English. You wouldn't be able to order groceries unless you spoke Italian or Hebrew, he said. Jews and Wops and old-country drunken Irishmen, and crowded with them. And you won't find a nigger to do for you the way you will back home. You'd best stay here and wait this out, I'll have my own store back home soon.

So the six-and-a-half walks in that afternoon about three in a black dress, a warm day in May and she's cool, just a little sweat beading through her makeup, a little veil from her hat brim shading her eyes, red lipstick, and stands there uncomfortably, looking sort of at him, sort of at the displays, and he can tell she's in way too small of a shoe, so he goes over and touches her elbow and says quietly, Good afternoon ma'am why don't you have a seat and let

me make your life a lot more comfortable for a change? And when
he eased her shoes off and gave a quick squeeze across the ball of
her foot and pressed a light and quick thumb into the arch and ran
it forward he could hear the barely audible exhalation that told
him, All right here's one for the plucking.

At the end of the bridge he hailed a cab and they took it to his
tiny apartment in Brooklyn. On the way up the stairs he didn't try
to time his steps to creak with hers as he had when he first moved
in and brought home a woman. He'd hear a lot of crap from the
landlord and landlady next day but they wouldn't have the
courage to say anything till then, so to hell with them. Always
threatening to kick him out but they didn't want to kick him out,
too much trouble to get someone else, just loved to shout and
shake their fists and claim they were going to kick him out. Fucking Wops. Genufuckingflect yourself over this.

He showed her the bathroom and bedroom and went into the
living room to open the windows and smoke while she got ready.
He was looking down on trees in smoky lamplight, the brick sidewalk showing through gaps in the leaves here and there, feeling
lucky as always that at least he lived in a place here where there
were a few trees growing from between the bricks. A man walked by
his shoes clopping, whistling something that might have been religious, one of those old hymns that sounded like a marching number, like "A Mighty Fortress Is Our God." None of his family except
Mama had ever given a damn about religion so she'd tried to make
up for them all. He'd told Birdie she could give a dollar a week and
he'd take whatever that would buy him in the next world.

She was on his cot bicycling her legs in the air next to a pale
patch of light slanting in like something from a painting. She was
peeling off her nylons and wiggling her toes and tossing the
nylons like ribbons to the floor. Her knees fell open to show him
the way. He pulled loose his tie and began to unbutton, pulled his

shirt off, unbuckled his belt, dropped the pants and pulled each shoe through the pantslegs one at a time and stood there in his drawers and socks and fairly new pair of Thom McAns, then stepped out of the drawers toward her nakedness, her shadowy tits and pale knees and black pouting bramble and eyes watching him like a driver waiting for a pedestrian to cross at the light, wanting to watch him. He crossed the room.

Ya not gonna take ahf ya shoes? she said, or something like that.

He knelt between her knees and held himself in one hand.

What do you care, baby, you interested in my shoes or this?

She smiled.

Whatavah.

He nudged it in.

Was thinking while they made the bedsprings creak slowly in the room so still he could see the dust motes suspended in the angled block of window light, so quiet otherwise he could distinguish individual springs on the bed and began to imagine each as having its own coiled and violated integrity, suffering the indignity of old brittling steel. He notched the toes of his Thom McAns into the edge of the frame at the mattress edge and began to push at her a little harder.

Oh-kay, she whispered, her head back and eyes closed, a half-smile on her lips.

It wasn't leverage, though, it was the stink he couldn't ever get rid of, embarrassing with him being a shoe man, but it was biological. Birdie made him take his shoes off outside the bedroom and sometimes still got up in the night and took them onto the back porch to get them farther away. Made him wash his feet in the tub with soap and water before coming to bed. Then still wouldn't give him any. Was it she just didn't like it, or she didn't like him? She seemed to respect him, treat him with respect.

Yeah, like that, whispered the six-and-a-half, teeth on her bottom lip, digging into his back with her nails.

She knew he fooled around but like with everything else pretty much just acted like she didn't. Acted dumb. She was naive, maybe, but she wasn't dumb. She knew a man had to have what he had to have, and when he wasn't poking around at her anymore she knew he was poking it elsewhere, but the subject did not come up, and would not. As far as Birdie was concerned, it would seem, the world would get along just fine without that. Maybe she thought it'd be better if grown women just played with baby dolls instead of having babies, if that was what you had to go through to get them, the babies. That family she came from had to be the most powdery dry and sexless family in the world, he was surprised they even ate meat they were so modest in their ways. A thing like that should enter a man's mind before he marries, should mingle with his knowledge of his own family's ways. Which in Earl's case included an old pussyhound of a papa and a mama obsessed in her own way, she might go off to every tent meeting in twenty square miles but her main obsession was sexual, all right, every woman did this or that was a whore. Wore makeup, a whore. Wore high heels, a whore. Wore short hair, whore. Smoked cigarettes, a streetwalking whore. Painted fingernails, toenails, don't even think it. Whore whore whore.

Now he wanted a cigarette, thinking about that, even with the six-and-a-half moving beneath him, making his prick bend up and begin to tingle. She began to get urgent, wanting to buck, and he put his whole mind to her. She had nice soft handles around her hips. He braced the heels of his Thom McAns against the cot's railing and held her in to him. They bucked together, walked the cot out into the room. A banging on the floor more than the cot's legs, Angelo and Angela hitting their ceiling with a broom and shouting below, the six-and-a-half shouting beneath. Even he was shouting something, huffing in a blind heat, the whole room suffused with the stink of his poor goddamn adulterous whoring feet.

Ah ha ha ha ha ha ha ha ha ha ha ha ha ha! the six-and-a-half was laughing, as tears ran down into her pale pretty ears.

~

TIME AND SPACE had no purchase on her. Just beyond the graveyard Birdie came upon a little glen she remembered as a child wandering off from the house to sit and look at the trees and their leaves turning and glinting in the breeze. On a little sawn trunk sat her pappy.

This is the way it happens, he said, glancing up. Like in dreams, like the way you wished it would happen in life, that you're going along and you come upon one you love and then you go together. As it happened with the prophets and the angels.

His long white beard was beautiful in this light. His eyes no more than little pieces of sky full of fragile light, his delicate hands holding a little hickory branch, the bark peeled off its smooth surface the size of his pale fingers, little twig knobs on it like his own knuckles. She noticed something about the way he worked it.

You have your arm back.

I never missed it too much, after I learned to write again.

You stayed old. I believe I'm younger.

I was happier, old.

They went to an old house falling in upon itself in the downtown as it used to be, seventy years before. Inside in a parlor where the old sweetly rotting wallpaper peeled away in poor light, in front of a cold fire, there was a reunion of sorts of the Urquharts, her tormentors. Their teapot sat cold on a little serving table, their hair thick and brittle with growing in upon itself and no outlet. A thickening and coarsing so that it became more like the fur of animals than human hair, and their features swollen like with some long night of debauchery, a permanent hangover of sorts it seemed. And no solace. At their entrance a barely audible low and mournful howl seemed to seep from one of them, she couldn't tell which. Old Junius squatted near the cold fire in a set of dirty white long johns, his pointed bald head with just the wisp of white hair on top no more than a bushy eyebrow's worth, and his mean little eyes unfocused and blind.

Who's there? he said.

His lascivious eyes put out, no light there, Pappy said. Remember how he used to could cry at will, get people to buy life insurance from him. He leaked the life out of them.

It's the old loony son of a bitch, Merry said, her voice like the dry discordant wheeze of an old squeezebox.

I don't like living in this house, little Levi said. He was that little boy again she'd had to carry all around Mrs. Urquhart's house, something wrong with his legs, or so he said. Must've been he almost had polio.

Was always a little actor, that one, Pappy said. And wanting to be taken care of.

I don't like this house, Levi said again. It was the repetitive tone of a pull-string doll, a simple recording he was reduced to, Levi.

She could have peeled away their gossamer clothing as easily as cobwebs. They were no more than a feather in weight, any one. This was just dust gathering into the bygone shapes, held together by her and Pappy here.

All time is in a moment, Birdie, Pappy said. These shapes are just the forms of memory and imagination.

Merry wheezed her disgust. She waved her hand and a little comet trail of dust motes suspended. She looked up at Birdie. Don't you think yourself so pretty, she said. I held up better.

Birdie became aware of something, the dry-rot stench of Merry's breath, even now unextinguished. If she'd known her herbs she could've chewed some parsley during her days anyway, she thought.

I could use a drink, Merry said.

Junius groaned at that, looked out the window, so dust-filmed the day outside seemed overcast and dull.

I think you all owe Birdie here an apology, Pappy said. All she ever wanted was peace on this earth, and to get along, and all you ever did was set upon her with lies, and jealousy, and thievery, and attacks upon her good name and character. I'll not have it, though. God will forgive you. Apologize and let's all go, now.

As he finished there became evident to her such an undercurrent of groans and something near quiet weeping, though all their faces remained unchanged, they dissipated into little shifting mounds of dust, sifting over the edges of their seats, and the dust of old Junius swirling in an indoor dust devil and gently up the chimney. She and Pappy followed him roaming down the deserted streets of town in which there was no one grown or prosperous but only streets full of tattered and beautiful angelic little beggars tugging and nipping at his fine suit, asking him for pennies and grabbing at his crotch and bottom, licking his hands as if to get some sweetness or else in a perversely erotic dumb show, who could say? He grew distant and diminishing, a fading figure slapping about himself as if beset with biting flies, a mere whirl of black and white receding below her and changing beyond her perception as there are ineluctable shifts of time and place in dreams, she was slipping from her own skin and felt an easy and effortless unmooring of her self here in an openness and was not fearful at all.

Finus Melonius
(the Ratio of Love)

THE WHITENING SUN up at the midmorning mark and black-rimmed. Finus felt its heat already prickling at his sensitive skin. He left the office, headed to Ivyloy's just down the block. A faded, pea-green Chevy stepside trundled past the courthouse, the figure inside but a shade in a town Stetson raising a hand. Finus waved, hardly noticing. Laughter made him look up and across the street at the courthouse lawn where a bob-haired teacher in a peach sundress gathered her small charges in the lean shadow of the monument, the little ones hopping like grounded fledglings. The young teacher's slim shoulders, white against the straps of her dress, gave shaded suggestions of her lovely bones. In the hard yellow morning light against the bright green centipede, they were all, teacher and little children, in motion and indistinct as a dream. He had turned to walk on when from the slanting scant shadow of a lamppost materialized Euple Scarbrough, the Man Who Knew Everything Because He Knew Nothing, wouldn't it be a skit writing him up one day, and couldn't be too far off. Euple now had that turkey look, head notched forward on the neck, mouth open, expression like a man just saw something mortally shocking, must've been his own shadow. Here he came, the mechanics of his walk resembling more and more that of an old steam locomotive, arms crooked like tie-rods and pumping, and moved as if on a track, no sharp turns. Here he was. Worked his jaw a silent moment to jar speech back into commission.

-Hello, Finus. His larynx a hollow dried corncob.

-Euple.

Didn't want to say anything more, get him started. Euple chewed his gums, blocking the walk and staring at Finus, looking all over his face like he didn't recognize him after all, in spite of speaking, his mind putting his memory of Finus back together in pieces. Worked his jaw a moment more.

-Well I'm never eating another can of pork 'n' beans if I live to be a hundred'n two.

Finus paused, to see if this one would die on the vine. But no.

-Was looking at the sauce. You know they use that gum from a special tree in South America, xanthan gum, drain it in little pipes look like your water faucet on the side of the house, naw, like they did the turpentine down here. Can turn it off anytime they want to, stuck in the bark of the—pause a long moment for a synaptic misfire—xanthan gum tree. Get buckets of it and that's what they use to make the sauce of things like pork 'n' beans. Called xanthan gum, I believe, I think I read that on the label. Seen it in salad dressing, even. And in stuff you can't even eat, like bug spray. It's an adhesive, something. They boil the bark, I believe. Euple paused again, his eyes wandered off into the park though his head didn't move, and Finus for a moment thought he'd fade out and allow an escape. The teacher in the peach sundress was now standing in front of the historical marker, the children clustered around her and moving something like Mexican jumping beans in a jar.

-Or could be the guar gum, they got that, too. Changes the texture of the skin of the bean, changes the chemistry of the skin of the bean, makes it like plastic, won't digest in your stomach, changes the bean meat into something like goat cheese, some kinda dairy by-product, something like bean curd. Harder to digest. And the gum in the sauce, with a little ketchup and sugar in there for color and flavor, it's a binder makes it hard for the stomach to absorb water at the same time, and working against digestion, and can lead to the spastic colon, you never know what'll come of that.

The two men stood there a moment.

Finus said, -Say you been thinking on beans.

-Yes I have.

-I tell you, Euple, I hadn't thought about it much, but you've truly been studying the bean.

-Guar gum, Euple said, looking over at the park as if distracted now. -No, it's xanthan. You look at a label, see it in just about anything. That's the key to life. Simple observation. It's what the scientist does. He might be watching in a microscope or he might be just setting beside the crick, but he's watching. He's looking at his little wife bending over to pick up the young'un, he's thinking fulcrum, lever, distribution of weight, density of bone, muscle mass. He's thinking all them things. If he's a philosophical scientist he's thinking about the ratio of love.

-The ratio of love.

-You'd know what I mean, eh, Euple said, his gaze wandering.

-Say I would, now.

-I believe you would.

The ratio of love: amazing and beautiful, whatever it meant. Maybe the ratio of love over longing, or longing over love. By God. That's why he'd given him the op-ed column, Finus remembered. The occasional weird jewel like this. He regarded Euple, who then nodded at him as if to confirm his thought. Finus said he had to go on. Euple nodded again and shuffle-turned to watch him go. For all Euple's turkey buzzard exterior there was still a glinting light in the old gent's eyes, they were still a hard blue and clear, as if his hard wiring were still clean and new, which maybe it was, maybe his particular imaginative visioning though of no practical value at all was genius of a weird sort. Even so, shoot me if I ever, Finus thought. So many things Euple had enlightened him and others on, from the invention of the shoelace eyelet to the reason birds can't swallow but just must raise their beaks to drain it down. A dog turns three times about his bed before lying down because it puts him in sync with the rotation of the earth, to which he has been on angle during his wanderings of the day, and it's why dogs are so easygoing as a rule and forgiving of others, because they are in sync and harmony with the world and the heavens. Clocks go clockwise because there is a natural gravitational pull to the right, though in England it is slightly to the left, just a hair, which explains things. A crack in the asphalt is the manifestation of one of the zillions of tiny natural fault lines in the rock formation miles deep in the earth, communicated by minute wave action to the surface, cracking the asphalt like chocolate frosting on a jostled cake. Finus let him write a column in the seventies, but after a while people just couldn't stand it anymore. Finus had titled the column Euple's Views. Privately he'd called it Euple's Screwy Views though he had never said it out loud to anyone but Lovie. Of course he would be the first to acknowledge that screwy views fit right into his paper, given his own whimsical approach to journalism.

He regarded Euple, who was standing there looking across the street at some pocket of air and working his jaw in a minor fashion, old desiccated lips parted and a crust of something pale in the corners, running through the grainy film of his days. He moved on.

Euple's discourse on beans had dislodged a pocket of breakfast gas stuck around Finus's ribs and it rumbled like a bubble in the

268 / *Brad Watson*

bathtub making for the surface, but downward through Finus. He
stopped, leaned a little against a building wall and let it brattle
out, went on his way. He hardly bothered to conceal a fart anymore, and hardly dealt more than one or two a day anyway. They
rarely seemed to have much odor beyond something akin to the
sweetfeed you give a horse—corn, with dank rich molasses. He
could track their progress through the tract. Sometimes on one
side of his abdomen a creaking would begin, and sound really like
the joyous squawks and burblings and intermittent drumming of
a woodpecker on a grubby old tree in the woods. Then directly on
the other side of his abdomen would answer the bird's mate, a little higher on the scale, of a different warble and rhythm, as if they
were just letting each other know where they dined. And then
brrraaapppt! like they'd both found the hot spot and hammered
away. Back before his surgery and the moderation of his diet he'd
had a big problem with gas, seemed sometimes his body existed
for nothing more than to produce it, as if he were fossilizing and
mineralizing like some ancient buried dinosaur in the brief span
of his earthly years. In that time he figured he'd produced just
about every variety of methane odor a human is capable of pro-
ducing, until Orin Heath had assisted Mack Modica in the
removal of several malignant polyps from Finus's colon, including
a large section of the colon itself. Before they'd done this they'd
irrigated him, cleaned him out with a pressure hose, it felt like,
and what had at first been simple discomfort, and then grave discomfort, had then progressed into a kind of relief, a sense of a
cleansing, which had then become a sort of euphoria, a moment
of absolute clarity, which had then intensified to the point that he
felt like his brain was on fire, tiny geysers of flame were firing from
the pores in his head, couldn't they see it? And also he had a pain
down lower, but not in his ass, instead in his groin, and he peeked
down to a teen boner, one of those threatened to split the skin. He

tried to reach down to hide it but his arms were gently pressed back to the sheet by the firm soft hand of a fleshy nurse whose breasts he could see straight through her clothing, like X-ray vision, saw her nipples grow hard and erect before his gaze, and he looked into her eyes and saw it was Adelphia Morrisette, the daughter of Blaise Morrisette, the druggist, a girl he'd often watched bend over to stock the shelving when she was just a teenage girl helping out after school, and in that moment during the visionary irrigation he could imagine with astonishing reality his rejuvenated prick poking its way through her wiry blond pubic hair and into slick glandular softness, young tight softness, and he felt her fingers press into the flesh of his head in a grip that could have been her manifest ecstasy.

-What's he trying to do? a nurse said.

-Hold him, he's bucking.

They held him. Lying there, in exquisite pain, he was recalling something from school, as a boy. Fellows out in the schoolyard, describing relations of the garden variety. Finus, who'd thought himself imaginative, was astonished.

-Come on, Bates, the farm boy twanged, back on his heels, a derisive squint, you can't *tell* me you've never fucked a melon.

~

HERE WAS IVYLOY'S shop now, Finus's own ectoplasmic reflection in the glass overlaying the image of Ivyloy himself, who stood at ease with one arm on the back of his barber chair in a dream, like a heron seeming to gaze at nothing just above Finus's head. He woke up, smiled and raised his eyebrows, just about the only hair on his big round head set up on a long skinny neck and tall bony frame. Must be a hard irony to live with, a bald barber, Finus thought, and walked on in.

-Hey, boy, have a seat. Ivyloy popped the apron out and when Finus sat he draped it over Finus's lap while he fastened a trimming collar around his neck, then he tied the apron, swung Finus around to look in the mirror.

-What'll it be, just a shave, or a trim, too?

-Shave, Finus said, appraising himself. -Used to be I needed a haircut every other day.

-Used to be lots of things I needed *every* day, Ivyloy said. He leaned Finus's chair back and laid a hot towel across his face. -Then I got married. He hummed to himself as he worked up a lather in the soap cup. Finus could see the TV reflected in the mirror. Three women were on a talk show set, fighting, two burly men trying to keep them apart. The big woman threw her chair at the littlest one, who deflected it with her own like a swashbuckling lion tamer.

-Why don't you ever turn on the sound? Finus said.

-I don't want to *hear* it, Ivyloy said. -Just like to have the pictures moving around.

Ivyloy bent to the task, stretching a bit of cheek here and there, taking care around the jawline, stretching the skin on Finus's neck where it dewlapped. He concentrated on the jawbone behind Finus's right ear. On the television two muscle-bound men came up behind the two women and put them into something like half nelsons. Ivyloy's razor skritched down into the low part of his neck, near the shirt collar, and gave Finus a pleasant prickling. He closed his eyes, to the television, to Ivyloy's fluorescent lightbulbs, to the slanted golden light through the barbershop's window. And in some space of time could have been years he felt the tug of a new hot towel dabbing the shaving soap away from his skin. He opened his eyes, back in time.

Ivyloy dried Finus's face, slapped a little Mennen onto his cheeks and under his jaw and chin, then rinsed and dried his own hands as Finus stood up and palmed out a ten, received his change.

-I heard you tell about Birdie and Midfield this morning, Ivyloy said.

Finus said, -I been writing them up.

-What's the high points?

-Nothing spectacular.

-Hmph, Ivyloy said, looking out the window. -I know you. Be writing it, *She once stood accused of poisoning her husband, her crazy in-laws threatening to dig up his body and hash it out.*

Finus just stared at him.

Ivyloy said, -Don't get riled, now.

Finus looked away. In a moment, he said, -And how's Miss Sadie?

-She's like you, you can't kill her. You could run that woman over with one of them big things flattens out fresh pavement, one of them big flatteners, you'd just have you a new pothole when she riz' up, shape of Sadie.

-Say she's a tough one.

-I done tried to kill that woman a thousand times.

-Go on, now.

-Run her over, shot her, tossed her off a cliff up in Tennessee, give her rat poison and buried her in the backyard, she just comes back in that evening while I'm having my coffee, whups my ass like a stray dog. Woman's tough, now. No, she's gone kill me with time, her life's mission is to outlive me.

Finus stood there nodding, looking at him.

-Now, I know you love that old gal, he said.

-Like my own life, Ivyloy said. -What there is left of it. Hey, you must a written me up years ago.

-I have not, Finus said. -You may be brain-dead but I can wait till you stop breathing, anyway.

Ivyloy looked a little pained, but he laughed.

-Aw, hell! he called out then, as if singing a note. -I don't believe it. You got files on ever one of us.

Finus ignored him and glanced into the mirror.

-You didn't even comb my hair.

-Did I cut it?

-No.

-Well, then, comb it yourself, your highness. I ain't no hair stylist, I'm a barber. I *cut* hair.

-You're not disposing me to knock out a good one on you when the time does come, Finus said.

-If you wait till I'm gone, which ain't likely to happen, as old as you are, it won't make a whole hell of a lot of difference to me, now will it? Ivyloy popped the apron in his hands and squinched his face up in the way he had that said, *So there.*

~

HE WAS GRAVITATED in a light atmosphere of aftershave down 5th toward the little hummock upon which old McLemore Cemetery received the earthly elements. A single small cedar tree remained on the downslope beside a family plot circumscribed by a low and time-scoured brick parapet, an undermined and sunken little wall. A solitary water oak, somewhat stunted but thick with limbs and hard green little leaves, hung on in the far corner. It must be old, Finus thought, left from when this little hummock clearing was edged by the woods around, out on the southeast outskirts of the town. The yard's old iron rail fence crooked along the borders, arthritic. He'd buried Avis there, along with his mother and father. Of course this became the last thing for which she could never forgive him. He knew he should have laid her out in Magnolia, the newer cemetery on the north end of town, where her own mother and father had bought a plot that sat waiting near their own, and where he and Avis had buried Eric. But at the time his thinking was her old man had held enough claim on the poor woman, right down to the way she could never trust a soul, could never open up and feel anything much beyond suspicion and disappointment and smoldering rage. Well, they could lay him out here in the plot next to her, let her complain throughout eternity, if she liked. He'd had Eric's grave moved over here after Avis's funeral. He lay beneath the cedar down below.

He opened the creaky gate and stepped through onto the dry, mown grass, its blades crunching beneath his shoes even this early, dew sucked in long before. They kept the grounds up but never watered. There'd been little rain. And this was the high ground here, nothing to drain down into the little hummock, a lone green patch in this neighborhood, with a view of the new overpass, the railyard, and beyond that downtown, looking small and upcropped and hazy. Just a short walk from here, where homes and little groceries and laundry and seamstress shops had cobbled up in the forties and fifties, the neighborhood had now declined: the shops empty, the homes listing with the topography, and housing what seemed the invisible poor. Their bare yards were littered with no broken wagons and Big Wheels, no rusted Pontiac hulls on concrete blocks. Old men and old women, probably, he didn't even know anymore. He'd known poor Jane Caulfield, a sexless maiden who'd lived with her aunt and her aunt's lover and partner in the dry cleaning business, until the aunt had died and Jane had been discreetly and kindly moved to a nursing home out on 39 North and stayed there until she died and was buried here in McLemore Cemetery, down the slope next to the big Schoenhof plot. She'd been a pretty young girl and no one knew exactly why she became almost a recluse and certainly an old maid after a lively youth of dances and running about, if not actual dating. Her wan smile had driven boys to fall in love with her, the first whiff of which sent her into a retreat so swift and silent it generally took them a year or two to get over it and date some normal girl.

He went to Eric's grave first. He'd refused the military marker the army offered, and put a nice modest stone down flat at its head. The boy was mute in there, a young voice now old in time and distant, the stone nothing to Finus but cold marble etched with what might as well have been Greek or Arabic, he couldn't read it anymore. After a minute or so he walked up the hill to see Avis. A wiry strange cat approached to arch and rub its side along the edge of her headstone, tail up and quivering while the cat turned its strange gaze upon him. The cat had an odd mouth, looked like, a cat with an underbite, you never saw that.

-You're an odd one, Finus said, and thrust his hands into the pockets of his khaki trousers.

You're an odd one, said the cat, its mouth quivering in the way a cat chirkling at birds will do.

-Copy cat, are you.

The cat said nothing then. It was an old tomcat he could see now, and its haunches quivered again as it sprayed a little urine on Avis's stone.

You tainted me off men forever, the cat said then.

Finus cocked his head for a new angle on it.

The cat said, Why'd you marry me, anyway, if you never loved me?

-Don't blame me for all that, Finus said. -You hated your old dad before you ever met me.

The cat stopped, still arched, and stared at him.

-Just because you could never stand up to him, Finus said, so you took it out on me.

You'll never be the man he was, the cat said, its underbite forcing the odd, high-pitched chattering of a cat longing to sink its teeth into some taunting bird.

-And I thank the gods for that, Finus said. -Poor old miserable son of a bitch, no wonder he went on those drunks, and no wonder he got mean and violent when he did. Scratching a living and then a fortune out of brambly land and marginal cattle, trading on his wits and growing hard-hearted just to feed all you young'uns, and your mother got the worst of it.

Don't even speak of my mother, the cat said. You cannot comprehend a strength like hers.

-No, Finus said after a moment, I'll give you that. She was an amazing, sweet woman, as sweet as he was hard. I loved her, too.

You never loved anyone but yourself.

The cat lay down on the grave, its back against the headstone, and began to groom itself.

-You're one to talk, Finus said. -You never even had that.

A little warm gust, the afterthought of a breeze, nudged his ear, an almost imperceptible rustle in the hard green leaves of the oak. Finus snorted in disgust.

-Old Mike was here, he'd shake you like a rag doll.

The cat said nothing, just stared at him. He sighed.

-I'll get some flowers out here, he said, as much to the empty granite vase at the stone's base as to the cat. The cat merely paused a moment, one paw suspended before its odd-shaped mouth, then resumed licking and combing its ears with the paw. Finus sighed again, wished for the first time in some fifteen years he had a cigarette, and turned back toward town.

The cat, its paw suspended midlick once again, watched him until his head disappeared beneath the cemetery's knoll, then settled in to see what else might flit or wander into the grounds. Squeezed its indifferent eyes together and began to purr in the delicious warmth of the morning.

Finus Impithicus

THE CUSHMAN GOLF cart seemed to sag half-melted in the hard overhead sunlight on the steaming asphalt there. Its white vinyl seat was hot as a woodstove through his britches but not unbearable. And it cranked right up, stuttering to life sounding as much like a gas-powered generator as ever, and it jumped as lively as ever when Finus kicked off the brake and whipped it back out of the space and down toward the doughboy soldier monument, his old Ben Hogans rattling in their bag on the back at every bump and turn. The accelerator pedal needed a good greasing, it was sticking and he had to give it a good pop to release it, and the cart would shoot ahead, but the governor kept the speed down once he got going. He kept both legs inside the cart. Wasn't one of those who liked to hang the left leg out, as he'd seen more than one idiot's knee turned that way. Seemed like fat men did that more than others, why was that? Lazy? Didn't want to have to swing more than one leg out when they stopped for the ball? Not enough room on the seat? Finus hadn't even taken up the game until Avis died, hadn't gotten the cart till he turned eighty, was holding up the other players, walking so slow. Turned out to be a good way to get around town on a hot, or a cold, day, too.

It had the old shaft-type steering mechanism, which Finus loved, was painted a plain off-white, no roof like the newer electric E-Z-GOs, and the biggest difference from them was its motor, the little two-stroke gasoline job that announced to anyone, on the course or on the streets of Mercury, that Finus Bates was rounding the bend.

As he was, past the World War I monument and onto 22nd Avenue, headed down 7th Street. He could see the jumpy reflection of himself and the cart in the plate-glass windows of the old Kress Building, where the town boys boxed these days, building gutted and adorned in the center of the old floor with an elevated ring. He honked his claxon in front of the fire station, where the boys all flung an arm up from their lawn chairs and hailed.

Looming now in a sort of plantation palatial splendor and unavoidable, Grimes Funeral Home basked in the morning's heat, its tall white columns like silent sentries, half a dozen large white rocking chairs on the veranda. He parked the Cushman at the curb and went on in. The air-conditioning quickly turned the sweaty parts of his shirt to coldpacks and Finus peeled it loose from his skin and jiggled it while he cooled.

He hated how funeral parlors went for opulence in the grand lowbrow middle-class fashion as if we all were shooting for such a parlor in heaven, but it served us right after the hymns about streets of gold. Here in Grimes's old foyer the windows were either leaded and colored glass supposedly from Italy, as in the front door and side panels, or clear and wavy with antique imperfection, as in all the other windows, and when one stood in the hushed, sunlit rooms and looked outward through the warped panes, the view seemed appropriately distorted when one considered he was standing in the halfway ground, an earthly equivalent to limbo, the place where we stood between the worlds of the living and the dead. This idea, the situation, was appealing to

Finus. If it weren't for the pretentious furnishings, the Italian or Victorian fainting couch (a divan, he supposed, or maybe a chaise longue), the high-backed stuffed chairs done out in embroidered crimson silk, the dolorous presence of an ancient pump organ in the foyer complete with hymnbook open to "Come, Ye Disconsolate," he would have thought Parnell's place quite pleasant. But he couldn't get past the ridiculous idea, reinforced by the luxurious Cadillac hearse, gleaming metal caskets with plush pillowy pink and blue linings, and the fat, florid, professionally mournful faces of Parnell's two young assistants, stationed at the parlor doors like courtly eunuchs, that some poor truck farmer or frame carpenter who never felt comfortable in a suit his whole life should want to be trussed up, made up, displayed like a mannequin, and then paraded through town as if he'd been the third duke of Ellington or whatever. Ceremony was important, sure, but ceremony could be as simple as washing a body with cool rags and laying it out on a plank.

He'd thought Parnell's place more interesting when his wife, Selena, was alive, her presence something like a silent screen tragedienne's, intense and weird but it had seemed appropriate to the setting, at least gave it a little flavor in Finus's opinion. Why shouldn't the parlor of the dead be a weird place? Though the dead be among the living at all times, they are not in their bodies, which people paid such as Parnell to briefly preserve as a strange totem to their own finite forms in a way not so different, as far as Finus could see, from the way in which they preserved sported beasts on the walls or in museums or, in a more subtle sense, the way they kept the images of those they loved or thought interesting preserved on little pieces of photosensitive paper. And the thing about photos was that as truly as they recalled the way light struck and rebounded from the object of our bodies at the time the camera's shutter blinked, it was still a lie. A piece of photosensitive paper was not a retina, was not attached to a brain, so the image was at best secondhand and all the immediacy of the image's vitality and meaning to the viewer was lost, reincarnated as a kind of art. There was its value and its limitation.

Here now came the little footballish shape of Parnell Grimes, these days looking partially deflated with his advancing years, advancing slowly toward Finus in the warbling light of the room, arm and tiny mottled pinkish greeting hand outstretched. He was bald on top but for a little tuft of down at the front of his head that he kept oiled to a dull silver and pulled to one side instead of straight back like anyone with a smidgen of self-awareness would have done. Well I can't criticize the bald, Finus said, running a hand through his own thick white hair and allowing himself a cool and calming moment of mortal smugness.

Parnell clasped Finus's large hand in both his own and drew close, looking up sympathetically, as if he couldn't break the habit.

-Finus. Good to see you. Come on back to the office and sit down.

Finus followed his little waddling shape out of the main parlor, casketless at the moment, past the other arched and stuccoed entrances to mournville where space awaited other dead, to Parnell's modest but beautifully decorated walnut-and-oak-furnished office in the sunny corner room back of the house.

When they were seated, Parnell leaned back in his chair, put his little hands before him in an attitude of contemplation or prayer.

-Now what can I do for you today, Finus?

Finus said well he thought he'd get the official word on the cause of death for Midfield plus an update on the services, and Parnell gave Finus his official grim nod, cleared his throat and shuffled through a few papers on his desk and said, well, it appeared to be cardiac arrest as he'd suspected, though just between you and me Midfield did have a fairly high level of alcohol in his blood and the cause may just as well have been liver failure, at least to some degree.

-Say he'd probably been drinking for a while.

-Quite a while, I imagine.

-Been on a drunk.

Grim nod.

-And Birdie? Her heart, too, I'm sure.

Grim nod. -A lot of fluid around it, as expected.

They sat in silence. A clock ticked on Parnell's wall and Finus glanced up to see his favorite object in this place, a cuckoo clock mounted in a little birdhouse. He remembered initially fearing to see what might pop out of there upon the hour, perhaps some little rattly skeleton or a little body tray to slide out as if from a morgue, the corpse sitting up to say Cuck-oo! After all a skull paperweight lay on papers at the rear of the bookshelf behind Parnell. Didn't look real, though. Too white. He'd never asked. Oddly indiscreet, it seemed to him, for an undertaker.

He wasn't ready to get on, yet, but couldn't think of much to say as Parnell was an odd one, not like undertakers Finus knew who were generally average citizens, interested in this and that, if possessed of a light-switch activation for maudlin gravity. Parnell and Selena had never had children, never went to a sports event, attended only the sermons at church and never Sunday school or Wednesday suppers, and never belonged to a weekend supper club. People said they'd often driven over to Jackson or up to Birmingham on weekends, to see movies and plays and so on, the occasional symphony concert. He supposed they were cultured, Parnell had that dignified air, and Selena, you'd have thought her an heiress if you hadn't known she was just a postman's daughter from Mercury, Mississippi, and married to a local undertaker there.

The way she always had one of Parnell's eunuchs drive her here and there in Parnell's Lincoln while she sat in the backseat to one side, staring ahead or reading a book, and was not going to the grocery store or the drugstore but to get her hair done or for a manicure or out into the country, as it was said every now and then one of the eunuchs would drive her to a little spot out at the old springs where she would swim alone for half an hour, dry off and then come back, her hair in a white towel, herself in a thick white robe.

-Well other than all that, how you getting along, Parnell? he finally said.

-Oh, fine, in general, Parnell said. -You? How's your health, Finus?

Always an ominous question from his ilk.

-Well as can be expected, Finus said. -Get much worse and I expect you'll know it.

They laughed.

-I was just thinking about your missus, gone all these years, Finus said. -I'm sure you still miss her.

-Yes, Parnell said, nodding, looking down for a moment, as you miss your loved ones, I'm sure. Then he said, -Sometimes it seems like she's not really even gone, even now.

-I know what you mean, Finus said.

-Do you? Parnell said with a little smile, looking up.

-Probably not the same thing, Finus said.

Parnell gave him a curious look, the smile gone and the old look of grief returning, except it looked like the real thing now and not his practiced expression, but said nothing.

-Mrs. Bates and I were not much the lovebirds, Finus said.

-Ah, Parnell said, nodding with a sad conspiratorial smile. -I heard you on the radio this morning, saying Miss Birdie had been your childhood sweetheart.

-An exaggeration common to the neglected, Finus said with his own sad conspiratorial smile.

Parnell added an actual wink to his own.

-I'm surprised, then, that you two never became the item in your later years, her a widow and all.

-Mrs. Bates and I never divorced.

-Yes, but after her death, Parnell said.

-Well neither of us was that keen on marriage, after our firsts, Finus said. -Poisoned by it, you might say.

-Yes. That old business, Parnell said, and the moment, somehow, turned inexplicably awkward. -Well, he said, with a nervous laugh, I'm certain *Mrs.* Urquhart wasn't poisoned.

-As opposed to Earl, you mean? Finus cocked his head.

-Ha ha! Parnell said. His smile tightened and he raised his brows.

-Something funny about all that, even now, ain't it, he said to Parnell, giving him the stare. -You know I always wondered if that man's goddamn crazy family didn't really do him in, you know, and giving Birdie all that grief about it. They're all gone, now, of course. Birdie outlived them all.

Parnell only pursed his lips and nodded shortly. Only glancing to meet Finus's gaze.

-Birdie always said the only way to get along with your in-laws is to outlive them, Finus said. He allowed a little smile to Parnell, which seemed to ease him a bit. But then it wasn't an easing. It was something else, like a heaviness descending on the strange little fellow. He took on an almost maudlin look. Guess that shouldn't be surprising, Finus said to himself, given his trade.

-Well, maybe it was just as well you and Miss Birdie never married, Parnell said then, meeting Finus's gaze in a way so open and uncharacteristic, so free of his professional demeanor, Finus felt he was seeing him for the first time.

-How do you mean?

Parnell sat there looking at him frankly, and seemed as if something like grief and regret rested solidly in his features. It made Finus feel oddly vulnerable, himself, just sitting there looking at Parnell looking that way. He wanted to look away from it.

Parnell got up after a moment and opened a filing cabinet drawer. He drew a file from the front, laid it on his desk, sat down again, and rested his short blunt fingertips on it.

-Off the record, of course. Finus nodded. -And just between us. If I share this with you, Finus, it is not for publication nor for any other sort of dissemination. My father's reputation, as well as Miss Birdie's, depends on it. It's weighed on my conscience, though, as I expect it weighed on hers.

Finus leaned forward now. He looked at the file, but couldn't read its subject heading from where he sat.

-This is a collection of articles and information I gathered over some years on the Atomic Energy Commission, Parnell said, and settled his own gaze on Finus then, as if he'd said something final. Finus looked at the file a moment, looked back at Parnell, then picked up the file and skimmed through it. From what he could gather, going fairly quickly through it, there had been a long-running government project to collect dead bodies and body parts, on the sly, for use in testing the effects of atomic radiation on the human body. He looked up after a minute.

-I've read a little about this, over the wires, he said. Parnell said nothing.

Finus said, -What could this have to do with Birdie?

The men sat silently a minute, looking at one another.

-This information, Parnell said, the possibility that my father was doing this, selling bodies and body parts to the Atomic Energy Commission in the early phases of that program, was used to blackmail me. The state forensics lab wanted to take a closer look at Mr. Earl's heart, after seeing the sample I sent them. He paused. -I talked them out of it.

-Are you saying you had sold them Earl's body? That makes no sense. He was in his casket till you closed it and put it in the ground, as I recall.

-I'm not saying that, Parnell said.

-Well what does this have to do with Birdie, then?

Parnell shook his head. Then he told Finus what had happened the night Creasie came to get Earl's heart. And told him about the sample he sent to the state lab, and his putting them off. About everything.

Finus looked down at the file in his hands. When he looked at Parnell again, Parnell's face seemed collapsed in a kind of baffled relief.

-What I don't understand, Finus said, is how in the hell Birdie would or could have known anything about all this—he tapped the file with his fingers. -That's what doesn't add up. Aside from the general macabre absurdity of the whole story.

Parnell sat down in his chair and blinked his eyes like a confused child.

-Finus, I have no idea. That, I have never understood.

-It was Creasie, her maid, who came by to get it.

Parnell nodded.

-And kept saying *she* said this and that.

Nodded.

-But never said *Miss Birdie said*.

-No, Parnell said. -She didn't.

-So maybe she didn't mean Birdie.

-Who else, Finus?

-Hell, Finus said, taking out his handkerchief and blowing his nose with a flatulent honk, I guess that's the question, all right.

Ten minutes later Finus let himself out, and stood on the sidewalk in a wind buffeting him and the Cushman sitting impassively at the curb, both bathed in fleeting shadows of something in the sky. He looked up. Dark baby cumulus drifting from the south as if in search of their mother. And there to the east beyond the Dreyfus Building's radio tower the mother cloud rose up like a billowing anvil, an atmospheric god.

Finus Magnificus

He DIDN'T KNOW what to do with himself, where to go. The Cushman sat there, mute and pale off-white. He heard the low loud drone of an old Stearman crossing town to land at the airport, some ex–fighter jock turned crop duster at the stick no doubt. At the stoplight a single car sat awaiting green. A new station wagon, windows rolled up and air-conditioned, vacation luggage strapped onto the roof. He couldn't tell what model car it was since they all copied the Japs in design, could've been a Ford or a Mitsubishi or a Mercedes for all he knew, and two nice-looking young ladies in big sunglasses and hair pulled back were chattering away at one another, the driver pointing at something down the street, and in the backseat a boy of about ten or so, looking straight at Finus, the boy's hair combed neatly as if he'd just been to the barber though that was unlikely, his face a small pale oval making his dark eyes seem large. There was no expression on the boy's face beyond frank curiosity over Finus, an old man standing on the corner looking lost. The light turned green and the car turned left toward the viaduct under the train tracks, no doubt headed for the beach highway south. Finus felt a nerve kick in his pelvis and could move his limbs again, unsure if he'd

seen this boy or if he was a vision and having nearly forgotten him
again anyway, lost in more reverie of his own son at a little less than
that age, looking down at him from the crook of a muscular live oak
where Finus had constructed a railed platform with a rope ladder
which little Eric could haul up after him to keep all others out, and
seeing in the boy's eyes that fascination with power and height.

A gusting moan from the Stearman turning final way over at
the field, carried in a sound pocket. A little puff of a breeze, as if
from the delicate faraway movement of its wing, carried the odor
of honeysuckle from some hidden patch and broke through the
lingering acidic exhaust from the station wagon with the woman
and the boy.

Finus looked up and blinked in the bright sunlight that allowed
no shadow in its merciless position straight overhead, no shadows
among the group of schoolchildren huddled into a jittery bunch
around the skirts of a young woman about to herd them into the
library across the street, same bunch he'd seen that morning, no
doubt on some field trip. Their motions as active and contained
as ants in glass. His vision blurred with sudden grief and self-
flagellation.

There was a sound from the cart groaning against its brake, as
if it were impatient, wanting to move on. Finus got in, kicked at
the stubborn brake, headed out. Not sure where he was headed.

To Knoll Creek, it seemed, the decrepit course that had thrived
in the twenties, when Mercury itself thrived, but which now was
as unkempt as a cow pasture, which it had originally been, with
knots and whorls of St. Augustine and clumps of Bahia corrupting
the Bermuda in the greens, johnson grass wild in the fairway
roughs, you might as well drop out of those suckers. It was like
playing golf on a farm. There was a par three on the back side
Finus had been trying to hole-in-one for years. The cart puttered
him to the north end of the town, hugging the curb, cars passing

and uttering little honks, whether in hello or watch out or move over he didn't pursue.

He veered off the road onto the fairway of number 11 and took the path down the hill across the street and sped down the long fairway of par-five number 12, on his way to the par-three water-hazard 13. The long flat fairway quavered in the heat and gave off ripply, otherworldy visions of the pines behind the far green. Passed two men and two women walking pull carts together. They all waved, hailed. Finus passed on. At the 13 tee a twosome had just hit. He'd have time to hit before the party on 12 got there. The course seemed pretty empty. Too hot to play, for most. Too hot for Finus, too, but all he wanted was a good tee shot, one try (with maybe a mulligan) at a one-holer here, to make his day, make his life. Hell he might not ever golf again if he made that shot, and so be it. The twosome, a couple of young fellows he recognized though didn't recall their names, had knocked respectable shots, one to the green, the other to the fringe. They motored down, chipped and putted, then waved to Finus as they replaced the flag, got into their electric cart, and drove up along the little copse path to the elevated number 14 tee. Out of sight.

Finus drove up the path and stopped beside the 13 tee, jammed on the parking brake. The Cushman sputtered to a halt and died. He took out his five iron and a ball and tee and walked up onto the tee. Used to be he hit an eight iron on this hole, a mere 130-yarder. Then later on a seven. Then he gave in and went on up to the five. He had no backswing to speak of anymore. Hell, if he kept playing, he'd be using a driver here before long. Took his best swing with the five now to green it, and that was rare.

He teed up a new Titleist and straightened up, hand to his lower back to assist the move, and stepped back from the ball. The flag was close today, near the tee side of the green, down from the little rolling rise in the middle. The hazard, a little pond laced with water lilies and a few cattails, stood unrippled by nary a breeze.

He stepped up to the ball, waggled the club, an old Hogan with a sweet spot the size of a dime at best. Squared off. Looked pinward, back down at the ball. Took a breath, hauled back, and hit.

Not a good one, toward the front of the club face. He felt it wobble when he hit. Looked up to see the ball go right of the green and low, roll toward and into the little dry trap there. All right, then, a mulligan.

He reached into his pants pocket and got out a second ball, a fairly new Pinnacle he'd found in the rough on 18 that winter. He looked around, found a tee broken near the point, that'd do. Teed it up and stepped back. Concentrate, he told himself. He took a look at the pin, squared up, and addressed the ball. Said, -Only you, you white and dimpled spherical son of a bitch. You were made for this hole only. He focused all his mind on the ball, on the club face resting perfectly before it. He drew back slowly, his feet planted firmly, and stroked through it, a nice smooth swing. A nice click he hardly felt in the shaft. Looked up then to see the ball arcing high and beautifully straight up into the cerulean blue. He sang in his mind to himself. Down it came, and he lost sight of it in the glare of noon and the backdrop of pale green washed-out summer foliage.

By God. By God, he thought, it *might* have gone in. Finus's blood ran hot and thrilling to every little vein end in his body. Like a mild induced electric current to his brain. He wanted to jump in the air with excitement. Held the club up in the air with one hand, a victorious gladiator with his weapon. By God.

He dropped the club where he stood and scurried, or something like that, down the tee slope to the cart and got in, cranked it. He hit the brake with his foot to unlock it. Hit it again. Stubborn brake didn't want to let go. He gripped the wheel and leaned down to check the brake pedal with his free hand. Wasn't thinking clearly. When he leaned down he accidentally braced his right foot against the accelerator pedal, which disengaged the brake and the cart shot forward, nearly tossing Finus out onto the path. He yelped and yanked on the steering wheel trying to right himself, and the cart veered, at out-of-the-gate speed, off the path, bumped down the front tee slope, and splashed at around ten miles per hour into the pond at a sharp angle and turned over. Finus, gripping the steering wheel with both iron hands, was trapped there on the muddy bottom of the pond in three feet of water. He'd had a leg out of the cart while trying to free the brake and the side of the cart now held it, not too painfully because of the soft mud, fast to the bottom of the pond.

He'd involuntarily closed his eyes upon impact. But now, in a panic at realizing he was under water and pinned there, he opened them again. He could see nothing for a second or two, with the mud swirled up in a cloud, but then it cleared and he could see his situation. His leg beneath the overturned cart. The dappled surface of the pond just out of reach of the hand he stretched tentatively toward it, as if he could grip the water's surface and thereby pull himself to air and safety. But before he realized he was suffocating for sure, the knowledge that this or no other miracle would save him settled in and he somehow received it calmly. All right, then. As good a death as any other, better than some. Only a few seconds more in these old lungs. He saw the pale and shadowed undersides of the lilies. The rippled and shimmering blue sky just beyond the still disturbed but settling surface of the pond. The ethereal limits of this beautiful world. A hole in one, by God. He had to believe, in this brief and finite moment, that he had put it in. The little projectile launched from his Ben Hogan five iron in a perfect arc into the realm of what we considered was no longer the firmament but an unfixed and evolving and volatile environment, that followed its planned, theorized journey down to the surface of green 13, to the little red-and-white pin with the yellow flag, and into the little hole with a sweetly satisfying earthly cluck. Birdie never gave a damn about golf, but still he wished he could have had her with him to see that.

A Pair of Boots

LATE AFTERNOON, A flurry of people coming to rap on the back door to the kitchen and dropping off cakes and pies, Lord knows where they come from, must have had them just waiting for Miss Birdie to die, and then a little later come hams and casseroles and extra coffee percolators, the big kind like little upright tanks, and plates of fried chicken and bowls of potato salad and big pitchers of ice tea. And for a while Creasie stayed in the middle of it all, shuffling here and there in her bare, dry, flattened feet, handing this and that, being handed, and then it got so crowded she had to get away and sit down.

She sat in her chair in the pantry sequestered from the buzz and clatter of the chattering, munching mourners, drinking a cup of coffee, and except for the little turn of her bent wrist that moved the cup to her lips, and the little pooch-out of her lips she'd make to meet the cup, and the slurping sound that came thereof, she was silent and still. And she wasn't thinking about all these white people milling around at all but about old Oscar the electric colored dummy Mr. Earl had owned when she was just a girl working for them early on. She was wishing she had asked Miss Birdie one more time about the dummy before she passed, but it wasn't something she could explain too easily because Miss Birdie would've never understood about Frank, because she couldn't have sensed the spiritual warp and weave that connected Frank and the dummy Oscar in her young and terrified mind at the time, and so now had her half hoping for some strange miracle that would make the world more alive than she'd come to fear it was, with just us flatfoots moping around day to day.

After the baby potion hadn't taken, just before Frank left, she'd stayed away from the ravine for two years. With Frank gone, she tried to resign herself to this fate, this life that was to be hers forever, as far as she could tell. She stayed her Sundays even in the cabin, sitting on her porch, took up dipping snuff herself, went to town sometimes when Mr. Earl would go in to check on his inventory, riding in the backseat of one of his new cars, closing her eyes so she wouldn't be scared half to death by the way he would speed.

The hardest times were when Mr. Earl would go to get his father, Mr. Junius, on Fridays and bring him over for the weekend. Old Mrs. Urquhart had died and they felt sorry for him. Creasie didn't. She wished him dead. She wished him pain and suffering. She wished she could administer such an end, herself.

He'd gotten older, fatter, balder, paler. No meaner-looking than before, really, still with his pale, pig eyes, thin lips, pointy head, foul mouth. Wandering from the guest room in the back in his suspender pants and T-shirt and house slippers, seemed stiffer, like age finally catching up to him all of a sudden, wouldn't be catching no girls alone in a shed no more, now. Couldn't bend his neck good, but would watch Creasie with those pale pig eyes when she had to pass him in the den or the living room, or bring a plate of food to the table when they ate.

Just a little simmer inside her, began to grow, till she was so angry it was into a boil. Hatred for that old white man. Hatred for what he'd done to her. He looked like some big boil himself, full of ugly, full of poison. That was what made her think of Vish again. She sat out on her porch Sundays, when she didn't have to go over to the house, and watched them load him in the car to take him back to his empty home in Alabama. And finally one Saturday night before she went home to the cabin she said to Mr. Earl that if he was going into town for inventory the next morning she'd like to get a ride to the ravine.

The old man rode along, sitting up front with Mr. Earl, Creasie rode in the back. She sat just behind the driver's seat, and though the old man couldn't turn his head to look back at her she could see his eyes cutting left trying to. Once he turned his shoulders and glanced at her, and she was looking at him. He scowled and turned back to face forward. Said not a word when Mr. Earl dropped her off, said he'd be back by around five that afternoon.

She carried a large bag with her, a tote bag, and stuffed in the bottom of it beneath some old clothes Miss Birdie had given her was her real gift for Aunt Vish.

It was early November. She made her way down the trail, still leaved but thinning, trees looking puny but arcing up scary and their colors darkening away from October bright. But morning sun sleeving through them fuzzy yellow and cheerful enough, though it was hard for this to warm her heart, bent on a purpose.

Vish was sitting on her porch in her rocking chair, saw her walking up and kept rocking, working her lip on the snuff. Didn't look a bit different, old woman was ageless. Time passed just through her, moving on, leaving her toughened and unmoved, she'd beaten it, looked like. Wearing a colorless old dress, a yellowed old piece of sackcloth looked like wrapped around her head, so she looked like some kind of black Arab, rocking and watching her. Creasie reached into the tote bag, pulled out the paper sack, and set it down beside Vish's old dusty bare feet, there like the roots of a blackened cypress pulled up and dried hard in the dry air. Toenails like black bark chips on burnt sticks.

-What's that, now? Vish said.

She didn't say anything, just stood there. Vish stopped her rocking, looked down at the sack, then leaned forward to reach it, pulled the top open and peeked inside. She leaned over farther, fished into the sack, and pulled out the pair of lace-up shoes, a pair of low dress boots.

-They bout your size, I figure, Creasie said.

She'd seen Miss Birdie wearing them and then didn't see them for a long time and had heard her say they didn't feel right on her feet, didn't like the heel, which was kind of high, about a two-inch heel. And they sat in the back of her closet long enough to be forgotten and then the last afternoon before they were going to take Mr. Junius home, while they were having their coffee after dinner, Creasie found them in there and tossed them out the bedroom window, sneaked over and picked them up late that night after they'd gone to bed, and took them back to the cabin.

Vish set the boots in front of her chair beside her feet and looked at them, working her mouth. She leaned over and spat off the porch, looked at the shoes again. She took the sole of one foot and rubbed it against one old withered bare shank, then did the same with the other. Angled them into the boots and pushed down into them. She lifted her feet and plocked them in the boots down on the porch boards a couple of times.

-Lace them for me, she said.

Creasie got down on her hands and knees in front of Vish and laced up the boots.

-Help me up.

She helped Vish stand up. Vish looked out over the tops of the trees and Creasie could see her flexing her old feet and stiff toes inside the soft leather boots. She bent her knees just the slightest bit and stood back up, then sat down in the chair.

-What you want, now?

She told her. And after a minute Vish said to help her up again. She went inside the cabin, stayed for a long time it seemed like, her new boots clopping on the pine floors, then finally came back out and handed Creasie a little pouch, just a piece of old fabric tied into a pouch with a piece of black thread.

-Just a little pinch in a cup of coffee be plenty.

-Yes'm.

-And child. You never got it from Vish.

-Yes'm.

She tucked the little pouch into the pocket of her coat and went over to her cabin and made a fire in the stove. She drank some coffee and sat in her living room looking out the window at the trees and the little glow of light around all the darkening leaves. There was a little breeze all day, that would come and go, and the tops of the trees seemed to jiggle in a secret and perverse delight at their imminent fall. It was nice sitting in her cabin again, which seemed abandoned forever of what she'd had there, the life with her grandmother and mother, the walls insulated with decades of the comics pages from the Sunday papers. Dust on everything like a light and settled, dried silt. Cobwebs and spiderwebs like glinting decorations in the fading light.

Toward the late afternoon she banked the stove, closed the cabin, and walked back up the trail and waited at its head for Earl and Junius to drive up. Pretty soon they did, she got in the back, they drove back out. She thanked Earl for the ride. He said he'd see her at breakfast, that Miss Birdie had some supper fixed for him.

-You need anything to eat? he asked her. -Papa's staying here tonight, I'm going to call it a day, take him home in the morning. You can come in and get a plate.

Junius was asleep in his seat, snoring.

-No, sir, I had something, she lied. She wasn't hungry.

She went to her place and took the little pouch from her coat pocket and put it up on the shelf in the kitchen beside her coffee tin. She went to bed early.

~

LATE NOVEMBER, WHAT was left of a hurricane down on the coast come through, cracked off the tops of two pine trees at the pasture's edge, pushed down one of the old oaks in the Urquharts' front yard, big roots exposed and clods of red dirt hanging from them. Mr. Earl hired some men to come out and saw the tree up to season for firewood, and Creasie had thought how Frank would be doing that, had he stayed. The chain saws whined and muttered for two days, and unsplit cordwood stacked up out on the north side of Creasie's cabin, under the shed along the fence line. And December then. She went to town on Christmas Eve and did some shopping for herself. She bought a little wristwatch with a gold band, and set it by the clock tower at the Catholic church, and she took a late supper at the bus station. It was a breakfast supper, scrambled eggs and a piece of sugar ham and toast and coffee. Then she hailed a cab as it was rolling slow past the monument. The driver got out to let her in, an old colored man wearing a cabbie's cap with the short plastic bill.

-Yes, ma'am, evening, ma'am, he said, closing her door and getting back into the driver's seat. -Where to?

She settled herself, touched the wristwatch on her arm, put her hands in her lap.

-The Urquhart house, out on the Macon highway.

The driver looked at her in the rearview mirror a second.

-Yes, ma'am, he said. -Yes, ma'am, that fare might be a mite steep.

-Yes, sir, I know it, that's all right, she said. -It's Christmas Eve.

He smiled and laughed, put the old station wagon into gear.

-Yes, ma'am, all right then, he said, and drove her on out, the radio tuned to a station playing Christmas music.

-Going to spend Christmas with your family, then, ma'am? he said.

-Yes, sir, Creasie said. -I am.

-That's nice, he said. -Me, too. He looked at her in the mirror, but she looked away, and he didn't talk anymore, and let her off in the dark driveway of the Urquharts' house. She paid him.

-You sure this all right, ma'am? he said. -Looks like nobody's home.

-Yes, sir, they just out for the evening.

He touched his cap in parting and drove off. She watched the headlights swing back onto the highway and stood in the darkened driveway a few minutes. Miss Birdie and Mr. Earl were in town with their children and grandchildren. They'd come in later, then get up in the morning and go over to Alabama, see old Junius. Then come back later that night.

From where she lay on her bed awake she saw their headlights swing into the driveway and then the garage. She kept no light, didn't want them to know if she was out there or not. Was a still night, and cold. She huddled under the covers in her clothes, shoes beside the bed. Woke up the next morning late and tired, and the Urquharts' car gone. She ate some cold cornbread with buttermilk, went back to bed. Late in the afternoon she went over to the Urquhart house and made some vegetable soup, ate a little, and left it on the stove warm for when they returned. She saw the car pull in, headlights on, heard the doors open and shut. A little later a knock on the door. She got up and spoke through it. It was Mr. Earl.

-Just checking to see if you're all right, Creasie, he said.

-Yes, sir, I'm okay. She mustered a little chuckle to reassure him. Oh yes, she was a happy nigger.

He said, -You have a good Christmas?

-Oh, yes, sir, I went to see some kinfolks in town.

-I didn't know you had kin in town.

-Yes, sir. Distant.

-Well, good, good. Well, we'll see you in the morning then.

-Yes, sir.

After a moment he said, -Merry Christmas.

-Yes, sir, she said. -Merry Christmas to you, too.

And next morning she was up, washed, and cooking breakfast for Mr. Earl, who went in to work early as usual, for the after-Christmas sale. And Miss Birdie up early, too, already had the coffee going when Creasie got there. She did some cleaning up. And through December, and January, no visit from Mr. Junius, until the end of the month one afternoon Mr. Earl announced he was going to get his papa and bring him over, he'd been feeling poorly, and was going to let him rest up awhile here and eat well, and visit with Levi and Rae and Merry. Next morning he went to get the old man and came back with him in the afternoon.

Old man had lost weight, was kind of ashy pale. Stayed in the guest room in the back for most of that evening and the next day, not much left in him she figured, but enough to blow on out like a bit of dust on the windowsill. She offered to take him some soup but Miss Birdie said no, she'd take it back to him. Offered to take him some coffee the next morning, Miss Birdie said -No he likes me taking care of him I think, getting sentimental in his old age. He finally came out of the room for dinner that day on his cane, walking slow and wearing pajamas and a bathrobe, shuffling his way down the hall and through the sunporch and dining room to the kitchen, and sat down at the kitchen table to have lunch with Miss Birdie and Mr. Earl. Creasie served them and went into the pantry to eat. She sat down and set her plate on a shelf and put her fingers into the pocket of her apron, where she had the little pouch Vish had given her. Brought it up and sniffed at it. It was a tangy rottenness in there, like some kind of noxious mushroom dust. She heard them clattering their plates, heard that die down, heard more talking. Got up and went back into the kitchen, poured coffee for Mr. Earl and Miss Birdie, took it to the table.

-You want some coffee, too, Mr. Junius, she said, no expression on her face.

-No, no, none for me, he mumbled, gruff and not looking at her.

She went back into the kitchen, stood by the window looking out.

-You sure you don't want a cup of coffee, Mr. Junius?

-I said I didn't. She heard him grumbling to them about her.

-I think I'll go over to the lake for some exercise, Mr. Earl said. -Cut some wood from that tree that fell last year.

-Earl, don't tax yourself, Miss Birdie said. -We got plenty of wood from that tree that fell in the storm.

-That's still green, won't be dry till next year, Earl said. -And we're a little low on seasoned wood here at the house. That tree's been down more than a year and I imagine it's ready. I just feel like getting out and doing it, anyway. Need some fresh air.

-I'd go with you, I was feeling better, old Junius grumbled, and headed shuffling back to his room.

Just her lot to live here, wait on these people, live in that shanty out back of their house, be at their beck and call. And nobody but them, anyway. Mama dead since she was so little, her daddy she didn't know where, gone off, could be dead, Vish never said. She stood at the window. She saw, out on the side lawn and in a flat dull ray of winter sun angling over the hedges through the junkyard across the road, the endless days of nothing but the same, and being nothing but a nigger in the world.

The others had left the dining room. She was alone. She poured a fresh cup of coffee, took out the pouch, poured it all into the cup, and stirred it. She took it back to Mr. Junius's room and tapped on the door. No answer.

She went on in. He was asleep. She set the coffee on the table beside the bed.

-Just in case you changes your mind, she said, in case he was really awake. He said nothing, breathing heavy. She went out, back to the kitchen, into the pantry, and sat in her chair. Waiting and hoping, and dreading, too. Didn't know how long she'd sat there when she heard Mr. Earl come into the kitchen in his boots, heard a clatter in the sink.

He stuck his head into the pantry, scowling.

-What the hell did you do to that coffee?

She sat there like a mute, frozen. Then she managed to say, -Is he all right?

Earl snorted.

-He's better off than I am. I'm the one tried to drink it. That's the worst cup of coffee I've ever had in my life. Tasted kind of like Birdie put some more of that goddamn sassafras in the pot again. Or something.

He just stared at her a minute, then shook his head, saying something to himself.

-Don't you bother him anymore, he said. -And make a fresh pot of coffee. Just coffee. I'll be back in about an hour.

-Yes, sir, she managed to whisper, after he'd gone out, the screen door slapped to, the truck door slammed, the truck rumbled off. The quiet came back, there in the pantry.

Last time anybody saw him alive.

Finus Resurrectus

HE WAS RESCUED BY the foursome he'd passed on the fairway of hole number 12. Pumped out, unconscious, and carried to the emergency room in the cart of one of the men who'd hit before him on 13. He lay overnight in a bed on the fourth floor of the hospital, and the next morning Orin Heath came up to give him a last check-over before letting him go home. Orin poured himself a flask cap of whiskey, opened the window, and sat in a chair beside it to smoke a cigarette.

-Looks like you'll miss Birdie's funeral, he said.

Finus nodded. -Might have to.

-How you feeling?

-Not too bad, considering.

-Did you have what they like to call in the *National Enquirer* a near-death experience?

-White light and all that? No. Birdie did, out at the rest home.

-I heard they had to revive her out there.

They were quiet awhile.

-Have a drink?

Finus shook his head no.

-Your daddy was quite a drinker, too, wasn't he, Finus said. -What was his name? He asked though he knew and Orin knew he knew this unless the hole 13 pond water had gotten into his brain.

-Cornelius, Orin said. -Yes, he liked the corn. Said his name gave him a predilection for craving corn whiskey from the getgo. I ever tell you how I got my name?

-No.

It was a game, almost a ritual, with them, came up every year or so in the regular banter. There was often some slight change in the story.

-I was an accidental conception, Orin said. -Papa said to me one day when he had a load of corn in him that I was conceived on a romantic evening out in a boat on the lake, and they had it rocking. There was a loon calling, round there. Heat lightning way off, purple sky. He had a moment there, forgot who he was with. Came the time to make a decision, to take it out or leave it in. Do I take it out, or leave it in? Looked down at her face in a flicker of lightning glare, she was a stranger, made him wild with lust. Out, or in? Out, Or-in? My name reflects the grave finality of his decision.

-That's preposterous. What's that about the loon?

-There was a loon. It's a strange and ancient, solitary bird. Got an egg the greenish color of tarnished copper, speckled brown. It was in the summer in the northeast, in New England, where he was at school. He brought her back here but she was never happy.

Finus said, -I believe I was named after an Irish chieftain, but I'm not sure. That or they decided I was just the finest-looking young'un.

-The loon's got a strange call.

-You sound like you been talking to Euple.

-He came in the other day.

-Was he talking about loons?

-No.

-Beans?

-Digestive problems. He fears it's cancer. I sent him for some tests.

-What do you think?

-Intestinal gas, Orin said. -Constipation. Talks about beans, eats nothing but meat. Never drinks water. He's dry as beef jerky inside.

-What did you give him for it?

-Nothing. Told him to drink some of those herbal teas, instead of drinking coffee all day. I used to use them for remedies way back, before they got into the stores. I had an interest back then in what they call alternative medicine these days.

-Just the old remedies.

-Yeah. Old medicine woman down in the ravine used to make me up herb tea leaves, roots, all that crap. Worked about as well as pharmaceuticals, then. She had a garden somewhere down in there, grew what she didn't find wild in the woods.

-Old Vish.

-That's right.

-She used to treat all the black folks back then didn't she.

-Well, some. Midwife, mostly. But hell she knew as much in her own way as we did, in those days. What, you want a remedy? Can't cure old age, my friend.

Finus stood up from the edge of the bed. After a moment he said, -I've never believed your papa's story. I believe Orin is derivative in some oblique way of Cornelius.

-Well, Orin said, I have rather liked being an accident. It's relieved me of some of the burden of accomplishment. You seem to be feeling better.

-I'm all right.

Orin got up, tossed his cigarette out the window, and closed it.

-You can go on home if you want to. I'll give you a ride. Your cart's in the shop.

-All right. Maybe I can get out to Birdie's later on, anyway.

-Nobody'd blame you if you didn't. It's not every day an old man crashes his golf cart.

-I feel all right, Finus said.

-Just take it easy, Orin said.

-I will.

-I fed your dog, let him out to do his business.

-I thank you, Finus said. -I'd like to get on home now.

-At your service, Lazarus.

~

HE WAITED, LOOKING out the window of his apartment, until Orin's car had turned the corner, then skitched his cheek at Mike. The old dog looked up with his sad vacant eyes.

-Come on, old boy, let's take a drive.

Mike followed him slowly down the stairs, taking one at a time on his old shoulders, claws clicking on the wooden steps, scratching on the sidewalk. Finus opened the pickup's passenger door and gave him a little boost to get him onto the seat, where Mike settled down and put his snout onto his forepaws again, just like he'd been on the floor. But he was alert.

Finus took old winding Poplar Avenue to the north end of town, out past the shopping center and up the long hill, pulled over in the little dirt clearing in front of the old ruined Case house and shut off the engine, went around and helped Mike down from the truck. Together they walked slowly, both of them a little shaky-legged, careful of exposed roots and gopher holes, down the path that led down into the ravine. Though the day was dry and had not cooled, he felt an instant drop in the temperature along the shady path, which had the softened and weed-edged appearance of an old path not used so much anymore. Finus was aware of birdsong all about him, and began to notice them flitting and fluttering in the low limbs and wild shrubs on either side of the path, and crossing the path ahead of him in short bursts of flight.

They came to the low and shaded clearing at the base of the ravine. The little leafy tunnel of the trail opened up into what could only be called a woodland cathedral, its ceiling the boughs and leaves of tall oaks, sycamores, sweet gums, beech trees, and pines. The floor carpeted with pine needles and brown leaves, and furnished with small shrubby trees and the remains of a half a dozen small plank cabins on brick and pine-stump posts. These all stood on one side of a tiny creek that wound down toward a dense-looking swampy area, and on the other side of which stood bamboo thickets and lower-limbed, moss-draped live oaks. All appeared to be abandoned, at first look. Then he saw something on the little porch of the far one, and a movement, and went that way.

She sat in an old paintless rocker, though not rocking, and her eyes though cataracted looked unmistakably at him. She was as knotted up as if she were actually a strip of cured leather someone had twisted into shapes resembling a head, shoulders, crooked arms and hands, and a pair of feet on shanks so thin they couldn't possibly hold her up. She was barefoot, though her feet were a blackened color such that he'd had to look twice to determine they weren't in some worn-thin pair of old leather soleless shoes. Her face like an old burnt knot of lighter pine from within which the two milky pools of hardened sap regarded him calmly.

-Afternoon, Finus said, standing there.

Her eyes cut momentarily to old Mike standing droop-headed at his side.

-Are you Miss Vish? Finus said.

She nodded again, continued to look his way without speaking.

-I'm Finus Bates, run a little newspaper in town. This is my old dog, Mike.

-I don't much like dogs, she said, her voice phlegmatic but strong for that. Then she said, nodding toward Mike, -You seems pretty healthy, yourself, for an old gentleman, but your old dog is ailing.

-Yes, I expect he won't be around much longer.

-I don't know much about treating dogs, she said. -Sometimes I treated a cat or a horse or a cow, but never could do much to help a dog.

-That's all right, I'll just let him go when he's ready.

She looked at him a moment, nodded.

-Yes, sir, what can I do for you?

Finus said Dr. Orin Heath had told him about her. She said nothing, working her mouth a little bit, then nodded.

-How he doing, then?

-All right, all things considered.

-Still drinking that whiskey?

-Yes.

-Well, she said after a moment, it ain't killed him yet. Maybe it keeping him alive.

-May be, Finus said.

-Them cigarettes gon kill him, though.

-I expect they will, soon enough.

-Yes, sir, soon enough. Is there something I can do for Dr. Heath, then? Ain't nothing I can give him make him stop that whiskey or smoking.

-No, I just wanted to ask you about a couple of things.

She nodded. -You knew Mr. Case, now, ain't that so.

-Yes, I did know him. I always heard he left this land open for the folks that lived here in the ravine.

She nodded. -He left it so can't nobody clear or build down here, so his children can't let nobody do it, for some time.

-How long he make that for?

-He ask me how long did I think before everybody live down here be moved out into town. I said could be just ten year, could be twenty, thirty, or longer. Just depend on how much the younger folks likes it, or if they gets restless or not. He say, You think could be forty year, Vish? I said, May be, but I doubt it. Well, he say, just in case, and make it forty year. That was near about forty year ago, and now I'm the only one left down here. I figure any day the Case children gon get a judge to let them change the papers, tear it all down, if they remember to. She laughed. -With me goes the ravine, I speck. I speck they gon put another shopping center right here someday.

Finus looked at this old woman looking at him like she'd watch a snake.

-You ever help out Mrs. Birdie Urquhart, lives out on the Macon highway?

She considered that.

-No, sir, don't believe I ever helped her out none.

-Did you ever know the woman worked for her, Creasie Anderson?

She didn't answer for a minute, then, -Yes, sir, she from down here in the ravine. I raised her. But she ain't lived here in a long time.

-How long she been gone?

-Moved out from here to the Urquharts' when she was just a girl, many year ago.

-Did she keep a place back here?

-Yes, sir, had a place. Ain't been back to it in a long time, though.

-When would you say was the last time she used her place here, then?

-Couldn't say, I reckon. Ain't seen her here in a long time.

Finus looked around at the other cabins.

-Which one was hers, then, you don't mind my asking?

The old woman cut her eyes without moving her head to look at the other cabins.

-That old green one over there was hers.

Finus looked. One of the cabins was a flaked and faded dark green color.

-You reckon it'd be all right if I took a look around it?

After a moment the old woman nodded.

-I don't reckon it make a whole lot of difference, she said. -She don't never come back here no more.

-I appreciate your time, Finus said. -You take care, now.

-Yes, sir. Tell Dr. Heath I said good day.

-I will.

Mike following stiffly, Finus walked over to the green cabin and mounted its rickety porch. He pushed on the old plank door and it gave way to a cobwebbed and ratty single room that gave way itself to what looked like a tiny kitchen in the rear, where he could see the edge of an old wood stove there. In the main room there was just an old stuffed chair, torn about the arms and cushion and backrest and stained with water and whatever. A little table stood near it, bare. The walls were covered with what appeared to be faded Sunday comics pages, torn and stained and splotched with age and water damage. In the kitchen the stove was bare except for a rusted cast-iron pan sitting on one of the heating plates. There was an old metal sink with no faucets but with a drain that appeared to run out through the wall. Above the sink there was a single shelf on which sat a salt box folded in upon itself, shredded paper in a mound of something could have been once flour or cornmeal. A lard tin. A mason jar stood next to it, shrouded in cobwebs and dust. He leaned in close to it, something inside. A black and gnarled little knot of something, like a

charred fist of an old monkey or something. Finus heard a huffing sound, Mike settling down on the floor beside him, old baleful eyes looking at nothing.

-Poor old Mike, Finus said, bending stiffly over himself to
scratch the dog's head. Mike's eyes moved to him but otherwise
he didn't respond. Finus straightened up and looked at the jar
again, took it off the shelf and wiped the cobwebs and dust away
and peered closely at whatever it was inside there. Shriveled ten-
donish piece at either end, looked to have been severed away. He
gently coaxed Mike up off the floor and led him outside. The
old woman was still on her porch in her rocker. Seemed to be
looking at nothing, just out through the woods. Finus stepped
carefully down the steps of the porch and, Mike slowly and stiffly
making his way beside him, walked back over and stood at the
base of the porch steps.

-Sorry to trouble you again, Miss Vish, he said. -I just wanted to
ask one more thing.

She nodded. Eyes cut just for a second to the jar he held in
his hand.

-Yes, sir.

-I was asking Dr. Heath about poisons, ways folks might poison
someone if they had a mind to do it.

She looked at him, even cocked her head just a fraction of
an inch.

-Poisons? she said. Then an odd little movement ticked at the
thin licorice twist of her mouth. The old lips opened a hair and
something between an enervated laugh and a wheeze came out.
-Naw, sir, she said then, don't truck in no poisons.

-Say you don't.

-No, sir, and her eyes went back to where they rested on something over his head across the tiny creek in the swampy woods.
-No sir, she said again, managing an emphatic little movement of

her head, the white straw and scarce hair there looking as if permanently blown and dried hard away from her face like a frost-driven shrub. -Poisons invented by the white folks. Black folks don't need no poisons.

-Why's that?

-Well, sir, she said, we got the white folks, poison enough. Then she bared her gums, gave that little wheezy laugh. -I reckon I can say that nowadays, cain't I.

-I reckon you can say whatever you want to.

She nodded.

-Ain't always been the case, she said.

Finus held the jar up a tad so the light caught it, seemed to be soaked up by the black gnarl inside it, a tiny black hole into which the fading afternoon light was sucked.

-You got any idea what this thing she was keeping on her shelf might be?

Old woman rocked once, using an old toe as black as the thing in the jar, about as gnarled, and seemed to regard the jar with her opaque eyes.

-I can't see too good, she said.

-It's just a mason jar. Got something in it I can't tell what it is. It was on Creasie's shelf, in the kitchen.

-Naw, sir, she finally said, drawing out the words. -Look to be some kind of old preserves, to me. Might be some old figs drawed up. Long past eating.

-I'll bet you're right on that.

-Might have something to eat inside, you hungry.

-Well, Finus said after a moment, I appreciate that. But I believe I'll pass. He nodded by way of saying good day, made his way with hobbling old Mike back up the trail toward his truck.

A Lost Paradise

S HE HAD NEVER been naked in public in her life. She had
been naked outdoors but not within sight of others aside from her
friend Avis. Now it felt naked but not quite the same, though who's
to say since she never went outside naked, not out in the open air
with no cover. This was not naked the same way, but she was getting used to it. And she wasn't anymore like walking, but more like
what you call flying in a dream, just sort of moving just ahead of
some awareness of the body or of moving itself, an effortless here
and there. She had no voice but a sound like a gentle wind rattling
dry fall leaves. Once in a moment she was frightened by the shadowy presence of tangled live oak limbs all around her. Then she
was near and among the presence of the little town of Silverhill
down near the Alabama coast, and the pecan groves in between
there and Fairhope, and then there was the bay and the sifting of
breeze through the wings of a flock of gulls who seemed to see her
and roll their beady eyes in her direction and nearly crash into one
another in distraction. She held her long dark hair out of her eyes
and gazed upon herself at that height and thought, Oh, I was beautiful, I look like, I don't know. It was like the brief moment in her
life between a child's comfort in her own skin, and the burning
new awareness of what she was to a man.

Here, the streets of Fairhope were like none of the streets

when she was a child and they would visit—all these homes had sprung up since then, none of the old waterfront homes survived, long gone, she had long ago mourned them and now their own ghosts lay over the newer homes like veils, or mosquito netting. She skimmed through the old live oak tops on down to the Grand Hotel, the ghost of the original Point Clear Hotel itself now barely visible to her among the broad oak boughs and the steam coming from the ventilation pipes in the roof of its successor. None of the long galleries and the swings, though the promenade was the same. On the bay, on the water's surface and out between two sunglint sailboats, a man leaning himself back out over the chop said *hah!* when his boat gave a tilt in her direction as she rose up to avoid a little wave. The man nearly fell out of his boat.

She spread her arms and legs and let the foamy tips of the chop skim into her navel, then deep into the water without the resistance to which she was accustomed, past the hulls of sunken fishing boats, the cracked beams of sailing vessels and the long bent and wrenched-off arms of hapless shrimp boats, the skeletal hulls of great tarpon resting in their long-quiet disgust, and automobiles, some she seemed to recognize from her youth, and she remembered the sinking of an early ferry taking travelers across to Mobile. She passed in through the rusted torpedo shaft of a submarine of which no one knew save those poor souls still locked inside, and drifted slowly past the stricken eyes of the crew boys who rode it to its death, and one said, Bless you, Miss Birdie, and she kissed his concave, whiskered cheek—he was all tears, in the briny deep. She left through the molecular lacunae of its old prop shaft and spinning blades. Seeing spindly legs ahead of her went to look, and circled with the speckled trout and a few lost snapper the beams of a natural gas derrick, and then swam away and left the water. Ahead of her lay the old fort. Through the decrepit buildings that were the captain's quarters and the officers' and enlisted men's barracks, she came through cracked panes which gave her some dread, and along the floors where boards had pulled apart from one another in age and ill health, these buildings propped up with the crude buttresses of those who would preserve them, their galleries gone as if from faces had fallen their features, poor noses and teeth and jaw, exposing the yaw of the corpse. She was caressed by the cool, clipped grass of the lawn inside the fortress itself, seeming ancient but no older than her father were he still alive. She drifted through the dark archways and chambers and then back into the yard, paused at the bloodstain on the steps where she'd had her picture taken as a girl with her sisters, where some confederate had died and left his ineradicable mark in the mortar. She slipped over the lip of the gun bay for the old disappearing cannon, no longer there, but its ghost too still lingering, even steel leaving its shape somehow in the air, a lingering particulate shade, collecting itself in her honor, to swing up and out over the water, and she entered its bore and followed its sighting above the Gulf itself and kept going, the earth receding, and she thought she must keep going into the lighter air and nothingness, but was drawn back in a dreamlike shift from there to here, the old lighthouse, in the balmy air currents moving east along the peninsula. Over the old site of Palmetto Cove. She heard cries and went down. There were the general calls of the animals once native to the shore, the wild hogs descended from the pigs the soldiers let go when the fort was first shut down, and the older, indigenous bears and panthers and even the shy, retiring ivorybill. The glow from the treasure laid in by pirates and sought by everyone and never found now called to her from beneath cypress but she paid it no mind. There were pirates hanging a man from the hanging tree, and whipping others back into the water. But those cries she heard first now became apparent to her in the spirits of two young girls who drowned in the storm of '06, huddled in the corner of a room in the house built by their father, who had earlier washed into the bay, their poor mother tumbled into a drowned thicket of scrub oaks whose dense branches held her by her clothing until the water rose and drowned her too. Soldiers would find their ravaged bodies in the trees in Bon Secour and would be ashamed at their own interest in the girls' bawdy contortions, long dresses lifted and twisted about their heads like murderous turbans, their drawers torn and muddy. A soldier unable to contain himself would begin to cry, as the others stared and drifted in the tide, and then discovered another girl alive and hanging from the high branches by her long blond hair.

This was a paradise, once, Pappy said. There, he was with her again.

It's all gone now. We had all our homes in here, you probably can't see it.

Though she did, now, free as she was to see all that had been in her mind's eye throughout her life, the little pine board homes with sheet tin roofs, and the smallish porches and wash sheds out back, the raked sand yards and the dogs roaming free and chasing off into the thickets after wild boar and deer. She remembered her grandmother once stepped out onto the front porch and shot a boar attacking their dogs, with a rifle she held seemed longer than she was. And all the homes separated by the dunes and the scrub oak thickets and some up on little hard dunes and the others nestled down into the flats between the shifting oblong mounds over which the children ran. And there were paths from there across the old fort road to the Gulf beach, and the children roamed them with the wildlife and stayed out of one another's way, human and animal, with a kind of natural grace.

You have no memory of your own, of the storm, I expect.

I remember the sound of the wind, and of being cold and in the water, in the dark, and being cold on the little hill by the oak trees.

She felt a cool breeze and they were a memory of hands clapping, a singing around the fireplace in his old home down on the coast, here on the peninsula, before the storm that blew it away, when she and her mother and father still lived with him and her grandmother there, before Pud and Lucy were born, and she smelled the heavy salt air, felt the cool freshness of the white sand outside the open windows, and heard the breeze in the tops of the longleaf pines, and the old heartpine house timbers groaned.

See here it is again, Pappy said. The sand white as sugar, the dunes high as the tops of the pines, and the little live oaks and the sea oats on them rustling and swaying, the tops of the little oaks swept back like wild women standing facing the wind so that their hair is blown back and their faces beautifully ravaged by it, and the white sand blowing in the little drifts and ribbing the upside of the dunes and in gentle swells down the sides toward the bay, stitched with the milkwort, the backdune drifts filled with the yellow flowering partridge pea and cropped up you see these wax myrtles and cacti and the yaupon holly, this wild rosemary, and you see these little holes for the ghost crabs and the beach mice, and their tracks leading to and fro. There was life everywhere, it was full and teeming with life, and with joy. There was no locks on any of our doors, which people say but it was true, here, there was simply no one and nothing to fear here, we knew everyone else and we knew the whole world here. We ate and lived on what was here, we needed nothing much from the outside. The fish from the sea. We kept pigs and cattle, a kind of longhorn which would feed on the palmettos and ranged the woods. And there were deer, chickens. Some things would not grow well and we traded for those from inland, but most what we needed we kept or raised.

The floor of the little bay there was full of sweet oysters you could scoop up in your hands, and the wild ducks came in the fall and stayed all winter long, part of the Lord's bounty. In the evenings in good weather the young people made fires of drift-wood on the beach and gathered to sing songs and talk and to hunt for the sea turtles when the moon was full, and the ones in love would walk the sandy paths among the dunes. We had dances for them. It was an innocence.

We truly were a happy people. Some said they didn't miss it after it was gone but I did, aye, I still do miss every leaf and little grain of sand. We were three generations here, going on four, and most of us bar pilots. We moved by water, every boy sailing small boats as easy as breathing, came natural to us. This is where we belonged, see. It was like being made to leave paradise and the only life we knew, when it was destroyed. But we couldn't go back for the very land itself was washed away, nothing left. Wiped off the face of the earth. Nothing to do but find another life some-where. That's why we moved inland.

It almost seemed it was a punishment. Like we had grown proud and inward. You can have a little world of your own but you cannot be so proud that you shut out the rest of the world entirely. Cousins marrying, such as that. A taking advantage of the bounty, it seemed it was. I don't know. A vague corruption, child. And then come the flood. It seemed like something terrible from the good book, to me.

The day before the storm it was raining hard and steady, and there was a blow. We watched it from the south beach and went home. Late in the evening there was a terrific crash in the sky, and a flash of light. We tried to go to the south beach again but had to take a rowboat where we'd walked earlier, the water was already so high. And by three or four in the morning it was blowing so hard the houses shook, and the water rushed beneath the houses, and the driftwood logs it carried bumped and crashed against the pil-ings and the floors.

Those who'd been back to the south beach later said the water had been like a great gray wall coming toward the shore, and it was all about us in that blackness later on. Not another flash of lightning, no more thunder, just a terrible roaring and howling of the wind. I and your father made our way to the Dixons' next house down to see how they were faring, pulling our way by the limbs of strong shrubs and the smaller trees. And when we arrived there we could see a lantern light in their upper floor and their faces in the dormer windows, and as we approached their gallery the whole house gave way and floated into the bay like a doomed ship departing, their hands reaching out the windows for salvation where there was none.

We made straight back to the house and gathered you all up, and lashed ourselves together with rope, and when we stepped off the gallery we had to hold you above our heads as the water was then shoulder deep. There was an old longhorn there at the edge of the gallery and we held to his horns and drove him to the edge of the yard towards high ground, to the fence, where we let him go and he was washed away. We knocked down the fence to get to the little hill where there were four strong oak trees, and when we got there we lashed ourselves to them, and each to the other. And others arrived there in the storm, finding some way, and they lay flat on the ground, and clutched onto us, trying not to be blown away by the wind. McCutcheon was struck in the face by a flying piece of driftwood and died there on the spot. Something struck me in the chest and your grandmother held me up as I was unconscious for a while, else I'd have drowned then as the water was for a while even up over the little hill itself.

We held on there through the night, and when dawn came the water had gone down some and the gale died a bit, though it was still strong. Still we found oranges lying about that had been knocked from trees in the grove, and we found potatoes there, and a single egg lying there, a single egg! On the ground. When the water had gone down a bit more we dug up fence posts that were miraculously dry and managed to make a fire and roast that egg and feed it to you and the other two young ones there with us. We found jars of preserves floating in a few inches of water in the kitchen and ate them from the jars with our fingers, they was the best thing we ever tasted. I'll bet you remember that.

After the soldiers came in their rowboats to rescue us and take us to the fort, after the waters had finally subsided, we returned to search for the dead. But all we could find was the body of poor Agnes Drummond, whose children and husband were lost and not to be recovered, in the ruins of her home, her hair which had been beautiful and rich in color now a tangled gray and matted about her stricken face and shoulders.

And where our home had been there was nothing but a little body of water, a still pond, and the high dunes were gone save the one that saved us. And the only home of the dozen or more that had stood there was the little plank house John Keesler had built with his own hands, and it skewed and bent like a freak house at the fair, you couldn't stand on its floors and keep your balance.

Some said we should find another place like this and rebuild, all together, those that survived, but we hadn't the heart to do it, child. This place itself was gone, disappeared, wiped off the face of the earth, and we couldn't help but see it as a sign that a time and place had ended and we should move on. That's when the Bateses helped us move up to Mercury. And so it's been, so it was.

If we have faltered as a family it is my fault, for letting the loss of this life I knew discourage me, so that I lost something of my sense of who we were, and I could not see life clearly from the new place that we came to live. I lived in confusion for some time, and was not wise as I should have been. If we had been here you never would have married Earl, though I think still he was not a bad man, he just had no vision, he plowed headlong into life like a man afraid, and I think most men are afraid. I cannot fault him for that for after we left here I knew some of that fear and lack of vision. It's the age, it's the way we live, it's difficult to overcome. I lost faith for a time in the ability of God to lead us, to give us that vision. I closed my eyes to his sight, and lost mine own.

Nobody faulted you, Pappy.

It's for no one else to do, Birdie. I fault myself. I don't condemn myself. I was human, like anyone else.

Where are you going? she said to him then. He was walking down a twilit white sand trail into the dense pine woods east of the house. He only raised his hand and was lost in the grainy light there. She was tired. She was drifting herself with a northern breeze to the Gulf side where gentle waves flopped and crushed themselves against the sand stained wet and draining. Two ladies lay on towels on the beach nearly naked, their skin glistening with oil. They seemed strange and familiar, too, like people she'd once known in a dream, and forgotten. Birdie went down and lay down on sand between them. They were sleeping. She looked up toward the deck of the beach house behind them and a young boy stood there, looking at her. She waved. He merely stared at her, and so she approached him and was there before him in the buffeting Gulf breeze. He was not afraid. He knew her, somehow. He put out his hand, and when he touched where she was he gave a start, and she wanted to say, it's only electricity, child, but she could not, and she rose away so that he would wonder for the rest of his life about the presence of this angel who visited him as he stood on a deck overlooking the Gulf of Mexico, when he was a just a boy.

Grievous Oscar

THERE WERE CARS everywhere, from the carport and down the driveways on both ends. Finus drove along the grass beside the driveway and parked by the sidewalk to the front door. But he chose to walk around back and go in the kitchen door, the familiar entrance, and avoid whoever might be playing gatekeeper at this event. Didn't really want to talk to Birdie's kinfolk or some righteous church woman full of baloney and saccharine goodwill. He went through the little archway between the carport and the kitchen door, opened the screen door, mounted the steps, and pushed open the stubborn door to the kitchen.

It was crowded, even in there, but at least those standing there were eating, occupied, and at best looked around with a chicken leg poised at their teeth and nodded, grinning at him, and kept eating. Howard Feckman did actually take a chicken wing from between his teeth a millimeter from biting in, set it down on the plate long enough to shake Finus's hand, then picked up another piece and bit on into it. In spite of all the congregated living bodies, which hovered over and around the tables of food, Finus could see and take in the impressive spread: dishes of broccoli and cheese casseroles, French green bean and mushroom soup casserole, apple crunch desserts, a coconut cake, several crusty pound cakes, large plates of cold fried chicken covered with plastic wrap, a massive ham, the cooling meat drawing up around a shank bone big as a severed sapling. Large aluminum pitchers of ice tea frosted with sweat, ice tinkling in tumblers as the tea was poured in. Sweet potato pudding with melted marshmallow topping. Dishes of snap beans cooked down and dark, sweet, and tartish. Baked squash with onion, soft as pudding. And tall slim sweating steel crankbuckets of homemade ice cream, vanilla and fresh peach, beside at least a dozen pies: glazed pecan, lemon icebox, sweet potato, custard, apple, chess, and what looked like a blackberry cobbler. The din from conversation and eating was considerable, almost made him smile.

He felt someone brush his elbow then and saw old Creasie standing there, eyes limpid and tired-looking, looking up at him. She wore a pretty pink dress with a clover print on it, and Finus was fairly sure it had been Birdie's once.

-Hello, Mr. Finus, she said to him.

-Hello, Creasie, he said. Finus wondered where this old woman would go now, what she would do. Maybe she had family somewhere, he had no idea. He wanted to ask her, but he didn't think he had the energy to listen, and he was certain she didn't much have the energy or will to tell him everything she could tell him. Same space, different worlds.

-Missed you at the services, Mr. Finus, she said then.

-Yeah, he said. -I wasn't feeling too well.

-Yes, sir. Better get yourself a plate, then, Creasie said. She reached over to the counter and got him a plate and some silverware. He took it from her hands, dark and weathered on the backs, light-colored in the palms.

-Thank you, Creasie, he said. -I believe I'm about to starve to death.

He got a plate and put some chicken, beans, squash casserole on it, and came back over by the sink and Creasie to eat it. He set the empty plate in the sink.

-You was hungry, she said.

They looked at one another for a minute.

-I was out to your old house in the ravine today.

She looked up at him as if not understanding his words for a second.

-Yes, sir, you was? What in the world was you doing way out there?

-Just exploring, I guess, he said. She nodded. -Had a conversation with old Vish out there. Was talking to Parnell Grimes yesterday, said some curious things, then Dr. Heath said I might talk to Vish about them.

-Miss Vish still alive, then, Creasie said. She nodded to herself and walked over to the sink and stacked a few small dishes in there. Finus followed her.

-I took the liberty of looking around your old place, he said. -Hope you don't mind.

-Umm, hmm, no sir, she said, running some water over the dishes and turning off the faucet, drying her fingers on the apron she wore over the skirt of her dress. -I don't never go out there no more.

-I was just curious, Finus said then, if you could tell me what is in that old mason jar in your kitchen. Strange-looking thing, aroused my curiosity.

She looked out the window, working at the snuff in her bottom lip for a second, then her eyes cut over at him.

-Yes, sir, what kind of old jar was it, now.

-A tall kind of mason jar, had some thing in it I can't even tell what it was. She was holding his eye then. -You know what I'm talking about then?

She nodded. Her attention seemed to wander a little and she sagged a little more in the shoulders.

-Fact, I got it out in the truck, if you'd like to see it, jog your memory.

She nodded again.

-I'll tell you, Mr. Finus. That was a long time ago. She stood there a long minute, seeming to think about something. -Yes, sir, I can tell you the story behind that jar, you help me do something here.

-All right, he said.

-You got a minute, then?

He nodded.

-Yes, sir, come on with me.

-Outside?

She nodded, motioning him to follow her. They went out the kitchen door, down the steps to the archway, and across the drive in front of the carport to the old shed out by the pumphouse. He followed her up to a door cut into the sheet metal siding, which was fastened to with an old hasp lock. Creasie reached up and shook the lock once, dropped it.

-I need to get in here for something.

-Do you not have the key?

-No, sir. Don't nobody know where the key to this old shed is. I didn't want to bust in there. You reckon it's all right to bust in, now?

She nodded toward the carport. -They's some tools in there back by the deep freeze, might be something that would work there.

He found a rusty-hinged toolbox and in the top tray a short crowbar, and brought that back over. He jammed the flat end behind the hasp lever and yanked and pried until the screws came out of the old wood, and the door swung free. He took hold of it and opened it wide, revealing a packed dirt floor with an old cylinder lawn mower and rusted child's wagon there, and shelves beginning chest high on which sat blackened hand tools and moldered collapsed cardboard boxes and wooden boxes topped with miscellaneous junk. On the shelf to their left sat a cobwebbed and rotten-clothed bizarre thing, a dummy of some kind with minstrel features, faded red lips and yellowed teeth and yellowed eye-whites, gazing at the space where the door now stood open, just over their heads. It almost made Finus jump.

-What in the hell is that thing? he said.

Creasie was standing there staring at it, something about her of the bereaved.

-Nothing but an old nigger dummy, Mr. Finus. What everybody done forgot about but me.

Finus Infinitus

HE SKIPPED THE council meeting that evening, sat at the kitchen table and sipped from a bourbon and water, and looked at the blackened heart inside the jar he'd set down beside his glass. He wasn't hungry after the plate of food out at Birdie's.

After staring at the telephone a while, he picked it up, called the press that printed the *Comet*, and told them not to run Birdie's obituary.

-Just pull it, he said. -I'll run it next week.

He took his drink into the living room, thought about turning on the television for late-night crap and decided not to. Mike shambled creakily in and humphed himself to the floor at his feet with a wheeze. About midnight he woke up with his neck in a crick from leaning it back on the sofa in sleep. Mike snored gently on the floor. He sat there awhile working his neck with his fingers, feeling tired to the marrow and last drop of old blood. Then he got up slowly, careful not to wake old Mike, and went down the stairs to the street and got into his pickup. He laid the jar from Creasie's house on the seat beside him and drove through town past the orphans' home and turned in at the cemetery, lights off, around to where he knew Earl Urquhart's grave was.

Wasn't hard to find, with the earth in a mound over Birdie's fresh grave. The air was cooler, though there was little breeze. Finus took the jar and walked over to the graves, not sure what he intended to do. But there lying beside Birdie's grave was a shovel, apparently left there by one of the gravediggers.

He read the stone. Earl Leroy Urquhart, 1899–1955.

-Well, old Earl, Finus said, I don't mean this as a desecration. Just a restoration, of sorts. If it's just an old pig's foot, I'm sorry, no disrespect intended.

He took the shovel and made four neat incisions in the turf at what he figured about chest level for the body of Earl down deep, and lifted it carefully and set it aside. Then he dug enough earth out to place the jar a foot or so deep in the hole. He replaced the dirt, packing it down with the sole of his Red Wing, leveled it, then knelt and placed the piece of turf back on top of it, pressing it and shaping it until as best he could tell the surgery wouldn't be too obvious.

He stood up, brushed his hands off on his pants, knocked the dirt off his boots with the shovel, and laid the shovel back down next to the mound of Birdie's earth where he'd found it. Stood there catching his breath. For the first time in his life he seemed to feel every one of his true and earthly years. Maybe it's coming my time, he thought, where my time here and the way I feel about it have come together and will take me out of this light and into another, or eternal darkness. He figured he could take it either way, wouldn't make much difference to the man he was here and now. That would be that and then, not this and now. He looked about. Down behind him in the area where he had used to park and rut with Merry Urquhart now there were neat lines of headstones just as there were in every other part of the cemetery, the place was about filled up. He looked up. The night was clear, and the nearly full moon he hadn't noticed but had worked by stood high above the magnolia trees at the cemetery's summit, between Finus and the dim penumbra of the lights in town. He heard something and saw it moving toward him along the narrow paved pathway from the street. Some kind of dog trotting along, veered away from him and through the stones between him and the magnolias and stopped there when it saw him watching it. It stood stock still, sideways, head turned his way, to see what he was going to do.

Finus stood stock still, too. It looked just like the dog in his death dream, the one he'd told Birdie about, charged with guarding his body while he slept. Though it was clear the dog didn't know him and feared him. A guilty, negligent dog.

-Hey! Finus called to it. The dog twitched but didn't run. Both stood still watching the other. Then after a minute or so the dog seemed to relax. He looked away from Finus, looked around the cemetery, feigning a casual manner, sniffed the grass at his feet, as if something interesting there had caught his attention for a second. It was a transparent attempt to look innocent. He looked back at Finus, as if Finus had said something else. He hadn't. Then the dog trotted on his way, weaving around headstones, crossed the gravel path at the crest of the hill and disappeared over it down into the lower parts of the cemetery out of sight. Finus watched him go. His heart was racing. When it calmed he looked around at where he was, at Birdie's grave, at Earl's stone, at the other stones shining dully in the moonlight, at his truck waiting stunned or suspended, incomplete without him.

~

HE SLEPT TILL two o'clock the next afternoon, took his time rousing, and went into the office at four, and finished rewriting her obituary early that evening. He took out the addendum about the poisoning, and inserted three new bulleted items:

- She was the best at making a little gumball out of sweet-gum sap of anyone yours truly has ever known.

- She developed later in life the ability to suck in her cheeks and make her lips into a funny little narrow pucker, made her look like a little mouse nibbling something, real comical, made all the children laugh.
- She once at age eighty speared an actual mouse using one of those sticks with a nail in the end of it, used for picking up paper trash, disgusted that everyone else had been too squeamish.

He put the copy in Lovie's basket, then put his overnight bag in the truck and helped Mike get up into the passenger seat. He filled the tank at the Shell station on the highway just south of town, then headed up the long hill that was the south ridge and rolled along the general decline to the Gulf coast.

It was a route he'd known since a small boy, though the roads had changed, improved. His grandfather accompanied them to the fort at the end of the peninsula, down on the Alabama Gulf coast, for dinner with the Commandant. His grandfather knew the Commandant, from the Spanish-American War. They ate by flickering lantern and candle light. Out the open, screened window, gentle summer waves flopped and crushed on the sand. Finus sat quietly as after dinner the grown-ups drank from small bowled glasses and his father and the Commandant smoked cigars that his grandfather leaned over and whispered to him came from Cuba.

-Go to the south window, Finus, and see if you can see the lights of Cuba.

He'd smirked at his grandfather, who knew he was too smart for that. His grandfather was big and open-faced, a bald and friendly giant, and his touch was gentle on Finus's shoulders and on his back, and when he tousled Finus's light brown hair. His parents were dressed in their best clothes, though he could not see his mother, she was eternally just at the edge of his eye. He was in his worsted wool suit, and the Commandant wore his dress jacket with the high collar and stars. The Commandant was a bachelor and had hired a Creole cook whose head at what seemed regular intervals appeared from behind the swinging door to the kitchen to look at him with oddly green eyes in her coppery face, and then disappeared again. The food was wonderful, fish in a sack, gumbo, fried grouper, bright white scallions like pearls with long green stalks, and boiled new potatoes so small and sweet they didn't even need butter. The Commandant gave him a very small measure of red wine. The others raised their glasses to him, love and admiration in their eyes.

~

HIS GRANDFATHER TOOK him just before dawn on horseback down the beach and turned in through a pass in the dunes toward the old lagoon. They rode around the lagoon and down a trail into the thick brush and piney woods and dismounted in a little clearing on the trail and tied the horse to a bush. Fragrant with citronella his grandfather had rubbed onto their faces and necks and hands, they made their way slowly in a cloud of mosquitoes, yellow flies buzzing fiercely about. It was first light, now, dawn seeping into the air. There were thick patches of saw palmetto they made their way around, stepping on hummocks of spongy ground around marshy spots. The faint blue light seeming to emanate from the little rounded clumps of needled branches at the tops of the pines. There were dense and compact water oaks draped with moss that in this light seemed gauzy veils hung from the arms of great skeletal ghosts. They came to the edge of a clearing smoked with low-hanging fog and haunted with gaunt old giants, suffering ancient leafless oaks and tall crooked poles that were once grand pines, and here his grandfather motioned for him to sit beside him on the grass and to be quiet. All else was quiet. The low fog moved almost imperceptibly within itself, a slow swirling with what breeze made its way into the swamp through the scrub thickets and saw grass and younger pines toward the water.

The birds had begun their singing and their calls, a tuning up of the world, and he began to see them dipping through the fog of the clearing from one part of the woods to another. Crows called from far off. He could hear the rooster doves lamenting. His grandfather touched his hand and motioned with his eyes to one of the old dead oaks, high up, and he looked in time to see a huge bird, its rakish red crest thrust from a hole there, and then the bird launched itself and flew high across the clearing in a loping manner, its body black but for the scarlet head and large painted patches of pure white on the wings, calling in a strange, strong but small-for-its-size-sounding *kent, kent,* like a piercing loud toy horn, and was gone in the mist. Then another bird, minus the crest but with the strong white slashes on its black wings and on its breast, followed, with the same call. And the woods seemed silent again after that, all other birds diminished to relative silence.

-That's the ivorybill, his grandfather said then. -Almost gone from this world. You should not ever forget it, Finus. You may not ever see them again.

He wouldn't. The big storm would wash the hotel away, his grandfather would die just two years later, and for some time his family did not go to the beach. Did he know this somehow, the vision of a child? He thought of the birds again as a teenager and tried for some time to find the spot. And when he finally did, after three early-morning attempts, and sat there the next dawn, he saw nothing but songbirds and crows. It was a part of the world that was gone for Finus, as was his grandfather.

-They're a shy bird, see, the old man had said. -Don't like people. And they need lots of woods, lots of old dead trees like this one around. They rip the old bark off and eat the grubs out of there. And when people cut down the woods and grow new trees, it takes too long for old dead trees to come around again, and the birds have nowhere to go. They need no one else but themselves.

They don't need the company of other birds, other animals. They're a solitary race of bird.

-Like you and me, Finus said.

The old man looked at him and laid a hand on his tangly brown hair.

-Ah, he said, you're too young for that, Finny. But you may be right. He smiled at him. -Don't be too hard on yourself, now. Don't be so hard to get along with.

-I'm not.

-No, you're easygoing. But you are a loner, aren't you?

-I like to be alone.

-I see it, his grandfather said. -It's too bad, but it's not so bad, after all. Just don't turn away from people so quick. Give them a long look, don't close up your heart, now.

-All right.

-An open heart will save you, but you have to be smart, too. You have to be careful who you open your heart to. Some people can't help but hurt you if they know it, he said, and kissed the young Finus on his forehead.

~

HE GOT THERE at midnight and found his key to the old cabin and climbed the creaking sand-blown steps to the shaky deck and let himself in and lay down right away in the main room. He and Mike slept together in one of the daybeds and while he slept the ghosts of those whose lives left some parts of themselves there visited him and laid their soft and fog-drifted hands upon him. They passed into him some of the energy that always generated within them but which they could never contain and gather to take shape in the world as they'd known it. He woke in the faint light and gull-calling of dawn. The air in the cabin was suffused with age, he hadn't been down there in decades. One front window was broken out, the glass on the dry wooden floor beneath it. A pair of beach sparrows flitted in and out of the window to a nest hole in the corner ceiling. He went over to the refrigerator, which was somehow miraculously humming. Inside he found two cold ancient Schlitz cans and drank one straight off, and carried the other with him out to the truck.

He and Mike made their way carefully down the deck steps and to the truck, and he drove down to what he thought was the old path road to the Palmetto Cove site, bulling through a couple of deep sandy spots and crashing through some low pine limbs until he broke out right at the bay shore and had to slam on the truck's brakes to keep from tipping into the water. When he stepped out there was a good breeze blowing from the north, and a good thing because otherwise he realized he'd have been attacked by yellow flies and mosquitoes and had brought nothing to protect himself from them.

He took off his shoes and socks and rolled his pants up and waded a few feet out into the bay and leaned over and began scooping at the sand of the bay until he came up with a good-sized oyster in each hand. He tossed them onto the bank where he'd stepped in and where Mike lay watching him. Mike sniffed the oysters and lay back down. Finus kept scooping till he had something like a dozen big bay oysters, then he waded back in and sat on the bank and opened them with the short blade of his pocket knife and ate them from the shell, drinking the salty water that clung to the oysters' edges. He drank the second Schlitz from the refrigerator, tossing the old tab top into the back of the truck from where he sat. The strong breeze cooled him and he felt so tired he had to lie down awhile. He fell asleep, lying there.

In his dream he was first with his father and mother and grandfather again at the Commandant's house down at the fort, and they were all around the table and happy. They toasted one another, and Finus was grown up in his mind in the dream but also still a little boy. He loved them so much. Some part of him was not just himself but was Eric, also, and he was so happy to have Eric within him and did not question how such a thing could be. The Creole cook was in the dream but he could not see her, and she was also Creasie, and he was aware of Birdie's presence somehow though he was not sure how, and he wanted to leave the table to see where she was but he also didn't want to leave such good company, but then he did and when he wandered out of doors it was not nighttime anymore, but a cool and sunny fall afternoon.

He wandered toward a spot of color in the distance and when he got close he saw that it was a bush filled with preening monarch butterflies, migrated there from South America, resting and soaking up the sunlight. He lay on the sand and looked up at them. They were like the leaves of the shrub, they were so numerous. They seemed to shiver under his rapt attention. He felt such an outpouring of love for them, he thought he would weep. They seemed hardly able to contain their delight that he was gazing upon their beautiful wings.

THE HEAVEN
OF
MERCURY

Brad Watson

PHOTOGRAPH OF MY GRANDMOTHER

My maternal grandmother, Margaret Maria (Maggie) Wells Watson, known to her grandchildren as Mimi, was married at sixteen—too young to know any better, according to her lights. My grandfather, a determined and persuasive young shoe salesman, had almost bullied her into marrying him, she said. A year into the marriage, this girl, who'd never been more than kissed on the cheek before her wedding night, was pregnant with her first child, my aunt Marjory. Mimi used to say her childhood just vanished.

I was always fascinated by Mimi, who lived to be ninety-three, and her hilarious stories. She told them in a disjointed, lighthearted, rambling fashion, punctuating them with gems such as the time I asked how she felt about my grandfather's infidelity (like his father, apparently, he got around), and she replied, "Well, it hurt, you know. But at least it kept him off of me."

She hadn't really wanted to marry at all, didn't want to have children, not as young as she did, anyway. She couldn't stand the Watsons, her in-laws. Earl's father, an insurance salesman, was a reputed womanizer who'd killed his brother-in-law in a fight many years past; he spent two years in the penitentiary for manslaughter. He carried a little pearl-handled pistol in his jacket pocket until the day he died. Earl's siblings were always envious of him, especially his brother Klein, with whom Earl fought all the time, sometimes in the house. Mimi said Klein would storm in, raging, and Earl would leap up from the table, and they'd be whaling at each other in the living room. Her sisters-in-law were catty

to her and insulted her all the time, took advantage of her, disparaged her character behind her back. According to Mimi, she was plagued by these people. Sometime late in her life, Earl's sister Myrtle wrote a novel (unpublished), a good portion of which was devoted to disparaging her sister-in-law, Mimi.

When Earl died of a heart attack in 1955, he left a wholly dependent wife who'd never worked a job, and a son (my father) he hadn't bothered to teach the business. Then someone began to mail her letters made of words cut from magazine headlines, accusing her of poisoning Earl. The letters threatened an exhumation and autopsy. "THE TRUTH WILL OUT!" one said. Mimi knew these letters came from Klein and his wife because Klein was furious that Earl hadn't left him a share in his two shoe stores. She was traumatized and embarrassed by these things, but nothing ever came of them. "Well, you know they're just crazy, Maggie!" her friends would say.

Only after Mimi's death in 1995 did I see this photograph, taken sometime in the mid- to late 1920s. I was trying to begin work on a novel that would become *The Heaven of Mercury*, and I had a vague idea that my grandmother could be the model for a main character, Birdie Wells Urquhart. But the book gave me fits, and I wrote the rough drafts of two other books in the meantime, just trying to avoid this one. I was finding it almost impossible to invent a story about someone who had been such a strong presence in my life, and so much herself, as an old person. I struggled to see her as a girl, flirting with boys, being desired by boys and men. This photograph, showing my grandmother in something like a flapper's dress, looking quite flirtatious as she leans coyly against the fancy car (no doubt my grandfather's—he had a weakness for new automobiles), allowed something of her old lady veneer to crack a little, and I began to imagine her life in a way I hadn't been able to before. And I began to weave some of her stories into a narrative, to elaborate upon them, and to invent others.

I also began more freely inventing things about characters based on other people in her life. I knew little about Mimi's housemaid of some fifty years, Velma Hubbard, but the woman was very sweet and kind, generous of spirit, and very rooted in the old ways of the racist South; I never could get her to stop calling me Mr. Brad. She and my grandmother were always arguing, bickering over little household things—they both got cantankerous in their old age. My grandmother fired Velma several times; Velma would simply let herself in the next morning with her key.

The character invented to become Birdie Urquhart's unrequited lover (Finus Bates) in the novel has no model, aside from sharing certain crotchety characteristics with me (I am not such an old man but act like one). So I was surprised when, after the book was done, my mother said there was a man who used to visit Mimi, and who cared enough about her to sit by her bedside when she was ill with various ailments. Mom didn't know if the man was in love with Mimi or not, but she wondered, even suspected he was. I was astounded: It almost seemed like life imitating fiction.

I don't think Mimi would mind my using her life as inspiration for a novel. She might tell me I got some things wrong, but she'd understand I was making those things up. She'd say she didn't want the facts, they were so awful, or that things weren't really so awful as that. Most likely she'd just repeat what she said after reading my first published story, when I was twenty-three: "Well, I know you're a good boy, anyway." Meaning in spite of the awful things I wrote.

Q & A WITH BRAD WATSON

Where, or what, is "The Heaven of Mercury"?

The title of the novel comes from Dante's *Divine Comedy*, in "Paradiso." I'm no Dante scholar, and I don't know the "Purgatorio" or "Paradiso" books as well as I know "Inferno," and I don't know it as well as I used to. But early on in writing this book, when I was working with the idea of communion between the living and the dead, it occurred to me that Dante could be a model of sorts. Reading the books again I came across "The Heaven of Mercury" in "Paradiso"; I thought it a lovely and fitting title for my story, and as it had to do with betrayal, all the better. The parallels, as it turned out, are a little vague, though Finus Bates is guided, in a sense, by Birdie Urquhart's spirit in his search for answers.

It's also everywhere in the book. In the characters' minds, their memories, in the presence of the dead in their waking and dreaming lives, in their communion with spirits, real or imagined, and in their ability to survive grief, loss, and rage with dignity and compassion for one another—for the most part. It is in a sense a real heaven, where those dead wander, which is near, what the character Finus Bates describes as their "presence in distorted slips of air that revealed, like the thin and vertical flaws in a lens, the always nearby regions of the dead."

Is Mercury a real place, or a mythic one, like Faulkner's Yoknapatawpa County?

I don't want to compare myself to Faulkner, but Mercury is like Yoknapatawpa in the sense that it is modeled after my hometown, Meridian, Mississippi, with many liberties taken. Mythic to the degree that certain elements are broadened or simplified, yes.

Your descriptions of Mercury cover the better part of a century—from about 1906 to 1989. How have times changed or not changed in that kind of Southern town?

They've changed a lot, even though in appearance many small Southern cities and towns seem not to have changed much. Demographics, economics, social cauldrons, these have all been modified by changes from the civil rights movements to increasing urbanization and the death of small farms, and the move away from cheap-labor manufacturing (it's moved on to more fertile fields in developing countries).

Like the rest of the country, small towns and small cities in the South are being overrun with shopping malls, strip malls, Wal-Marts, Kmarts, and new supermarkets. The family-run hardware and lumber stores struggle or are forced out of business by Home Depot and Lowes. Restaurants fail often because people would rather eat at the chains, such as Western Sizzlin', Applebee's, Pizza Hut, or McDonalds.

In Meridian, many of the family cleaning businesses, paint stores, clothing stores, barber shops, lumber yards, scrap yards, bakeries, and specialty shops survive. The plumbers, builders, Peavey Electronics. I believe the newspaper, *The Meridian Star*, is still privately owned, though I may be mistaken. There has been a largely successful effort to revive the historic vaudeville theater downtown, though the little movie theaters (and the monumental Temple Theater, now used for special events) have given way to the chains around the downtown's perimeter. The churches thrive, of course; the South is still largely a region that respects and practices its religion. Meridian, for one, is not without an eclectic representation, with all manner of Protestant churches, an old and respected Catholic church, and a long-established synagogue that survived a Klan bombing in 1968; there may even be a mosque there now, for all I know. I moved years ago.

One thing that's changed, obviously, is race relations. How did that affect your portrayal of the book's African American characters, Creasie and Frank, and their relation to their white employers?

It didn't. 1950 is 1950, and the changes that have come since then have no bearing on the way things were then. I tried to write honestly about it. It was more difficult and risky, of course, to write from Creasie's point of view, to write about her and Frank from their perspective. I did the best I could, as any fiction writer would, to put myself in their place when I was writing about them. If 1950 is 1950, human beings are human beings; fundamentally, we are all alike in love, loss, disappointment, greed, desire, sympathy, and so on. Of course Creasie, like the character Birdie, is modeled after a person I knew, whereas Frank was entirely invented. So it was actually a little more difficult to write about Creasie, since I had to allow her character to go beyond or transcend the limited knowledge I had about the woman who inspired her.

Race relations are of course much better in the South these days, as they are in most of the country, but like elsewhere they're still far from perfect. There's a residual racism that lingers in this country, and small to mid-sized Southern towns and cities are no exception to that, though it may be more obvious there because racism is more of a tradition in the South. I say that ironically, but it's true.

The celebrated Southern tendency toward politeness has come to include racism; that is, it is there but it is not spoken of, mostly.

Faulkner's great novel Absalom, Absalom! *famously ends with Quentin Compson in a cold dorm room at Harvard protesting to his roommate, "I don't hate the South! I don't hate it! I don't hate it!" You also left the deep South for Harvard—to teach there, after your first collection of stories,* Last Days of the Dog-Men, *was published. What were your own feelings about the South, looking back at it from Cambridge? Did you also feel you had to defend it?*

Occasionally, the need or opportunity arose. Once at a dinner party, someone mentioned hunting, and all eyes swung to me, as the token Southerner who must obviously be the resident expert on such a barbaric topic. Of course, I was, even though I'm not a very good hunter.

I do think living here has given me a broader perspective on my home region. It helps sometimes to get some distance and look back. Mostly, it helps you to understand yourself a little better through seeing your home from a different place. When you go home to visit, you see and hear things you may not have noticed before, cultural tics you took for granted, and it gives you a different perspective on yourself. That's always good. I go home, and for the first few days I'm chafed by the Southerners I run into, their accents and manners or lack of them, their taste, their music, their cars, their big manicured lawns, the heat and humidity, the lack of things to do. But then I settle in and I love it again. I go back to New England, to Boston, and I am appalled by their particular nasal accents (some Southern accents are quite nasal, too), their gruff manners, the traffic, the noise, the crowded sidewalks, the parking nightmares, the sense that they really don't care if you come there or not and would prefer you didn't. But after a few days I settle in, begin to like the sense of anonymity, that my neighbors don't know or care what I'm up to, that there are several good coffee shops, pubs, and restaurants to choose from in walking distance, and I begin to pick up on the occasional presence of a certain real Yankee charm. There are things I love and hate about both places, depending on my mood.

We've already referred to Faulkner twice in this discussion. Other readers compare you to Flannery O'Connor and Eudora Welty, saying your work is funnier than O'Connor's but darker than Welty's. Is the great Southern literary tradition a legacy or a burden? How did it influence your writing? Who would you like most to be compared to?

If those things have been said, I'm flattered, though I'd never consider myself a better writer than either of those two, in any sense. Harder to be funnier (or darker, for that matter) than "A Good Man Is Hard to Find" or "Good Country People" or "The Life You Save May Be Your Own." If I'm darker than Miss Welty, maybe I'm just more crude. I love the lovely darkness of "The Hitchhikers," "No Place for You, My Love," "Death of a Traveling Salesman," the comic darkness of something like "June Recital." I really don't believe I'm worthy of comparison to either writer, but I'd love to believe I've learned some things from them, and certainly both writers have influenced my own writing. The way Welty's stories plumb the mysteries without simplifying them—she leaves the mystery and the wonder intact, doesn't violate it but enhances it. O'Connor—I just wish I was nearly as smart as she was, as she is in her stories. She and Welty both, what beautiful minds. I have discovered that it is very hard to be funny in the way that O'Connor is funny; I've failed at trying a few times. But I do love her black humor, and the merciless way she exposes the truth in her stories. Who could not love the moment when the Misfit says the grandmother would've been a good woman if she'd had someone to shoot her every day of her life?

So I don't think of the tradition as a burden at all. Thank the gods for it. I read Faulkner, O'Connor, Welty, Robert Penn Warren, and listen to their sentences as I read, try to understand their visions of the world on their own terms as well as how they may give language to my experience. I want their language and vision to inform my own, to educate me about what I already know on some level and about what I did not know before reading them. I think Eliot was right in "Tradition and the Individual Talent"; there is no way we cannot be a part of and extend a tradition, in some sense, as writers. I'm embarrassed when I see someone obviously straining to be different because they think it's weak-minded and boring not to be different. Did Cormac McCarthy adore Faulkner? I don't know him, but it seems to me that he did, and his first novel sounds very much like Faulkner, to me. By "Suttree," he'd taken what he learned from Faulkner and made something entirely his own, though the influence is still obvious. Now we have writers who sound like McCarthy, and that's okay with me. They're learning something new from him.

One of the most beautiful aspects of the novel is the way you capture the thoughts of older people, and the physical aspects of aging. You're not such an old guy yourself . . . how did you research that?

In the company of old people, listening to them, watching them. And by being something of an old soul, myself. I'm a cranky old man in a middle-aged body. I always loved and respected my older relatives, though, loved to listen to them talk, tell their stories, vent their anger over long-held grudges and disappointments. Most of my older relatives—though not all—were cheerful and bright, but they all had some tough stories. These people were the most alive of all the people I knew; they lived more in the moment than young or middle-aged people, even though they loved to revisit the past. The spoke directly, they told the truth and didn't care about the consequences. They didn't have time for polite lies, anymore. I loved that. If I could get away with acting like an old man all the time, I would.

So your grandmother was a model for Birdie Wells Urquhart—how do you think she'd take to your publicizing her secrets this way? If she is watching from heaven, aren't you in trouble?

Unlike my grandmother, I don't subscribe to the notion that people go to a heaven that is much like earth (conceived apparently by an earth-bound mind), only grander and less troubled. (See answer to question one, above.) But if Mimi's spirit is with me, in some sense, I sense humor as well as admonishment. She used to tell what she considered awful things about herself, as well as others, and be horrified by them, and then laugh at them. Maybe you live to be ninety-three by not being so resistant to the things that happen in life, I mean by accepting them and moving on. She, for one, did not hold a grudge, even against those who had mistreated her terribly, and did not excessively mourn her losses, until her last years, when she grieved most that she was still alive while her children had already died. She complained about that, thought she was living too long. I loved her very much, still do, and she knew that I loved her.

Besides, the secrets she told me weren't really secrets, and I invented the rest. Mimi didn't read fiction, but I'll never forget what she said to me after reading my first published story, which was a little bawdy: "Well, I know you're a good boy, anyway." She meant, "in spite of what you've written."

The novel blurs the distinctions between life and death in interesting ways—most provocatively, in a scene with the undertaker's young son that some people might find offensive—what's that all about?

I hope not too many people find Parnell Grimes's latent necrophilia (as I call it) offensive. Parnell knows his desire is wrong, perverted, grotesque, and he seeks some kind of salvation from it, which he finds in his wife, Selena (who understands him and does not condemn him). And I tried to write about Parnell's troubling desires in a way that shows him to be a fundamentally good man, one of the most compassionate people in the novel, in spite of his problem and being a kind of weird, goodhearted fool. In a strange way, his great love for other people, his compassion, contributes to his problem. It's a darkly comic vision, of course, this character. I enjoy certain kinds of morbid humor; I can't be alone in that, in a country that made Edward Gorey a bestseller. Maybe Flannery O'Connor would have written about such a character, had she been born thirty or forty years later, and done a better job of it. I don't know.

Concerning the scenes when the world of the dead and the living merge in other ways, such as when Finus sees his dead wife in a chair in his bedroom, or hears her voice through a stray cat in the graveyard, I was playing with some sort of notion about the ephemeral nature of earthly life, I think, and the sense that we commune in all kinds of ways with the dead, ways that aren't spooky or supernatural or weird; they're with us always, in a real sense, if we cared about them.

In the scenes with Birdie after her death, I like to think a reader can see her spirit travel as either real or as a moment of compressed time and brain travel in the moments between life and death, the moments when the body has given up and some sort of residual energy still exists in the brain. A hugely imaginative time, I would think.

How exactly do you describe the relationship between your two main characters, Finus Bates and Birdie Wells? If this is a kind of love story, why didn't you let them get together and live happily ever after?

I think all too often people don't end up with the love of their lives. They end up with someone they love okay and they stick it out, or they don't. Finus and Birdie never get together, and to some extent it's a result of the bad timing, the odd luck of timing, that so often keeps people who seem right for each other apart. We've all had it happen: a love at first sight that tears our hearts out instantly, but we're committed to someone, or they are, and we don't act. Same with these two. It's a shame, when that sort of thing happens. But there usually are shameful consequences, sometimes ruinous, that follow if we do act.

I didn't have a real vision of Finus and Birdie as a couple, a vision of what their lives together would have been, until one night late in the time I was revising the book. I'd met some friends at a nice restaurant in Cambridge, and this older couple kind of shuffled up to the hostess to inquire about a table. They stood there a while, waiting, holding hands. They were older, and kind of frail, but there was something obviously beautiful about them, individually and as a couple. I had the strongest sense that these people were as much in love as when they first fell in love, and it seemed to me that they were in a sense Finus and Birdie. It added something, I think, to the last draft, seeing that couple.

DISCUSSION QUESTIONS

1. Barry Hannah, in a comment on Brad Watson's first collection of stories, *Last Days of the Dog-Men*, wrote: "Watson's people are the wretched dreams of honorable dogs." In this, Watson's first novel, what seems to be his view of human—and animal—nature?

2. Would you describe Watson's writing as earthy or lyrical? What characteristics dominate in his prose and how do they affect his portrayals of individual characters? How do elements of his style influence the book's intermingling of the living and the dead? Does Watson's prose evoke or suggest a larger world view?

3. How does Finus's radio broadcast set the stage for the rest of the novel, in terms of both narrative and theme? Did Finus's cosmic reflections strike you as profound or eccentric?

4. Some of Watson's characters seem to have an intimate connection with a world or dimension beyond the strictly material world of the present. How does this affect their ability to relate to the "real" world? What is it about Watson's prose that makes this "other" world seem normal and understandable to the reader? Would you describe this other dimension as magical or spiritual in a conventional sense?

5. Time, memory, and desire are traditionally construed as elements of earthly existence that are no longer relevant in the afterlife. Would you say that Watson turns that idea on its head? Is there some way in which time, memory, and desire in this novel are elements of a "life beyond" that surrounds us even while we're living?

6. Is this identifiably a "Southern novel"? Why? How is the Southern literary tradition distinct from writing from the rest of America? Is this related to the issue of race?

7. Did you find Watson's portraits of Vish, Creasie, and Frank offensive? Why, or why not? Is the reader invited to see these characters differently from the way the white characters in the book see, or don't see, them? Do we get any idea of how they might see themselves?

8. How do Watson's influences show themselves, and do they add to or subtract from the originality of his novel? Do the "ghosts" of Southern literature overwhelm his work or does he manage to keep them in their place, and how? What elements remind you of Faulkner, Welty, O'Connor, or other writers?

9. "The heaven of mercury" is the second circle of heaven in the "Par-

adiso" of Dante Alighieri's fourteenth-century religious allegory, *The Divine Comedy*. What was Watson trying to achieve with such an allusion in the title of a novel about twentieth-century Mississippi? One reviewer commented that the title was the weakest part of the book—do you agree? What about the author's choice to use mock Latin chapter titles—does that work with, or against, the "Southernness" of the novel?

10. Does the community in Mercury change from the beginning to the end of the novel or does it seem to be suspended in time? How, if at all, does the outside world affect the way the story plays out?

11. Fellow southern novelist Larry Brown was one of many who compared Watson's novel not only to Faulkner but also to South American novelist and Nobel Prize winner Gabriel García Marquez. What does Watson have in common with García Marquez? Are the fabulistic elements in the book examples of "magic realism," or are they really fantasies of the individual characters? What is the role of dreaming and fantasy in this book?

12. Does Watson effectively combine an intimacy with his individual characters with a larger overview of their lives? What is gained and what is lost in his narrative strategy?

13. Is the narrator omniscient? How does the novel's use of various points of view shape the narrative and, ultimately, the book's view of the world, or your view of the book?

14. Finus is an old man when we are told the story of his love for Birdie Wells and of life in Mercury. Watson claims that his older relatives were the most alive of all the people he knew. Why do you think he chose Finus as the main character? How do you think his age affects the tone and pace of the book?

15. In an interview, Watson explained that when he first started writing this book, he was thinking about the idea of communion between the living and the dead. Does this novel believe in an afterlife, or transcendence? If so, of what kind?

THE "WATSON" POEMS

Even an author can become a character in someone else's work and imagination. A long-time friend of Brad Watson's, accomplished poet Michael Pettit, has been writing "Watson poems" since the days when both were in graduate school in creative writing at the University of Alabama, and Pettit, his life in transition, was spending nights on Watson's couch. In a comparably transitional frame of mind, Watson was considering leaving graduate school and becoming a navy fighter pilot. Thus the genesis of "Blue Angel," reprinted below. Over time, however, like most fictional characters, Pettit's "Watson" began to take on an independent life of his own. (Unlike Pettit's Watson and Watson's Finus, the author of *The Heaven of Mercury* was never assigned to a newspaper's obit page.)

BLUE ANGEL

It goes time, indolence, boredom,
depression and Watson figures his way out
is at twice the speed of sound. It's booze
tonight though, sitting home with thoughts
of Navy jets, Mach II, and the blues
he'll leave behind like the sudden sonic boom

that shatters the farmer's rain gauges,
drives his milk cows and wife crazy.
Watson uncorks his bottle, already over
the next flat state, delighted and busy
doing a swift 1,500 miles per hour.
Glassy-eyed, he turns the pages

of a glossy book: F-104 Starfighters,
the XP-86 Sabre jet, an F-4 Phantom.
Behind each dark-tinted canopy
he sees his own face: composed, handsome,
heroic. And it's there amid the debris
of an airshow disaster, the four fires

on the desert, the four perfect black
columns of smoke. O to be a Blue Angel
burning, becoming wholly and finally air!
Watson knows how, step by step, the soul
can die in the living body. He'll make sure
they go together, and when they do, go quick.

PERDIDO KEY

Watson's found work, like a dime on a sunny street,
a happy accident. Salaried, living by the sea,

he's writing half the weekly news the Gulf Shores
Independent prints. It's not the Sacramento *Bee*,

not the Boston *Globe*, but he's got a new used car
and a white fishing cap his press badge flashes from.

By dumb luck his beat is the water: the whole Gulf
is his, from the Miracle Mile to Mobile, every wave,

every beauty on a beach towel his to cover.
O happy Watson! O his deep tan, his bright smile,

his sharp pencil! So what happens? No news but what
he hunts up: shady sewer schemes, rapacious condo lords,

worthless lives of sleaze and greed. Current hot story?
A threat to the habitat, a threat to the very life

of the beach mouse. Diminutive, less than an inch long,
beach mice don't have half a chance without Watson.

He's discovered Perdido Key developers want high rises
rising where the beach mice roam. O none of that!